Burn All The Bodies

Five Tales of
Violence and Vengeance
and Topher's Ton, a novel

James Noll

PULP!
Horror, Post-Apocalyptic, and Science Fiction

Book and Cover Design by James Noll

Cover Illustration by Bri Bevan

Author Photo by Haley Noll

ISBN: 0692391606
ISBN-13: 978-0692391600 (PULP!)

For my parents, Don and Judy Noll, who put up with a lot of nonsense from me when I was younger and still loved me anyway.

ACKNOWLEDGMENTS

Thank you to *WHURK!* and *the Fredericksburg Literary Review* for exposing my work to a larger audience. Visit these wonderful publications at www.whurk.org and www.fredericksburgwriters.com. Also thank you to the many people at PitchSlam! who provided me with invaluable feedback and support.

CONTENTS

1 The Legacy of the Monster Diego Tomas, Part I   1

2 Coming Home   5

3 The Legacy of the Monster Diego Tomas, Part II   15

4 It Steals Things   23

5 The Legacy of the Monster Diego Tomas, Part III   27

6 Topher's Ton   37

The Legacy of The Monster Diego Tomas

Part I

Ramon stood shirtless in front of the open window, dripping sweat onto the warped pane. It was two in the afternoon, the worst part of the day, when the sun angled in and beat and beat and beat. At ten floors up, there was no relief, no escape from the heat, even if it rained. Rain this time of year was tropical. All it brought was more humidity.

He stared at the flooded avenues below. Skeletal awnings, rusty and broken, poked up out of the oily water, catching errant debris—flotsam from yet another building that had collapsed in some far off part of the city. The Barquemen fished the narrows, shouting and scrambling as they hauled in another catch. They weren't going to eat any of it. Nobody would. They used it for oil. For their lamps. And their bombs. Stupid Barquemen. They stank like fish. They fucked like dogs. They were animals.

"Be glad we live up here, Ramon," his father, Diego Tomas, used to say. "The air's fresh and we're clean, not like down there with those fucking wetbacks."

It made perfect sense to Ramon when he was a kid: Barquemen hauled the fish, so they reeked and were inferior. Roofers tended the garden, so they smelled like earth and were better. He always struggled to classify the Generators. They didn't smell like anything, yet Diego Tomas called them stupid for choosing to live in the middle of the building. It created dissent, he said. They were always fighting the Barquemen or the Roofers, striving for position, respect. Now that they could no longer keep the electricity running, Ramon knew that they weren't just stupid. They were stupid and desperate. He experienced that desperation first hand when the bastards broke through the fifth-floor barrier and tried to take over the building.

He rested his elbows on the sill, wincing at the pain from the pellets in his back, pellets his own son, Michal, shot at him. While he was downstairs defending his people, fighting off the idiot

Generators, Michal did their job for them, took over the roof, made his own barricade. Ramon tried to talk some sense into the boy, but after the battle, his anger was difficult to contain. He couldn't get the image of his son's eyes out of his mind, how they went dead and blank as he raised the shotgun.

"How much longer?" Ramon asked.

His wife, Zoryana, said, "Almost ready."

Ramon turned back into the dark apartment. The wood floors were worn and warped. A few turquoise drapes hung over the windows. Zoryana, her long black hair draped over her shoulders, came toward him with a knife and a bowl, bandages and honey. He pulled up a chair and sat in it backward so he could look out the window while she worked on him.

"You have to go down and talk to her," she said.

"I don't want to go down and talk to her. I want to go up and beat some sense into my son."

"That sounds productive."

"Yes. Productive for me."

Zoryana pushed the tip of the blade into one of the puncture wounds, withdrew a metal pellet, and dropped it in the bowl with a plink.

"Didn't you try that already? Why am I picking these things out of your back?"

"I was too fast for him to hit me in the face, that's why."

"Psh."

Plink.

"I wouldn't even have to go through the barricade," he said. "I could grapple up the side. It's only three floors."

"No, Ramon."

"It's the only way."

"Not if you talk to her. Alone, you're weak. But together."

"Zoryana. I just killed four of her people. We fought, she and I. One on one. I . . . her arm."

"You have to talk to her, Ramon. She's the only one who can help. You know Michal's already done it."

Someone in the distance zip-lined between two buildings, a black silhouette against the red sun. A stray bee buzzed by, followed by a message flying down on a string from the roof to the fifth floor. Michal really was talking to the Generators, talking to her, planning a coup. Ramon sucked his teeth and shook his head.

"I want to strangle him." Zoryana jabbed him a little too hard with the knife. "Aye, Zory!"

His foot rubbed against something, and he looked down to see what it was. A shoe. A little white shoe with a yellow flower on the heel. It belonged to Mia, his daughter.

"How is Mia?" he asked.

"Fine. She's in her room."

"I want to check on her."

"Don't. She's finally asleep. She was terrified when you left."

Ramon let his wife work. After a while, he said, "How long has he been building that barricade?"

"Since you went to down to fight her."

"And you let him?"

Another jab, another pellet.

"He took your gun, Ramon. What was I supposed to do? Why did you leave it up here anyway?"

"I left it for you, for him," he said. "Just in case."

She stopped, and he wondered if she was mad or thinking. He knew better than to force it. After a few minutes, he heard her unscrew the lid to the jar.

"He better be taking good care of my bees," he said.

She spread honey on his wounds, massaged his shoulders.

"Of course he will."

"How do you know?"

"He's your son. You trained him."

Ramon put his chin on the sill and closed his eyes. Lately, when the sky finally did open up, he and the others had had to haul in the big flats of corn and peppers, the grape vines and melons. First it was enough to store them in the rooms on the twelfth floor, but now the roof leaked, had even crumbled in places, and he wondered how long it would be before it vanished entirely, just rotted away. How long would their building last? How long before it listed and fell and turned into so much debris floating in the narrows? What were they going to do?

"This is madness."

"He's just mimicking you, Ramon. How many times did you tell him the story of you and Diego Tomas?"

"I'm not Diego Tomas. Diego Tomas was a monster."

"And what are you? What did you just do?"

"What was I supposed to do? They broke through the barrier."

"Your son sees it differently. He's in love."

"With some pale, midlevel slut. How did they even meet?"

"They climb the elevator shaft, the old trash chutes."

Ramon knew this. He did the same when he was a child.

"It's dangerous."

Zoryana turned his head and took his face in her hands and gave him a sweet kiss.

"It's how we met. Remember?"

"I remember. But you were one of us."

"In love, what does that matter?"

"I'm his father. He should listen to me."

Zoryana stood up and started to gather her things.

"Go see her. Go talk to your sister."

Ramon emptied the bowl into his hand before giving it back to her. The metal painted little dots on his skin. He looked out the window. The sun pounded down, fat and red. The Barquemen continued their haul. Ramon watched them. He shook the pellets in his fist.

COMING HOME

The enemy came from Salvation. They came in the fall. "The Knights of the Book". They told us we were sinners, that we had to be punished. They set fires and raised ladders, but our walls, the walls of Gabriel, were too high, and we rained down a reckoning so fierce that they were forced to pull back. Out of anger, they launched our own people into the city, the poor farmers and cobblers and merchants who couldn't make it in before the gates closed. Their bodies looked like seabirds as they flew through the air, those clumsy types that got blown in by the storms every now and then, all legs and beak and belly. Nobody could tell if they were dead before or after they were sent flying, but they sure were when they splatted on the stones.

It didn't take long to deal with them. We piled them up in the market square. Then it became a question of what to do about it. Some of the dead were so torn apart that it didn't matter, but there were more than a few that could have caused problems. They'd have wiped us out in a day. Worst part was that we couldn't send them to sea, not as long as the enemy was out there. We didn't have any wood to spare for boats, or fabric to spare for sails, so our soldiers carted the bodies into the barracks and burned them. Soon a thick black cloud plumed over the towers.

The siege lasted for days, weeks, months. They poisoned the streams. We starved. Parents died in their homes and their children had to drag them to the barracks to be burned. Some waited too long, and the soldiers had to wipe out entire families. Toddlers wandered the alleys. The black cloud became eternal.

Gabrielites were strong. We were people of the coast. We survived typhoons and tsunami, drought and disease. We told stories of the winter when the ice fog blew in off the sea, froze people where they stood. We thought we could survive anything. But to not see the dead off properly, to not sew the sail, stitch the X, say the words—it nearly broke us. Some people threw themselves off the west wall and smashed on the rocks below, their bodies sucked away by the tide. We worried about them, hoped that the current would wash them away, tear them apart before they could come back.

Then one spring night after almost a year of siege, the Knights of the Book disappeared, just up and left in a whirl of dust. We waited a week to make sure it wasn't a trick, but when it was clear that they weren't coming back, we flung open the gates and celebrated. People called for a feast. I didn't know what they planned on eating, but I didn't want to go. I just wanted to get out of the city, away from people, away from the stink and the death, so as the preparations for the celebration advanced, I snuck out of a side gate and headed for the woods.

Of all the things I'd missed during the siege, I missed the pond the most. I always thought of it as "my pond," but wasn't like I was the only one who knew about it. Everybody went there. I just loved it more than most. People were kinder to me there. It was quiet and calm, and they left me alone. It was big, too, and in the winter the ice froze so thick that people could walk clear across, one side to the other like it was solid earth. The older folks said it sank clear to the other side of the world, and when I was a little girl I believed them. But one winter I cut a hole in the middle like I was going fishing and sounded it out. It was only a hundred feet deep.

Once I got there, I stripped off my dress and dove in. The water still held the winter's frost, so I didn't have to go too deep to cool off. I shivered through icy pockets, backstroked around the edges to warm up. When my shoulder stump began to ache, I grabbed onto one of the roots and pulled myself out. There was a spot where the water made a little corner cove, and it was shallow and warm, and the roots hollowed out like a chair. I liked to wend my good arm through them and lean back and take a nice, long soak.

Lying there in the warm little cove, I couldn't help but notice how skinny I'd become. My ribs stuck out like a xylophone, my arm looked like a twig, and I could feel the roots burrow into the bones of my butt. After a while, the scar on my stump began to itch. It was dry and flaky, so I got out and found an aloe bush and rubbed some in the cracks and crevices. Then I got back in the water. I thought of what the Abbess used to tell me about my arm when I was a girl. She wouldn't tell me anything else, nothing about my brother and the old man, nothing about my old home, but she couldn't talk enough about my arm.

"That old witch didn't care much for a clean cut," she'd say. Over and over. "It's a miracle you didn't die of infection."

"Yep, that's me. Your miracle girl."

Any of the other sisters would have scolded me for that, called me insolent or rude, but not the Abbess. She just smiled.

"We had the devil's time cleaning it out. Had to cut more bone to make it even. Still wasn't enough flesh."

"Uh huh."

The best way to get her to stop talking about it was to ask her who brought me to Gabriel. Then she'd get all quiet and pretend like she didn't hear. Eventually, she'd say, "The knights brought you" and that was the end of the conversation.

I looked at the mulberry-colored patch on my thigh where they took off the skin to cover what was left of my arm. It was kind of like a dent. Wasn't too big, but enough to make me look like a regular rattled soldier, even at the ripe old age of nineteen. Through the water it looked all wavy. I ran my finger along it. Poked it. The sun peaked out over the tops of the trees and warmed my face, and the rocking water made me drowsy, so I leaned back, smiling, and dozed off. When I opened my eyes there was a man standing over me.

I started to scream, but he clamped a dirty hand over my mouth.

"Hush girl."

I bit down as hard as I could, bit until I tasted blood, just a drop, and he grimaced but didn't let go.

"I'm tainted, girl. You'd best spit that out."

I did. I spit and spit and spit, and when I was done he yanked me out and pinned me to the moss-covered roots. I thrashed under him and he struck me in the temple so hard that I saw stars. All I could think about was the coppery taste of his blood on my tongue. He thumped me around some more, and suddenly I remembered what the Abbess always told me about men, something that saved me so many times from the drunks in the alleys and the perverted priests.

"Kick them down there, Lily. They'll drop like a stone."

My left arm might have been gone and my right pinned, but both my legs were whole and free. I brought my knee up as hard as I could, right where the Abbess showed me. The knight made a sound like a whipped dog, and I shoved him over and stood up and dove for the water, but he lunged after me, grabbed my foot, and yanked me back. Then my head hit a knot on one of the roots and I blacked out.

When I was little, I used to get into fights all the time. I didn't know what I was and wasn't supposed to do. I wasn't born in Gabriel.

I didn't know the rules. The thing that got me in trouble the most was that I liked to play sports with the boys. They thought it was funny, a girl with one arm trying to keep up with them. But when I started to score for my team? All hell broke loose. They'd slide tackle me, try to clothesline me. By the time I was thirteen, it got to where half the time I was ducking an attack as much as I was playing the game, even from my own teammates! It didn't have the effect they were going for. All that ducking and running made me real good, and that only made the boys madder. Most of the time I ignored it, but this one time I scored and some skinny little jerk tackled me and shoved my face in the dirt and ran away, laughing. I'd just about had enough.

"Hey!" I cried, and popped up off the ground.

I was on him before he could even turn all the way around. Knocked him down, pinned his shoulders with my knees, and started slamming his face into the ground. I would have killed him if the Abbess hadn't dragged me off.

I didn't care. No way I was going to let anybody push me around like that.

Back in her room, she said, "Lily, you can't—"

"I can't nothing. He started it."

"Yes, Lily, but—"

"I was just fighting back. Like the Book says, 'An eye for an eye'."

"Lily."

"Every word in the Book is true. You said it. 'An eye for an eye'. I shouldn't be punished for fighting back."

"I know, Lily, but it's not just that. It's everything else, the back talk, the strange ideas, the words you use. It's not how we do things here. You know that."

"You wouldn't say that if I was a boy."

"You're not a boy, Lily."

"I don't care! Anything a boy can do, a girl has the right to do better!"

She looked at me like a spider just came out of my mouth.

"Where did you hear that?

"I-I don't know. It just came to me. I think, maybe, my mother?"

She reached out to comfort me, but hesitated and drew back.

"Lily, you know a lot of things people around here don't. Things you learned before."

"When? From who? I don't remember anybody from before."

"It just seeped in. Like the ocean."

I took a deep breath, tried to calm down. And then it came to me. A melody. I remembered it clearly. The smell of cinnamon, something baking. I started to hum.

The Abbess listened for a while, then she said, "What song is that? Is it a hymn?

"No," I said. "Maybe it just seeped in. There's words, too."

"Will you sing it?"

I shrugged. Why not?

"Singing to an ocean, I can hear the ocean's roar. Play for free, play for me and play a whole lot more. Singing about the good things and the sun that lights the day. I used to sing on the mountains; has the ocean lost its way?"

For a second, she looked happy. But then she frowned.

"The melody is beautiful, but the words are . . . unusual."

"I'd say poetic."

She suppressed a smile.

"Lily, listen. You need to be careful."

"Why?"

"Because you're different."

"What's wrong with being different? Being different is what makes the world interesting."

She couldn't stop the smile this time.

"I know. I know that. But as enlightened as Gabriel is, it's not ready for someone like you. Everybody's afraid of you."

"But I'm just a girl." I shrugged my stump. "I only have one arm!"

"People are afraid of change, Lily. That's what you are to them. Change."

When I came around, it was night. The moon was about to rise. The man had built a fire and was sitting across from me, warming his hands. I could see the shadow of the bruise my teeth left. Just thinking about it made my stomach cold. The temperature had dropped since the late afternoon, and I was sore and shivering. He'd found my clothes and covered me up. My dress with the arm sewn shut, the shirt I wore over it like a shrug. My sandals sat next to the fire. The lump on my head swelled above my eyebrow, pulsing like a tumor, and my ankles were bound with rope.

"You're a knight," I said. "From Salvation."

He grimaced like he was embarrassed.

"Put your clothes on," he said.

I sat up, holding my dress to my chest.

"Look away, please."

At least he afforded me that little dignity. He gazed out over the pond.

"That's the problem with you people," he said. "You're too close to the sea. It loosens your morals."

I let the dress fall over my shoulders, shrugged it into place, pulled it down over my hips.

"I don't see how nearness to water makes a person more or less sinful."

"The salt air warms the blood."

"Oh, so this is about heat, is it?"

"Heat is a temptation."

"Isn't Salvation on the Grand Prairie?" The knight studied the water. "Average low on the Grand Prairie's seventy-eight degrees."

"Shut up, girl."

"That's just during the winter. During the summer it's over ninety."

"I said shut up!"

I tested the rope.

"That's an interesting knot you got there." He grunted. "Mister, what do you want from me?"

"How do you know I want something?"

"Because if you didn't, I'd already be dead. Or worse."

"Maybe I'm waiting to kill you."

"Aw. You don't want to kill me."

He seemed to really look at me then. I couldn't tell if he was angry or not. I'd like to believe that he was more embarrassed than anything else. He seemed to swallow it and gestured at the pond.

"This is a beautiful place," he said.

"I know a way it'd be a whole lot better."

He smiled like he understood.

"I can't let you go. Not yet."

We sat for a little, silent. I could hear the far-off roar of the ocean.

"How long have you had it?"

"It doesn't matter. I won't last the night." His sword sat unsheathed on the roots. He reached out and rested his hand on the blade. "Do you know how to use this?"

"I think I can figure it out."

His eyes fell on my stump, doubtful, and he lay back.

"Salvation's gone, isn't it," I said. He nodded. "Everybody?"

"Everybody."

I let that sink in. The whole city of Salvation wiped out; the sickness burned through them like tallow. I guess they got it wrong about who were the sinners.

I played with the rope. It was thick hemp, well-woven.

"How'd you get out?"

He seemed to not want to answer that at first. When he spoke, it was short.

"Brother Oliver. He sent us to warn you."

"Who's Brother Oliver?" He didn't answer again, so I said, "You sure you got it? I knew a girl who got sick, had her black X stitched up and everything. Right when they were ready to start the ceremony, the fever broke. Now she's going to get married. Well, she was."

"Why are you telling me this?"

"You might not have it. There's plenty of sicknesses that look like it but aren't it."

He swallowed, grimacing.

"Would you like to come over here and see?"

"I'm just fine where I am, thanks."

We all knew what the first stage was supposed to look like. Purple lumps under the jaw popped up overnight, swarms of them, like insect eggs. They were tender at first, made it hard to swallow. Some people got feverish. Just as many didn't. Everybody knew how it ended, though. Only took a day. Sometimes less. Once the bleeding started? Once they coughed it up or sneezed it out? Only a few minutes to do anything after that happened. If too many got to that stage all at once, it was all over for the rest of us. So at the first sign, we sent them to sea. Fathers and mothers and brothers and sisters. That's what we called it in Gabriel. We didn't kill them. They were "sent to sea". There was a station, the Abbess said, set up a long time ago. "It's on the ocean. They go there to heal," she told me, and when I was little I believed her. Now I knew better. In the twelve years I'd lived in Gabriel, I'd never seen a ship return.

"Wait until I'm done," the knight said.

"Why don't we just get it over with now?"

He shook his head.

"It is a sin to die before I am called back."

"The first or the second time?"

I didn't expect his grim laughter.

"Such glibness from someone so guilty. I had a family. My wife, Siobhan. My two little babies."

He couldn't finish. I knew he was crying without even seeing it. He took a deep breath when the fit passed.

"Make it quick. Don't linger. Burn my body."

"We don't have to do this. We could just set you out to sea."

"Set me out to sea? What is this?"

"You don't know?"

"Know what, girl? Tell me."

I thought it was funny that he didn't know about it, but then again, none of us knew too much about Salvation. We knew they followed the Book more closely than we did, and we knew they hated us, but the two places might as well have been on opposite sides of the world. So I explained it to him, our custom, and as I did I could see him grow more and more agitated. When I got to the part about the station in the ocean, he burst out laughing, and then the laughter turned into coughs. He leaned on his side and retched. I knew it was blood. When he was done, he lay onto his back.

"I'm not dumb," I said. "I know it's a fairytale."

"How long?"

"How long what?"

"How long have you been doing this?"

"As long as I can remember. Why?"

He didn't answer for a long time. Then he said, "We were wrong to try to bring God's wrath upon you, and we were punished. We didn't know. We didn't know he was going to do it Himself."

He died choking.

I tried to sit him up so he could spit it out but he wouldn't let me, just shook his head and pointed at his sword. When he was finally still, when his eyes were fixed on the sky, I grabbed it. I'm pretty strong for a girl, but having only one arm had its limitations, and I couldn't pick the thing up all the way. Had to kind of rest the point right on his throat and push it down and saw it back and forth until his head was off. Then I built up a fire around him and let it do its work. I washed off in the pond, dried everything out in the sun next to it.

Right when I was getting ready to leave, the city bells started to ring. Didn't take long for me to make it to the cliffs. There stood Gabriel, its sandstone walls tall and proud, a barrier against the sea, the wind, and the storms. The bells pealed. People lined the towers and the west wall, pointing out at the ocean. I shaded my eyes, straining to see. Around front, the gates were closing. Entire families were caught outside. They ran for safety, crying out, but it didn't matter. When the gates finally slammed close, they fell to their knees, pounded on the iron, begging to be let in.

If you couldn't tell before, I never was much of the churchly type. The Abbess made me go, and I listened and I thought, but I can't ever say I really believed any of it. But standing there, looking out over the ocean, I remembered something I heard one of the priests say. Something like, "Every knee shall bow, and every tongue shall give praise, and each one of you will account yourself to Me."

Pretty, in an angry way, I guess.

Standing there looking at the golden horizon, I think I finally understood what it meant.

There were thousands of them. Sails. Torn and tattered, all bearing the black X of disease. Every dead mother, every dead father, every dead son and daughter. Heading our way.

Coming home, at last.

James Noll

The Legacy of The Monster Diego Tomas

Part II

Ramon stood in the stairwell with his back to the wall. Around the corner sat the fifth-floor barrier. He could smell the blood, the death. Marijke's people murmured to each other as they cleaned it off the tiles: two men and a woman. He had to plan this carefully, had to give Gazini enough time to gather his men and oil, set up the catapults. If he spun around the corner too fast, Marijke's people would startle and jump on him. If he waited too long, she would see what the Barquemen were up to and fight back. Either way, Gazini's attack would fail, and his wife and daughter would die.

Lamps smoked and sputtered in the stairwell, casting a brown light over everything. Ramon winced. Why was she wasting her oil here? Better to let the stains remain, a reminder for her people, something she could use when she needed them to fight again.

He took a deep breath. Counted back from five. Four. Three. Two.

"I am Ramon Cruz," he called out. "I mean no harm. I want to talk to my sister."

He waited a beat, then turned the corner, hands raised.

The soldiers had already drawn their long knives and crouched side by side, ready for a fight. The woman jumped up and grabbed a spinner leaning up against the wall. She hunched down behind the soldiers, who closed ranks to protect her.

Ramon eyed the spinner, four sharp blades bolted to the end of a long pole. The woman turned it slowly, deliberately, to show him she knew how to use it. He knew what she was thinking. One jab to keep him back, one to weaken him. If he somehow got under it, if he grabbed it, the men would slice him to bits, and as he stumbled back, the spinner would find his eyes, his throat. Excellent for one on one fights. Useless everywhere else. He kept a wise distance.

"I'm here to talk to Marijke," he said. "I'm here to offer a truce. An alliance."

The woman snorted.

"Bullshit. I've seen what your offers look like. Look around."

"You don't understand."

"I understand fine, *cabron*. You came unarmed?" As a unit, they advanced two steps. "That was stupid."

She spun the blades faster, trying to intimidate him. They weren't close enough yet to hit him, and he could always run, but that wasn't an option. He had to finish this, had to finish it tonight.

So he stood.

Stood with raised hands and a raised chin as the spinner cut the air in front of him. The trio inched forward as if he were a wild animal, expecting him to charge at any moment. The woman feinted once, twice. He closed his eyes. Gathered his strength. One more inch. One more inch.

"Xi! No!"

Ramon's eyes flew open. The blades tickled his shirt, stopping a centimeter over his heart.

Marijke, his sister, was standing in front of the barrier. She was battered and bruised and bloody, her right arm held in a sling against her chest, her left eye filled with blood.

"Ree-ree," Ramon said, smiling.

"Don't call me that."

"It's what I've always called you."

"My name," she said. "is Marijke." Ramon chuckled. She seethed. "What do you want, *cabron*?"

"Again with the *cabron*? You people need to read a dictionary. Get another insult."

"I don't have time for this."

She turned around as if to crawl back through the tunnel, but Ramon said, "Marijke. Wait."

"Why?"

"I want to talk."

"Talk? Talk about what? The people you murdered?"

Ramon swallowed his protest, saying instead, "No. There's something else. Something new. A new threat."

A hint of a smile pulled on his sister's upper lip. She squashed it.

"A threat? So soon?"

"Yes."

She started to say something, something harsh and bitter, but then she stopped. She saw something, something she hadn't seen in a long time, not since they were young. Not the anger and hardness that marked their adult life together, but heartache and desperation, swaddled in sadness. He needed her. It was strange to feel sorry for a man as brutal and cruel as him, a man who had slaughtered her people, most certainly doomed her to gangrene and amputation. She strived to hate him, to feel contempt. She wanted to harden, to spit in his face, to stomp on his false humility, but couldn't. There was no point. She couldn't back it up with anything anyway, so she swallowed the acid and forced a smile.

"Okay," she said. "We'll talk, Ramon." She let out a small breath, nodded back at the barrier. "But in there. Where you can see what you've done."

Ramon watched the blood blossom on his sister's sling as they walked down the hall. They walked in a line: first Marijke, then him, then Xi, taking up the rear, staring daggers into his back. There were dark stains on the walls, spatters, and thick smells, too—the typical rot and mold that he was used to, but under that something rank, death or dying or something worse, something in between. He stepped in something soft and squishy and sucked in his breath. Marijke enjoyed every step.

"Don't like it down here, do you big brother?"

"No."

She gestured with her good arm.

"But this is all yours. You created this. You should take pride in your accomplishments. Isn't that what Diego Tomas taught us?"

"Diego Tomas was a monster. I'm no Diego Tomas."

Marijke stopped in the open door of an apartment where a woman and three children wept over the body of a man with a hole in his chest.

"You're not?"

Ramon bit back his response. He wanted to remind his sister that it was her people who broke the truce, her people who pushed up to the seventh floor, but she'd just throw it in his face, show him more filth, more children weeping over fathers, brothers, as if he had anything to do with their bad choices. Did she think he was any better off? He stopped himself from letting the dark thoughts take over. He didn't have enough time. He had to get her back to her apartment. They needed to be in there together. Gazini was counting on it.

"Fine, Marijke," he said. "Fine. You win. This is all terrible. Can we just get moving?"

She paused a little longer, just to make him squirm.

Finally she said, "Okay."

She led him to the end of the hall, to her apartment, and opened the door.

"Please, brother. Come inside. Let's 'talk'."

It was no better lit than the hallway, and no better smelling, too. She left the windows open and uncovered, letting in the pale light of the moon and the warm yellow of the Barquemen's fires. Xi went to the kitchen where she lit a lamp. Beneath the dirty face and torn clothes, she was actually quite beautiful. Wide set eyes and full lips. She caught him looking and glared as he took a seat at a battered old card table. The fake leather top frayed at the edges, and a tear ran the length of one side. The chairs were rusty metal fold-ups. Marijke sighed and adjusted her sling as she sat down.

"I'd offer you something to eat, but we don't have any food."

Ramon tried to ignore the barb. "We have water. Xi. Get my brother a glass."

Xi ignored the order.

"Fuck him," she said.

Ramon pushed back from the table.

"Little girl, you don't want to take me on. No spinner. No guards." He stood to his full height. "Come on."

She smiled and took a step forward, but Marijke pounded on the table.

"Godammit, Xi!"

The girl snapped out of her spell, and her eyes locked onto Marijke's.

"A glass of water. For my brother."

"I don't know where—"

"Gabriella has some."

Xi hesitated.

"Now!"

She nodded and turned and stalked out of the apartment. Ramon sat down, laughing.

"Really, Marijke. Where do you get these things?"

"Xi's parents came all the way up from the gulf."

"The gulf? Why didn't they just head for Boulder?"

"Boulder's not letting anymore people in."

"Since when?"

Marijke shrugged.

"They posted guards, put up a fence. Xi's parents were shot dead trying to climb it. She made it all the way here by herself. You wouldn't believe what she had to do."

Ramon pondered.

"She's pretty."

"Don't let it fool you."

"Oh I wouldn't dare."

Xi returned with a pitcher of water and two cloudy glasses. She plunked them down on the table and retreated to the kitchen to lean on the edge of the counter and cross her arms. Neither Ramon nor Marijke reached for the glasses.

"So Ramon," she said. "Talk."

Ramon had planned out what he would say as he stood on Gazini's balcony, how he would make a long speech about their father, create some common ground, how he would plead for peace, for forgiveness, anything to buy more time. It would be hard playing that part, especially with that girl glaring at him. Before he could start, his sister said, "Did your wife send you down here? Did she make you come?"

Something must have shown in Ramon's face, because Marijke laughed.

"The great Ramon Cruz, son of the monster Diego Tomas, tamed by a scold of a wife."

"Don't talk about Zory that way."

"She must be quite a fuck, Ramon."

"Marijke. Listen to me. Something's happened with Michal."

"Oh, really?"

She gestured for Xi, who sat down on her lap. She stroked her hair with her good hand.

"Yes," Ramon said. "It's serious."

"Mm-hmm."

Marijke pulled Xi's face down toward her and planted a full kiss on her lips. Ramon watched for a moment, then, disgusted by the display, slouched in his seat, let his eyes wander over the torn surface of the table. They broke the kiss after a moment, and Marijke said, "I know all about my nephew, brother." She reached for her glass, and Xi got off her lap and filled it with water from the pitcher. Then she filled Ramon's glass. Ramon put his hand on it but didn't pick it up.

He wanted to. His mouth was dry, and after the day he'd had, the fight, the meeting with Gazini, he desperately wanted something nice, just a small drink, something to cool his throat, but he had to wait. He had to wait for his sister to drink first. Xi drifted over to the window.

"Did you contact him?"

"*He* contacted *me*, Ramon."

Xi leaned on the sill.

"Marijke," she said. "The Barquemen are—"

Ramon cut her off.

"What did he want?"

"He wanted a truce. To put a stop to the violence. Said he was sick of it, sick of everybody dying. He promised to give me the sixth and seventh floor if I agreed."

"Michal said this?"

"Xi, give him the note."

The girl tried to explain again, saying, "But Marijke, they're moving the oil."

"Xi! Go get the note."

Xi pulled herself away from the window and went to the kitchen. She picked a scrap of paper off the counter and slapped it down on the table in front of Ramon. He glanced at it. It was written in Michal's handwriting.

"Those floors were not his to give."

Marijke sighed.

"That's what I told him."

"The roof is mine."

"Just as I thought. Still, he is a Cruz. He is your son, your favorite. Just like you were father's."

"Marijke, with that again?"

She ignored him.

"I took him at his word. I told him if he could deliver me what he promised, no more fighting."

Ramon thought of Gazini's son. The butcher's block.

"That's not what he was doing, Marijke."

"Of course it wasn't. So I took out some insurance."

She motioned to Xi, who produced a ripped plastic bag and put it on the table between them.

"What's this?" Ramon asked.

"Take a look, brother." A cry came up from the Barquemen outside.

"Fishing?" Marijke said. "This late?"

"That's what I was trying to tell you," Xi said. "They're out there, loading up their boats."

"Who is?"

"The Barquemen."

"Yes, but who? The fishermen? The gutters?"

"All of them."

"What?"

Marijke jolted to her feet, wincing at the pain in her shoulder, and she and Xi ran to the windows.

Ramon knew what was coming. He'd given Gazini the time he needed. But the bag, it bothered him. What was his sister up to? He pulled it to him and let it sit there, unopened. Just looked at it. A thumb, maybe? An ear? The Barquemen let up another cry, deep and guttural. The room lit up with a great red light. Before he died, before the world erupted in flame, he had to see what it was. He opened the bag, carefully, as if it held a bomb. Peered inside. Then he gasped and leaped to his feet, knocking the metal chair to the floor.

"What have you done?" he said.

Marijke turned from the window.

"I should ask you the same thing."

"Marijke! What did you do?"

"Nothing you wouldn't do, brother."

The building shook with the first explosion. Something crashed through the windows, striking Xi and sending her sprawling to the hardwood. She grabbed her neck, gasping, clawing at the shard of glass sticking out of it. A second explosion rocked the building, knocking the table and chairs over. The bag fell to the floor, spilling its contents at Ramon's feet. People in the hall cried out.

"They're coming! They're coming!"

Ramon ignored everything. The crashing windows. The roaring fire. The screams, the battle cries. The floor buckled beneath him and he didn't care.

The thing in the bag wasn't a thumb. It wasn't an ear. It wasn't a head or an organ or any other body part. It was a shoe. A little shoe. White with a plastic yellow flower on the heel. And it was covered in blood.

James Noll

IT STEALS THINGS

Ben rubbed the fog off the windshield with the cuff of his windbreaker, succeeding only in smearing moisture all over the glass. Rain washed down in sheets, and his struggling wipers did no more than slop it back and forth.

"Can't see a goddamn thing," he muttered.

It had been twenty-nine years since he escaped Partlow. Twenty-nine years of lying about where he was from, of adopting the accent and attitude of wherever it was he ended up. He remembered little of his childhood, and what he did recall was nothing more than a strobe-light of faces and names, blurred moments and sounds. His cousin, though. Mike. How could he forget him? They'd been so close, but when they were little something happened and Mike changed. He didn't see him for years. Then in high school, he snapped and stabbed someone. A teacher or an administrator. He remembered his mother saying "thank goodness nobody was killed," and his father saying "he's better off where he is." The details were moths, but one thing was certain: he never saw his cousin again after that.

Then out of the blue, he got a letter in the mail. It was from Mike. "Please come home," it read. "I need help." It sat on the passenger seat under his overnight bag.

The road twisted and turned, and Ben struggled to stay in his lane. Then a burst of static exploded out of the radio and he jabbed at the power button right as the road button-hooked. His car started to hydroplane. He'd only experienced that kind of fear and panic once before, on a Jetbus that dropped two hundred feet in two seconds as he flew across the country. He gripped the wheel, eyes clenched, jaw clenched, 360 degrees of pure terror, then the car hit the grass shoulder and cracked into a tree. When he finally opened his eyes and saw the road he now faced, he couldn't help but laugh.

Dunwich Drive.

Mike's road.

The garage sat open like a yawning mouth. The car's headlights lit upon the contents inside: drifts of newspapers listed in one corner, a workbench buried beneath a landslide of tools and plastic, a bag of kitty litter, an axe balanced atop a mound covered by a leather tarp. Underneath the tarp blossomed a dark, oily stain. Just as Ben cut the engine, lightning burst in the sky, illuminating the form of a man standing right outside the door. He was wearing a hunter green rain poncho and a wide-brimmed camouflage hat, and Ben couldn't see his face.

The man ripped the door open and grabbed his elbow.

"Get inside!"

"Jesus!"

"Tornado warning."

It was Mike. Just Mike. Ben pulled his arm from his cousin's grasp.

"Okay, okay," he said, reaching for his bag.

The garage door entered into the kitchen. Mike took his bag and dipped away without a word, and Ben walked into the living room and back in time. Candles sat everywhere, on the coffee table, the mantle, the sills, the floor, lighting the room with a warm, yellow glow. Everything looked exactly as it had when he was a kid. He stopped in front of the wide front windows, straining to see the fields. Memories flooded.

When he was little, he used to eat cereal on the front step, watch the crows hop in and out of the green stalks. He remembered the dust swirls in the air as his uncle steered a tractor up the driveway. He remembered the sun peeking out over the treetops, the sunflowers in the garden. Now all he saw were the shadows of dead corn, gray and silver in the night, and the black outline of the trees beyond. Mike's reflection appeared in the window. He was standing right behind him, still wearing the rain poncho, his eyes obscured by the brim of the hat.

"Do you remember the farmer's market we used to go to?" he said. "The one in town?"

Ben turned around.

"The one in Spotsy?"

"No."

"Fredericksburg?"

"You know the one."

A strong wind shook the windows, pressed down upon the house. Ben looked over his shoulder. The trees swayed dangerously

"Shouldn't we get down to the basement?"

"We'll be fine."

"But the tornado."

"We'll be fine. Do you remember the farmer's market?"

"Mike, what's this about?"

"I remember it." Another rumble of thunder, distant, low. "When we were little, they used to build the straw maze."

The straw maze. The smell of wet hay, of apple cider. Ben had loved that market, loved everything about it. The moon pies, the pumpkin juice, even the bland natural peanut butter. Maybe something changed in Ben's face, something that Mike recognized.

"You do," he whispered. "You do."

"Mike, are you okay?"

"I was nine. Do you remember, Bennie? I was nine when it happened."

Ben winced. He hadn't been called Bennie in twenty years. Another hard gust pressed against the house. The siding popped, sticks pattered on the roof. He turned again to look out the window, worried.

"Don't look out there," Mike said. "Look at me." Ben did as he was told. "Do you remember, Bennie? When I was nine?"

"Mike, I don't remember what I did last week."

"You told me to go in. You told me to go in. 'Just try,' you said. Called me names. So I did. I went in. It was dark. I couldn't breathe. The mud wetted my knees. It ruined my new corduroys. It smelled, Bennie. It smelled like . . . like someone had . . . ."

Something clattered and banged on the roof. Ben jumped.

"Bennie, I was only nine. I was only nine, Bennie."

Hinges whined in some distant part of the house. The basement door.

"What is that?" Ben asked.

"You know in the middle? In the middle of the maze? It's pitch black in there. It sits on your chest. It steals things."

A soft thump, then the subtle susurrations as something dragged itself across the floor.

"Is there someone else here?"

"I could hear you and the other kids above. You were laughing. Screaming."

The noise grew closer. It sounded like someone dragging plastic across the hardwood. Shhh. Shhh. Shhh. Ben peered into the flickering candlelight.

"Mike—"

"It steals things, Bennie. It stole something from me."

Ben's legs flooded with adrenaline. He felt the urge to get off the floor, to leap onto the furniture.

"When mother finally found me, I hadn't moved from that spot for an hour. I was shivering. You were gone but I didn't care. It stole something from me that night and I didn't even know it and never really cared because it was gone."

They stood there like that for a long time. Mike's head lowered, the brim of his hat masking his face. Ben in a slight crouch, his hands balled into fists. The thing from the basement slid nearer and nearer.

Morning dawned with all of the warmth and cool clarity of early fall. The woods were alive. Birds flitted through the trees, lighted on the dead stalks in the fields, dive-bombed the yard to peck at ants and worms. Puddles from the night's rain potted the asphalt in front of the garage, the doors of which remained open.

Mike was kneeling in front of the leather tarp, the poncho draped over his shoulders, the hat askew on his head. He grunted as he tried to push something all the way under. When he was satisfied, he pulled the last corner down as tight as he could. He tried to tuck it in, but the edge wouldn't reach so he just let it hang there.

Someone called from inside the house.

"Hold on," he said, pondering a stain at his feet. He reached for the kitty litter. "I'll be right there."

The Legacy of the Monster Diego Tomas

Part III

Michal and Natalia zipped down the lines, two black dots against the red sky. The alarm was raised, and Ramon's guards fired off a few halfhearted pot shots, but the pair expertly threaded the old broken windows in the building opposite and landed unscathed. They sprinted down the eleventh-floor hall to the first opening (a hole blasted into the bricks), clipped to the new lines, and sped down another story. In this way they reached the third floor on the other side of the building, out of sight and out of range of his father's snipers. Night fell. They squatted in a busted up kitchen, the moonlight filtering through the shattered windows, illuminating the broken pipes and shredded wiring. Natalia bit into a red pepper, and Michal sucked his teeth.

"What?" she asked.

"The peppers."

"What about them?"

"They're smaller and smaller every year."

She pointed it at him as an offering, and when he refused she shrugged and took another bite.

"Isn't that why we're here? To level things out?"

"Yep."

She watched him pull something out of his pocket and shake it in his hand. The ring. That stupid, silver ring. He liked to play with it when he was thinking, and it drove her crazy. If she said anything, he got ugly.

It belonged to his father, Ramon Tomas, the pillar of his life and the source of all his anger. Natalia saw the old man once when she was little, carving a path through the soldiers in the hallway as she cowered against a doorjamb. He slashed and chopped. Blood sprayed the walls. Then their eyes met. It was only for a moment, but the terror lasted long after her mother snatched her up and fled back into their apartment. From that point on, Ramon Tomas was the bogeyman, the murderer hiding around the corner, the thing in her dreams. No wonder Michal barely ever laughed. He was raised by a monster.

"How many kegs of oil did you say we can get away with?" she said.

"Enough."

"You sure you can do it?"

He fixed her with an icy stare.

"You provide the distraction, I'll kill that stinking Barqueman chief."

She finished the pepper, seeds and all, and wiped the knife off on her pants. Then she grabbed him by the back of the head and planted a kiss on his mouth.

"I've got this," she said.

It was so quiet at night that Abrafo could hear the water lapping against the crumbling bricks of the old buildings. He liked the sound. It was the only thing that soothed him. Everything else about his life, the endless heat, the crowded apartments, drove him crazy. He was the son of Gazini, chief of the Barquemen, and it shamed him to feel that way. He'd heard of dry land to the West, places where people didn't live like he did, squeezing the life out of every last thing until it finally disintegrated or broke and crumbled back into the narrows. He wanted out, and the monster's son, Michal, was going to help him. They were going to burn it all down.

He skimmed along the surface on his skiff, using his long pole to guide it through the water. Every now and then something bumped him from beneath, testing the platform; every now and then he saw eyes glitter in the moonlight. One of the other night patrolmen, an older boy he didn't know, whistled and pulled his skiff out of the shadows next to his.

"Stupid!" the boy hissed. "Didn't you see it?"

"See what?"

"Ha. Some chief you'll make."

Abrafo scanned the dark lane before him, but still couldn't see anything.

"There it is again!" the other boy said.

"Where?"

"There! Open your eyes."

They paused, listening, but all Abrafo could hear was the gentle lapping of the water. Five seconds passed. Thirty. A minute.

"Shh," the other boy hissed.

Abrafo ignored the temptation to knock him off his skiff. Then, out of the corner of his eye, he saw movement. A shadow flitting in past one of the broken windows. The other boy leaned forward to stare at the water, stupidly putting him in a position where he could easily lose his balance.

"It's not in the water," Abrafo said. "It's up there."

"Shh!"

Then a shadow plunged into the water from above, rocking their skiffs, and the other boy tumbled overboard with a shout. Abrafo felt his foot yanked from beneath him and down he went. When he surfaced, the attacker had already climbed into his skiff and was using his pole to steer it away.

"Get it!" the other boy yelled.

Then he was jerked under the water.

Oh god, Abrafo thought.

He lunged away, trying to put as much distance between himself and the monster under the water. The boy resurfaced again.

"Help!" he gasped, and grabbed Abrafo's forearm.

Abrafo yanked it out of his grasp, and then the boy was dragged under again and didn't come back up. He turned and swam for his life, trying to focus on his body. Scoop the hands, roll the shoulders. His arms were pistons, his legs on springs, and before he knew it he ran into the side of a half-submerged awning and scrambled up.

His attacker was only a few feet in front of him, struggling to steer the skiff. He leaped for it, landing aft, gained his footing, and scooted forward. One arm thrust around the neck, one around the chest, and . . . wait—

"You gonna feel me up all night?" Natalia asked.

Abrafo released her.

"Michal said you were supposed to come quiet, not like this." He grabbed the pole out of her hands. "You could have gotten me killed."

"You were supposed to be alone. Had to make it look real, didn't I?"

Abrafo lay the pole across the skiff and took his machete out of the loop on his belt, flipped it so that he was holding it by the blade, a smooth, practiced movement. Natalia tried to back up, but she was already standing at the prow.

"What are you doing?"

"I have to make it look real, don't I?"

Natalia stumbled through a second floor hallway, her clothes soaked, her head whirling. Her eye had swollen closed and black spots swam in the other so all she could see were her feet slapping on the soaked carpet and the occasional face of a child staring out from an open doorway. Abrafo kept a tight grip on her wrists as more and more people filed in behind, whispering and murmuring the whole time.

"Who is this?" someone asked. "What did she do?"

"Mid-level bitch tried to kill me and break into the building," Abrafo said.

"Are they attacking?"

"Who knows. I'm taking her to my father."

"A wise boy. Gazini will know what to do. Gazini will protect us."

Natalia was a little shocked. They weren't as filthy as everyone in her building said they were. In fact, they looked fresh and clean, and they wore colorful clothes decorated with shells and bits of metal. Abrafo pushed her up an open stair well, leaving the group behind. Glass lamps had been screwed into the crumbling walls. Oil burned in them, providing dim light. Natalia struggled to climb, but waited until they turned the first corner before she leaned up against the wall and sank to the floor.

Abrafo gave her a bladder filled with water and she drank from it, dribbling some down her chin. She handed it back, shifted her feet and tried to stand, but her legs shook and she plopped back down again. Abrafo held out his hand. She slapped it away.

Raised voices from below, shocked cries. Abrafo craned his neck over the rail to see what was going on.

"What is it?" Natalia asked.

"I don't know."

Then he saw him. The boy from outside, the one he thought was dead. He was standing at the bottom of the stairs, all of the people from the hall gathered behind him. His chest and arms were covered in blood, and his face looked like something had taken a chunk out of it. His one good eye fixed on Abrafo. Abrafo turned and grabbed Natalia's arm.

"We have to go," he said.

She saw the expression on his face and didn't resist. They ran, Abrafo in front, yanking her up the stairs. Below them she heard more astonished cries, voices raised in argument.

"Impossible!"

"The chief's son?"

"Yes! Yes!"

Natalia did her best to keep up, but Abrafo took two steps at a time and her head hurt so bad that she felt like she was going to pass out. They made it up one flight, then another, turning corners as fast as they could, the boy widening the distance with each step. She slowed down to pull out her machete.

"Hurry," he called.

"I'm trying!"

The mob below grew louder, angrier. Natalia's stomach twisted. Dozens of feet pounded up the stairs.

"Abrafo! Traitor!"

Abrafo sprinted up and away, and Natalia lurched and struggled, conscious only of the burning in her lungs, the ache in her head. One step at a time, one step at a time. She tripped and sprawled forward, picked herself up and pushed on. The mob behind her grew closer. Their cries echoed in the stairwell, blocked out even the sound of her own breathing until it filled her head. How many more flights?

Someone grabbed her foot and she slashed back with her machete. She heard the familiar *phut phut* of the Barquemen blow guns, felt the darts strike her back, her legs. One more flight and then she'd have to turn around, have to face them.

The thought of it gave her strength, made her strong again. She scaled one set, then another, moving faster and faster, yanking on the rails, putting more steps between her and the mob. The voices fell farther behind, and then suddenly she reached the top. Abrafo was arguing with a muscular man guarding the door to his father's floor. Natalia stumbled forward and the guard put his hand on the knife in his belt.

"Who is this, Abrafo?" he said. "What do you want?"

"I caught her trying to break in."

"So? Take her to the basement and throw her in the pit."

Natalia fell against the wall next to the guard, her machete clattering on the floor. She pulled a dart out of her leg and tossed it aside. He recoiled.

"What do you think will happen if we kill her?" Abrafo said. He pointed down the well. "Listen to them! They've gone mad. They want blood."

"I don't think—" the guard began, but Natalia interrupted him.

"He's not going to listen," she said. In one swift movement, she scooped up her weapon and buried it in his stomach.

The guard stumbled back, startled, confused. He started to withdraw his knife, but Abrafo kicked him onto his back. They were inside the door in seconds. Abrafo locked it against the crowd.

Gazini's floor was dark and squalid. He'd opened up the entire thing, tore down all of the walls, pulled all of the pipes, yanked all of the wire, every fixture, knob, scrap, everything had been dismantled and put to better use. Even more incredible was the light. Oil lamps burned in great pots in each of the four corners, sending black smoke into metal ducts that carried it out into the night. Smaller lamps lined the floors, hung from the ceiling, burning more oil in a minute than Natalia had ever seen in her lifetime.

A chopping sound echoed in the dark. They followed it around the corner of a support beam, careful to avoid tripping on the lamps that lit the way. There he stood, Gazini, Abrafo's father, a hulking figure bending over a chopping table covered in fish parts and blood. He'd surrounded himself with lamps, so many that Natalia could see every muscle in his back ripple as he worked on the meat in front of him. The butcher's knife thunked into the wood, he made his cut, then pushed the meat aside. Natalia couldn't see what he was working on, but judging by his grunts and effort, it was big. A shark, maybe? A mutation? Whatever it was, she didn't want to be there anymore. If Gazini was alive, it was a bad sign.

They stopped a few feet away. The butcher's knife thunked one more time into the block, and Gazini leaned on the table with both hands. He sighed.

"It was a beautiful night, huh Abrafo?"

Abrafo frowned, wondering how to respond. He started to say something, but a dozen stout fists slammed on the door behind them. The mob cried for blood. Gazini ignored them.

"You were born on a night like this," he said. "Your mother on a cot in the corner." He grabbed the handle of the butcher's knife and yanked it out of the block, dragging it across the wood. "Nature," he said, twirling it in the air. "Punishes you for success. Once you think you've made it, once you think you have everything you want, she takes it away. Not all at once, but little pieces."

He grunted and chopped into the meat again.

Abrafo said, "Father."

The door behind them cracked. More fists pounded.

"Do you know what your mother told me before she died?" Gazini asked. "She said, 'take care of him.' Like I had a choice."

Natalia swayed on her feet.

"What's on the block?" she asked.

Gazini reached out behind him with the bloody knife.

"Tell the mid-level bitch if she opens her mouth again, I'll cut it off."

Abrafo looked at her, shook his head.

"I took care of you, Abrafo," Gazini said. "That's what fathers do. That's what men do. They take care of their sons."

"Is that what you call it? I'm a prisoner here."

"Abrafo, you're going to be the chief one day."

"Oh. Yes. 'The Chief'." Abrafo spread his arms wide. "Of all this. Of this magnificent kingdom."

"Son—"

"I'm not your son, I'm your slave! I don't want any of this."

"There it is! The fire. The anger. When I was young like you, I had it, too. So much piss and vinegar. I leaped and ran. I climbed these walls, wrestled net after net out of the water, fought off that stinking Diego Tomas and his fucking zip-liners. But now? Now, I'm paying for it. My body hurts, Abrafo. I can barely walk up a flight of stairs."

A fist punched through the top part of the door.

"Abrafo! Traitor!"

Natalia took three steps forward, raising her machete over her head. Abrafo could only watch, frozen.

Gazini said, "The pain keeps me up at night. Which was why I was awake when your friend tried to kill me."

She stopped, and finally the old man turned around, revealing the mangled form on the block. She dropped her weapon and fell to her knees with a moan. Gazini reached back and picked something out of the ruck, held it up for her to see. It sparkled in the light.

"I think he might have wanted you to have this," he said, and flipped it to her.

It pinged as it turned, end over end, landing beside her on the floor, bouncing once, twice, coming to a rest just as the mob broke down the door and flooded the room.

~

Gazini stepped out onto the balcony, carefully closing the door on a high pitched squeal. Pots of oil burned on the rails, hung from the platform above. He withdrew a cigar from his pocket and used one of the pots to puff it to life. The cherry glowed red in the dark. Another scream erupted from inside, knifing through the angry shouts of the mob. Behind him, a voice said, "Is that her?"

Gazini chuckled. He turned around. Ramon stood with his back to the wall, still in the shadows.

"I asked you a question," he said.

Gazini took a languorous draw on his cigar, filling his cheeks. It was a rare gift, given to him on one of his yearly trading convoys to the mountains. He savored it, closed his eyes, blew a great gray cloud out into the night.

"I got rid of your problem for you."

Ramon remained in the shadows, his face unseeable, unreadable, but his reply was terse, as if he spoke through clenched teeth.

"Thank you," he said.

"We old men, we have to stick together, you know."

"I know."

Ramon took a step out of the shadows and Gazini took a step back and put his hand on the door knob.

"All I have to do is open this door."

Ramon's eyes didn't move.

"Relax, barqueman."

"I'll relax when when you've taken care of my problem for me."

"I told you I would."

Gazini took another puff on his cigar.

"And your wife? Your daughter?"

"They're safe on the eleventh floor. It'll only be me and my sister."

"Are you sure you can even talk to her? Her men will hack you to pieces."

"She'll let me through."

The Barqueman was unimpressed. He gestured at the door.

"If she's anything like you, I'd bring some kind of weapon."

He laughed at his own joke, and Ramon stepped up on to the railing and clipped onto a zip line. He turned his head, a sneer forming on his lips.

"Give me an hour."

"Okay, Ramon."

Ramon looked like he was about to say something, thought better, and jumped off the railing and into the night.

"I'd love to attend a Tomas family reunion!" Gazini called after him. "What a party that would be, huh?"

James Noll

Topher's Ton
The Final Chapter
of the Topher Trilogy

CONTENTS

1 Survival of the Fittest   43

2 Someplace Safe   75

3 Liam Chris   171

4 Raleigh's Redux   227

"Should the whole frame of nature round him break,
In ruin and confusion hurled,
He, unconcerned, would hear the mighty crack,
And stand secure amidst a falling world."
—Joseph Addison

"Sometimes even to live is an act of courage."
—Seneca

"I may not have gone where I intended to go, but I think I have ended up where I needed to be."
—Douglas Adams

"Nuclear apocalypse-who do you need? Actors are probably not top of the list. What can I do for you? I can pretend to be somebody who can grow you some nice crops."
—Christian Bale

SURVIVAL OF THE FITTEST

It was the end of the world, and Topher needed a new linen suit. Unfortunately, some maniacs from the west attacked his caravan before he could find one, so he had to put off the search until later, unless he died, of course, in which case the point was moot. But at least he'd put on clean underwear, not that going into battle wearing soiled undergarments was even an option. It was a longstanding Bill family tradition to put on clean underthings before all major life events, stretching back to the days of Wilhelm Bill the Mangler who, having married into French aristocracy, fought against his homeland during the Franco-Prussian War, thus earning the title Wilhelm Bill the Sonofabitch. Besides, Topher considered himself a gentleman, and gentlemen did not die while wearing dirty drawers.

But he wasn't dead. Not yet.

He had a battle to win, crazy people to kill, so he did what great leaders did: he strode through the maelstrom of bullets and grenades, Molotov cocktails and flamethrowers, arsenic-laced bullets, whip-cracks, moans, shrieks, and cries, and barked orders until his voice went hoarse.

Then a spear zipped by his head and he nearly soiled himself.

To make matters worse, a gust of wind kicked up dirt all around him and dirtied his beard. He passed through it, cursing, coughing, wiping his eyes with his sleeve. It occurred to him to do something impressive, perform some kind of daring feat, so he removed his Panama hat and knocked it against his thigh.

"Mayor Bill!" someone shouted.

A short, skinny young woman ran up to him. She had smooth, olive skin and a thin, angular face, and she wore thick, oversized glasses that perpetually slid down her nose. Her curly thatch of black hair was tangled and filthy, and she hid it beneath an old Redskins baseball cap. Her name was Saanvi.

"Saanvi," Topher said. "I told you to man the flamethrowers."

Saanvi struggled to maintain her composure. The shouts and screams, the occasional bullet, all of them wreaked havoc with her sensory issues. Plus, she was afraid of dying. She blinked and flinched with each bullet fired and each explosion, but squashed the desire to run. This wasn't her first firefight, and the best cure was exposure. The best cure was exposure. The best cure was—

"Saanvi!"

She shook it off.

"We're out of gas."

"What? We can't be out of gas. We had plenty before."

"We ran out. We were just trying to use the flamethrowers, but—"

"Goddammit!"

"What do you want us to do?"

"I don't know. Throw the flamethrowers!"

Topher stomped away, Saanvi trotting close behind.

"Throw the flamethrowers?"

"Why do you think they call it a flame*thrower*?"

"But that's stupid. We'll find gas somewhere else. What if the enemy has some?"

A bullet ricocheted off the top of a nearby truck. Saanvi ducked. Topher didn't.

"There's no way they can have any gas."

"They probably thought the same thing about us."

"Not anymore."

Saanvi blinked hard, forcing herself to answer rather than react.

"Mayor, they're going to breach the ring!"

"Then throw rocks at them. And stop calling me 'Mayor'."

"Rocks?"

Topher stopped abruptly and spun around.

"Yes. Rocks. And when they breach the ring, break their skulls with your fists, and when they break your fists, tear them apart with your teeth, and when they break out your teeth, head-butt their eye sockets, kick them, lick them, spit on them, *do* something! Do something! Do anything except follow me around repeating every suggestion I make like some kind of deranged cockatiel!"

Saanvi opened her mouth to argue but thought better of it. She snapped a quick salute and turned on her heel.

"Wait," he called after.

A white flash interrupted him, followed by a roar and then black silence.

Topher gasped awake, head pounding. The battle was done, replaced by nothingness. No bullets, no enemies, no explosions, no dust. Somebody cried out in the distance. He sat up and looked around. To the left, hunks of metal and glass entwined with body parts. To the right, blackened frames of cars. A burning rubber tire rolled by, turned, and wound to a stop like a quarter on a table. He watched it.

My God, he thought. *It's over. It's truly over.*

He thought maybe he should feel something. Anger, perhaps? Rage? Fear? Guilt? He'd let everyone down, after all. His men were dead. But he didn't feel anything remotely close to any of that. In fact, all he felt was relief. He always knew the day would come, the day when he lost, when he would die, and waiting for it was worse than it actually happening. Now he didn't have to worry anymore about anything, about his men, about the children, about the illness, about gangrene, about dehydration, about getting an infection, about losing an arm, about hunger, shelter, or someone slitting his throat in his sleep. He stood up, giddy, and swayed in place. A body lay nearby, and he stumbled over to it, stuffed his boot under its chest, and flipped it over.

Not one of his men.

He did the same to the next body and the next. Not his. Not his. None of them were his. So wait. The idiots had somehow bombed their own people. They'd bombed their own people and didn't even know it.

He sighed.

He'd won again.

The stupidity was galling. He might be ready to die, but it wasn't going to be at the hands of morons. He looked around for a weapon, something with which to brain a skull, or stab a gut, or slit an artery, and there, a few feet away, lay a morning star made out of nails and a piece of rebar. He picked it up.

"Perfect," he said, and weighed it in his hands.

But before he could plot anymore, before he could mock his enemies and praise his superiority, a familiar voice rang out. He paused, listening, and there it was again, cutting through the screams and the pain and the moans of the dying.

"Onward, you apes!" it cried. Topher swung in its direction. "Don't stop until your hands have wrung the necks of every last one! Don't stop wringing their necks until your palms meet! Cry havoc, and let loose the dogs of war!"

He was in shock. That voice. Could it be? Saanvi suddenly appeared, her face covered in soot, her glasses hanging at an odd angle. She grabbed his arm.

"Mayor, we're done. We've got to run."

He shook her off.

"We're not going anywhere."

He broke into a trot, heading for the voice, leaving her there.

A savage leaped into his path, all wild hair and ululations and bad teeth, and Topher buried the rebar in his chest. Another flew at him and he clothes-lined him. A strong wind collapsed upon them. Storm clouds rolled in. Fat drops of rain spattered on the asphalt.

Topher jumped up on the hood of a burned-out wreck. There, in the midst of all the carnage, stood a bearded man wearing fur pants and a fur jacket, screaming into the wind.

"Where are you?" he cried. "Fight! Fight!"

Then he spotted Topher and froze, amazed, petrified. His beard flew up into his face and he clawed it away.

"Oh dear god, no. Not you," he said.

Topher let up a whoop.

"Zorn!" he cried. "Zorn, you idiot! It's 'let *slip* the dogs of war'!"

Topher sent Saanvi to retrieve their people, the horses, the food truck and the children, while he and the surviving men set up camp by the side of the road. The worst of the storm had passed, washing the highway clean, and a fine mist took its place as evening settled. The peepers in the woods started to sing. When she returned, Saanvi wove through the tents, looking for where Topher had set his up. She'd lost her cap, and the mist dampened her hair, decorating it with little crystal dew drops. She paused for a moment to take a breath before going inside, and she was just about to say something when Topher erupted with laughter from inside.

Laughter always made her feel uncomfortable. In fact, of the many things that made her feel uncomfortable—facial expressions, abstract art, disorganized closets—humor made her feel the worst. No. That wasn't entirely true. She liked humor when she was the one responsible for it, but when it came to discrepancies, particularly those for which she was unprepared, she possessed the tact of a sledgehammer. Why was Dali considered brilliant? All he did was make things look weird. And what was the deal with puns? There was nothing funny about homonyms. Why was the Mayor laughing after dozens of people were killed? War and death weren't funny.

One of the enemy savages passed by. He was all beard and belly and wild hair, but he'd changed into khaki pants and a tattered blue Oxford. He stopped when he saw her and said, "Barry."

He held out his hand. Saanvi looked at it. She knew she was supposed to shake it. Social niceties demanded acceptance of another's presence via rigorous digital manipulation. But of all the appendages on the human body, the hands and fingers harbored the most disease, and in this post-antibiotic world, one could never be too careful. She clasped her hands behind her back.

"Saanvi," she said.

Barry faltered and let his hand drop.

"I was a dentist."

Saanvi nodded.

"I was in a mental institution."

Barry laughed.

"Then I guess things haven't changed very much for you at all, have they?"

Saanvi watched him as he walked away. Of course things had changed. One, she never slept in the same bed twice anymore. Two, no more Tapioca Tuesday. Three, living outdoors resulted in a distinct lack of hygiene. Four.

She stopped herself.

The list could have gone on forever if she didn't. Her hand automatically went for her right sleeve, which she always kept buttoned around her wrist. Nobody needed to see her arm. It led to questions, and rather than answer them honestly, she lied, which was hard for her to do because it wasn't real and things that weren't real made her anxious and anxiety reminded her of father and his rules and his punishments and his expectations, so rather than give anybody the opportunity to ask her about her scars, she kept her sleeves buttoned. When she needed to, she felt them over her shirt. She decided to repeat the number four times and then stop.

Four.

Four.

Four.

Four.

And that was it.

She balled her fists, tensing up the muscles in her arms and back, held it for a few seconds, then let it all go with a ragged breath.

The compulsion was gone.

Her mind was clear.

The Mayor laughed again at one of his own jokes. He often did that, but this time she decided that it might actually make sense. From what she understood, he and the savage leader were old acquaintances, college roommates or something. If they had truly found each other, then they would be happy, and when people were happy they sometimes laughed. She smoothed her dirty clothes and knocked on the tent flap.

From inside a voice said, "Did someone just knock on the tent flap?"

It was the savage leader. The Mayor said his name was Zorn, but that was an odd name because she'd never met anybody named Zorn before. It didn't help when, after the battle, he explained to her that Zorn was his friend's last name.

"What's his first name, then?" she'd asked.

"Michael."

"Then why don't you call him Michael?"

"Because I call him Zorn."

"But that doesn't make sense."

"Saanvi, what's your last name?"

"Fickerald."

"Fickerald? Your name is Saanvi Fickerald?"

"My father was white."

Topher took a breath.

"If you don't stop talking to me about this, I'm going to refer to you as Fickerald from now on."

"But why?"

"Does it make you anxious?"

Saanvi thought. Her hand trailed to her cuff.

"It makes me very anxious."

"Then you have your answer."

Saanvi knocked on the flap again.

"It's probably Saanvi," the Mayor grumbled. Then, in a louder, exaggeratedly pleasant voice, he said, "Enter, Saanvi. No need to knock."

She ducked inside. The Mayor and Zorn were propped up in lawn chairs, each holding a jar of Ton Brew. A small fire crackled in between them, and a thin line of smoke rose up into the air and out of the little circular hole in the top. It was quite warm and cozy.

"Zorn, this is Saanvi."

Zorn said, "Hello."

Saanvi looked at him.

"Your name is Michael but the Mayor calls you Zorn."

"Yes. People have called me that my entire life."

"I understand nicknames. The Mayor says people use them when they're friends. He said it is a 'term of endearment.' But that's not how people used it on me."

Zorn took a sip from his jar.

"How did they use it on you?"

"My last name is Fickerald, but they called me Fucktardal."

Topher suddenly felt horrible. As strange as the woman was, he hated bullies, and she'd obviously suffered more than one in her past, and he had reminded her of it, before, when he threatened to call her by her last name. He put his jar on the ground and leaned forward, resting his elbows on his knees.

"What can we do for you, Saanvi?"

"I made a report of the damages and casualties, Mayor."

"You didn't have to do that."

"Right now I've counted thirty-seven injured and two dead. Six of the cars are destroyed, and we'll have to replace almost all the tires. But the animals are safe, and our supplies and civilians."

Topher gaped.

"Only two dead? Are you sure? I could have sworn I saw more."

"I was only counting our people. We're okay. Michael Zorn's people, though . . . ."

Zorn remained silent, pressing his lips together until they were white.

Saanvi said, "I met a man named Barry outside. He was a dentist."

"Barry's alive?" Zorn asked.

Saanvi glanced at him, confused. Hadn't she just told him that? She was about to explain this to him but remembered what the Mayor had told her about stating the obvious. Instead, she said, "Would you like to know the names of the dead, sir?"

Topher thought for a moment, then said, "No."

"But, sir."

"All I want to know is if you've burned them yet."

Saanvi's face turned red.

"It's wet out, Mayor."

"So?"

"We're out of gas. You know we're out of gas. I told you we were out of gas. Before. During the fight. You told me to throw rocks."

"Saanvi, I don't have to remind you what happens if we don't burn them."

"No, sir."

"Then find a way."

Saanvi gave him a clipped nod and left without another word.

Zorn took a sip of his beer.

"I can't believe this is happening," he said.

"Me, too."

"The last time I saw you was on Riddle's couch."

"Did I show you what that crazy bastard did to me?"

"No."

Topher took off his boots and socks and showed him what was left of his toes.

"Why?" Zorn asked.

"He was going to use me as fertilizer." He put his socks back on, navigating the holes with his remaining digits. "Said he was a 'connoisseur'. Had a trophy case with decapitated heads in it. Reinholdt was there. Well, his head was. Can you imagine how horrible that would have been for me? Spending eternity next to that dumb bastard?"

Zorn grimaced. He finished his drink and set the jar on the ground.

"I don't know what he had in store for me. One moment I was on his couch, dropping off to sleep, the next, I woke up in a basement in California."

"My God."

Zorn looked around the tent, listened to the rain patter outside.

"You seem to have done well."

"Riddle had a bunker," Topher said.

"What?"

"A bunker. Under the pump house. It's how I survived. After the radiation died out and the flood waters receded, I had everything I needed. Seeds. Books. Guns. Ammo. He actually had a press and bullets, powder and casings. I've got it all here, too."

"Of course you do."

"What's that supposed to mean?"

Zorn shrugged.

"It means that these things just have a way of happening to you. I bet the next thing you'll tell me is how you've created a sanctuary to save the world, and that you were on your way there when we tried to kill you."

Topher paused.

"Well, actually . . ."

"Oh for god's sake!"

"It's not exactly like that, Zorn."

"Really? Good."

Topher told him about how he used Riddle's supplies to establish The Ton. How it took him two years to fight off the raiders, grow the food, attract a population.

"We even put up walls," he said. "But it wasn't enough. Disease doesn't care about walls. It found us and burned through us like we were dry grass. There was nothing we could do about it. There wasn't even enough time to kill everybody again or burn the bodies after they were dead. We just ran. That was a month ago. And now we're here."

He picked his jar up and settled back into his chair.

"Topher, that's horrible," Zorn said.

"Survival of the fittest."

"Sure. Sure. But, why even try? You had everything you needed in the bunker. You didn't have to save the world."

"Nobody else was doing it."

Zorn felt the old, familiar bitterness rise up in him again.

"It always has been about you, hasn't it?" he said. "Nobody is smarter than you, better than you."

Topher rubbed his face.

"I don't know where that's coming from, but I suppose I deserve that."

"You do."

"I'm different now, Zorn. I've changed."

"I'll believe that when I see it."

"How do I explain this to you?"

"That's not my problem."

"You know, my whole life I've felt like a fool. Like my ideas were stupid. Like nobody should take me seriously."

"Come on, Topher. You? You're the most arrogant person I've ever known."

"I hid behind it. It was my armor."

Zorn snorted. Topher reached behind him and held up a jar of mayonnaise.

Zorn said, "So?"

"A little girl gave this to me, right before you attacked." Topher put the jar back down. "It told me all I needed to know. I'm not that fool anymore. I'm sure of it. People die for fools all of the time. People die for fools, they die for monsters, they die for idiots. But they never give the last jar of mayo in the world to one."

Zorn tapped the arm of the lawn chair.

"You know, it doesn't matter if you're an idiot or the smartest person in the world. If they die for you, then it's your fault."

Topher didn't answer, and they sat in awkward silence for a while. Finally, Topher said, "I was thinking that you'd like to join us."

"Join you? Are you serious?"

"Yes."

"You're not going to kill us?"

Topher looked startled. Kill them? The thought hadn't even crossed his mind. It wasn't an invalid question, he supposed, but still.

"No. We're not going to kill you."

"I'm not sure what to say," Zorn said. "We didn't really have any goals beyond surviving. What's your plan?"

Topher could have lied, said that he wanted to start again, that he was looking for a new place to call home, but he didn't have it in him.

"I don't have a plan, Zorn," he said. "I'm out of ideas. I don't know what to do next. The only thing I know is that there are people out there who are following me for some reason and I feel responsible for them, so I'm just kind of winging it here."

"Don't you think they'll see through that?"

"It's not like I'm lying to them. Before you attacked us, we were heading up north. There are suburbs there. Maybe they haven't been looted yet."

"That's a long shot."

"But it's at least some kind of shot. Don't you understand? I have to give them something to hold on to. Hope, a mission, something. Otherwise, they have nothing."

"That makes sense."

"Zorn, you have to come with me. I can do this alone, but I'd rather not. I need a friend."

Zorn thought for a while before he responded. A friend. He hadn't thought of Topher Bill in over twenty years, and even before that, he didn't think of him as a friend. An arrogant madman who constantly got him in trouble and exposed him to situations in which he was attacked first by monstrous wolves, then by zombies, and finally by a serial killer. Just thinking about it made him angry. All of his people, they were good people. Now they were dead. But then he was partially to blame for that, wasn't he? Topher had plenty of good people, too, and in this kind of landscape, the only true safety was in numbers. Unless some other group had more people than he did and oh Christ, he could go on forever about this, couldn't he? In the end, he said the only thing he could think of. The least committal. The least inflammatory.

"Okay."

Before they left, they burned all the bodies.

They wandered up I-95 for a week, hunting in the woods, catching rainwater. The suburbs in Northern Virginia turned out to be a treasure trove. So many apartments and McMansions. They spent a week looting Springfield, then headed west to avoid the contaminated zone around D.C. In Vienna, they nearly ran into a band of outlaws outside the Metro station. Zorn wanted to engage, but Topher didn't want to waste bullets, and by the time the argument ended, the outlaws had vanished.

It was there that they first saw the warnings. Sometimes it was a red ankh painted on front doors and traffic signs. Sometimes it was something simple, like a sheet of plywood with the words "SHE IS HERE!" painted on it, also in red. Once, scrawled on a sheet hanging from the roof of a house on Lawyers Road, they saw this:

"WHEN SHE COMES, RUN."

They stopped in Reston to take inventory. The caravan separated good food from bad, classified weapons and ammo, and shed their dirty old clothes and shoes for fresh new ones. Topher found a linen jacket in a townhouse that overlooked a lake. He brought it out to show it to Zorn.

"Look what I found!" he said.

Zorn, who was holding an unopened can of peaches, said, "Peachy."

He opened it with a knife and sniffed.

"Doesn't seem to be bad," he said, and guzzled it down.

He pointed the empty can at another red ankh, this one painted on a boarded-up window.

"What's with the symbol?"

Topher squinted.

"I'm not sure. It looks Egyptian. Does it matter?"

"Maybe it's the government."

"What government?"

"A new one?"

"A new one that uses Egyptian symbolism?"

Zorn chucked the empty can aside.

"I think we should leave."

"Are you kidding?"

"No."

"Zorn, look around you. This place is a gift. All the food we want, no bandits, no rapists, no crazy cult leaders. There are schools we could rebuild, a library, lakes. Lakes!"

Zorn pointed at the ankh.

"And that."

Saanvi walked up behind him.

"It's the symbol of Isis," she said. "The blood goddess."

"Blood goddess!"

"The blood of life, of rebirth. When Seth cut Osiris into a thousand pieces and threw him in the Nile, Isis took the parts back into herself and gave birth to him again. She's a symbol of resurrection."

Zorn pondered this.

"I suppose in that light, it's not so bad."

"The cult of Isis sacrificed people the same way," she added. "They used to cut them up into little pieces and throw them in the Nile."

By the end of the spring, they'd completely restocked their food truck with all kinds of canned goods: fruit, tuna, beans, peas, carrots, soup. They found more ammunition, bullets and rifles and handguns locked up in gun safes or tucked away in shoeboxes. They did not, however, find any medicine. No aspirin, no Neosporin, no antihistamines, and certainly not anything more serious, like morphine or insulin. They didn't even find any good drugs.

"I know the potheads didn't make it out alive," Topher grumbled to himself. "Some hippie has to have a stash somewhere."

They did, however, find a huge cache of Adderall and Ritalin, Prozac, and Zoloft, as well as an inordinate amount of Cialis and Viagra. More importantly, they found a single round of antibiotics. One round. At least one of them wouldn't have to worry about getting an infection.

Gradually it all began to make sense. The end struck so fast and in so many different ways that nobody had time to react. Most people were drowned or burned or swallowed up almost immediately, and those who didn't find immediate shelter afterward were eaten during the ensuing CZA. Desperate men wiped out the rest. Nobody had time to eat or fire a gun. Nobody had any time to do anything other than kill or die.

They headed north on Rt. 15, spent the August and September in the cool climes of the mountains. In the fall, they traveled back to I-95 where Topher told Zorn he wanted to head to the ocean.

"Why the ocean?"

"Why not?"

"I can think of a few: Hurricanes, earthquakes, tsunamis, the fact that most of the coast is underwater."

"We don't have to stay there. I just want to see it. Kind of like a farewell."

"Farewell?"

Topher gave him a look.

"Don't worry. I'm not there yet."

Zorn didn't press him about it. He was too busy thinking of the best route to get to the beach. He fished an old road map of the East Coast out of his backpack and spread it out on the ground. The edges were tattered and torn, and the map was ripped at the folds. He found some back roads they might use, but back roads were always a gamble; they were either washed out or blocked by fallen trees or, even worse, hunted by bandits. The interstate was only slightly better, but at least it was out in the open and relatively dry. They'd have to avoid Philadelphia altogether. It was always a good idea to stay out of the big cities. He traced his finger over his proposed route.

"I think we can head north to Wilmington. Head east on 295, then take the Atlantic City Expressway."

"Alright then."

"When do we leave?"

"I don't see why we should wait. Why don't you go rally the troops?"

Zorn was more than glad to help, and Topher watched him as he folded up the map and left. He wished he could share his friend's enthusiasm, but all he could think about was Robert Burns and Steinbeck.

His name was Scotty, and he was eight. He was only a year old when the Catastrophes happened. He'd never known a home other than a tent, had never been to school, had never passed a day when his stomach wasn't grumbling. He didn't know what electricity was, had never seen a television program or gone to the movies. He didn't know it, but the woman he called his mother wasn't his mother, and the man he called his father wasn't his father. He was tough and smart, but young and full of questions, and one morning he got it into his head that he was going to explore. His mother always told him to stay close, to wake her up if he got up before she did, but she seemed so comfortable in her sleep, breathing heavy as the sun lightened the sky, and he didn't want to bother her.

First, he was just going to pee. That was okay, wasn't it? He went to the edge of the woods where they made camp and made water there, staring into the dark, his breath fogging the air. It was so beautiful, so still. He'd just finished when he heard the crack of somebody stepping on a stick, the thump of something heavy nearby. He held his breath. Nothing. Daddy always said to be careful, and Scotty had seen some red work in his short life, so he knew it wasn't an idle warning. But if he ran, he'd make noise, and whatever it was would come after him. After another silent moment, he began to relax. Nothing more to be heard. Just the rustle of the wind.

"H-hello?" he asked, then clamped his hand over his mouth.

Stupid! Why did he do that?

Another crack, another thump.

He strained to see what was out there, fighting the urge to run back to his tent. He was brave. He was strong. Noises were nothing, right? He swallowed his fear, even as his hands trembled. Daddy wouldn't be afraid. Daddy would fight the monster and kill it. Another breath of wind stirred the dead leaves, and then the thing stepped into sight.

Scotty gasped.

It was the most beautiful creature he'd ever seen. Brown and white fur covered its body, which was sleek and strong and made for speed, and it had a little ball for a tail and nubs pushing out of its head. He marveled at how it seemed to emerge from the woods, like magic. It stopped when it saw him, and they stared at each other for a long time. Then another thump came from somewhere else and the beautiful creature bounded away, shooting between the trees and brush with athletic leaps.

Scotty couldn't help himself. He ran after it.

He tried to keep up, but it was too fast, too agile. Little branches whipped his face, the undergrowth tore at his jeans, and he quickly lost track. He ran farther and farther in, turning here and there when he thought he heard it nearby, but after a while, he grew winded and had to stop. He leaned over and put his hands on his knees, trying to catch his breath.

How far in had he gone? Was he lost? The camp couldn't be too far back. He'd run in a straight line, right? All he had to do was turn around and head back out. He was about to do this when he heard a scream. A woman's scream. It sounded like it was coming from in front of him. She must be in trouble! He turned back the way he came, thinking. Daddy wouldn't run back. Daddy would help. She screamed again, clearer this time, and Scotty made up his mind.

He only had to walk another hundred yards or so before the woods ended at another road. He popped over a rusty guardrail and walked across it. There, down below, was the most terrifying thing he'd ever seen. He looked at it, heart racing, then turned and ran back through the woods to tell his parents.

Topher and Zorn scooted under a rusted metal barrier at the edge of the road to get a better look at what they were dealing with. Double layers of winding highway twisted before them, bending through itself like a fat black snake. Some of the overpasses were as tall as skyscrapers. Philadelphia sat gray and dead in the distance.

The first beams of the morning sun shone on their faces, which were dusky and dirty with endless travel. Ever since the Catastrophes, there seemed to be more dirt in the air, and the days stayed hotter longer, and the wind sometimes swooped down out of nowhere, bringing with it dust storms that blackened the sky even at noon. This, however, was no such day. The landscape was as white as bleached bone, and though it was fall, they could feel the heat gathering above, pushing down on them, cruel and heavy. All was still.

Topher surveyed the road before him with a pair of binoculars. She was there. Just like the boy said. Naked. Seemingly bound to the pole.

She was surrounded by a circle of crushed cars stacked atop one another, forming a ten-foot wall of metal shards, exposed wiring, and broken glass. Although the boy said she'd been screaming, her chin now rested on her chest.

"She's dead," Zorn said.

"Or faking it."

"How could she be faking that?"

Topher handed Zorn the binoculars.

"Look. See how she's holding her arms behind her? It's so we can't see if she's really bound or if she's hiding a weapon?" He sighed wearily. "Obviously a trap. You'll get used to it, you know."

Zorn put the binoculars down, placed his right palm under Topher's chin, and smacked his head up into the guardrail.

"Ouch! What was that for?"

"I've stayed alive this entire time, too, you know. Did you fight off the Elk-Men of Montana? Did you escape from cannibals in Aspen?"

"Boys playing cowboy and starving yuppies. Nothing compared to what she has in store for us."

"They were cannibals! And the Elk-men weren't playing at anything. They screwed actual elk horns into their own skulls. It sounds ridiculous until you find yourself impaled on one of them."

"Now you're just making things up."

"You're such a dick."

"So?"

"So what about morality? Goodness? Art? I thought you wanted to start civilization again?"

"I do, but for now it's gone, and we have to be realistic. We're all eating each other. A splinter could be a death sentence, and if you die, you come back and eat other people. Even worse, nobody knows how to read anymore. The next generation will be populated by illiterate cannibals who flinch at anything made out of wood. So I'm a dick. Who cares. I'm a living dick, aren't I?"

"I'd rather be a dead dick than a dick that lost his morals."

"Dead dicks can't do anything to start again. Living dicks can. At this point, selfishness is morality."

Zorn opened his mouth to argue but stopped himself. Topher was right. Everybody was too focused on survival to think much beyond the next threat. Maslow's hierarchy, right? Math and art were wonderful, but who could think about literature or geometry when someone was trying to impale you? What was the point in painting anything unless it was with blood? It was enough to make someone commit suicide.

He wouldn't be the first, too. How many basements had he come across with swinging undead? How many times had he and his men found piles of them beneath tall buildings, skulls cracked open and leaking? Wouldn't he have gone through with it if he didn't think he'd come back and make someone else suffer? He saw it so clearly. They were barely holding on before the Catastrophes, and that was with the benefits of medicine and refrigeration and video games. Now they had nothing. They were nothing.

"We're doomed," he said.

Topher suddenly felt bad.

"Don't worry," he said. "Can I tell you something without you getting angry?"

Zorn shrugged.

"In the beginning, when I was just setting up The Ton, there were these gangs that used to come around. Young guys. Cocky, violent. At first, they left me alone, thought I was just some old quack trying to farm in irradiated soil. Then I reaped my first crop and people started to join me. That got their attention. One day, a group of them came by and demanded my harvest. I refused. They beat me half to death and burned everything. Kidnapped women and children."

"Jesus."

"I know. I was devastated. It was my fault. I'd promised those people protection and food and I failed. In the darkest pit of that night, I seriously considered just killing myself. But I couldn't do it. I wasn't brave enough. So that next morning I set off with a few of the survivors in search of another place. And we found one, and again we built it up, and again the bad men came.

"This time we were ready. We fought back. They took some of our food, but they didn't take our people. We killed as many of them as they did us. Word got out. There is a man in the South who will fight. When they came around the third time, we outnumbered them four to one. We lured them into camp and butchered each one, cut off each head and spiked them on stakes around the settlement."

They fell silent. The wind blew. Birds cawed.

"Why are you telling me this?" Zorn asked.

"Because I don't want you to let this get you down. Bad things have happened, and bad things are going to continue to happen, with or without us. That woman? She might actually need our help. Or she's a trap. Either way, it's depressing, but there's nothing we can do here but walk away and live another day."

Then he scooted out from under the guardrail and headed back to camp. Zorn shot a look back at the woman, then scrambled out himself.

"Wait!" he called, running to catch up.

"Forget it, Zorn."

"How can you just leave her there? The Topher I knew at Raleigh's Prep wouldn't have done it. Topher the Transcendental Tracker would have cut down legions of monsters to save a woman in distress, and damn the consequences. Remember Chainwrought? Remember Fredericksburg?"

Topher ignored him. They walked on, sweating lightly. A lone carrion bird circled above. They took a moment's relief under the shade of an overpass, then cut back into the woods, hopping a rusted chain link fence wound through with weeds.

"So we're really not going to save her?" Zorn asked.

"Didn't I explain this already? The cars are the barrel. We're the fish. She's just bait."

"What good is rebuilding civilization if we can't behave like civilized people?"

Topher snorted.

"What good is rebuilding civilization if we don't have any people to rebuild it with?"

"That's my point exactly!"

"That's not what I meant."

Up ahead they saw the tent city. The food truck was in the middle, guarded by men armed with clubs and spears. Children played on the median, squealing. Their mothers watched in groups from a distance. They'd parked their vehicles, which were nothing more than stripped frames on wheels, in a semicircle around the camp. The horses were housed in the back to protect them from scavengers. Topher's SUV sat in the lead, facing north. It was the only one that hadn't been scavenged for metal. It had no engine, of course, and all of the unnecessary parts—the exhaust system, the radiator, the transmission —had been removed. But the body was intact. It was drawn by twelve horses, like a stagecoach from the wild west. He justified the extravagance as all men with power did. He was in charge, so he got the perks.

Saanvi had brought his team to the car and was squatting around them, straightening the trace lines, preparing to leave. Topher was immediately irked. How many times had he told her not to do this? How many times did he have to explain that the horses needed to be protected? Saanvi was so engrossed in her task that she didn't even notice his approach. He stood beside her, his irritation mounting.

"What are you doing?" he finally said.

Saanvi didn't jump as he'd hoped, which made him even more irritated. She straightened a line. Paused. Checked another.

"I just want to straighten them out again," she said.

"Do the horses need to be here?"

"I need them to be."

Topher grimaced, holding his tongue.

"And this has to be done now because . . ."

Saanvi held up one of the lines.

"They're frayed. We need to repair them."

"Dear God." Topher turned to complain to Zorn. "Can you believe this?"

But Zorn wasn't paying attention. He was looking at the trace lines, trying to figure out what Saanvi was talking about. The leather didn't look frayed at all. In fact, it looked rather well-maintained. Saanvi didn't seem to think so. She smoothed the lines out on the road, peering intently, looking for signs of wear and tear. To Topher it looked like both of them had gone crazy. He threw his arms in the air, exasperated, and marched away, heading toward a group of children playing in the middle of the road.

"Why are these children screaming!" he yelled.

Saanvi watched him go, then resumed her work.

"He's always been like this," Zorn said.

"I know."

"He was actually worse when we were younger."

Saanvi pulled another line clear and lay it flat on the ground. She untwisted it, inspected a slight tear.

"Why do the lines have to be straight?" Zorn asked.

"They just have to be."

"Will they break if they're not."

"No. Yes. Eventually they will."

She ran her finger over the leather.

Zorn tried again.

"How long have you been with him? Topher, I mean."

"The Mayor?"

The Mayor? Zorn wanted to scream. *Seriously?* Instead he said "Sure."

She shrugged.

"Were you there at The Ton?" he asked.

"Yes."

"From the beginning?"

"No."

Zorn let out a breath. Well this was pointless. He patted one of the horses, the lead. It nickered. He liked the smell, the animal warmth, but he wasn't sentimental. If it came to it, they'd have to eat them. He gave the bridle a gentle little tug and the horse looked at him.

"This one has a saddle," he said.

Saanvi didn't say anything.

Zorn strolled around the animal, calculating, and Saanvi breathed a sigh of relief. Some people just didn't know when to shut up. She picked up the first line and threaded it through its hasp, trying not to twist it. She brought it to the second hasp, then the third, making her way up the team, focusing on her work, intent, blocking out all sounds. She loved feeling this way, the dropping off of all distractions, noises, sights, and sounds. Being able to zoom in on what she was doing was so rare, so pleasing. She was about to thread the line through the last hasp when Zorn jumped onto the lead horse and slapped it on its rear.

"Yah!" he cried.

The horse didn't move.

He tried it again, "Yah!" but it still didn't move.

"What are you trying to do?" Saanvi asked.

"What does it look like I'm trying to do? I want to ride the horse."

"But I'm using it. Get off."

"No."

Saanvi's stomach clenched, and the anxiety rose in her chest. She needed the horse to finish, but Zorn was on it and he said he wanted to ride it. He was also bigger than her, so there was no way she could get him off unless she hurt him, but if she hurt him, the Mayor would get upset.

"Where are you going?"

"I-I just want to to try it. I've never done it before."

"Will you bring her back?" she asked.

"The horse? Of course."

"Okay." She took a deep breath. "Pick up the reins."

Zorn did as he was told.

"Now squeeze its sides with your legs and say 'Walk on'."

Zorn did it, and the horse started to walk.

"It worked!" he said. "How do I make it go faster?"

"Squeeze your legs again and tell her to run."

"Run, horsey."

The horse sped up.

"Try it again," Saanvi said.

"Run, horsey! Run!" The horse started to trot. "Oh my god."

"One more time."

"Run, horsey!"

The horse broke into a gallop, faster and faster, and soon Zorn was a figure in the distance, bouncing in the saddle like an idiot. He aimed it down the highway toward the ramp, a cloud of dust pluming in his wake.

Zorn, who once fell off a perfectly stationary bicycle, quickly realized that the only way for him to not fall off a speeding horse was to cling to its neck. The screaming was optional. He hurtled toward the entry ramp, the one that would deposit them on the interstate, wondering if the horse knew where they were going, or if he would have to steer, and if he did have to steer how this would be accomplished, and whether or not it would end like one of those Internet car-wreck videos he used to watch when there was an Internet, before the meteors, the tsunamis, and the bombs.

"Right!" he screamed.

The horse did not turn right.

"Turn right!"

The horse continued not to turn right.

He pulled hard on the horse's ear. Nothing. He swatted its shoulder. Nothing. He wanted to be brave but couldn't figure out how to do it. Topher had put him in situations worse than this, situations in which he confronted monsters and psychopaths, and each time he faced the enemy down, cool and calm, the consummate professional. But the stupid horse addled his wits until all he could do was shut his eyes and wait for it to be over. And then it happened. Topher's voice rang in his head. "Zorn, you idiot!" it said. "Are you trying to ride that horse, or hump it?"

He sat bolt upright, gripping the reins. If he was going to die, it wouldn't be doing something that would give that linen suit-wearing bastard more material that he could use to mock him at his own funeral. He pulled the reins steadily to the right, and to his great surprise and wonderment, the horse began to indeed turn in that direction. Once it saw where he was leading, it adjusted and zoomed down the ramp. The rush was exhilarating, and Zorn thought he finally understood that the attraction of equestrian sports was somewhat more than owning leather goods and playing cards with ranch hands.

They shot out onto the highway. The wall of cars was a half mile away, but it was astounding how fast a horse could cover that distance. He reached it in little less than sixty-seconds, zipped through the entrance, hopped off the horse, and ran for the woman.

"I'm here, I'm here," he called.

She hung there motionless, her chin still resting on her chest. Zorn took off his coat and draped it over her. She moaned. Her eyes flickered.

"You're alive," Zorn said.

Her voice slurred when she spoke.

"Get me off this thing," she said.

"You're not going to kill me? This isn't a trap, right."

"What?"

He checked behind her, half-expecting to encounter an axe to the face, but instead saw that her hands had been nailed to the pole. Her feet, too. They'd crucified her. The rumble of hooves sounded in the distance, and Zorn shot a look over his shoulder. It was Topher and five other men, each leading teams of horses pulling cars filled with more men. He knew it! He knew he'd change his mind. He just needed a little prodding.

"Oh my God, they're here," the woman said.

"Nothing to fear," Zorn said. "They're with me."

"Not them." Her eyes searched the sky above. "Them."

Zorn followed her gaze to the overpasses that twisted and turned overhead.

Lines of barbarians stood along the edges.

Hundreds of them.

He couldn't be exactly sure from his vantage point, but they looked like something out of a George Miller movie. Hair cut in mohawks, skulls and teeth hanging from their necks. Their weapons were long and sharp and glinted in the sun. It was worse than the Elk-Men of Montana. A *thousand* times worse than the Elk-Men of Montana.

"Oh dear," he said. "Topher's going to be so angry."

And indeed he was.

"Zorn, you idiot!" he cried, pulling his team into the ring.

The barbarians on the overpasses let up a brutal war cry, and Topher ran up to Zorn and smacked him across the face. Then he turned around to issue orders.

"You, you, and you! Block the entrance."

His men maneuvered three of the cars outside the wall in a semi-circle, filled up the narrow gap with the last two. They moved the horses to the back, keeping them as far from the center as possible. Topher turned his ire back to Zorn.

"Zorn! Don't stand around like a scolded child. Do you want to be flensed?"

Another cry rang from the overpasses, bloodthirsty and booming. Zorn rubbed his cheek.

"Who are they?"

Topher said, "How am I supposed to know." Then, to his men, "Break all the remaining glass and throw it over the side!"

Zorn returned his attention to the woman on the pole. The nails, while long, didn't appear to be too difficult to work with.

"I think I can pull them out," he said.

She nodded, bracing herself.

"Okay."

"I'll start with your hands."

"Okay."

"It's going to hurt."

"Just do it!"

Zorn took a deep breath and let it go.

"One. Two. Three."

Her screams were lost in the roar of the barbarians as they streamed from the exits and onto the highway. She slumped to her knees, pulling her feet right off the nail, and passed out, blood pooling in the dirt. Zorn's fur had fallen off, so he picked it up and draped it over her again. He didn't know what to do about the bleeding. Pack the wounds with dirt? Don't be an idiot. No, a tourniquet! He ripped off his shirt, tore it into strips. He wrapped the holes, then he tied off her wrists and ankles. He couldn't be sure if this would stop the bleeding or if the clothes would just sop it all up, but what else could he do? A spear chunked into the earth to his right and he yelped and leaped away.

"Zorn!" Topher cried. "Stop molesting that poor woman and help us get out of this mess!"

Zorn rearranged his coat, making sure to cover her as best he could, then jogged over to Topher, who was standing by the entrance. The car frames didn't look particularly effective at first, not by themselves. Then he realized that they were too tall and spread out to jump completely over, and that the barbarians would have to work their way through, one at a time. Topher had made a trap in a trap, a funnel through which they could pick the enemy off one at a time. The walls were thick, too, consisting of two concentric circles: a ten-foot outer portion buttressed on the inside by another about six feet tall. The idiots had built them a castle.

"Line the walls," Topher ordered. "Up! Up! Up!"

The enemy stormed forward, the bones and skulls that hung from their necks bonking, their bare feet slapping on the pavement. The Reaper's rhythm section, the cacophony of death. Zorn had dreamed of his own demise before, and if his independent study of Native

American lore was to be believed, his would come in the teeth of millions of miniature purple bunnies. Now, however, he thought he might perish to the musical tune of human calcium. Topher's men rested their guns, on the wall and aimed.

"Steady!" Topher cried.

More men took position in the entrance, gripping their axes, their maces, their knives.

"Steady!"

The horde broke against the wall, howling as they cut their feet to ribbons on the broken glass. A wave of spears took out two of Topher's people. One of his men jumped down to decapitate them, then clambered back up to his position. Topher was just about to yell "Fire!" when a club hit him in the shoulder and spun him around and he screamed "Fuck!" instead.

His men fired anyway, cutting down the barbarians' front line. Topher whirled about and fired his gun into the horde. Ladders clanged against the walls, and soon dozens of the brutes were scampering upward. Topher's men picked them off, but for every one who fell, three more took his place. A few crested the top, some managed to thread through the cars or jump into the ring, but they were shot or clubbed and thrown back over.

Soon the enemy was just as busy dealing with the undead as it was trying to kill Topher and his people. Though they were certainly angry enough and ready to kill, Topher marveled at how poorly prepared they came to the fight. Maybe they didn't count on their prey being armed with working guns. Maybe they didn't care. They didn't have any firearms of their own. Machetes, yes, and augmented rebar, clubs, maces, daggers, spears, even a few swords, but not guns. They were forced to retreat and set up position a hundred yards out, waiting for reinforcements. And the reinforcements did come, pouring in from all directions, but they didn't attack. They encircled the wall of cars, chanting and jeering and throwing rocks.

Topher glanced up at the sun.

"What time do you think it is, Zorn?"

"I don't know. Late morning? Why?"

Topher didn't reply. He just stood there, thinking. Then a sound like thunder echoed in the distance. They heard the missile before it struck, a high-pitched whistle that ended with an explosion just beyond the fortress. Asphalt and metal rained down, and everybody dove to the ground, covering their heads with their hands. The horses reared and panicked, breaking into a frenzied gallop around the inside of the ring, trampling anybody in their way. The barbarians let up a massive cheer. Topher peeked over the top.

A dozen savages appeared the horizon, spread out over the highway, seeming to lean forward into thin air as if struggling against a strong wind. Soon another line of twelve men crested the hill, also leaning forward. Then a third row appeared, and a fourth, and more and more, dozens upon dozens of them, forty-eight, sixty, seventy-two, eighty-four and more and more, and he now saw that were holding chains over their shoulders, pulling something behind them.

Then it came into view.

"It's a tank," Topher said.

Zorn's head popped up over his right shoulder.

"A tank?"

"A tank."

Topher dodged a spear and a few rocks, squeezed off a few rounds. He checked his clip. Three bullets left.

"Where did those assholes get a tank?"

Zorn didn't have an answer, and for good reason.

First: hundreds of mohawked and pierced barbarians had surrounded them, all standing perfectly still, gazing reverently in the same direction. Second: what a beautiful morning! The red and oranges and blues and ooooh that's so pret . . . Third: a dozen lines of a dozen men had been harnessed together to pull a tank. A tank. They were pulling a tank. And atop the tank was perched a boy. He was perhaps thirteen years old, and he was wearing an old pair of cutoff jeans and nothing else. Things had gone from weird and frightening to weird and terrifying.

Then it got weirder. The enemy started to chant the boy's name, just a few voices at first, but one by one they joined in until they were all crying out in synchronicity, "RA-SHEED! RA-SHEED!"

"Apparently his name is Rasheed," Topher said.

Rasheed indeed. The boy god of Philadelphia. He observed the creatures beneath him as they pulled his tank forward, tilting his head back like a true monarch. He'd painted his face crimson, with black eyeliner defining his eyes and black lipstick defining his lips, and his body was skinny but muscular, and his skin was so pale as to reflect the sunlight, and he was perfectly bald all over.

The men pulled the tank to within a hundred yards of the wall of cars and stopped. Rasheed allowed the chanting to continue for a few minutes, then held up his hand for peace. His people stopped at once.

The wind whistled in the silence. Then he called out to his people, and his voice was pure and high, beautiful and terrible all at once.

"Who is your Lord, God, and Savior?"

And his people answered: "RA-SHEED! RA-SHEED!"

"Who is the ruler of this land, the supreme deity, and punisher of all who dare trespass?"

"RA-SHEED! RA-SHEED!"

"And who is the judge, jury, and executioner of this land, who will smite all heathens, sinners, and followers of false gods?"

"RA-SHEED! RA-SHEED!"

He gazed coldly upon them, absorbing their adoration as a snake does the sun.

"Then let them all die!"

The barbarians let up a final cry, one to deafen the dead, and with it, the tank roared to life. Another explosion rocked the ground, and the next thing Topher knew he was flying through the air.

Of the many horrific things he experienced in his life—the patricide, the incarceration, the werepyres, the bullies, the administrators, the succubi, the zombies, the squid monsters, the serial killers, the Catastrophes—nothing horrified Topher as much as waking up in the dark and not being able to move. Something huge and soft and heavy lay across his chest, but he couldn't see what it was. Then there were the sounds, the screams and moans and explosions and gunfire. The battle was raging on all around him, but somehow he was protected. Not knowing what was going on was terrible. He imagined the horrible ways his men were being slaughtered, or raped, or both, and all of the sudden he thought that, yes, perhaps perishing in the dark beneath something soft and furry was preferable. He'd stay there, fading in and out of consciousness, quietly dehydrating, and then starving, and then he'd just fade away.

Then the thing on top of him moaned, and Topher discovered that his arms were pretty much free. He poked at it, prodding here and there. It wasn't really all that soft and furry, now, was it? In fact, it felt rather fleshy and hirsute.

"Zorn," he croaked. "Get off me."

No response.

Topher poked him in the ribs again.

"Damn you, Zorn. Wake up."

Zorn snorted like a horse, so at least he was alive. He'd come around. Or not. What if he'd suffered a traumatic brain injury?

Topher had a strict "Do Not Revive" policy when it came to such matters, thought it humane given the shortage of medical resources and complete lack of licensed psychotherapists. And if someone happened to revive by himself, bully for him. At least until the PTSD began to irritate everybody, or any sort of basic psychopathic behavior manifested itself, or the body mistook "revive" for "reanimate," at which point his "Do Not Revive" policy became a "Stab in the Brain" policy.

His eyes adjusted, and he realized their great fortune. They were buried beneath a pile of crushed cars, of course, but the cars that were supposed to have crushed them, or at least severed them in half, landed in a way that created a small, protective pocket. It really would be best to just stay there a while, let the battle burn itself out, let Rasheed and his crazy people do what they wanted to his men and leave. If Zorn ever woke up, and if he was of sound mind and body, they might be able to push the cars off and, with any luck, escape this hellhole.

But then what?

That familiar boulder of despair formed in his chest. How many more times could he do it? How many more times could he cut his losses, write off those he knew and loved, pretend that everything was going to be okay? Everywhere they went, they ran into groups just as desperate as themselves, men and women turned into animals, or cannibals, or idiots like Rasheed. If it wasn't people trying to wipe him out, it was disease: dysentery, malaria, anthrax, sonambum, pneumonia, smallpox, cholera. He'd watched children wither right before his eyes. Watched their parents do what needed to be done before the child came back. What was the point of enduring that again?

Zorn huffed into the dirt, and then suddenly he was awake.

"What happened?"

"Get off me."

Zorn pushed up too quickly and banged his head on metal. The pile above them shifted.

"Careful, you oaf," Topher snapped. "You'll get us both crushed."

"We're alive?"

"That's a stupid question."

Zorn pushed off his friend, found just enough space to sit and pull his knees to his chest.

"My head is killing me."

"Seems appropriate."

Zorn stared around their shelter.

"This is incredible."

Topher sat up. Miraculously, his hat was on the ground next to him. He put it on and slapped forlornly at his torn linen trousers.

"It really is incredible."

"What are the odds?"

"No, not that. My pants."

"Don't be a moron."

"I'm not a moron. Do you know how easy it is to find a good linen suit these days? Of all the things in the world that we need right now, food, medicine, shelter, weapons—we can barely find any of it. But this," he opened his jacket. "This is a Bianco Brioni. I have no idea what the thread count is. Probably two thousand. Torn to shreds. Found it in a closet. Easy as that."

The sound of the battle outside escalated: gunfire, screaming and grunting and yelling, all the details of a nasty fight.

"We have to get out of here," Zorn said. "We have to help." He looked up. There was, at the peak of the pocket, light coming through a crack. "Could we crawl through there?"

"I suppose," Topher said. "Or we could just wait it out."

"Get serious. They need us."

Zorn pressed gently on the car above him. It creaked. Dust sifted into his face.

"Do what you like," he said. "I'm getting out of—"

A tremendous screeching and whining drowned out the rest of his sentence, and the cars creating the pocket were ripped apart in either direction, leaving the two exposed in the middle of a clearing, shielding their eyes from the light.

Topher blinked away the sunspots. Small skirmishes played out all around him, but he couldn't tell who was winning. Sometimes a savage went down screaming, sometimes one of his own men. Still, for all of his sudden despair, he was happy to see that so many were still fighting. It relieved a bit of the burden, even if they all were going to end up dead. And then dead again. He and Zorn stood up as the savages surrounded them, snarling and pressing in with their spears.

"Not yet," came a fey voice.

The boy, Rasheed, appeared as if out of nowhere, carried upon a litter by six slaves. Up close, Topher could see that he was a little older than he thought, maybe sixteen or seventeen, but his size and thinness made him look like little more than a child. How had he ascended to such power? How was he able to control all of these people?

Rasheed stared at them, his cold and dispassionate glare turning to anger when he realized that they were not going to glance away, or quail, or fall apart

"Who are these creatures?"

Topher looked around him.

"Do you want us to answer?"

One of the savages jabbed at him with a spear.

"Don't speak unless commanded."

"I asked you a question!" Rasheed cried.

Nobody spoke.

The savage jabbed at Topher again.

"Answer the lord!"

"I thought you told me not to speak unless commanded."

"He asked you a question!"

"No, he made a statement about the fact that he asked a question."

The savage cracked him across the skull with the end of his spear, knocking him to the ground. Zorn hurried to help, but Topher pushed him away, yelling, "Get off!" as he struggled to his feet. He felt his ear, and his hand came away covered with blood. "God DAMMIT!"

"Kneel to me," Rasheed said.

Topher shot him an irritated look.

"I can't hear you. Your idiot minion destroyed my hearing."

"I said kneel!"

Another savage struck Topher in the back of his legs, sending him to his knees. He was barely able to catch himself with his hand before another spear, sharp end first, chucked him under the chin and guided him erect. Topher clenched his jaw, breathing heavily. Rasheed eyed Zorn.

"Okay, okay," Zorn said, holding his hands up. He joined his friend in the dirt.

"Did you really think you could defeat me?" Rasheed asked.

Topher said, "Should I answer that?"

"How dare you! I am Rasheed!"

"You've made that perfectly clear."

Another blow to the skull sent him face down into the dirt, and his hat finally fell off his head. After a long moment, he huffed and pressed himself up. Wiped his beard and eyes.

"What are you doing?" Zorn hissed. Then he smiled with his teeth at Rasheed, who said, "You *will* bow to me."

Topher frowned.

"Bow? We're already kneeling. Isn't that overkill?"

"YOU WILL BOW TO ME! YOU WILL ACCEPT ME AS YOUR LORD AND MASTER."

Topher chuckled and shook his head. He patted his pockets as if looking for his keys. His hat. Where was it? Ah, over there on the ground. He leaned over and swept it up, snugged it down over his balding pate.

"Boy. I'd cut off my own head before I bowed to you."

Rasheed's eyes went wide with anger. He hopped off his litter, lips curling into a snarl. Topher held up his hands.

"Oh no! He's off his litter!"

He couldn't stop laughing. It was all so perfect. He made it all this way only to be killed by an adolescent bully.

Rasheed grabbed one of his minions' machetes.

"Bring them to me."

They hauled the two men up by the elbows, Topher giggling, Zorn horrified, and threw them at his feet. The boy hefted the machete above his head, his eyes glittering, maniacal. One of the cannibals forced Topher's head down and he let it happen. Rasheed took a deep breath, muttering some vile incantation, calm, poised, enraptured, then his eyes flew open, he summoned his strength, neck muscles straining, veins throbbing, and just as he started to bring the machete down, just as he was about to sever Topher's head from his body and once and for all end his miserable life, his eyes went wide and his mouth went wide and the end of a spear burst out of his chest. He dropped his weapon and stared confused down at the hole, the spear, the blood dripping from the head. His men took a step back, shocked. Then the spear was ripped back out, and the boy collapsed into the dirt. Behind him stood the woman Zorn had saved, draped in his fur coat, gripping the spear in both hands.

"Arrogant little prick," she said.

Rasheed's men, suddenly understanding, started for her. She grunted and took a step back, but before they could do anything, gunfire exploded all around, and Topher and Zorn threw themselves face down in the dirt, covering their heads with their hands. When it was over, Topher peeked out from under his hat. Their enemies lay all around him, torn to pieces.

"Ha!"

He slapped Zorn on the back, and they both stood up.

Saanvi was standing behind what was left of the boy-god's litter, smoke from the nose of her shotgun trailing up in a thin line into the air. A dozen more of Topher's men stood on the car wall, picking off what was left of Rasheed's men, those who hadn't fled already.

"Sorry about the wait," she said.

Topher got off the ground.

"Where the hell were you? I was nearly decapitated by a boy in cutoffs. Zorn's an emotional wreck."

"You said 'around lunch'. I'm actually early."

"How do you know that?"

A screaming savage ran for her and she fired her last shot. His chest exploded.

"I made a sundial out of a stick. It's really easy. All you have to do is stick it into the ground and count to sixty sixty times, then put a rock down at the top of each shadow."

"Of course. That makes perfect sense."

He squatted down to address the woman, his savior. She was sitting on the ground, shaking, hugging her arms around herself. He held out a hand.

"Madam?"

"Don't touch me!"

"Very well," he said. He stood up, meaning to assess how they were going to get out of this when a rock crashed into his jaw. He stumbled back a step. Something else slammed into his right shoulder and he grunted. My goodness, that was painful. He felt like he was falling, or that he had already fallen, but he couldn't be sure. The next thing he saw was the bright light of the sun, and then Zorn was hovering over him, looking shocked and scared.

Topher said, "What?"

And then all was dark.

SOMEPLACE SAFE

Topher woke up in the back of his SUV. It was hot and he was parched, and his shoulder was in horrible pain. Someone had dressed it in an old rag. He peeled it aside, took a peek, and winced. They'd cauterized the wound. His skin was twisted like beef jerky. He struggled to sit up and nearly passed out again. It took all of his strength to crawl to the door, even more to open it. He simultaneously slid and fell out onto the pavement, managing to prop himself up against the rear wheel where he closed his eyes and fought back the nausea. When he opened them, he beheld the most curious thing. The enemy had been arranged, somewhat artistically, on hundreds of metal stakes. Impaled, really. And their heads had been cut off and lay rotting on the highway.

Zorn came up beside him, and Topher gave him a little glance.

"Interesting layout," he said. "Very concentric."

"That was Isa's idea. She made us organize it in a very specific pattern."

"Isa?"

"The woman."

"Ah. Is it meant as a warning?"

"It's meant as revenge."

A small group of children burst onto the highway from out of nowhere and ran squealing through the maze of bodies. They pulled on dangling feet, threw rocks. Their horrified mothers came rushing after them, scolding and angry. They snatched up their wriggling progeny and ushered them away, shooting Topher ugly looks all the while.

"Probably not the best thing for kids to see," he said. "Do you think we should burn them?"

"What's the point?"

"Just in case."

Zorn thought for a second, then he said, "Nah."

Topher ordered them burned anyway.

A black gash of smoke scarred the sky as the caravan creaked away.

They made camp a little south of Bellmawr. Topher convalesced on the bench seat of his SUV. He was just optimistic enough to think he might escape with a broken shoulder, that the worst he'd have to face was a poorly healed bone and a slight stoop, that maybe when it rained his muscles would ache "from the old wound." As the week passed and he didn't feel a fever or see the telltale red lines creeping down his arm, his optimism turned to confidence, and he decided to give the woman, Isa, the only round of antibiotics. Zorn didn't think that was such a good idea.

"Are you sure? We hardly know her."

"I'm fine, Zorn. Besides, you said she refused to cauterize her hands and feet. She needs it more than me."

"Still."

"She saved us, Zorn. I can't forget that."

That evening, Isa visited him. She knocked on the SUV's door and Topher called for her to come in. She hovered outside, uncertain, the bottle of antibiotics in her hand. She'd scavenged clothes from the men she impaled: a loose, white tunic that was too big, even for her muscular frame, and a pair of cut-off khaki cargo pants. The boots seemed to fit perfectly. How long did it take for her to find them? How many corpses did she undress?

"Please," he said. "Sit in here."

She checked out the interior, then stepped in, wincing, and sat on the middle bench.

"How are you?" Topher asked.

She stared at him, amazed.

"I'm fine."

"And your feet? Your hands?"

She looked at her hands. She'd wrapped them in what looked like a torn up old shirt. A little red patch bled through on each palm.

"They hurt. But I think I'll be okay." She held up the antibiotics. "Thanks for this."

"No need."

"Are you sure you don't need them?"

"I'll be okay."

Her eyes flitted over his mangled shoulder.

"You don't look okay."

"Your name's Isa?" She nodded. "Isa, you saved me from that crazy boy."

"You saved me, too."

"You don't understand. I didn't want to. I wanted to leave you there. Zorn forced my hand."

"Oh."

"So those are for you."

"But—"

"No. Take them. Zorn was right. It was the right thing to do. I want you to have them. Plus, I think the cauterizing worked." He gave her a brave smile. "No fever yet."

It hit him a day later, swift and brutal, his temperature pushing 100, then 101, 103, and it was clear that they were going to have to do something. They discussed it that night around the campfire, Topher, Saanvi, Isa, and Zorn.

"You can have what's left of these," Isa said. "I've only finished a day's worth."

"No," Topher said. "You have to finish the full round or they're no good."

"So what are we going to do?"

Topher noticed that she said 'we' and not 'you'.

"I don't know. We either cut my arm off or go looking for more antibiotics."

Saanvi said, "We should cut it off."

"I wasn't serious about that one," Topher said.

"But sir!"

"No."

"But it's the easiest option."

"Easy enough for you."

"But—"

"I'm keeping my arm."

"If it will save your life, you should do it."

"What if the amputation causes another infection? What if the infection's already gone deeper than just my shoulder? What are you going to do then? Carve a chunk out of my neck? Chop my head off?"

"Fine. Where will we find any antibiotics? We spent a whole season ransacking Northern Virginia and only found one round."

Isa said, "I know where we can find some."

"Where?"

She turned and pointed at the skyscrapers in the background.

Philadelphia.

"Are you kidding?" Saanvi said. "He's not going in there." When Topher didn't immediately agree with her, she said, "Sir, you can't be serious. What about those things?"

After a moment, he said, "We've heard rumors. That's it."

Saanvi looked at him, stricken.

"I'm not losing my arm, Saanvi. If there are antibiotics in the city, why wouldn't I go?"

"You're in no condition to do anything. Let me go instead."

"No. I don't have enough time." Topher looked at Isa. "You're sure you know where we can find some?"

She nodded slowly.

Zorn finally spoke up.

"Well, if you're going, I'm going with you."

Saanvi took refuge with the horses. She talked to them, rubbed their limbs, brushed their coats until they were sleek. The rhythm of the chore calmed her down, soothed her. She counted one hundred strokes each, one hundred strokes one dozen times, and then a dozen more, and when she was done her back was tired and her hands and arms were sore, but she felt centered and grounded. One by one she led them to a grassy median where they ate. When the sun started to set and the air grew cool, she covered them in blankets. She was putting the brushes and other gear away in an old leather bag when someone stepped on a stick behind her. She dropped the bag and spun, her hand flashing to the Bowie knife on her hip.

It was the woman. Isa.

Even Saanvi couldn't help but notice how beautiful she was. Her long, brown hair, her honey-colored skin. Her eyes were striking, one blue, one green, and her lips were full and red.

"What do you want?" Saanvi said.

Isa pet one of the horses, which stopped eating and looked at her. She whispered something to it, and it went back to its meal.

"Your horses are lovely."

Saanvi relaxed a little.

"You shouldn't sneak up on people."

"I know."

"Then why did you do it? I could have had a gun. I could have shot you."

A hint of a smile flashed across Isa's lips.

"I was watching you. You have a way with them. They love you, and you love them, don't you?"

"Answer my question."

"I didn't mean to scare you. I thought you heard me."

"I didn't."

Saanvi leaned over to pick up her bag.

"Don't go," Isa said. "Not yet."

"Why?"

Isa took a step closer. Saanvi tensed. She didn't even like people she knew getting too close, let alone strangers.

"Stop," she said.

Isa took another step.

"It's okay. I just want to talk."

"Then talk." More than any time in her life, Saanvi wanted to leave, but fastest way back to camp was past Isa. She could circumnavigate the horses, go entirely around her, but she knew that the woman would cut her off. She had that look in her eye. She recognized it from before. From the boys at school. From her stepfather. From the orderlies at the hospital. She let her hand fall on her knife again. Isa saw it.

"Are you going to hurt me?" she asked.

"Are you going to make me?"

Isa shook her head.

Saanvi felt the urge to trace the scars on her arms, to count them, but she promised herself she'd never do it again in front of someone else. A knot formed in her chest and her breathing quickened.

"I want to go back to camp," she said. Isa took a third step toward her. "Please."

"Who did this to you?" Isa asked.

Saanvi found it hard to concentrate. She started to count her breaths, and the more she did, the faster her heart raced. A light sweat broke out on her forehead.

"I want to go back to camp."

"Was it a man?"

"No. Yes."

Saanvi grew dizzy. A rushing sound filled her ears. She closed her eyes. It didn't help. She tensed her muscles, but that made her feel like she was going to pass out. And then she felt something on her cheek, something cool and light and dry. She gasped, but the touch was delicate and fine, and her breathing started to even out.

"It's okay, Saanvi. It's okay."

Her heart slowed. The rushing sound faded, and along with it the desire to trace her scars, to count, to run.

"Saanvi, open your eyes."

She did. Isa's face was inches from hers. She hadn't been this close to anybody since she was a child. The coolness on her cheek was Isa's fingers.

"Do you know what your name means?" Isa asked.

"It's Indian. It's another name for Lakshmi."

"The goddess of love and wealth."

"Yes."

"My name is short for Isabelle."

"Isabelle," Saanvi said. "It means 'devotion'."

She could understand that. Being devoted to someone like Isa. So beautiful, so strong. Isa put her other hand on Saanvi's cheek, and Saanvi didn't even flinch. It felt good, natural.

"It also means love," Isa said. "Love and affection."

A small smile twitched on Saanvi's lips.

"We're a good match," Isa said. "The goddess of love, and love itself."

Saanvi had heard words like that before, and it was always followed by something horrible. Isa saw it, felt it, and before it could spiral out of control, she said, "Saanvi, you don't have to go there. I'm here. You're better now."

And remarkably, just like that, she was. The dizziness dissolved, the compulsion, the anxiety. She felt centered, anchored.

"Can I take touch your hair?" Isa asked.

"Okay."

She brushed it out of her eyes, tucked it behind one ear.

"It's so lovely. You're so beautiful."

Saanvi frowned.

"What do you want?" she asked again.

Isa caressed her cheek with her thumb.

"I want to ask you about Topher."

"What about him?"

"Is he the one? The one who did this to you?"

Saanvi hardened. She pulled her face away from Isa's fingers.

"You don't know what you're talking about."

She pushed by, angry now, but entirely in control. Was the Mayor the one who did this to her? He was the only man she'd ever trusted, the only man who made her feel like she was more than just a body, the only man who let her be herself, who let her show how capable and smart she was and asked nothing in return. Who the hell did this woman think she was?

"Saanvi, wait. You don't have to protect him."

"Yes, I do."

"You don't. You can leave if you want. He doesn't own you. You don't have to be afraid. He can't hurt you. You can come with me."

Saanvi stopped and spun, her anger spewing out of her before she could stop it.

"He's not like that! He's never . . . he wouldn't even think . . ."

Isa seemed confused.

"Okay. Okay. I'm sorry."

Saanvi turned to leave, but Isa called out, "Wait!"

"What?"

"Can you tell me?"

"Tell you what?"

"What he did? What he did to deserve you?"

Saanvi took a quick breath.

"He saved my life."

"When? Where?"

"Always. Everywhere."

Then she walked as fast as she could back to camp.

Topher didn't feel strong enough to travel for a few days. He slept, he ate, he rested. He watched Isa. First, he was suspicious, then he was intrigued. People felt safe around her, comforted. They were drawn to her. She bathed them in the glow of her attention. Perhaps it was her beauty or the way she made someone feel like he was the only person around. Perhaps it was the little touches she bestowed. She did it to everybody. He'd seen her touch Zorn the same way. She let her fingers brush up against his arm, and Zorn turned and smiled at her. It was a friendly smile, innocent and pure, devoid of all guile. Everybody smiled at Isa.

She even charmed Saanvi. Over the course of two days, they seemed to grow close. Conversations at first, short and clipped in Saanvi's fashion. Isa helped her with her seemingly endless lists of duties, quiet most of the time, with little bits of chit chat here and there, commiseration over difficult or mundane tasks. And in the tedium, a bond was born. The night before they left, the pair sat by the fire, eating, and Isa leaned in and whispered something in Saanvi's ear and Saanvi giggled. And then she was laughing, and then they were sharing discreet glances, and then she looked Isa right in the eyes as they spoke, the tips of their fingers brushing.

Topher was entirely amazed.

Saanvi did this. Saanvi, who didn't even like to be looked at. Saanvi, who leaped as if stung if anybody accidentally grazed her skin.

On the evening of the third day, Topher realized that he wasn't getting any stronger and that he might have made a mistake by waiting so long. He told Zorn and Isa that he wanted to leave as soon as he could.

"When?" Zorn asked. "Now?"

"I need the night. Just the night."

"I'll get the horses ready."

"No."

"Why not? It'll be faster, and you won't have to walk."

"We can't spare them," he said.

"What's the worst that can happen?"

Topher didn't reply.

"Okay," Zorn said. "We can ride as far as city limits. Someone can come with us, take the horses back."

"Who?"

"I don't know. One of your men? Saanvi?"

But Topher was already shaking his head.

"You don't understand, Zorn. Nobody will go within five miles of that place."

So walking was their only option. They left that morning before anybody woke up. Isa took the lead, and Topher noticed that she'd found a gun and a holster and strapped it around her hips; it stuck out, blocky and dangerous. Zorn followed her. If he had a gun, it was hidden in the folds of his fur. Topher came last, feeling weak and useless. He struggled to keep up, slowing their progress. Philadelphia seemed unreachable. It was noon before they made it within city limits, early evening by the time they made it to the Delaware. The river ran north to south, black and eternal, rushing past the rusting construction cranes that sat on the banks like ancient sentinels. There were only a few cars left on the bridge, and they'd almost crossed over to the other side when they figured out why.

The military had built a barrier, twenty feet high, spanning all eight lanes. It was made out of bricks and tires and barbed wire and dirt and iron pillars and anything else that could be found to block the way. Four machine gunners' nests were anchored at even intervals: two in the west lanes, two in the east. It took the three of them a good fifteen minutes to climb to the top. They kept slipping and falling, which, Topher supposed, was the whole point. But they didn't give up. Dirt shifted, exposing sharp metal edges and dead things. Zorn slipped and uncovered a pale, rotting face.

Topher, whose arm had taken on a yellowy-green hue, was on the verge of passing out. He couldn't really straighten it for the pain, and he couldn't catch his breath or see without spots obscuring his peripheral vision. His fever intensified. By the time he reached the middle of the climb, he was more pallid than ever (if such a thing were possible), and his lungs felt like they were on fire. Christ. If this continued, death would come a lot sooner, merciless and sweaty, filled with vomiting and embarrassing flatulence, and though he wanted to express his feelings, though he wanted to tell Zorn how scared he was, all he could say was "I think I might barf."

Then he barfed.

The sun set behind the broken skyscrapers. Zorn finally made it into the nest; Isa waited for Topher at the top. She seemed especially attuned to his illness, his creeping fever, his mounting weakness. She planted her feet firmer into the barrier, making sure she wouldn't slip or fall, and leaned toward him, extending her hand. Topher scrambled again as the barrier shifted, sliding down a few feet. Isa, wincing, stepped forward and wedged her boot against an old tire. She said, "grab my hand," but Topher slapped it away.

"I can do it myself."

He lurched up, slipped, and slid down another foot. Isa stretched even farther.

"Take it."

Topher swallowed his pride and did it, and she pulled and he scrambled and together they made it to the top and collapsed into the nest. They leaned up against mouldering sandbags.

"Christ on a crutch," Topher gasped, holding his arm against his chest. He closed his eyes and tried not to feel nauseous. After a few minutes, he shrugged his pack off his shoulders, gritting his teeth when one strap rubbed against his wound.

"Let me see it," Isa said.

He slapped her hand away again.

"It's fine."

"It's not fine. You're going to be lucky to keep it."

"I told you all before. Nobody's amputating anything."

She sighed.

"At least let me change the dressing."

"With what? Another dirty shirt?"

"Better than what you have on now."

Topher set his jaw.

"Don't be stupid, Topher," Zorn said. He unzipped his pack and took out their last three water bottles.

In the end, he let her. It was painful and humiliating, but Isa was good and she worked fast. She removed the old dressing, cleaned the crusty blood off the maculation, told him not to look.

"I'm going to have to move it, okay?"

"It's going to hurt, isn't it?"

"Like hell."

"Such bedside manner."

She smiled, and he was struck again by her beauty. He couldn't place it. It wasn't just the way she arched her eyebrow when he teased her, or how she bit her lip when she was concentrating, or even in the perfect symmetry of her features. She was just beautiful. It was hard not to look. He felt butterflies in his stomach, like he was in middle school again.

"Just close your eyes," she said.

He did, and she started to hum. He didn't recognize the tune, but the melody was sweet, reminding him of rainy afternoons, fingers entwined, shy smiles. She lifted his arm, and the pain shot up his shoulder. He sucked in his breath.

"Okay, okay," she said. "Relax. Take a deep breath."

He did as she instructed.

"Now let it out. Feel your body let go."

He did, and she sang to him, the words following the tune she had hummed before.

"Baby, remember on the bus when your hand was on my knee? When you love somebody it's hard to think about anything but to breathe."

"What song is that?"

"I don't know. My mother used to sing it to me when I was little. Before."

"How old are you?"

"Not as old as you."

"How old do you think I am?"

"Not old. Not old at all."

Topher sighed.

"I am old. I'm bald and old."

She laughed, then she said, "Finished."

He opened his eyes. She'd done an expert job, using the new shirt to wrap his arm against his chest. It was comfortable and tight, and it took the pressure off his shoulder, which had been aching.

"I didn't feel a thing."

Isa scooted over to her side of the nest.

"Good."

He leaned back on the sandbags and rested his eyes. Though all he wanted was to catch his breath, get a moment's respite, he started to think. He wondered whether or not the infection in his shoulder had spread too far, about how long it would take him to die, but mainly he thought about the people they'd left back in Bellmawr. He hoped they were okay.

Zorn snapped him out of his reverie by saying, "what a dump."

Topher looked around the platform. The plywood floor was green with moss and rotten in the corners, and the metal sides were strung with barbed wire. A dried out body hung over one side, its fingers melted into the metal. The sandbags were stacked three feet high in the corners, sagging and torn, but the two tarnished .50 .50's mounted into the metal looked angry and efficient. Zorn patted one with his hand, flicked the barrel with his finger. It made a metallic ting, and rust flaked to the ground.

"They're pointed in."

"It's that way everywhere," Isa said.

"Really?"

"Everywhere I've been."

"And where is that?"

"Baltimore, Frederick, Hagerstown."

He used a buck knife to open a can of peas. They shared it, passing it around, using their fingers to scoop out the food. When they were done, Topher held the empty can up to the other two.

"We'll need to learn how to do this. Farming, I mean."

He flicked the can over the side.

Zorn said, "Seems simple enough. Seeds. Land. Water."

"Well, we know it's possible," Isa said.

"My grandmother canned tomatoes. At least, that's what my father used to say." He glanced at her, then away. "I'm afraid of botulism."

"What's to fear?"

"My father used to tell me about his dog. Bubbles."

She giggled.

"Your father named a dog Bubbles?"

"I know it's ridiculous." His smile faded as he remembered. "Bubbles ate an old can of strawberry preserves once and died of it. His stomach exploded."

Topher saw little spots in the corner of his eyes. He said, "Nonsense. Nothing to be afraid of. My Uncle Byron Bill survived a case of botulism while in the prison camps in Vietnam. He ate a live snake."

"Was that the cure?"

"No, the cause, I think. He never really elaborated on it, just said, 'Got botulism in Vietnam. Ate a live snake'."

At one point in his life, Zorn might have tried to get his friend back on track, but he didn't have the energy for it anymore. Isa didn't seem bothered by it. Or she just didn't care.

"I always thought that was the most impressive thing I'd ever heard," Topher continued, more to himself than the others. "That a human being, and someone like Uncle Byron for that matter, could be so hungry as to eat a live snake. A live snake!" He paused, thinking. "You know, if a meandering little punk like him could survive food poisoning and viper-eating in the jungles of Vietnam, I should be able to survive this."

Isa said, "I don't want to argue, but this is worse than Vietnam. This is worse than anything that's ever happened before."

"It is."

She looked at Zorn.

"Do you want to know how I got caught? By that thing, Rasheed?" Zorn seemed unsure. "It's okay. I want you to know. I didn't get caught because I was stupid. I didn't get caught because I was careless. I got caught because everyone's given up. Because there are lunatics out there like him, and there are lunatics out there like all those men who followed him, and they don't want to do anything more than hurt other people."

"We're not doing that," Topher said.

"That's why I'm telling you this. You're good men."

"Well, I'm good. Zorn masturbates to pictures of women in bunny suits."

"Topher!"

Topher started to laugh but it ended in a fit of coughing.

"Serves you right," Zorn said. "Plus, I never masturbated to Delmont and Bunny. I have nothing but good childhood memories of them."

"You're both so odd," Isa said. "But I guess that's not a crime."

"Nothing's a crime anymore," Topher noted.

Isa considered this. She poked around with her toe at the sandbags, ran her finger along the barrel of the .50 .50.

"What do you think Rasheed would have done if you'd lost? If Saanvi hadn't shown up?"

"It's a moot point," Topher said. "We did win. Saanvi did show up."

"Just play along. What do you think he would have done?"

Topher shifted his weight and sat up straighter.

"Well, I'd be dead, that's for sure. Zorn, too." He thought for a little while. "I suppose he would have tried to hunt Saanvi and the rest down. Probably would have killed the children. They're useless. If he did keep them alive, he would have used them."

"And me?"

He paused uncomfortably.

"How many men do you think he had? A hundred and fifty? Two?"

"At least."

"And you're a woman."

She took a sip of her water, replaced the cap.

"What if I told you that there was someone out there worse than Rasheed?"

"He's about as bad as it gets."

"No," she said. "He's not. The group I was with. We were worse than him."

"Okay."

"You know what we would have done if we would have found you?"

"I'm sure I can conjure something up."

"Think of that, and then think of something a million times worse."

She was quiet for a while, seeming to think of a way to say what she wanted to say. A tear ran down her cheek and she wiped it away, disgusted with herself.

"When I left her, when I left them all, I left everything behind. My husband, my son. I couldn't do it anymore. She kept us safe, she kept us fed, but it was wrong. My husband, he was totally under her power. And Daniel, my son, he wasn't . . . he wasn't a human being anymore. None of us were."

"If we had caught you in that ring, there wouldn't have been anything left. The men, the women, the children, the horses, everything. We would have destroyed it all."

"Is that why you left?"

"Yes and no. Things had to change. I needed to change. I-I'm looking for something."

"Have you found it?"

She met Topher's eyes.

"I think so, but I'm not sure yet."

Without another word, she gathered up her things and stepped over the barrier.

Half an hour later, she stopped and looked around.

"We're in Schuylkill. If we head west for a mile or so, that'll take us to South Broad. There are a few hospitals on that street."

"How do you know this?" Zorn asked.

Isa looked away.

"I know the city pretty well."

The streets were cracked, and the cracks were filled with weeds, and the weeds were two feet tall and brown, and some of them had bugs on them, and when they passed the bugs shot up into the air and swarmed around Topher's arm. Many of the windows in the buildings were broken and jagged. The wind whooshed and barreled down the avenue, bringing with it all manner of dirt and dust and scraps of paper. A sulfuric stench burned in the air at one point, and ash sifted in the ruined gutters.

Zorn thought he saw something bob up and down on top of the townhouses to his left, something small and round, like a head, but when he stopped to look it wasn't there. Then he saw a few more red ankhs painted on the boarded-up doors and windows. There was a curious absence of automobiles. He chalked it up to looters. Isa knew better. Topher was too sick to care. When the wind brought the sulfur smell towards them again, Isa bent down to the gutter and rubbed handfuls of the ash onto her face, arms, and legs, even in her armpits. She motioned for the other two to do the same. Zorn obeyed immediately, but Topher resisted.

"Do we have to? I'm feeling sick enough already without rubbing that all over me."

"Topher, you need to do this," Isa said. "Better to feel a little nausea than your guts pulled out."

Topher took a careful knee and reached out for the gutter.

"A compelling argument."

Zorn spied another bobbing head soon after. He saw the third one a few steps later, this time on the other side of the street, silhouetted against the early evening sky.

"Isa," he said.

"I know."

He turned around to Topher.

"Are these the rumors you heard about?"

"Yes."

"You need to tell me what you know. Now."

"Nobody's sure what they are or where they came from," Topher said. "It's hard to sort through the exaggerations to find the truth."

"What exaggerations?"

"I've heard all kinds of things. That they're monsters with five-inch claws. That they have green skin. That they eat people alive."

Isa shook her head. She pushed forward.

"It's impossible to know," Topher said. "Anybody who came into contact with things like that wouldn't live to tell the tale, but every now and then, we'd come across someone who said they did."

"C'mon," Zorn said, hurrying to catch up to Isa.

Topher struggled to keep up. His face was now entirely red, his neck muscles roped, his breathing ragged and labored. He thought of the nature programs he used to watch on the Discovery channel, how the predators picked off the young, the old, and the lame. He was two for three. Five more bald heads, oval and overlarge, popped up on the townhouse to their left. This time they remained in place, eyes glittering. Heart in his throat, he scanned the street for possible escape. Nothing but boarded-up row houses and narrow alleys clogged with old dumpsters and fire escapes. Isa started to jog, and as soon as she did, drums sounded all around them, loud and booming. A flash of light arced out into the sky, then another, and another.

She cried, "Run!"

There was some kind of official building at the intersection ahead: stairs sweeping up to a colonnade. Zorn grabbed Topher by his good arm and yanked him forward. Red fire and glass exploded not five feet from where they just stood, slicing Zorn across the cheek. Topher grunted in pain. Two more balls of flame to the left, two more to the right.

Isa made it to the stairs, pausing only to shoot a panicked glance to the sky. Another red finger arced out into the night, and she dashed up several steps, ducking behind a column just as it exploded.

Zorn and Topher followed as more bombs struck. Glass peppered the air, and their faces were soon streaked with blood. The drums churned a raucous rhythm. They made it to the top, and Topher sank down to his knees, exhausted. Three sets of sturdy wooden doors spanned the colonnade, and Isa was already pushing on the far left set. They were locked tight.

"Chained from the inside!" she yelled.

The drums suddenly stopped, leaving a terrible silence its wake, the rush of wind, the crackle of flames. Then, underneath it, Topher heard something. He cocked his head.

"What's that? Did you hear that?"

Zorn frowned, listening.

"Hear what?"

Topher shushed him, straining to hear.

"There. That sound. It's like—it sounds like rats."

They all hung there, waiting. And then there it was, plain as day. Feet slapping on concrete, nails clacking on wood. Not just a few, but dozens.

"Those aren't rats," Isa said.

She pulled her gun out of the holster, and almost as soon as she did, the monsters burst out of the townhouses across the street.

Topher's jaw dropped. The reality was worse than the rumors.

They were human. Or somewhat human. Hairless and emaciated, but with strong, ropey muscles. Their pale green skin glowed in the moonlight, and their fingers ended in inch long claws. They scrabbled forward on all fours, hissing, eyes tracking their prey. Some wore scraps of clothing, torn hospital pants and tattered robes. Most were nude. More poured in from the side streets, galloping toward the stairs. Isa fired into the horde. Zorn, too. Topher turned to launch himself at the center set of doors and nearly cried out with both fear and relief.

A man was standing just inside, holding the way open for them.

"Hurry!" he yelled.

Topher leaped within, followed Zorn. Isa had just reached the jamb when one of the monsters grabbed her leg. She cried out and shot it in the face. Another leaped for her and she fired again, catching it in the gut. It crumbled in midair and struck her and they both tumbled inside. The stranger slammed the doors against the tide, pulling on the handles, anchoring his feet against the frame. The first wave struck and found the handle, and he was yanked forward.

"Help!"

The other doors shook with the assault, but they were still chained tightly. Glass shattered. The frames groaned. Arms waved through the broken windows. The monsters' squeals filled the entry, bouncing off the marble, the domed glass ceiling. Zorn grabbed the handle next to the man who'd saved them and pulled with all his might. Together they slammed the door shut. At his feet, he noticed plywood and two by fours, something someone might have used to board up the windows. Or was trying to use. Behind him, Topher fired his gun at the beast that had gotten inside, but it weaved and ducked, galloping in a full circle before zeroing back in on him. His arms shook as he held the gun up. Sweat ran into his eyes. It leaped, fangs bared, claws out, and he could smell its stinking breath, ripe with rot and death, and then Zorn struck it in the head with a two by four and it hit the wall and lay still, its skull crushed.

"Run!" the stranger cried. "Go!"

Zorn pulled Topher off the wall and they ran in the only direction they could. Deeper into the building.

They made it only a few feet in when they heard wood cracking and glass breaking as the beasts burst through the doors. They turned left, sprinting past shadows of desks and bookshelves, heading for a set of double doors. A monster spun out behind them, crashing into mangled chairs and broken study carrels. It scrabbled erect and bolted forward. Two more turned the corner behind it. A broken desk sat just inside the doors, and Zorn threw it against them. He pulled an errant bookshelf down over the desk. Then he grabbed Topher's hand and pulled him forward again, not daring to look behind. They were in a hallway now, and the overhead lights guttered, then burned low and brown.

"Electricity?" Topher gasped. His eyes swiveled around as they ran. "The walls."

A red arrow had been painted on either side, pointing down the hall. They passed a second, then a third, then the word "Salvation," the paint dark and dripping and eerie in the flickering, dead light. The doors burst open behind them, and the beasts leaped over the broken furniture. Zorn pulled Topher left into another hallway, another set of flickering lights, more red arrows. One last set of doors sat at the end, and they pushed through.

"Don't leave me," Topher said.

"I won't."

In the next hall, the overhead lights shut down, and when they flashed back on there stood the stranger again, the man who rescued them, a vision of messianic hair and beard and blood red robe. He put a finger to his lips as they pushed past and into an open space (an operating theater?) filled with men in women in green scrubs, all of whom stopped and gaped at the two brutes covered in blood and ash that burst into their midst.

"Help us!" Zorn cried.

As they ran forward, Topher felt suddenly lighter, like his feet were no longer connected to the earth, and the lights grew brighter and brighter all around him, washing everything in its pale glory, consuming him, infusing him, shooting out of every pore and every orifice, his eyes, his nose, his mouth, burning him up from within, devouring each cell, melting bone into muscle and flesh, and he was no longer himself but a part of the light, falling forever forward into pure and terrible nothingness.

Ages passed.

Shadows formed in the white void, weak, pale green outlines, and every time he let his lids crack open, even if it was just the slightest bit, pain shot through his temples and ricocheted around his brain, so he kept them shut. After a while, he was able to hold them apart, though only for a few seconds. The forms emerged again, more defined this time: oval, hairless, green. Now he could see faces, three of them. They were wearing full surgical gear, gloves, gowns, masks, and caps, so that the only things visible were their eyes. Sounds morphed all around, low and distorted. He felt his body jerk back and forth, as if they were moving something around inside of him.

". . . eel," he said. "M'arm . . ."

One of the faces disappeared, then he felt a slight prick on his shoulder, and his vision darkened.

Later. He could open his eyes without pain. Zorn's face hove into view. His wonderful beard! His marvelous curls! His magnificent nose! All of it unmasked.

". . . onderful news!" he was saying. ". . . trude . . . live . . . ive . . . ive . . ."

Topher tried to sit up, his heart leaping, and a machine somewhere began to beep. Soft hands on his shoulders pushed him back into blissful darkness.

Awake again. A voice, official, formal, was in the middle of saying ". . . removed all the bits of metal, doctor."

A nurse?

"He seems to be responding to the anti-venom."

A second voice, deep and assured, said, "Very good, Nurse Smith."

Topher's lids fluttered open, and his eyes rolled around in his head.

"Ah. He's awake."

Beige walls, lime green couch, blank television anchored in the corner.

Hospital.

He was in a hospital room.

"Water," he croaked.

He sat up, stronger this time, but the doctor, unmasked, stepped forward and put his hand on his chest, pushing him back down, firm but gentle.

"Not so fast. You've been gravely wounded."

"Where am I?"

The doctor raised his eyebrows, and Topher couldn't tell if he was amused or angry. He turned around to fiddle with some instruments.

"The scratches and cuts on your face will heal easily enough, but the puncture wound in your right shoulder did a lot of damage. Whatever pierced it was poisoned, and you still had pieces of metal left in the tissue. You're lucky to have an arm at all."

"Get out," Topher whispered.

"That's right. We had to get it out." He smiled with his teeth, which were large and white, and gripped Topher's left arm. "Tell me. What are you and your friends doing in our fair city?"

"Antibiotics."

The doctor smiled thinly.

"Just the two of you?"

Topher nodded.

"No other reason?"

Topher tried to think. His mind was a fog of painkillers; words evaded his grasp like flies.

"No?"

The doctor hovered over him for a menacing minute. Then he gave a curt nod.

"Very well." He flashed another big-toothed smile. "Have it your way. Now it's time to get some rest. Group begins early tomorrow morning."

He spun on his heel to leave, nodding at the nurse to open the door. She punched a few numbers on the pad, there was an electric buzz, and the lock released. Topher snatched at the doctor's sleeve before he was out of reach, and, though he had to use all of his strength to do it, managed to hold on. The doctor stiffened and glared down at Topher's hand as if it were something nasty.

"Yes?"

"Zorn?"

The doctor cocked his head.

"I'm sorry, what?"

"My friend. Is he okay?"

"Zorn? Your friend's name is Zorn?"

Topher nodded, and the doctor and nurse exchanged a glance.

"Zorn's safe," he said.

He tried to pull away but Topher clamped down even harder.

"Doctor?"

"What is it?"

"Where am I?"

The doctor sighed. He rubbed his eyes under his glasses with his free hand. Then slowly, very slowly, he prized Topher's fingers from his sleeve and let his hand drop.

"Someplace safe," he said. He wiped his hand on his pants. "Nurse Smith?"

The nurse held the door open for him and they left.

A few days later, Nurse Smith pushed him out of his room in a wheelchair. He was, according to her, "still too weak to walk," and though he at first resisted (hadn't he made it to the bathroom and back several times by himself already?) she refused to let him go anywhere until he got in the chair. He looked up and down the hall, nervous, full of anticipation, and then Zorn turned the corner.

"Topher!" he called. He hurried over and knelt in front of the wheelchair. "You're alive."

"Barely." Topher cleared his throat. "Where are we?"

Zorn started to answer, but Nurse Smith inserted her body between them and began to fuss with the footrests.

"Honestly, Mr. Bill. How do you expect me to push you if you don't keep your feet off the ground?"

"My feet were nowhere near the ground."

He allowed her to put them back into the rests, studying Zorn's face for an answer, but Zorn only shrugged.

Nurse Smith stood up.

"There we go." She put her hands on her hips, admiring her work. "Ready for Group?"

The halls were completely empty, the rooms unoccupied. Nobody at the nurse's station. Nobody in the lobby. Nobody in the church. Their footsteps echoed. They passed a visiting area that had recently been cleaned and straightened, with plastic flowers in glass vases and new bags in the wastebasket. Someone had fanned out magazines on a coffee table.

"What is this?" Topher asked. "A ghost hospital?"

Nurse Smith pursed her lips and stared straight ahead. She didn't seem like she was in a rush to get them anywhere, pushing the wheelchair with careful, measured steps. Topher tapped the armrest.

"Can't we go faster? I'm a man, not an eggshell."

She said nothing.

He turned to Zorn, who was ambling beside them.

"Honestly, Zorn. What's the last thing you remember?"

Nurse Smith jerked the chair to an abrupt halt and said, "Here we are!"

The door she stopped at looked like one of the dozens of empty doors to the dozens of empty rooms that lined every empty hallway. She motioned to Zorn, and he hopped around to open it. To Topher's surprise, a waiting room sat on the other side. Empty, of course. Behind a sliding glass window, a secretary tapped away on an antiquated manual typewriter. The nameplate on her desk said her name was Doris.

Doris was middle-aged and, as far as Topher was concerned, plump in just the right ways in just the right places. He stared at her as she typed, and nearly fell out of his chair when she stood up and leaned over to put something in the bottom drawer of her filing cabinet. Unlike the rest of the staff, most of whom either wore pale green scrubs or those ridiculous patterned pajamas (ducks, bunnies, basketballs), Doris was dressed like a professional. Her cream-colored blouse plunged, and her beige skirt clung, and her glasses perched upon the end of her nose, and right then, right when she turned back around and rested her palms on her desk to read something, she took them off her face and let them hang from a chain that encircled her neck, and they nestled into the wedge of her perfectly shaped breasts.

A gray box of crackers sat on the ledge of the glass window, open. Some had fallen out of the package, leaning like dominoes. Topher salivated. Premium Saltines. How had she found them?

As Nurse Smith rolled him up, Topher noticed another door to his right. A black plate affixed to the wall announced it as the "Athenaeum". Nurse Smith cleared her throat, and Doris squeaked as if she had not noticed them, then shuffled around and slid the glass aside.

"Hello," she said. Her voice was high but matronly. "Is this your first visit with us?"

Topher glanced at Nurse Smith.

"Tell her the truth," she told him.

"Okay. Well, er, yes?"

"Okay then," Doris piped. She presented him with a clipboard to which a handful of forms had been clipped. "Please fill this out with your information. Make sure to sign here, here, and here. And make sure you've updated any changes in your medical history and insurance. As soon as you're done, we can get you started on your therapy!"

Puzzled, Topher took the clipboard and pen as Doris swished back to her desk to peck away at her typewriter. He flipped through the forms. One asked for personal details, and the rest inquired after his insurance information. He thought briefly about lying about his name but decided against it. What did it matter? Were they going to steal his social security number? He wrote "transient" for his address and N/A for everything else. He scowled at the line that asked him to leave his signature, leaving a big, black X in its place. When he was done, he held out the clipboard, and Doris stopped typing and bustled over to take it. While she looked over what he'd written, he glanced around her and saw a mini-refrigerator humming next to her desk. His stomach grumbled. Surely a woman of Doris' healthy attributes kept it stocked beyond necessity.

"I'll be with you in a minute, Mr. Bill," she said, still reading. "Please go over there and wait."

Nurse Smith started to push him but he snapped, "I'm more than capable of pushing myself, thank you."

She stopped but didn't take her hands off the handles, struggling with the correct response. Should she respect his spunk or unhinge her jaw and bite off his head? Topher twisted partially around and said, "May I?

"Certainly, Mr. Bill," she said. "Be my guest."

She watched him as he wheeled himself away, then turned to Zorn and said, "You can take him from here" and left the room. The moment she was gone, Topher carefully wheeled himself back to the glass window and swiped a handful of crackers. He ate one, then quickly put the rest in his robe pocket.

Zorn skipped over to the coffee table.

"Oh! They have *Cat Fancy*!"

He sat down at one of the cargo chairs, pouring over the table of contents. "Everything You Ever Wanted to Know About Feline Kidney Stones," he read aloud. "Remarkable."

Topher snuck another cracker.

"Zorn, please. We're in a lot of trouble."

"Mm-hmm."

"Did you not see that crazy nurse's clumsy attempts to keep you from answering me?"

"You mean Nurse Smith? I think she's dreamy."

"Look at this place. Electricity, functioning medical equipment, *Cat Fancy*. It's the end of the world and we're enjoying climate control."

Zorn buried his face in the magazine.

Topher tried again.

"I mean, can you believe it?"

"I'm reading."

"Curse your feline fetish!"

Zorn looked up from his magazine.

"The ancient Egyptians regarded cats as gods."

"Please. Everyone knows cats are the spawn of Satan."

Zorn went back to his magazine.

"What article are you reading now?" Topher asked. "Are you reading an article about cats?"

Zorn turned the page.

"Does *Cat Fancy* have personal ads for cats?" Topher asked. "I would imagine that would be especially difficult for a copywriter to write personal ads for cats, as cats are illiterate."

Zorn ground his teeth.

"Though I wouldn't put it past a hack job like *Cat Fancy* to give something so stupid a shot."

Zorn slapped the magazine down in his lap.

"*Cat Fancy* is a highly regarded national publication!"

Topher opened his mouth to reply, but when he did another voice said, "Topher?"

Both men looked up, startled.

Doris was standing next to the door to the Athenaeum, looking around the waiting room as if it were full and she didn't know who Topher was.

"Topher?" she asked again. She checked the clipboard. "Toph —"

"Yes?"

Her eyes found him and she smiled.

"Well, there you are! We're all ready for your now."

By definition, an Athenaeum is a sacred building that serves as a place of learning. Centuries ago, great men used them to hold forth on complex issues of deep philosophical import. They strolled from column to column, gracing their students' ears with the logic and reason that established the very foundation of western knowledge and culture. Here, truth trumped blind faith, Socrates developed his method, and *The Republic* and *The Five Dialogues* were born. They were beautiful and open and proud—fortresses of reason, citadels of enlightenment.

The Athenaeum into which Zorn pushed Topher was a filthy warehouse littered with broken furniture and shattered electronics.

Brown light from chipped fixtures cast a pall over the room. In the middle of the chaos, the three-legged couches, the mouldering upholstery, the ancient, cracked monitors, the dismembered VCRs and DVD players and video game consoles, someone had made a circle of seven bare wooden chairs. A small group of men sat there, tense and silent. Behind them stood an orderly.

One of the patients was probably the angriest looking man Topher had ever seen. He slouched in his seat, chewing on his thumbnail with such fervor that he might have gnawed it to a stump. His bald head might have gleamed were there enough light, and he wore his robe open, exposing a T-shirt that stated, in large, bubble letters, "Liberals are Pussies!". He simmered and seethed. He fumed and fulminated. When he saw Topher staring at his shirt he popped his thumb out of his mouth and said, "The fuck you looking at?"

Topher ignored him and took in the rest of the group.

A bug-eyed man with a chin so weak that it looked like his lips were hanging free in space. His spectacles took up half of his face.

A weasel-faced man with a bushy mustache. He wore a comb-over that did little to cover his baldness.

A fat man with a mole on his cheek, also bald, smiling in adoration at the nail-biter. His belly poked out of his robe.

The Saltines leaned forward, elbows on his knees, about to burst.

"Hey!"

Fatty giggled, his belly jiggled.

The orderly, a muscle-bound jock in a sleeveless T-shirt and jeans, took a step forward as the Saltines scooted up to the edge of his seat.

Topher might have responded had the final group member not so arrested his attention. He was muscular, round, and (like many of the others) completely bald. He slumped in his chair, staring off into space. There was something about his largeness, the shape of his head, and his massive hands and feet.

No. It couldn't be.

The Saltines popped to his feet.

"You want a piece of me?"

Fatty started to laugh, throaty and hoarse, like an old man.

"Gertrude?" Topher said.

He wheeled himself forward.

The biter couldn't take it anymore.

"That's it!" he cried, but before he could lash forward, the orderly clapped a meaty paw on his shoulder and shoved him back into his seat with a thud. The biter threw up his hands.

"What? What? I was just welcoming the new guys!" He waved at Topher. "Hiya, faggot!"

Topher pushed through the circle, ignoring Zorn, who said, "Topher, wait!" and wheeled up to his old friend. When he saw his face, his wide grin faded.

Gertrude was sitting in very much the same state as the weak-chinned man across from him. Eyes vacant and fixed, mouth ajar, hands resting on his knees. Topher turned to Zorn.

"Why didn't you tell me he was alive?"

"I did. Before."

"When before?"

"When you were crazy on drugs."

Topher waved his fingers in front of Gertrude's face. Nothing.

"What's wrong with him? Why is his skin so pale?"

A door on the other side of the room whined open, and in walked a small, dainty man wearing a fatherly beard. His cardigan was worn at the elbows, and his green corduroys were worn at the knees, and his shoes were worn at the heels. He moved in a way that seemed to indicate timorous serenity.

"Doc Smythe!" the biter said. "Howdy!"

Smythe's eyes shook over the men, jittering a little too long on the biter and the orderly standing behind him. He addressed the latter first.

"Is there a problem, Tre?"

Tre, in a voice like an elephant with a head cold, pointed at the nail-biter.

"Ask Shawn."

Shawn, however, had resumed his relaxed posture: legs stuck straight out before him, one arm draped over his stomach. He gnawed absently at his thumb.

"I'm fine," he said. "I'm fine."

"Good," Smythe said. "That's what I thought."

He let out a shuddering breath, then turned and started at the imposing sight of Topher and Zorn.

"Oh, my. You're the new arrivals. I'm Doctor Smythe."

He nosed toward his seat and sat primly on its edge. Then he pulled a green binder from his bag and studied it for few minutes, exhaling through his nose. The giggling fat man watched him, shocked and amazed, as if he had no idea what was about to happen, no idea of what to expect next, but was, all the same, happier for it, like a baby anticipating a fart. Finally, Smythe opened his mouth to speak, but the voice that filled the room was not his own.

"What would we like to talk about today?"

It was Shawn, his voice a smooth, goofy parody of Smythe's posh accent.

Tre, who had retreated into a corner, bridled at the disrespect, but Smythe held up his hand.

"That's very funny, Shawn," he said, smiling. "But don't you think it rude to mock me in front of our new friends?"

Shawn played with a rough patch on his pajama bottoms.

"No."

Fatty giggled louder and Shawn joined in, enjoying the attention. Even the Mustache seemed to vibrate a little. Smythe folded his hands in his lap.

"No? You don't think it's wrong to mock somebody in mixed company?"

"Somebody? Yes. You? No."

Fatty could contain himself no longer, and he barked out a hysterical laugh. Smythe shot him a look and he swallowed it.

"You are a difficult man, Shawn," Smythe said.

Shawn might have said, "I'm sorry, Dr. Smythe," but it was too difficult to hear him through his laughter.

"Well, as wonderful as your apology may be, Shawn, I thought we agreed that I was to commence and convene all meetings, and that I was to set all of the topics, and that I was to lead this group. Not you." He jabbed his finger at Shawn, then at each of the other patients. "Not you, not you, not you, not you, you, you, and you!"

"And I thought we agreed that you're a complete asshole!" Shawn said.

The room erupted, and Smythe sat back, stunned. Then he nodded at Tre, and Tre stalked over to Fatty and put him in a headlock. Fatty gasped and his face went red. Tre squeezed harder. In a second, Shawn's demeanor changed. He growled and launched himself at the orderly, mouth wide, screaming, and sank his teeth into his shoulder. Tre grimaced but didn't release his hold.

"Is this what you wanted, Shawn?" Dr. Smythe asked. "Are you happy now?"

Shawn bit harder.

"Get him off me," Tre said.

Dr. Smythe regarded him, calm and impassive.

"Why, Tre? Can you not take care of it yourself?"

Tre glared, but instead of talking back, he stomped on Shawn's knee. Shawn crumpled to the ground, his eyes wide with pain, his leg at an odd angle. Tre returned his attention to Fatty.

"It's really such a shame that you pushed it to this point," Smythe said. "If you had only just followed the rules." He turned to the rest of the men, who were watching in horror "Do you see? Do you see what happens?"

Fatty gargled. His face turned maroon, then purple.

"Now Tre," Smythe said. "That's enough."

Tre squeezed.

"Come now, Tre. Let the man go."

Fatty's eyes began to flutter, and his hands, which had been grasping the orderly's forearms, fell limp.

"Tre?"

Tre squeezed harder.

"Tre!"

Suddenly, Gertrude's left arm shot out, grabbed the orderly's wrist and ripped it away. Fatty slumped to the floor.

"Jesus!" Topher said. "Did you see that, Zorn?"

Tre yanked his wrist out of Gertrude's grip and rubbed it, weighing his options. Should he punch him? Choke him out? He wasn't sure he could win. Usually they were too weak or near the end to put up much of a fight, but this one was nearly catatonic and almost broke his hand. Must not have been as far along as they thought.

Smythe was breathless.

"My goodness, that was good," he said. "That was very, very good." He gazed down at Shawn, who was cussing and spitting on the ground. "Does it hurt?"

Shawn groaned something through his teeth.

"I can't hear you, Shawn. You'll have to speak up."

"Fuck you!"

Smythe tsked.

"Mind your language."

"Cocksucker! Motherfucker!"

"Okay, well, I must say that I disagree with you." He motioned for Tre, who picked Shawn up and threw him back in his chair. "Can we begin, now? Today I'd like to talk about emotions."

Shawn said, "Sure," hopped up on his one good leg, and lunged for Topher, snarling.

Smythe watched it happen.

"Goodness," he said. "Goodness me."

Shawn crashed into the wheelchair, tipping it over and sending them both to the ground. Topher tried to fight back, but his shoulder flared, and his other arm was pinned to the ground. Good Christ. The crazy bastard was going to tear his face to pieces, and there was nothing he could do but clamp his eyes shut. Shawn jammed his mouth to his ear, breathing heavily.

"Please," Topher said.

"Don't take the meds," Shawn whispered. "Don't eat the food."

Then Tre yanked him off.

Shawn spun out of his grasp, still hopping, and, with a bestial growl, fell upon Smythe, bit his cheek, and ripped out a chunk of flesh.

And as the doctor's screams escalated in pitch, and as Shawn bit again and again, and as Tre rained down blow after blow, and as Fatty slumped to the floor, Gertrude remained in the exact same position as before, his eyes empty and hollow, his arm rigid and horizontal, hanging there in midair as if waiting for someone to tell him what to do.

That night Topher probed his room. He didn't know what he was looking for, he just knew he was looking. The room was filled with standard hospital furniture. Cheap bed, cheap dresser, cheap couch. He tapped on the television screen, pushed a few buttons on the remote. Maybe there was a special hospital channel, or maybe he could tune into some rogue signal being sent out by . . . who? Rebels?

Survivors? Good guys with guns? What a crock. The damn thing didn't even turn on, anyway. He chucked the remote onto the bed and swiveled the set aside. The power cord had been cut. There was just a little nub poking out of the back. He put his hands on his hips, staring around him. What else could he investigate?

He'd just pushed his bed aside and was trying to remove the air vent cover on the wall behind it when Nurse Smith barged into his room holding a tray filled with small white paper cups.

"What do you think you're doing?"

"Please," he said, looking up from his work. "Come in."

She seemed uncertain as to how to react. Anger? Disappointment? Playful scolding? Rather than choose, she said, "Tre."

The orderly muscled his way into the room. When he saw what Topher had done, he said, "Goddammit" and stomped over and knocked him against the wall. "You're a pain in the ass," he muttered, shoving the bed back into place.

Topher struggled to his feet, and Nurse Smith presented him with the tray full of paper cups.

"Time for your vitamins."

Topher eyed the cups, remembering Shawn's warning. The man was clearly deranged, but still, things felt a little off here.

"Vitamins? Shouldn't I be on antibiotics? Opiates? Viagra?"

Nurse Smith paused, assessing him.

"You think this is funny." She put the tray down on his bed. "I heard there was a commotion during group?"

"Yes. One of your patients bit the psychologist's face off."

"Dr. Smythe is not a psychologist."

"Guidance counselor, then?"

Her lips twitched up in the corners.

"Such a strange little man you are."

"You have no idea."

"Tell me, Mr. Bill, what did you do before?"

"Before I got here?"

"You know what I mean."

Topher almost told her. Almost told her about Raleigh's, Mr. Floyd, the werepyres. About Fredericksburg, the zombies, Riddle. But something stopped him. He didn't want her to know anything more about him than she already did.

"I was an appliance salesman," he said. "SEARS."

"Really?"

"Oh yes. Michelin. Firestone."

"Those are tires."

"I sold them, too."

She gave him a long, cold stare.

"I see."

"Listen, I'm very grateful for what you all have done for me. I can't begin to tell you how much I am in your debt." She locked her blue eyes upon his brown ones. He suppressed a shiver. "But I was wondering when you might let me go. Us go. Zorn and I, that is."

"Zorn?"

"Yes, my friend. Zorn. It's his last name. It's what I call him."

That little flicker of a smile tugged at the corners of her mouth again, but rather than answer, she picked up one of the paper cups from the tray on the bed and offered it to him.

"You were gravely wounded, Mr. Bill. You need to rest and recuperate. Please take your vitamins."

Topher took the cup. There were three tablets sitting inside: two small ones, blue and oval, and one large one, white and round.

"Hmm," he said, picking out the white one. "Can you tell me what this one is?"

"It's your vitamin."

"Yes, but which one? Vitamin A? Vitamin C? Magnesium?"

Nurse Smith smiled sweetly.

"Don't you want to get better?"

"Of course, Mrs. Smith."

"*Nurse* Smith."

"Nurse Smith, I'm just feeling uncomfortable about this."

"Are you saying you won't take them?"

"Not necessarily. I just—"

"Are the pills too big?"

"That's not the problem."

"Then what is it?"

He opened his mouth to speak, shut it, then said, "I guess I'm just uncomfortable putting something in my body without knowing what it is."

"I told you. They're vitamins."

"They don't look like vitamins."

"Are you calling me a liar?"

"No."

Nurse Smith pressed her lips together.

"The way I see it, you have two options. Would you like to hear them?"

"Does it matter whether or not I do?"

"It's a simple yes or no question. Answer it." He didn't speak. "We have other ways of inserting them, you know." He remained silent. "You are a child. Tre?"

The orderly took a small step forward and Topher said, "Okay, okay. Fine."

He upended the cup into his mouth and dry swallowed.

Nurse Smith gave him that tight little smile again.

"Good boy," she said.

She picked up the tray and followed Tre out of the room, but before he shut the door, she turned around.

"Lights out in five minutes."

It was a pointless order. In less than three, Topher was on his bed, face down, barely able to hold his eyes open. Right before he blacked out, he heard an electric buzz followed by a thunk. They'd locked him in for the night.

The next morning, he woke to find his wheelchair gone and the door wide open. The P.A. clicked on, and Nurse Smith's voice came through a speaker in the ceiling.

"Group therapy has been canceled until further notice. All patients please report to breakfast immediately."

The cafeteria, like so many of the rooms, was filled with an assortment of mismatched furniture. Lounge chairs, duvets, and recliners shared space with rickety tables and three-legged stools. Dust swirled and twinkled in light made dingy by the dirty windows. The paint on the walls was faded and yellow. Cracked pillars and carvings and pediments decorated the murky corners. Only three of the chandeliers worked; the rest, about a dozen, swayed above like pendulous sacks, knitted with frayed wires and broken crystals, coated with cobwebs.

Two steam tables lined one end of the hall, presenting Topher with a melange of maddening smells. Grilled steak. Buttery potatoes. Baked beans. Creamed corn. Pasta Salad. Tomatoes, green beans, red peppers, sliced onions, croutons, chocolate pudding, apple pie, Jell-O. His mouth watered and his stomach gurgled, and he didn't want to eat it, wary as he was of Shawn's warning, but he couldn't help himself. He and Zorn snatched up trays and plates and spoons (the only utensil available) from a stack by the door and proceeded to load up with every single offering. There was only one clean table in the place, and to get to it they had to weave through a maze of broken furniture.

Zorn was already eating as they sat down, shoving a spoonful of corn and beef into his mouth with a moan. Topher was ready to follow suit. He scooped up a spoonful of peas and put it right up to lips. All he had to do was open the hatch, chew, swallow, repeat, but he couldn't do it. All he could think about was Shawn's hot breath on his ear.

"Don't take the meds. Don't eat the food."

Oh but the smells. The textures. His stomach gurgled again and he closed his eyes. Then, as if he were lowering a box filled with iron weights, he put the spoon back down on his plate.

Zorn elbowed him and, through a mouth filled with food, said, "Topher this is really good you should eat it."

Topher tried to ignore him. He inspected the food. The steak was too brown, the corn too yellow, the Jell-O too neon. He poked at a chunk of chicken floating in sauce the color of red crayons.

Zorn swallowed and said, "How could you not be hungry?"

Topher drove his peas around the plate and pushed the tray away.

"Don't eat it, Zorn," he said.

"Are you crazy? Look at all of this." He cut off a hunk of chicken and put it in his mouth. "You're crazy."

"Shawn told me not to. That and the meds. 'Don't take the meds, don't eat the food' he said."

"Yeah well, he's crazy. The next time you see him, tell him that."

"Tell him yourself," Topher said, nodding at the entrance.

Shawn limped into the cafeteria, a muzzle fastened to his face and a brace strapped to his knee. Tre followed close behind. He limped over to the steam tables, piled his tray with food, and wound his way back to where Topher and Zorn were sitting. Tre took position behind him, arms crossed over his chest. Fatty arrived next, followed by the Mustache, then the Lips, and finally Gertrude, each one escorted by a nurse. The nurses filled their plates, guided them to the table, and put spoons in their hands. For some reason, though, that was where the service ended; once the utensils had been distributed, they left.

Zorn shoveled a mound of peas into his face, then a spoonful of steak, then another spoonful of steak, then he took a bite of a biscuit, then a hunk of potato, then a spoonful of steak.

"Slow down, Zorn," Topher said. "You'll impact your bowels."

Zorn stopped long enough to point at Topher's untouched breakfast.

"Unna ea at?"

Topher shook his head.

"I've lost my appetite." A pea rolled out of Zorn's beard and hit the table. "For some reason."

Zorn chewed thoughtfully for a moment.

"Really?" he finally asked.

"Have at it, Big Mac."

"Ahnk ooo."

Zorn grunted pulled the tray to him and dug in, double spooning it.

"Not eating?" a pleasant voice asked from behind.

Topher craned his neck up around. Nurse Smith was standing there, hands folded primly over her waist.

"Oh. Nurse Smith," he said.

"Not eating?" she asked again.

Topher was suddenly reminded of his mother. When he was younger, she was always questioning him about world events, calculus, geography, expecting—no, demanding—for him to understand concepts he couldn't possibly fathom. Once, when he was ten, she asked him his opinion regarding the "Israeli/Palestinian conflict."

"Oh," he responded. "I'm all for it. Father always extols the virtues of physical fitness."

"What?" she replied, horrified.

"We're talking about soccer, right?"

His mother had regaled him with the same tight smile now splayed across Nurse Smith's lips, then smacked him across the face.

Which was exactly what he told Nurse Smith

"You remind me of my mother," he said.

"Oh? How sweet."

"She was a harpy."

"I'm sorry you think so."

"She died in a horrible fire."

Nurse Smith paused.

"Is there something wrong with your food?" she asked. "Would you like me to get you another plate?"

Topher glanced around the table. The Mustache slowly and mechanically brought spoon-load after spoon-load of mashed potatoes to his mouth. Fatty appeared to have molested an entire blueberry pie with his face. Shawn studiously fingered tiny morsels through the feeding hole in his mask. Their skin was so pale, and they were all *bald*, dammit, or balding, all except for Zorn, of course. At least he still had his beard and his long curls.

Zorn reached up to scratch his head and pulled out a small clump of hair.

"Dear Lord," he said, staring at it. Then he gave Topher a sheepish look. "Middle age." He fell upon his food again. Through a mouthful of peas, he said, "Surprised I lasted this long!"

Tre appeared and deposited another full plate before Topher with a thunk.

"Eat it."

Topher glared at it, then relaxed into his chair. He slowly crossed his arms over his chest.

"If you don't eat," Nurse Smith chimed. "We'll have to force feed through a catheter."

"That's not how you force feed someone."

Nurse Smith bent over and whispered something in his ear, and his eyes widened. She stood and patted him on the shoulder and walked away, saying, "It's up to you."

Topher grumbled and scooped some carrots into his mouth. Though he didn't want to eat it, and though every part of his soul wanted to reject it, his stomach gurgled and his hunger took over. Soon he was halfway through his meal, scooping faster and faster.

"What did she say?" Zorn asked.

Topher stopped long enough to say, "Not the way we do it."

One week passed. Then two. Topher lost track of time. One night in his room before lights out, he emptied the half-masticated remains of his dinner from his pocket into the toilet. He had to eat something, put on a show, but he didn't have to eat it all. The flush roared like a plane engine. He closed the lid and stood on the toilet so he could remove the metal vent cover in the ceiling and felt around inside. He found the spoon he smuggled out of the cafeteria, the husk of a dead insect, and, ah, his crackers. He took a few out and ate. Palmed water from the sink into his mouth.

It still amazed him that they had running water, even if it didn't always work perfectly. Sometimes it was brown or smelled like gas. Once they lost service for two days and they had to use honey buckets, but the very fact that they'd managed to make it work at all was impressive.

Standing in the bathroom, chomping purloined crackers, Topher started to get nervous. If he spent too long in there, Nurse Smith and Tre had a habit of showing up unannounced, so he reached up and put the vent back in place, got down and flushed the toilet, took a deep breath, and opened the door.

Nurse Smith and Tre were standing next to his bed, staring at him.

Nurse Smith said, "You spend a lot of time in the bathroom."

"Yes." Topher forced a chuckle. "You feed us so well."

He patted his belly, which had actually shrunk since his arrival, no matter how much they made him eat. He tried to justify the weight loss. He was still recovering from a terrible trauma. His body was adjusting to the new routine. But the fact of the matter was that something was off, and it wasn't because of his shoulder. He felt like he was wasting away, like there was already less of him, and not just in body but in mind.

It had started slowly. He struggled for words, forgot dates and times. Sometimes he would think of something, then head off to do it, only to forget where he was going and what he was trying to achieve. Again, that didn't bother him. Middle-aged men often complained about these kinds of things. He didn't really start to worry until one morning he found himself standing in a room with no recollection of how he got there.

"Yes, we do," Nurse Smith said. "We do everything for you here."

"You've been more than kind."

Nurse Smith gave him a thin smile.

"Not that you people appreciate it a bit. Without us you'd still be out there, scrounging for food, fighting off rapists."

"I'm grateful. Such wonderful food. Steak and chicken. Crackers."

She gave him a queer look.

"We don't give you crackers."

"Oh! I meant biscuits. Where I come from we call them crackers. Heh."

She stared at him for a solid beat, his eyes, his chin, his shoulders, his stomach.

"Come here," she said.

"I'm fine where I am."

"I want you to come over to me. Now."

Topher swallowed his anger. He crossed the room to stand in front of her. She reached for his face, stopping when he flinched.

"Why," she said. "Are you afraid of little old me?"

He shook his head, a mere twitch. She reached out and caressed his cheek and he closed his eyes. Such revulsion. He wanted to vomit. She turned his chin left and right.

"Your beard is so thick," she said.

When it was clear he could endure no more, she let her hand fall to his shoulder and swept something unseen from his robe.

"Tre," she said. "The vitamins."

Topher took the paper cup and toasted them with it.

"Heh-heh. Must get stronger!"

They left the room before he even swallowed.

A wild idea struck him. He waited a full five minutes before he dared to move again, then strode directly to the bathroom and spit the pills into the toilet. He was still awake an hour later. The bed, he realized, was fully adjustable. Why hadn't he noticed it before? He played with the remote. First his knees went up, then his back, and then he was a Topher sandwich. He flattened it out again. Time to pretend like the pills were working, or Nurse Smith and Tre might come back in and give him more. Worse still, they might search the bathroom and find his stash. He rolled onto his side and looked out his window. He saw what he always saw: the roof of another part of the hospital. He wondered if he was even in Philadelphia anymore.

His digital clock read eight oh seven. Every night he was dead asleep before eight, like a toddler. Every morning he was up at five. But now, without the aid of the drugs they'd been giving him, he couldn't sleep at all. He almost got up to retrieve them out of the bowl, but he couldn't do that, no. He had to stay awake. Perhaps an idea would come to him. Perhaps something would happen that would further his knowledge of his surroundings. Or perhaps he would just stare at the ceiling and worry and fret and let his mind spin around the hundreds of millions of things that had happened to him in his life, from the terror of his cold-war adolescence to the terror of his supernatural young adulthood to the terror of his post-apocalyptic later years.

He worried about the food. He worried about Zorn. He worried about Gertrude. He worried about Isa. He worried about his people. He worried about his arm. Was it really healed? He wiggled his shoulder, pressed it and flexed it against the bed. It was stiff, yes, a little sore, but they'd done a remarkable job. He could, when he stood, nearly demand a full range of motion. The swelling had long dissipated, and the bruising faded until there was nothing left but a shiny slug of a scar.

He looked at his clock. It was cheap. It was the cheapest clock he'd ever seen in his life. At least twenty years old. The numbers flickered. The cord was crimped and dusty. It didn't even have a radio on it, but it did tell the time. Eight eleven. Eight twelve. Eight thirteen

Good God. There was no way he could keep this up. He'd fling himself out his window.

He tried to mentally reconstruct what he knew of the hospital's layout. It seemed to him that most of what he was allowed to see remained in close proximity to his room. The Athenaeum was only three halls away to the right, and the cafeteria two halls to the left. Zorn's room was around the corner to the right, and he'd seen the Mustache in a room around the corner to the left. He didn't know where the others were. If he were to somehow escape at all, first he'd have to get past his locked door. He supposed he'd hit Zorn's room first, and they'd need to have already figured out where Gertrude's room was, of course, and get him next. Fatty, the Lips, and the Mustache were dead weight, but Shawn might prove handy with his teeth. He might know some things that could help them get away . . .

He startled awake. The room was pitch black. He checked the clock to see what time it was, but the clock was dead. Then he heard it. A sound that unnerved him, formed a ball of anxiety in his chest.

Nothing.

He heard nothing.

Even in the stillest moments, something could be heard around here. The buzz of the overhead lights. The distant chug of the generators. The white noise of the empty hospital. But now it was gone, and it felt like something terrible was about to happen.

And then it began.

A noise from somewhere deep in the hospital. A thunk echoing in the hallways. It rattled around the corner, louder and louder, heading right for him. Topher rolled off his bed and covered his head. Three doors down, two, then it hit his and continued on.

More silence.

He dared to uncover his head. The door creaked open and a crack of light fell upon his face.

Realization spread across his face. The drugs. The silence. The dead clock. The door. He smiled. Suddenly, he knew how to get out.

~

Saanvi started to worry after a couple of days. Not that this was unusual. She worried about a lot of things, a constant ball of anxiety that spun in her chest, but she never really worried about people. Routines, yes. Order, yes. People? But Isa, Isa got to her. Saanvi was well aware of her inability to connect to people emotionally, especially women, so for someone, especially a woman, to be able to affect her in such a way was more significant than she let on. She found herself thinking of Isa's hair and eyes, her voice, the way her fingertips brushed her skin, which made everything worse when two days turned to three, four, five, and then it was over a week and they still hadn't returned. She distracted herself with her duties, did her best to hold the caravan together, put off questions about what they were doing and when they would leave. It worked for a few days, but soon she heard them grumbling, saw the veiled glances, felt the whispering when she passed.

The rebellion started with little things. Insects were always a problem, specifically ticks and mosquitos, but deer and other wildlife had begun to thrive again, and nobody was used to it. Saanvi told everybody to clean up their sites to keep the pests away, but some refused. Some wouldn't bury their waste or made water too close to camp. Others wandered off during the day, scavenging on their own. Sometimes they returned; sometimes they spent a night or two away before eventually straggling back. When she called a meeting to discuss the problems, only a handful of people showed up. Most crossed their arms and glared at her while she spoke. The days dragged.

One day, a small band of men, starving and violent, attacked the camp. It was the only time the caravan banded together, and for a moment, as they fought off the intruders, Saanvi saw a spark of the former unity and brotherhood Topher seemed to so effortlessly inspire. But it was short-lived, and after the fight, they returned to their families and their cliques to nurse their wounds and curse their condition.

A few days later, one of the hunters tracked and killed a deer, but he was combative when he returned and didn't want to give any away.

"It's my meat," he said. "*I* tracked it, *I* killed it, *I'll* eat it."

Saanvi tried to reason with him. This is a collective. You didn't find that can of beans you ate last night. Someone else did. You didn't make the bullets you used to hunt the deer. Someone else did. This only made the hunter angry.

"I did this, I did this," he snarled.

She didn't understand. Her logic was sound; she used clear examples and proper diction, but the more she spoke, the more hysterical he became.

Fortunately, the rest of the caravan sided with her, and it was only after he saw that he was outnumbered that he agreed to share. He was raw about it, though, and took to sleeping on the edge of the camp. She was sure he hunted more after that. He must have been keeping the meat somewhere else.

Saanvi cursed herself. Topher would have been able to both congratulate the man on his skills and distribute the booty while making everybody feel good about the situation. He would have had a feast in celebration of the victory. Everybody would have loved him, felt needed. He was just one of those people. She wasn't. All she could do was sow discord.

One day, two weeks after they left, she was patrolling the camp when she passed the hunter and his friends. He muttered something under his breath as she walked by and she stopped, incredulous.

"What did you call me?" she asked.

The other men wouldn't look her in the eye, but the one who called her a name did.

"I didn't say anything," he said, smiling.

"Yes, you did. You said, 'Here comes the bitch'."

His friends laughed out loud, and he joined them, basking in their attention.

"No, no, sweetheart. I didn't say 'Here comes *the* bitch.' I said, 'Here comes *his* bitch'."

Saanvi was speechless. Her face flushed, which only spurred them on.

"I remember your name," she said.

"Oooohhh! I'm so scared."

"You're Brody. You came here with your daughter."

Then she turned and walked stiffly away.

"How long he tell his bitch to wait for him, huh?" Brody called after her. "How long we gotta wait around here?"

She found refuge in the food truck. There were still enough cans that she could count and count and regain her breath, and so that's what she did, even counting the empty shells sitting in a box on the bullet press, and when she felt better, she left and sat down on the rear bumper. Another group, both men and women, had gathered in the parking lot. They talked quietly amongst themselves, occasionally glancing in her direction. Apparently, a decision was reached because one of the men detached from them and started walking toward her.

Great.

She stood up, her hand trailing for the gun on her hip. She didn't have too much ammo left, and she didn't want to use it on her own people, but she would if she had to. Things were getting out of control. Somebody had to put a stop to it, or there would be no more caravan left. The man glanced at her hip as he approached, and he put up his hands and stopped.

"I only want to talk," he said.

"Okay."

"My name's Jamal."

"Talk, Jamal."

"Look, I know it's been tough these last couple of weeks. I know he left you in a tight spot."

"I'm doing fine."

"I saw that. What happened with Brody. I just want you to know that not all of us are like him."

Saanvi weighed this.

"Okay," she said.

Jamal took a deep breath.

"We all know what your man did for you, for us, and we're on your side. But something's gotta change. We're low on food. We're camped out here in the open. The kids, they're . . . something's gotta change."

"I know."

"We just want some information. We need to know what's going on."

"What do you want to know?"

The man looked at her gun.

"If I put my hands down, will you take yours off that?"

Saanvi thought for a second.

"Okay."

He did and she did.

"How long he tell you to wait on him?" Jamal asked.

"Three weeks."

"Three weeks? He told you to wait three weeks?"

Saanvi nodded slowly, knowing it sounded like the lie it was.

Jamal thought for a moment, then he said, "Okay. Three weeks. Well, it's already been two weeks yesterday. You got a plan for when it gets to three?"

"Yes," she said, lying again.

"That's it? You got a plan, but you're not going to tell us about it?"

Now that she started lying, she found that the next one came easier.

"I'll wait until it gets to three weeks. It's what he told me to do."

"Alright. Well, look. You gotta know that Brody's fixing to take over. He's got a good-sized group with him. But there's just as many of us who're willing to back you up. Maybe more."

"Why?"

Jamal seemed confused.

"Why what?"

"Why do you want to back me up?"

"Well, you were his right-hand man, sorry, woman. I trusted him, so I trust you. Long as you got a plan."

"I do."

He measured her face, but Saanvi had always been able to keep her features plain and controlled, even in the darkest twists of her compulsions. Finally, he nodded, satisfied.

"Well okay, then."

Two nights later, she found one of Brody's men stealing cans from the truck.

"What are you doing?" she said.

He smirked at her.

"What does it look like?"

"You can't do that. We set up a schedule. You have to stop."

"Or what?"

Then he walked away, laughing.

She set up guards, Jamal and some others. She tried not to think of them as "loyalists" (the idea was laughable), but there it was. The next day, two and a half weeks since she was left in charge, she was mending one of the trace lines again when a teenage girl came running up to her and said, "They're killing him."

Saanvi ran with her to the food truck, where a group of shouting men had gathered in a circle. She pushed her way through to the middle where she saw Brody straddling Jamal, pummeling him in the face. She didn't know what else to do, so she pulled out her gun and put it up against Brody's temple. He stopped immediately and put his hands up. More guns were drawn: Brody's men, Jamal's friends, anybody who was armed. Brody risked a smile.

"Looks like we have us a bit of a standoff," he said.

Saanvi said, "Get off him."

"You gonna take that off my head."

"No."

He stood carefully, the barrel still pressing into his temple. Saanvi waited until he was standing to back off, keeping the gun trained on his head.

"Turn around."

He did.

"You're not the only one with a gun," Brody said.

"No. But you don't have one."

"I can change that."

Saanvi stepped forward and pressed the barrel against his forehead.

"Okay, okay," he said, raising his hands higher. "Come on now. We were just having a little spat, that's all."

"You were stealing food."

"Well, you may look at it that way. Or you can say that I was taking what's rightfully mine."

"The food belongs to everyone, Brody. That's the rule. We all agreed."

"We did. You're right. But that was before your man disappeared. It's pretty clear he ain't coming back. Now, I hate to break this to you, sweetie, but this whole thing we got going here? It's falling apart. I'm just trying to make sure I get what I need before it does."

"It's not falling apart."

Brody laughed.

"Oh, it's not, is it?" He gestured around him. "What do you call all this then? Family dinner?"

"Keep still."

He waved his arms up and down.

"What, you don't like that?"

"Stop it."

He spun around.

"Whoopee!"

"Brody!"

He spun again, and right when he made the full turn, he reached out and grabbed Saanvi's wrist. Her finger squeezed the trigger, and one of Brody's men went down screaming. After that, it wasn't hard for him to wrench the gun out of her hand. Now it was his turn to press the gun up against her forehead.

"How's that?" he asked. "Don't feel too good, do it?"

Jamal was up now. He spat a mouthful of blood into the dirt.

"Brody, don't take it out on her," he said. He could barely speak through his split lip. "Whatever problem you got is with me."

"Oh, you're going to get yours, too, boy. Don't you worry."

"Let her go, then. Give it to me now."

"Oh no, goddammit. First I'm going to give it to this bitch."

"No, you're not."

"I'm not, huh? You gonna stop me?"

Saanvi found her voice.

"Brody, if you put down the gun, I promise I won't tell him anything when he gets back."

Brody burst out laughing.

"Tell him anything? Who? 'The Mayor'? Ain't you heard a thing I said? He's dead. Or gone. Whatever."

"I remember the first day I saw you," Saanvi said. "Do you?"

"Yeah, you remember me."

"I do. I remember how scared you were. How you begged to be let in."

Brody's cocky facade crumbled at that, and he hauled off and slapped her with his other hand.

"Shut up."

Saanvi continued.

"You were both naked, you and your daughter. Just came up to the gate one day, hysterical, screaming about how somebody had—"

"I said shut up!"

"He gave you clothes, fed you, put you to work. No questions asked."

Brody pressed the barrel of the gun harder into her forehead, and she closed her eyes. The end would be quick. Maybe there'd be a moment's pain, but that would be it. For that she was grateful.

Murmurs came from the edge of the circle, then gasps, then people started saying, "She's here," and "It's her."

Brody yelled over his shoulder, "What's going on?" Nobody responded, and he said, "Who is it?"

Somebody said, "Put the gun down."

Saanvi's eyes flew open. It was Isa. Standing right there in the middle of the circle. Everybody had lowered their weapons, Brody included. Saanvi snatched it away and ran to her, stopping a few feet away. Isa's clothes hung off her in strips, her arms and face cross-stitched with scratches and deep cuts, her skin coated with black ash. She held one arm against her ribs. In the other, she gripped her gun.

But even though she was clearly in pain, she still stood up straight and proud.

"What happened?" Saanvi asked.

Isa looked at her like she'd never seen her before, and Saanvi saw the change that was wrought by whatever horror she encountered. She'd hardened.

"What's happening here?"

"It's nothing," Saanvi said. "I'm handling it."

Isa didn't seem to believe this. Her eyes searched Saanvi's face, looking for cracks. They flicked over to Jamal, and she went to him. Jamal squirmed in the glow of her attention. He shuffled his feet, put his hand over his lip. She gently pulled it away, tracing the bruise forming around his mouth.

"Did he do this to you?"

"No, I—"

She turned away again, impatient, and strode up to Brody.

"Jesus, lady," he said. "You look a mess."

"Let me see your hands."

He put them behind his back.

"Ain't nothing of mine you need to see."

She let it go and turned around. Saanvi wondered at her ability to command a crowd just by showing up.

"We went into the city," she said. "We were attacked."

Someone from the crowd said, "Was it Rasheed's men? Are they still out there?"

"No," Isa said. "It was something worse."

"What?"

She thought before responding, considering how much information to reveal. She looked down at the scratches and bites on her body. Brody saw her do it and said, "Holy fuck, lady. You been bit."

The crowd gasped, took a collective step back. A few of the men, both Brody's and Jamal's, partially raised their weapons.

Isa shook her head ruefully.

"It wasn't that," she said. Nobody budged. "If it were, do you think I'd still be here now? I've been gone for two weeks."

This seemed to mollify a few.

"Then what did it?" Saanvi asked.

"I don't know what they are. Not people. Something else. Something none you have seen before."

She told them about the attack, how the stranger saved them.

"There were too many," she said. "One attacked me. That's how I got these. Then the doors broke and I had to run."

The crowd fell silent. Saanvi looked around. Some nodded or bashfully toed the ground. Others crossed their arms and frowned.

"Is he dead?" she asked.

"No. The last I saw, he and Zorn were running away."

"Running away where?"

Isa paused. Then she said, "I thought it was a library at first, but . . . but I don't think so anymore."

Brody couldn't take it anymore.

"Oh, this is so much bullshit!" He looked around him in disbelief, finally settling on Saanvi. "Are you really going to listen to this? Look, your man got himself killed. More'n likely, she's the reason for it."

Saanvi said, "You don't know that."

"C'mon, sweetheart. Your girlfriend set them up."

Saanvi blushed.

"She's not my girlfriend."

"Maybe she don't know that, but I seen the way you look at her."

"Shut up," Saanvi said.

"She set them up and you know it."

"Shut up!"

"Led your man right into that city and took him out herself."

"That's crazy."

"No crazier than the bullshit she's trying to sell you."

Without pause, Isa took two steps forward and put her gun up to his face. He gasped. She pulled the trigger. It clicked.

Brody let out a combination sigh and moan, and Isa turned her back on him.

"Topher's a good man. He saved my life. He saved your lives. He protected you. Gave you hope. And now he's in trouble. I'm going to find him. I know how to save him. If you don't want to help, you're welcome to leave." She turned around to look at Brody, who was bent over with his hands on his knees, pale. "But if you leave, if you leave this group, you're no longer one of us. And if I ever catch you out there on your own, I'll make sure my gun is loaded."

~

One morning, Nurse Smith strolled by during breakfast and informed everybody that she would be running group therapy from now on and that they were all to finish their food and proceed immediately to the Athenaeum.

When they got there they found her sitting prim and erect in her chair, a clipboard on her lap, her uniform crisp and pressed, not a spot on it, not a wrinkle un-ironed, not a button undone. If she were any more rigid she would have turned to stone. They all took their familiar seats and she crossed her legs and said, "Shall we begin?"

Shawn was still wearing his muzzle. He told them all that they let him take it off when he slept, but as long as he was around other people he was going to have to keep it on.

"Where's Dr. Smythe?" he asked.

"*Mr.* Smythe is no longer with us."

"Is it because I chewed off his eyeball?" Nurse Smith didn't answer. He tried a different approach. "How are you going to run group? Aren't you just a nurse?"

"I, Mr. King, am a registered nurse, yes." He snorted. Fatty started to giggle. She turned her daggers upon him. "Is there something funny, fat man?"

This made him giggle even more.

"I loved me some nurses when I fought in the war," Shawn said.

"You're talking about the Gulf War."

"Oh yeah. Nurses in the Gulf War. Nurses in the Gulf War. And when I got hit and sent back home, the candy stripers. Mmm. You know what we used to do with the candy stripers?"

Nurse Smith grew a little flustered.

"Don't be disgusting."

"Most of them were fine with it. They wanted to help us. Did whatever we asked. But sometimes we got one that didn't want to. Those were the best."

Fatty whinnied.

"Are you saying you raped these girls, Mr. King?" Nurse Smith asked.

"Oh no. They loved it. It's not rape if they cum."

Topher said, "Jesus, man."

Nurse Smith shot him a look.

"Do you disapprove?"

Topher squirmed.

"Yes. No. Whatever."

She returned her attention to Shawn.

"Mr. King likes rape, it seems."

"Love it. Love it."

"You're fifty-three years old, are you not, Mr. King?"

"I'm always twenty-one, baby!"

"Twenty-one. Of course. Mr. King, did you ever have yourself checked for prostate cancer."

The room grew cold and silent. Fatty's laughter died on his lips.

When Shawn spoke again, his voice was ashes.

"What?"

"I didn't think so. I'll have you scheduled for an exam immediately. Never can be too careful in this environment. All of those bombs, the ozone layer."

"You can't do that."

"Mr. King, dying of prostate cancer is a very unpleasant experience, as I'm sure you realize. And since you seem to like rape so much, I didn't think you'd have any problem with it. In fact, while I don't think Tre here has any medical training, I'm sure he'd be happy to do it for you."

Tre, standing in the shadows, cracked his knuckles. Shawn went silent and still.

"I'd like to remind you, Mr. King, of who is charge here," Nurse Smith said. She let an uncomfortable minute pass. "Do you still want to talk about rape, Mr. King?"

"No," he whispered.

"That's what I thought." She let out a sigh. "Well. Let's try to start this on a fresh note. Since you doubt my abilities, Mr. King, I would like to offer an olive branch. Would you like your muzzle removed? I could do that, you know."

Shawn muttered something.

"I'm sorry, Mr. King. I can't hear you."

"I said, 'No way in hell'."

"I see," she said, leaning back in her chair. She shuffled through her papers and said, "It appears as though Mr. Smythe was more ineffective than I originally thought."

"He was an idiot."

"For once we agree, Mr. King. I mean, look at you people. I've never seen such a gathering of such layabouts and slugabeds. Today we will move forward in Group for once."

Shawn stirred uncomfortably.

"What . . . what would you like to talk about?"

"Ah, Mr. King! A proactive gesture. How kind. Well, since you asked, I want us all to talk about something we all have in common. I want us to talk about the past."

"The past?"

"Yes, Mr. King. The past. I want to know about your lives. Your lives before. Who were you? What did you do? Were you rich and powerful? Were you poor and powerless?" She looked at Topher. "Were you lost and alone?" She looked at Zorn. "Did you have a family?"

A hush fell over the group.

"Oh," Shawn said.

Nurse Smith smiled, and for once Topher didn't feel like she was going to eat him.

"Very good. So, shall we start with you, Mr. King?"

Shawn wagged his head back and forth.

"No, not me. Please."

"But you've done such a good job today."

Shawn continued to wag his head, harder and harder.

"Please, no. It's too painful. Dr. Smythe said."

"Smythe was an idiot. You said it yourself. Look at what he's done to you. I can help you get better. Don't you want to get better, Mr. King? Don't you want the pain to end?"

"Yes."

"Then why don't you tell us about it?"

"I can't."

He was rocking back and forth now, tears wetting the muzzle.

"Why not, Mr. King?" A stray lock of hair fell from beneath her cap, and she tucked it back up, neat and efficient. "Did you have children?"

The very idea seemed to calm him down. He stopped shaking his head, took deep breaths.

"Children," he said. "Yes, I had children."

"You did? Mr. King, how wonderful! Isn't that wonderful everybody?" Fatty laughed, uncertain. Even the Mustache's mustache seemed to move. "And how many children did you have?"

Shawn was now entirely still, staring at he feet.

"Mr. King? How many children did you have?"

Shawn whispered something.

"I'm sorry, I can't hear you."

"Twenty-seven!"

For the first time, Nurse Smith seemed taken aback. She began to flip through the notes on her clipboard.

"Mr. King, I think you're mistaken."

"I was a teacher, you stupid bink. Elementary school. Third grade. They were my students, my children. I was responsible for them."

Nurse Smith straightened up. Topher could see that she was upset, though he couldn't understand why. She acted as though her ignorance were an affront, like it took something away from her, and of course it did. It rebuked her authority and sapped her power. Authority and power. A powerful person never admits what she doesn't know something, never admits her guilt, never takes the blame.

Shawn leaned over, sobbing.

"Please, Mr. King. You've made so much progress here today. You can't stop now."

"No, no, no."

Fatty uttered half a word, a short "buh." The look of pity and terror on his face was heartbreaking. Then a different voice entered the conversation, a voice nobody had heard until now.

"Tell us."

It was no more than a whisper, but everybody heard it. Topher was amazed. It was Gertrude. His mouth, which he usually kept wide open, was now only slightly parted. Fatty placed a hand on the Shawn's back and patted it gently, patted it until the sobs slowed and dwindled. Shawn took a deep breath and sat up.

"Okay," he said. "Okay, I'll tell it."

"Very good, Mr. King."

"But only if you take this thing off my face."

Nurse Smith paused.

"Mr. King I don't think that's a good idea. Not until you give me something. Think of it as a deposit."

The rage burst out of Shawn so hard and so fierce that his whole body shook.

"I won't say a fucking thing unless you take the fucking thing off my fucking face! I won't say a fucking thing! I won't say a fucking thing!"

"Mr. King." A warning.

"Take it off my face! Take it off my face!"

"Mr. King!"

She looked horrified, as if she'd never experienced such behavior. Everything hung in the air, like falling leaves. There was a moment when Topher was sure her jaw would unhinge and she'd leap upon the poor man and swallow him whole. Then something seemed to thaw, as if the rod anchored in her soul melted just a bit. Her eyes snapped over to Tre and she gave him a curt nod. He hesitated a moment, but stepped forward and unbuckled the straps and took off the muzzle.

Shawn gasped with relief. He rubbed the red circle around his mouth. Then he yawned and stretched his jaws. Finally he looked at Nurse Smith and said, "Okay. I'll tell it, but not for you. Not for you, not for him, or him or him, or any of the other lunatics here. Got that?"

"I'm not sure I like your tone, Mr. King."

"I don't care."

"Would you like Tre to put the muzzle back on?"

"No."

"Do you want to get better?"

"Yes."

"Okay, then. Prove it."

He took a ragged breath and let it out with a frenzied sigh.

"It happened late in the morning, remember? We ate lunch at ten thirty. I remember what I ate that day. A turkey sandwich, light mayo. An apple. Bottled water. We'd just sat down to learn about state history, the state bird, the state flag, all of that garbage, when the first one hit. There was this tremendous pressure. Some of the children began to cry. I had no time to think, to figure out what to do next. The windows just exploded. Glass flying everywhere. John Bradley was in the first row and his face . . . . I stood up as fast as I could, and the whole wall was just gone, torn to ribbons. A huge wind was blowing through the classroom. Kids were screaming, running everywhere. Off in the distance, I could see it, this . . . well, you know what I saw."

He fell silent, and Topher couldn't tell if it was because he was overcome with emotion or because the implications were obvious. Nurse Smith, though, was smiling.

"And what happened next, Mr. King?"

"What do you think happened? They died. We tried the best we could, but they died."

"Everyone? But you're here. If everyone died, how did you survive?"

Shawn glared.

"We managed to get a lot of them in the basement. Then the lights went out and the children screamed, dozens of them, all at once.

"We stayed down there for a whole day. Twenty-four hours. It began to stink. Mr. Shelby, the gym teacher, went up to investigate.

That's how he put it, 'I'm going up to investigate. I'll be right back.' He never came back. After a week it became clear to the rest of us that we to do something. Look for food, look for help, something. We voted, the rest of the teachers, and decided that two of us would go the top of the stairs, one to actually leave and see what was going on, and one to stay behind and report back if the first didn't make it.

"I drew the short straw, along with Mrs. Plainview. I'd go out, she'd follow behind. Most of the hall up to the stairs were lined with children. Some were asleep, some weren't. They watched us pass but didn't say anything. It was the longest walk I'd ever taken in my life. I felt the metal door before we opened it and it was warm. I undid the latch, told Mrs. Plainview to step back a few feet, took a deep breath, and pushed it open with my shoulder. And then we saw it. What happened to the world."

He was done. He leaned back in his chair and sighed.

Nurse Smith watched him impassively.

"And the children? What happened to them?"

"I told you what happened to them."

"You know what I mean."

"No, I don't."

"Are they here with you now, Mr. King? Are the children with you now?"

He clamped his mouth shut and tightened his jaw.

"Would you like the muzzle back on, Mr. King?"

"No."

"Then tell me what happened to the children, Mr. Smith. I want details."

"Details?."

"Yes, Mr. King. About your students."

"I told you. They're gone."

"Where did they go?"

"We were there for weeks. We had no food. We had no medicine. Some of the kids were drinking from these pools, these nasty pools. We tried to keep them corralled, but they kept wandering off. Some just disappeared. Some just dwindled away. One little girl had asthma. It was horrible."

Nurse Smith glanced down at her notes.

"And then?"

Shawn glared at her for a long time. Finally, he chuckled, nasty, rueful, bitter. His face screwed up into a sneer and he said, "The rest were taken."

Zorn's mouth fell open.

"Dear Lord," he whispered.

Nurse Smith seemed pleased.

"Taken? By whom?"

Shawn shook his head. He leaned back in his chair.

"Men," he said. "I don't know who they were. They were armed. They came in one day and took them. Not all of them. The older ones. The healthy girls. The healthy boys."

Nurse Smith smiled.

"Don't stop now. It's just getting good."

Shawn began to cry again, but Nurse Smith was unfazed. She leaned forward, put her elbows on her knees.

"Weren't other teachers there? Didn't you try to fight back?"

"Some of us did, but we had nothing."

"What happened to them, Mr. King? The ones who resisted."

"They were killed."

"All of them?"

"No, not all of them."

"Which ones were spared, Mr. King?"

"I didn't see."

"Which ones, Mr. King? Which ones were spared?"

"The women."

"What happened to them?"

"You know what happened."

Nurse Smith nodded, satisfied. She allowed his story to sink in a bit. He cried until he couldn't anymore, then he sat there and stared at his hands. Fatty and the Mustache watched him, jaws hanging open. Topher and Zorn exchanged glances.

"One last thing, Mr. King," Nurse Smith said.

"I've got nothing left."

"I just have one last question."

"Jesus."

"Because you see, there's one thing I'm confused about in your story. One little detail that doesn't make any sense."

"Fine."

"So you say all of the male teachers were killed, right?"

He nodded miserably.

"Well, then. If all of them were killed, what are you doing here?"

He took a deep breath and stared at the floor.

"I escaped."

"Escaped? Is that really the word you want to use?"

"Yes."

"I don't think it is. Tre, get the muzzle."

"No! Don't! I ran! Okay? When the men came, I ran. I ran and hid. But I couldn't get far enough. The things I saw. The things I heard."

Nurse Smith was finally completely satisfied.

"Thank you, Mr. King, for such a wonderful tale." She paused to look at all of them again, slowly, staring at each man until he could no longer return the gaze. "Here, then, is your tough rebel. Your impudent, disrespectful, foul-mouthed leader, exposed for what he truly is. A coward. He left his friends and those children to suffer at the hands of murderers and rapists and now he's here, like the rest of you."

Shawn let out a pitiful sob.

"Let that be a lesson to you all," she continued. "Heroes don't exist. No one's coming to save you. None of you ever will escape this place. None of you will ever be free. You are weak. You are ours."

And with that, she stood up and walked away through the circle, past the broken furniture and other junk, straight from her seat to the door, which she opened with a whine, heels clacking on the tile all the way.

That was how life proceeded for the next three weeks. Every morning he left his room for breakfast, then they visited the Athenaeum for Group, Nurse Smith picked away at Shawn until he was no longer able to speak, then they broke for lunch. After that, they were confined to their rooms until dinner. Topher began to adjust to his captivity, which frightened him. The calluses of life on the road wore off. The routine of the hospital smoothed and softened him; should he ever escape (when he escaped, when he escaped), he might not actually be able to survive as well as he did before, or at all. He did at least start to get a feel for the layout of the one wing to which they were confined. There were no other patients, at least none that he could see. All of the other doors remained closed and locked, but he noticed one that doctors were continually exiting, dressed in scrubs, covered in blood. The plate next to the door read Suite 101-113.

He took to staying up past midnight, training himself, finding his center, his energy. After the power went out he sometimes heard grunts and shrieks from the floors above and below him. Every now and then they came from outside. One time he heard an engine growl to life, a bus or a tractor-trailer. He stood on tiptoes at the window as it roared away from the hospital, but he couldn't see it, and it never returned.

A few weeks into his captivity, the Mustache superseded Gertrude as the resident catatonic. Nurse Smith tried several times to snap him out of it by actually snapping her fingers in front of his eyes.

"Dear Lord," Topher said. "Is that the extent of your healthcare training?"

She ignored him, took the Mustache's blood pressure, felt his pulse. After making a few notes in his file, she gave Tre a knowing look. On the way to lunch that day, Tre grabbed the Mustache by the upper arm and led him to suite 101-113 and knocked on the door. Topher watched until they turned the corner, but the door never opened and the two of them just stood there, waiting. He never saw the Mustache again. Gertrude, however, stayed just lively enough to avoid being taken. Some days he merely stuck out a leg. Other days he whispered something: a response to a rhetorical question posed by Nurse Smith, an admonition for her to leave Shawn alone. Nurse Smith would always make a note in his file and continue with the day's harassment.

As for Group, Topher found that if he cooperated, if he gave Nurse Smith just enough information about his past or related some kind of painful detail, she left him alone. He discovered what she knew and didn't know by lying. When she asked for his parents' names, he gave her Zorn's parents' names, and when she said, "Really?" and called for Tre, he relented and told the truth. After that, Group became a breeze. Bit by bit, he realized that she had no information about his life after he was sent to Raleigh's Prep. Because of this, he came to understand (with great relief) that his escape from the school had gone unreported. But it was bittersweet and short-lived, tempered with consternation. All of those years of running from place to place, hiding, covering their tracks, worrying about being tracked down and sent to prison, were for nothing.

He took a similar approach to his food intake. All he had to do was look like he was eating, look like he was getting seconds or thirds, and she left him alone. And though he did eat, and though it was difficult to stop, he forced himself not to swallow it all, spitting the half-chewed steak or chicken or peas into his hand, or scraping the contents of his plate onto Fatty's. Fatty, who at this point had stopped laughing and who had lost so much weight that his excess skin drooped off his bones. Fatty, who didn't even notice the extra flank or leg or mound of potatoes. Fatty, who shoveled it in like a robot, his arm on greased ball bearings, his mouth on hinges. When he got back to his room, Topher flushed whatever glop he held onto down the toilet and retrieved a cracker from his stash in the ceiling. It didn't work.

He lost weight. His hair started to fall out.

Zorn fared worse. He lost every hair on his body. His face, his head, his arms, his legs. Skin hung off his triceps like melting wax. He hadn't seemed to lose any of his strength, though, which was odd.

One night, Topher lay in bed reading *Cat Fancy*, absently petting what was left of his own whiskers. He didn't really like cats and couldn't care less about their grooming habits, but there was nothing else to read and he was bored out of his mind. Still, the prose was drivel, and the letters the readers sent in so twee he nearly vomited whenever he read them. How many cute little anecdotes about cats could possibly exist? Kitty played with a rubber band. Kitty chased a laser pointer. Kitty decapitated a mouse. The poor storytelling appalled him, but not as much the syrupy tone. Better than nothing, he supposed, so he read and petted his beard.

At 11:15 he looked down at his hand and saw that it was full of hair. Then his stomach grumbled. He went to the bathroom to wash his face, and after toweling off saw that nearly all of his facial hair was gone. The remainder stuck out in odd tufts like weeds in a dirt field, so he scrubbed his cheeks and chin until the rest fell out and looked at himself in the mirror. The face staring back at him was a wraith. Dark pouches hung under his eyes, and his cheeks were sunken. Some men looked good bald. Their heads were round and perfectly symmetrical. But not his. Weird spots punctuated his skull (birthmarks, red spots, puckered skin), and while one ear was tucked back tightly against his head, the other popped out like a . . . like a . . . well, there was no proper simile for it. He just looked ridiculous.

He decided right then to explore the hospital. There had to be something out there he could eat other than Doris' crackers. Nurse Smith, Tre, the other staff, they weren't losing weight or going bald. He sat on his bed until midnight. The generators wound down, the locks on the hall thunked, and the doors whined open. Topher peaked out into the shadowed corridor, then slipped out and padded away.

The cafeteria was dark and spooky. The tables and chairs and all the clutter hulked in the shadows, seeming to breathe. Topher sped through the dining room and ducked behind the serving line, marveling at the smell of bleach, the cleanliness of the floors and equipment. He supposed there hadn't been a run on custodial supplies when the end of the world happened, but that didn't mean they were easy to find. He pushed through the swinging doors separating the dining hall from the kitchen, stepping into near darkness. Somewhere in the back, an emergency light glowed, right next to the EXIT sign. The electricity was on in here, of course. They had to keep the food cold. He felt it now, the subtle vibration of power, the low hum of the refrigerators, two of them on his left, industrial sized, stainless steel. Next to them was a walk-in freezer.

He took one step toward them and knocked over a whole tray of kitchen knives.

"No," he gasped, spreading his hands.

Butcher's knives, steak knives, butter knives, knives for shaving, knives for slicing, knives for hacking, knives for stabbing, all of them exploded in a pile on the tiled floor. Some bounced, some scattered, creating a musical, metal cacophony. The tray, however, was the loudest. It ricocheted up against the stainless steel legs of one of the tables, then rolled in a wide circle around and around, clipping one of the fridge doors right in front of him, finally winding down like a pot in a vaudeville skit.

Topher dropped to his knees and pushed down on it, trying to silence the final circle, but it was wet and his hand slipped off and into the pile of knives, slicing open his index finger. He popped it into his mouth and waited for someone to come and get him, for someone to haul him away. Would Nurse Smith kill him for this? Maybe. If so, it wouldn't be direct. No hanging from the hospital walls or staking his head on a stick as a warning, no public beheading or crucifixion. Most likely she'd devise some kind of psychological torture, something that would end in suicide.

But what would it matter if there weren't many of them left? The Mustache was gone. The Lips disappeared a few days before, and just that morning he saw Tre standing with Fatty outside Suite 101-113. Now it was just him, Zorn, Gertrude, and Shawn. There was no point in trying to humiliate him in front of the first two. They knew more embarrassing things about him than he could remember. Shawn barely spoke anymore.

Topher counted to sixty, and when nobody came, he took his finger out of his mouth to inspect the wound. It was long but not deep at all. In fact, it had already stopped bleeding. He picked up a butcher's knife and a thickly serrated cleaver, thought briefly about taking them back to his room, then thought better. At one point in his life, somewhere between escaping Raleigh's and becoming a Transcendental Tracker, he worked in a kitchen as a line cook. Every "chef" he worked with, no matter how incompetent or asinine, owned a set of perfectly maintained knives that looked exactly like the ones he'd knocked over. These people were highly particular about their tools. Nobody was allowed to touch them. Nobody was allowed to even look at them. Some used knife sharpening services, but more often than not they did it themselves. Every day at the end of the shift, the lead chef would clean his set, dry them, and lovingly wrap each one in soft, chamois cloth before zipping them up in a leather case. One even confessed to sleeping next to his kit. If Topher stole one from the hospital kitchen, somebody would most certainly notice, and that somebody would tell Nurse Smith, and Nurse Smith would employ Tre, and Tre would find his stash, and then it would all be over.

So he picked the tray up and placed it back on the table, put the cleaver and butcher's knife back on it, then carefully rearranged the rest. He polished a few with a rag he found drying on the lip of the sink, flicked a few specks of dirt off the silver surfaces. Then, sucking on his cut one last time, he turned his attention back to the refrigerators.

It couldn't have been easier.

On one someone had scrawled, in black magic marker, the words PREPARED FOOD. On the other, UNPREPARED FOOD. When he opened the first door, it, too, was divided into two different sections: PATIENTS and STAFF. The shelves were stuffed with tinfoil-covered pans. He lifted the foil from the closest one on the STAFF shelf. Lasagna. One of his favorites. He gorged. He shoved handfuls of it into his mouth, trying (unsuccessfully) to avoid dripping sauce onto his hospital robe. A glob of ricotta plopped on the tile. The next pan contained green beans, also one of his favorites. He ate them by the fistful. Then he found a container of potato salad (favorite), a dish of apple crisp (favorite), peaches and oranges (favorite, favorite), two tubes of salami, sliced carrots, sliced turkey, a jar of jam, a jar of pickles, a jar of blue cheese, and blocks of cheddar, pepper jack, muenster, and oh it was glorious, an orgy of tastes, textures, and smells, and he couldn't stop eating, he was so hungry he just kept shoving it in, shoving it in until finally he grabbed a jug of lemonade and chugged the whole thing and collapsed on the floor, spent, breathless, his face a rainbow of sauce and dairy and jam and meat and vegetables.

It felt like the nutrients and vitamins were coursing through his veins. His mind, which had been cloudy with fatigue and hunger, cleared. Even his vision felt stronger. He couldn't take any back with him, but there had to be dry goods somewhere that he could use. Nuts, almonds, sunflower seeds, maybe some chocolate bars or salad or something? He looked at the glob of cheese on the tile, the blob of sauce on his robe. He had to clean up the mess.

He found some bleach in a cabinet and had just finished when the cafeteria door banged open and he heard voices in the dining hall. He darted around the kitchen, seeking a hidey-hole or a nook or crevice into which he could squeeze, but there were no hide-y-holes, no nooks, no crevices. Even the shelves under the prep tables were too small. Then the door swung open and the lights flipped on and he hit the deck. He was exposed. All anyone had to do was look around the kitchen and he'd be caught.

"There, see? There's nobody here."

Nurse Smith.

She was standing with her hands on her hips in front of the refrigerator, right where he'd just gorged himself. Tre, arms folded, muscles bulging (as usual) stood right behind her. Both of them had their backs to him, and both were dressed for bed, she in a flowing white gown that reached to her feet, hair unfettered, streaming down her back in an icy white flow, he in athletic shorts and a sleeveless shirt that showed off his biceps. Topher wanted to feel dirty for seeing her in this state of undress, but he couldn't. Even barely clad, she was cold and imposing.

He had to take a chance. He scrabbled behind the nearest table and peeped over the top. Nurse Smith had turned to face Tre and was staring petulantly up into his frowning face. Maybe she was trying to be endearing or playful, but it only came off as terrifying. Tre ignored her, peered around the kitchen, his eyes gliding toward Topher's hiding place. He ducked.

"I know what I heard," Tre said.

"Ooh, I love it when you're assertive."

"Not now."

"Fine, Trevor. Have it your way. What did you hear?"

"I don't know. Something clattered."

He heard the sound of metal dragging on tile, and he knew Tre had picked up one of the knives he'd knocked over earlier, one that he missed. Oh, God.

"What's this?" Nurse Smith asked, more of herself than of Tre.

"A knife?"

"Not that. This. Over here by the refrigerator."

What else had he left out? Another knife? A pan of food? He couldn't resist looking. If they were by the refrigerator, they'd have their backs turned to him. He peeped over the top of the table again, and there they were, partially bent over, investigating something on the floor.

Nurse Smith said, "Ricotta cheese. On the floor. On the floor!"

"It's just a spill."

"Just a spill? Do you have any idea what this costs us? How much we have to trade to get this?"

"It's not that much."

"It's everything! And now he wants more."

"Well, at least you took control of King."

"You have got to be kidding."

"What?"

"King has been here longer than that drifter, and he's not responding at all! All he does is rile up the others."

Tre sighed. Nurse Smith went to a nearby sink and used a rag to scrub the ricotta off her hands.

"You'll have to flog the kitchen girl," she said, trying to regain control. "Every drop, *every drop* must be accounted for."

"Don't you think that's a little much?"

Nurse Smith slammed both palms down on the edge of the sink.

"Fifty!" She threw the rag into the dry sink. "That's how many he wants this time. We only have six. The fat one can barely keep down the formula, and the dosage is only making him more moronic. The only one of worth is the drifter, and he's resisting."

"Should we up his dosage? Put more in his food?"

"You know that kills them." She sighed. "Tre, I'm scared. If we don't give him what he wants, that's it. We're done."

Tre snorted.

"What's he going to do? We have the formula. If he kills us, he's done, too. He knows that."

"I know, I know."

"Plus, if he sets foot in the city, *they'll* get him first. He doesn't even know we have our own."

"But we still need to conserve. I don't want to . . . I don't want to live like this forever, Tre."

"Live like what?"

"Like this! With those horrible men. Just surviving. We have to get out. We have to move on."

"Why? We have everything we need here."

"Until he decides to take it from us. Think, Tre. How long do you think it will be? We're nothing but a drain on his food supply, a nuisance to be dealt with when he has enough power."

Tre took a step forward and put his hand on her shoulder, and she melted into his arms. Topher dry heaved.

"Shhh," Tre whispered. He kissed the top of her head.

She couldn't stop the tears, but she could hide them. He held her tighter and she burrowed into his chest. They remained that way, her back hitching, for quite some time. And then suddenly she cut it off, wiped her eyes on his shirt, and tried to pull away, but Tre held her and leaned down and kissed her. She resisted at first, but then she relaxed. Their mouths worked, their breathing grew heavier. They stopped, and Nurse Smith hugged him again.

"We'll find a way," Tre said, his cheek resting on the top of her head.

She took a brave breath, wiped away her tears, and looked at her wrist.

"Oh God. I've got to check on him."

She broke the embrace and walked toward the door.

"Right now?"

"It won't wait," Nurse Smith said over her shoulder. "At least this one's responding. Who would have thought it'd be him, with that dopey mustache. If we can send him over, say that he's the beginning of the next batch, it'll buy us some time."

"Okay."

She stopped and turned and held out her hand.

"Come. Walk with me over there. This place makes me nervous at night. Thank goodness they're drugged."

He followed her out. The lights switched off, and Topher was left alone in the dark. When he was sure they were far enough away, he stood up and snuck out of the kitchen, intent on seeing where they were going.

~

Dennis loved getting out of the hospital compound. As safe as he felt there, Nurse Smith freaked him the fuck out. She was one cold-ass bitch as far as he was concerned, and if she didn't have that black bastard for a bodyguard, he would have taken her out a long time ago. Dennis served his time in the ARMY. Went to Afghanistan. Knew how to use a gun. And he knew plenty of guys like that bodyguard. Big and ripped, wore their pants saggy. Probably sold crack and had about a dozen baby mamas. Not that he'd ever say it that way to Oliver, who was riding shotgun. He wouldn't appreciate the "baby mama" comment for starters. So instead he said, "I mean, seriously, that is some grade-A, fucked up shit they're pulling in there, you know?"

Oliver barely acknowledged him. He kept his eyes on the road, his hands firmly wrapped around the rifle on his lap. Dennis might have been offended if it was anybody else, but with Oliver, he didn't mind. Oliver was a badass. More of a badass than he'd ever been. Must have been a bounty hunter before. Or a SEAL. Something like that. Plus, from what Dennis understood, he'd gone through a shit-ton during the Catastrophes, a lot more than most. Had to be. People didn't act like Oliver for no reason. Probably lost a wife and kids. A son and two daughters. Yeah, twin daughters. Cute little tykes. Even if they were, you know, like Oliver. Probably they were burned up by the meteor or drowned in the tsunami. Or even worse, maybe they survived that and were eaten up after. Or even worse than that: vigilantes.

None of these things were true.

Oliver never had a family. He never tracked down any fugitives, and he never served in the military. In fact, before the Catastrophes, he wrote copy for an online marketing agency. It was the perfect job for him. Minimal meetings. Hours of time alone. He wasn't antisocial. If any of the people who really knew him heard someone describe him that way, they would have laughed out loud. Oliver? Antisocial? He was one of the funniest people they knew! Loved to hang out, have a few beers. He was pretty smart, but he never rubbed it anyone's face. He had a small, tight group of friends. He had a dog.

No, Oliver was not antisocial. He was not a misanthrope. He was not shy. The reason he was so quiet around Dennis all the time was because he fucking hated the guy. Dennis was loud and obnoxious, prone to endless, pointless talking. He laughed at his own jokes. Referred to himself in the third person. He was a moron. Being stuck in the cab of a tractor-trailer for the monthly drive into the mountains with an idiot like Dennis was like a four-hour prostate exam.

Oliver had a different partner once. Andre. Andre was the best person he ever had to work with, mainly because he was just as quiet as Oliver. And he was competent. But Andre took off one day. Found out what was going on in the main wing of the hospital and split. He'd even tried to get Oliver to come with him.

"Come on, man," he said. "That shit is fucked up and you know it. You have to come with me."

Oliver had honestly thought about it. He liked Andre. They made a great team. They just might be able to make it out on their own. But at the time, he just couldn't do it. The compound was too much of a sure thing, his place in the hierarchy a done deal. It would have been beyond stupid to ditch it.

Andre could tell that he was on the fence, so he said, "How long do you think it'll be before she comes for you, huh?"

"It won't come to that."

"It won't? You have psychic abilities I don't know about? You'll know when she drugs your food?"

"It's not going to happen."

"Oh, it's going to happen."

"Why? She needs us."

"To do what? Drive that rig? Anybody can do that, man. Jesus. If she thinks your ass is a candidate for a good fucking, your ass will be good and fucked."

It was a good point, but Oliver didn't go with him. Nurse Smith let him make the deliveries on his own for a while, and then three months later Dennis showed up and his life had been miserable ever since.

Which was why he decided to kill the asshole.

On this trip.

Had it all planned out. He was going to wait until they made it to Lake Ariel, where they usually stopped to eat and take a piss. Dennis liked to piss in the lake. Called it "my own gigantic toilet!" Oliver was going to follow Dennis out to the water. He was going to put his shotgun against the back of Dennis' head, and he was going to pull the trigger.

Unfortunately, he didn't think they were going to make it there in time. Once they unloaded the old man's cargo, Dennis asked him for a tour of the facilities, even though Oliver said "no."

"We've got to get back," he said. "I'm not driving on the side roads in the dark."

"Oh, come on, Ollie!" Dennis said. "It'll only be, what, twenty, thirty minutes?"

The old man delighted in Dennis' attention, laughed at his jokes, smiled and nodded at the nonstop monologue, interrupting every now and then to show him a field or a water tank. That was thing Oliver could never understand. People liked Dennis. Not everybody, but more than he expected. Reasonably intelligent people. The old man liked him so much that the tour took more than twenty minutes. More than thirty minutes. It took three hours. Now they were late and it was getting dark out. Too dark and too dangerous to stop anywhere. They'd have to blow right by the lake.

"I mean, I'm sorry we took so long," Dennis said. "But can you believe that place? All that water, and the fields, and way up there in that mountain? He even has a dairy! I mean, that guy's set. It's crazy that he's able to keep it up all by himself, but I guess he's got enough protection, right?"

Oliver stared out into the darkness. He scanned the road, the trees on either side. The interstate was impassable up to the lake (just one of the ways the old man secured his place), so they had to take the side roads, which were twisty and full of hills, and the woods were tight all around them. Driving a huge tractor-trailer laden with the spoils of their trade, vegetables, meat, bread, eggs, cheese, did not make for a relaxing ride. At least Dennis was a good driver. He took the turns slowly, didn't overdo it on the straightways, tried to conserve fuel.

"He's a crazy old coot," Dennis said. "Kept saying that they were 'almost ready'. I mean, I guess he was talking about the next harvest, you know. Gonna be a big one, it looks like. Not that we got fair exchange this time, right?" Oliver grunted. "Yessiree. Smith is not going to be happy with the haul. How many we give him this time? Thirty? Forty? We should have gotten more than what he gave us for that. But I guess we can't do anything about it. He's the boss!"

"Twenty-five."

"Huh?"

"We gave him twenty-five this time."

"You don't say! Twenty-five. Really?"

Oliver didn't respond. Dennis downshifted as they headed into an S-curve, and up ahead he saw an incline. A steep one.

"Well, I guess I'm not all that keen on details, you know," he said. "Never was one for that kind of things. Data. Numbers. I'm more of an intuition man. I like to feel things. People say I'm a pretty good synthesizer. I like to listen to other people, talk to them, get to know them. People say I like to listen."

"Empathizer," Oliver said.

"Yeah, I'm really good at synthesizing. My boss liked me. My old boss. He said, 'Dennis? You're a real good talker, you know that? You talk a good game.' And he was right. He was a great boss. We really understood each other. That's why I didn't take it too hard when he had to let me go. Economy, and all. I understood."

"Dennis shut the fuck up."

"Course, that's the push I needed to start my own business."

They started the slow climb to the top of the hill.

"It's like a rolly-coaster!" Dennis said. "We used to go to Six Flags when I was a kid. Man, I loved it there. You think it's still around? I wonder if we could go."

Oliver's belly tightened. The hills were the worst. Not because of the incline, although that was bad enough, and not because of the possibility of stalling in the middle, although that was bad, too, but because of how slow they were forced to climb, and how he couldn't see over to the other side. He and Andre had encountered their fair share of trouble on this particular stretch. Raiders who came sprinting out of the bush with their clubs and spears, bashed in the windows, tried to bust into the payload. It was easy enough to shoot them down, and Andre was pretty good at using the trees to scrape them off the cab, but it was downright terrifying.

Sometimes they set traps at the bottom of the other side, blocked the way with flaming cars or sections of Jersey wall scavenged from the turnpike. Andre, though, he was always cool as a cucumber. Rammed the blockade, shifted, and took off, leaving the savages in the rearview, chucking their useless spears. There was only one time Oliver could remember that he freaked out and hit the barrier wrong, sent them skidding. He remembered the look on his Andre's face as the trailer started to jackknife, that cold fear. But he recovered, straightened the rig out. And even though they'd come to a shuddering stop in the middle of the road, and even though some of the marauders set fire to the trailer, and even though Oliver had to hang out of the cab and empty his weapon again and again, taking a spear to the thigh as he did so, Andre still put the rig in gear and brought it up to speed and left the bastards howling behind them.

Fortunately, he hadn't encountered any such thing with Dennis. Not yet. He looked over at the man, chuckling and hooting like he really was riding the Teacup at the county fair. Dennis claimed to have been in the military, but Oliver couldn't tell for looking at him now. He was pear-shaped, all of his weight hanging around his middle. His shoulders were narrow, his muscles flabby. Not that he needed any of that to pilot a rig. And if he read did drive a Humvee like he claimed, they should have been fine. But that was the problem. Oliver didn't believe a fucking word that came out of the fucking guy's mouth. If they were attacked, if something like what he and Andre went through happened to them now, they were dead for sure.

"It's like that part when you're going up the hill, you know," Dennis said.

"We are going up the hill."

"Hahahahaha! Right! It builds the suspense. And then they pause at the top, just to build it a little more."

"Shut the fuck up, Dennis."

"Oh, come on, Oliver. We're fine."

"Don't stop when you hit the top."

"Why not? It'll be fun."

"Goddammit, Dennis!"

They were almost there. Just fifty more yards. The rig chugged along yard by yard. Oliver's hands were sweaty on the rifle stock. Dennis started to sing the theme to Jaws.

"Duh duh. Duuuuuhhhh duh."

The truck slipped over the edge so that the trailer was still facing up but the cab was facing down. Then it came to a hissing stop.

"Jesus," Dennis said.

At the bottom of the hill stood a woman. Her clothes were torn, hanging off her in strips. And she was all alone.

"Just go," Oliver said.

"What if she needs help?"

He engaged the valve brake and opened his door.

"She's bait, Dennis, don't—Dennis! Fuck! Fuck!"

Oliver slid across the cab to the driver's side and stood on the metal step, aiming the rifle into the woods, while Dennis trotted down the hill, waving.

"Hey, you okay?"

The woman waved back.

"Help me," she said.

"You need help?"

"Yes. I need help. Will you help me?"

Dennis jogged down to her, already breathing heavily. Oliver kept his eyes on the woods.

"Dennis! Get the fuck back in the truck!"

Dennis ignored him.

"Are you hurt?" he asked the woman. He was halfway down.

"They hurt me, yes. Help me, please."

Oliver ducked back into the cab and scooted across the seat to the other side, stuck his rifle out the window.

"Dennis, you idiot," he muttered.

Dennis had nearly reached the woman now, who stretched out her arms for him.

"They hurt you?" he asked. "Who?"

Oliver heard something crash through the woods. He caught the movement out of the corner of his eye. Oh, Christ.

"Them," the woman said, and a great howl sounded from all around.

Dennis stopped, adopting a slight crouch, hands out on either side. Men and women poured in from all around them, fully armed. They were shouting at Dennis to get down, and he fell to his knees, lacing his fingers behind his head.

Oliver ducked back into the cab. Slowly pulled the door close. Maybe they hadn't seen him. Fuck. At least the truck was still running. All he had to do was put it into gear and he could take them all out, Dennis included. What luck! It would take away from the pleasure of seeing the guy face down in his own piss, of watching his brains plop into the lake, but it would have to do. Nurse Smith would understand. Dennis ate like a pig. Maybe she'd even raise his rations for saving food. He put the rifle on the seat, stretched his legs out to reach the pedals, and was just about to disengage the valve and put the truck in gear when the passenger side door was ripped open and he felt a gun press against his temple.

"Hands off the stick."

He did as he was told, letting his eyes wander to the right.

It was a woman. Dark skin, long, black hair. She put a finger to her lips.

His eyes went immediately to the gun on the seat between them. The butt was on her side. She followed his eyes.

"Don't," she said.

He grabbed her wrist, pushed it away from his face, and she squeezed the trigger and the windshield exploded.

"Fuck!" he cried, putting his shoulder to his left ear. The pain was excruciating, but he managed to maintain his grip. He yanked the gun out of her grip, flipped it on her.

"Get the fuck out," he said.

"No."

He extended his arm and was just about to fire when the door behind him opened and someone yanked him out of the cab. His head hit the asphalt and his vision went black. When it cleared he saw a man standing above him, aiming a rifle at his forehead. Typical survivor. Scruffy beard. Greasy hair. Tattered clothes. The woman came running around the front of the cab, Oliver's shotgun in her hands.

"Brody, don't."

"Shit, sweetheart. He was like to blow your head off. Now you wanna save him?"

"We can interrogate him."

"Interrogate? Girl, let me explain something to you."

"Shut up, Brody. I want him alive."

She aimed the gun at him.

Brody seemed more irritated than afraid. He sucked his teeth. Thought about it.

"Okay. You're right."

She didn't lower her weapon.

"Put it down," she said.

"Well, he don't need to be conscious just yet, do he?"

But before she could answer, he slammed the butt of his rifle into Oliver's head.

~

Zorn loved shoving meat into his hole. Meat for breakfast, meat for lunch, meat for dinner. Meat meat meat. Shove it in. Shove it in. For a time, that's all they let him eat. Meat. Then Nurse Smith and Tre became more distracted and lax, and suddenly vegetables and pasta returned to the menu. And sweets, all kinds of sweets: cookies, cake, pie, fudge, ice cream, donuts, chocolate. Their days began to free up as well. Gone were the group sessions. Gone were the random room checks. They let him visit Topher and Shawn, and sometimes even let them play basketball in the gym clear on the other side of the wing, almost on the other side of the hospital. A month passed. Basketball games started earlier and earlier, lasted longer and longer, until their lives basically consisted of sleeping, eating, playing basketball, and lounging around in between.

There were other things happening to him, too. Dark things. Disturbing things. His dreams turned bloody. His thoughts dissolved into violent fantasy. He had blackouts. Sometimes he woke up as he was walking down a hallway. Sometimes he found himself just standing somewhere—in a corner, in an unlocked room, in a closet—not thinking anything, not doing anything more than staring, completely unaware of how long he'd been there or where he'd come from or what he set out to achieve in the first place.

He needed to tell someone about it, to get it off his chest, so one evening after dinner, he asked Nurse Smith if he and Topher could visit a rooftop courtyard he'd noticed near the gym, and Nurse Smith, who was going over what looked to him to be a handmade spreadsheet filled with numbers and lists of ingredients, gave him an irritated "sure" and waved him off.

It was sunny out, with a bit of a chill in the air. A paved path ran in a square around an overgrown lawn. At one end grew a tree, beneath which rotted dozens of crab apples. On the other end, a wooden bench had been anchored into the concrete. They sat down on it and turned their faces to the sun. Zorn ran a hand over his soft, bare skull, cheeks, and chin.

"I haven't been this hairless since I was born." He felt his chest and arms, then let his hand wander down his pajama bottoms. "It's all gone."

"You sound happy about it."

"Happy? I'm ecstatic. I didn't realize what a pain all that hair was until it was gone. I feel free. And smooth. And slick. The blood would wash clean off. I could kill anything I wanted and nobody would know!"

The next thing he knew, his hands were around Topher's throat. He couldn't remember how he got to that point. One second he was talking and happy, and then he was overwhelmed by a glorious wave of hate. It was bliss. It was more than bliss. It was like the first time he ever got high (Topher's fault), or the first time he ever had morphine (also Topher's fault). He could see that he was strangling his friend, he knew that his thumbs were pressing down on his windpipe, but it all seemed right, like sex, like sex with someone he loved, only better, like sex with somebody he hated and wanted to kill and have sex with after.

The image of his friend struggling beneath him was wrapped up in a haze of yellow and pink, with angels singing atonal melodies, and all he wanted to do was keep pushing until his thumbs punctured the pipe, and then he wanted to push all the way to the spine, and then he wanted to tear the throat out because wouldn't that be fun? Oh yes, so fun, so pretty, and hot. And he would have done it, too, had Topher not jammed his own thumbs into Zorn's eyes and the pain spiked through his brain and the illusion dissipated and he fell back, enraged but aware of what he'd done, and the joy turned to horror and confusion. Topher fell off of the bench, coughing and sputtering. It took a while for the pain to go away, but when he could breathe again, he sat back and hugged his knees.

"Topher, I'm sorry," Zorn said. "I don't know what got into me."

"It's the pills."

"You mean our vitamins?"

"They're drugs, you idiot. Sleeping pills and something else. I don't know what. It's in the food, too. It's changing us, turning us into something."

Zorn thought of the reason they were up there. The dreams and thoughts he'd wanted to tell Topher about. His mouth went dry.

"Turning us into what?"

Topher gave him a quick glance, uncertain how to answer. He'd seen them, of course, scrabbling across the dark Philadelphia street, and again the night he followed Nurse Smith and Tre out of the kitchen. He just didn't know what they were. He felt his throat again. It was already sore. If he told Zorn what he saw and wasn't able to explain it, would he choke him again?

"I heard a truck leave a while back. Sounded like a big semi."

"What does that have to do with anything?"

"I don't know. I mean, I know its connected, I just don't know how."

Zorn couldn't wrap his mind around it. It didn't make sense. A semi? But what was in the semi? Food? This was a hospital, not a farm. The more he thought the more confusing it became until he felt the anger and violence bubble up in him again.

Topher stood up and brushed the dirt and leaves off his robe.

"Look," he said. "I saw something and I think you need to see it, too. I can't explain what it is, so I'll show you tonight." When he saw Zorn's face, he trotted a few feet back. "Zorn?"

Zorn's cheeks were growing increasingly crimson, and he'd started to breathe heavily. Topher waited, quiet, trying not to draw his friend's attention. A cool breeze shook the leaves in the tree, sweet and refreshing. Zorn closed his eyes. His breathing steadied.

"Who am I?"

"What?"

Zorn looked at him, his face blank.

"You're Topher."

"Yes. I'm Topher."

"And I-I'm Zorn."

"Yes."

Another breeze cooled his skin.

Zorn said, "I want to go back to my room."

"Okay."

Topher led him back inside. Zorn was weak and unsteady, as if all of the energy had been sapped from his body. Topher wasn't sure what was happening, didn't know if Zorn would remember anything they'd just talked about. This was a great concern. They needed each other to escape. It was the only way. When they reached Zorn's door, Zorn turned slowly around and said, "How will I get out of my room?"

"Palm your meds. Wait until midnight."

"But the doors."

"Don't worry. If you can make it past midnight, you'll see."

He palmed his meds just like Topher instructed, but nothing noticeable happened. Except he didn't immediately fall asleep. And his thoughts started to clear. And he didn't feel as angry. He sat on the edge of his bed and thought about what happened on the roof. He'd never experienced such violence. Even worse was the forgetting. It was the worst moment of his entire life. Worse than what he did to his parents, worse than being attacked by those horrible creatures at Raleigh's, worse than any of the monsters he'd ever tracked and killed. It was like his soul had been replaced by a cavernous black pit. If Topher hadn't fought back, he was sure he would have killed him. He might have been still sitting out there, his friend's body lying broken at his feet, seething and fuming, listening for the call of his family. Wait. Family? Call? What family? What call? He didn't know what it sounded like, but he knew it would come, that they were out there. He'd hear it when he was ready.

He was glad that he couldn't sleep because his dreams terrified him. He wished he could have told Topher about them. At first, they consisted of sounds. Grunting and panting and screaming. But gradually images began to form. Pale, round heads and sickly skin, a confusion of teeth and claws, and he was always running in a pack, galloping through dilapidated hallways, tunnels, dirty alleys, broken city streets. The pack was his family, his brothers and sisters. Somehow he knew this. There were hundreds of them, a stinking mass of flesh. It felt good to be one of the many, not having to think or worry or make decisions, and he just ran and ran, hunting, his prey just head, right there, some weak, fleshy thing trying to get away but the pack was too fast and descended upon it, swift and brutal, and right before he woke up screaming, right before the terror snapped him out of his nightmare, his teeth found the soft of its neck, and his tongue sang as the salty blood filled his mouth.

He ran his hand over his head. So supple and smooth. The clock read nine. Three more hours. Maybe exercise would help pass the time? He stood up against the door and lowered himself into a squat. Before all of this, he might have been able to hold such a position for as long as two minutes. Now he barely felt anything after five. After twenty he thought he felt a twinge in his thigh but realized it was only a mosquito. He squashed it and wiped up the blood with his finger and sucked it clean. At forty minutes he gave up. His legs felt as strong and sure as when he started, so he dropped to the floor and performed twenty push-ups. Then fifty. Then one hundred. Then five hundred.

He exercised until ten, read *Cat Fancy* until eleven, and then sat and stared at the door until eleven fifty. He went to the bathroom to pee.

Eleven fifty-five. He looked in the mirror and examined the sole hair he managed to find on his body. An eyelash.

It fell out.

He went back into his bedroom.

Midnight.

Nothing happened. No electrical winding down. No thunk as the locks turned off. Nothing. He counted to fifty, watched his clock turn 12:01, and groaned in disbelief. Had Topher pranked him? Goddammit! Even after the end of the world, after everything they'd been through, he was still an immature little . . .

The electricity wound down. The digital clock faded. The lock thunked and his door opened with a creak.

He met Topher in the hallway, and they went immediately to the kitchen. When Topher showed him the staff food, his eyes lit up. They gorged. Caesar salad, broccoli, pasta, meat sauce, peas, corn.

When they were done, they leaned back against one of the cutting tables.

"So how does this work?" Zorn asked.

"I tried to tell you before. I think they're trading with somebody on the outside. Someone up north."

"Who?"

"Who knows. But he gives them all this fresh food. They rely on it."

"But what are they trading? Medication?"

Topher stood and clapped his hands clean.

"Let's straighten all of this up. Then I'll show you."

He led Zorn down a series unfamiliar hallways, stopping at every corner to bend down and check a part of the wall.

"What are you doing?" Zorn asked.

"I marked the way," Topher said. "Before."

The hallways were dark but for the occasional emergency light, and every now and then they heard doors opening in some distant wing, a creak and a bang that echoed in the emptiness. Sometimes they spun around a corner only to see a shadow flit through the next intersection; sometimes a door slammed behind them, forcing them forward. Creatures scrabbled in the ceiling above. Water dripped from cracks in the cinder blocks. They got lost, backtracked, backtracked again, each time seeking out the mark.

Topher picked up the pace, turning left, right, left, left, right, seemingly at random, no longer checking for his mark. They came across a section that had been flooded out entirely. Zorn thought they were going to have to wade through the mess, but Topher turned into a room with a collapsed ceiling, and they climbed up to the floor above them, scrambled forward, then dropped back down through gaping hole. Zorn noticed the courtyard from the day before. Then they passed the cafeteria. The gym. And suddenly they were in the hall to the Athenaeum, standing outside Suite 101-113.

"Are you kidding me?" Zorn said. "What the hell?"

"I don't know," Topher said. "Just felt like running. That was fun, wasn't it?"

Before Zorn could reply, the door opened and a doctor in full scrubs, surgical mask, hat, gloves and all, walked out, letting it slam behind him. He drew up short when he saw the two.

"Oh my god," he said, and leaped for the door.

Zorn was quickly overwhelmed by rage. It was just like in his dreams, just like how he felt when he nearly strangled Topher on the roof, a cocktail of fear, anger, and euphoria. Everything seemed to move in slow motion, especially the doctor. Zorn grabbed his arm before it even got close to the handle, twisted it, broke the wrist. After that, all he knew was teeth and cracking and screams, and though he felt that he should have been horrified by what he did, he saw it as beautiful, as art, a masterpiece he needed to complete, just a chunk here and a break there, rearrange the limbs just so, take this part off, put it on backward. So much blood to paint with. So much delicious squelching. They panted and groaned, contorted and flipped. Then he found himself standing over a mutilated lump of flesh, holding a severed arm in his hand.

"Dear Lord." He dropped the limb as if it was on fire. "What do we do?"

Topher, who had retreated into a shadowy corner, gulped. Had he really just seen one of his oldest, dearest friends dismember a living human being right in front of him and put all of the parts back on like some kind of perverted performance art?

"Um," he said. "Take it away?"

"Where?"

"Over there." He pointed down the hall from which they'd just come. "Away from the door."

Zorn looked down at what he had done. If only he hadn't been so violent, he could have dragged the poor man away by a limb, but there weren't any more limbs left. None that were attached, that is. Pity. It could have used an extra one over here, just for symmetry *oh god, stop it!* As it stood, he had to get down on his hands and knees and push the mound around the corner, like a lineman leaning into a blocking sled, leaving a thick trail of blood in his wake. The door rattled again, and Topher stepped farther back into the shadows, a silhouette in the dark. It opened, and another doctor stuck his head out.

"Doctor Smith?" he said.

Topher had to say something.

"Er, um, yes?"

"You okay?"

"Yes, I just slipped a bit." He looked at the smear of blood left by the lump Zorn had pushed away. "Hallway's a little slick."

Another voice from inside the room asked the man in the door something, and he ducked his head back in to shout, "Okay, just a minute!" He exited the room completely, letting the door close behind him. Now he, too, was nothing more than a dark shadow. "What are you doing? We told you to get the extra straps."

"Extra straps. Of course."

A sickening thud sounded from around the corner.

"What was that?" the doctor asked, taking a step forward.

"Don't come any closer! You'll slip, too."

"What are you talking about? Slip on what?"

"Your own blood!"

And he leaped for him.

Had Topher known that his intended victim was holding a scalpel, he might have changed his approach. Not that it mattered. All it took was one slash and Topher lost control. It was nowhere near what Zorn was going through (palming the meds and refraining from eating the tainted food had seen to that), but he had enough poison inside him to enjoy a surge of aggression and power. The doctor slashed him again, and again and again, and then Topher grabbed him by the back of the neck and slammed his head into the wall. He slid to the ground, unconscious, and Topher picked his feet up and dragged him around the corner just in time to see Zorn trying to pull a pair of scrub bottoms off what looked like legs.

"Dear Lord, Zorn. There's no time for that now."

"We'll need a disguise."

Then the doctor Topher was dragging grumbled and shook his head. Zorn's eyes blanked. He stalked over, straddled him, and punched him in the face until Topher pulled him off. It wasn't easy, but he did it, mustering all of his strength, pulling with power that seemed to come from somewhere else, and when he was done, he'd pinned his friend up against the wall. Zorn's eyes were still empty. He wouldn't look at him, focusing all of his attention on the beaten man on the floor, like an animal torn from its prey.

"Stop it!" Topher hissed. "Stop!"

Zorn didn't respond, just breathed and stared, breathed and stared. He took a step forward and Topher slapped him in the face. Zorn's eyes snapped onto him, and Topher's belly filled with ice. There was nothing there. Just darkness. He prepared to bolt.

"Hey!" he said. "It's me, Zorn. It's Topher."

The eyes didn't waiver. Topher smacked his face so hard that his head rocked, then, before he could do anything else, he started tickling him under the arms. When Zorn's head came back around, Topher smacked it again, then resumed the tickling. He repeated this until Zorn started to giggle, and when his head swiveled around again, Topher smacked him one last time, just to make sure.

"Snap out of it!"

"Okay, okay. Stop tickling me."

Topher tickled him some more.

"I said stop!"

He grabbed Topher by the wrists and shoved them away. Then he just stood there, breathing heavily.

"What's the matter with you?" Topher asked.

"I am not well."

Topher turned around and prodded the dead men with the toe of his slipper. He pointed at the second doctor, the one Zorn had punched to death.

"We're going to do something about this one."

"We don't have any fire."

"No. But you could do something about it, right? You know, with the bloodlust."

"It's not that simple. I can't just turn it on."

"I just saw you do it."

"That wasn't me. I mean, it was me, but, well, we were in danger, and I just felt it surge up."

Topher thought of what happened to him. How it rushed through his system like pure adrenaline, like unadulterated wrath.

Zorn said, "Pain seems to help it, too."

Topher considered this for a moment.

"Well, we don't have very much time before he turns. What if I do this?"

Then he kicked Zorn in the balls and sprinted away and hid around the corner. Seconds later, he heard the unmistakable sound of a skull being crushed.

The thing was wiry, with pale green skin. Its veins bulged in its neck as it strained against the thick leather strap fastened around its feet, legs, chest, and forehead. One of its arms had gotten free, though, and it pounded on the gurney with its fist. Zorn stared at its head, its completely bald head.

A doctor in a hazmat suit was trying to subdue it. He grabbed a circular saw, something they must have used for amputations or autopsies, and was about to brain the beast with it when he noticed Topher and Zorn standing there in their blood-spattered scrubs.

"The fuck are you guys doing out there?" he said over his shoulder. He tossed the saw onto the table behind him. "You get the straps?"

Zorn peered around the room. Five more of the monsters lay unconscious on metal gurneys in the back, where another door stood open. An escape route, perhaps? The doctor turned around, about to bark out an order, but stopped when he saw them.

"You're covered in blood."

This was an understatement.

"Yes," Topher said. "We are surgeons." He couldn't read the other doctor's expression through the mask, so he said, "I got a nosebleed?"

The thing on the table continued to writhe and hiss.

"That looks like Tahir," Zorn said.

"Tahir?"

"Yes, Tahir. The Mustache."

Topher peered closer.

"My God, I believe you're right."

"Oh shit," the doctor said. "You're one of them."

He bolted for the door in the back, tripped, slammed his head on the side of a table, and fell to the ground, out cold.

"That was unexpected," Topher said.

Zorn looked down at the thing that used to be the Mustache, the thing that, should he stay any longer in that place, he would someday become. Suddenly the dreams made sense. The anger and the hairlessness, the weight loss and the super strength. He found his gaze settling on its taloned hands, its rigid, curled fingers. At least that hadn't begun yet. He felt angry again, but not like before, not the rage, the uncontrollable wrath that flooded his veins, but calculated fury, boiling disgust. Vengeance. Vengeance was the thinking man's carnage. One had to have a brain, one had to feel.

He said, "Topher, I have an idea," and unbuckled the leather restraints holding the thing down. It launched itself off the gurney and leaped on top of a cabinet on the other side of the room, knocking over a tray of medical instruments. Its talons punctured the drywall. Topher edged back to the door.

"Great idea, Zorn," he said.

But Zorn ignored him. He walked over to the other monsters and started to unbuckle their straps, too. Topher crept around to the other side of the room, and the thing on the cabinet watched him, hissing.

"Shh," Topher said. "Quiet now."

His back hit the corner of the table and his hand found something hard and heavy and metal. The saw. He picked it up, triumphant, and held it out before him.

"Ha!" he said, and pulled the trigger.

Nothing happened. Crap. It wasn't plugged in.

The monster leaped at him and he jumped aside, bludgeoning it on the head.

"Zorn!" he yelled, scrambling for the back door. "I'm fairly sure your idea is a bad one!"

Zorn leaped from gurney to gurney, unbuckling the monsters.

Topher pounded on the frame.

"Let's go!"

Zorn finished the last buckle and bounced away, following Topher out the door. He turned before he left, making sure to leave it open just a crack, and saw the thing that used to be the Mustache stand up and woozily zoom in on the doctor. It stumbled over and straddled him. The doctor moaned and opened his eyes.

"Oh god," he said.

And then it was upon him.

~

Oliver woke up to the sound of Dennis laughing at his one of his own jokes. He sat up and regretted it. His head pounded at the base of his skull, bam, bam, bam. He dry heaved. After a few minutes, the pain softened enough for him to look up. It was dark, well into the night, but the stars were out, bright and full. If there was any benefit to life after the end of the world, it was the stars. He could see each one. He never knew there were so many before. It made sense to him now why ancient man looked up into the sky and invented the gods. Or why modern man looked up there and thought, "I wish I could reach them."

The idiots hadn't tied him up. They'd taken him back to their camp and left him alone in the dirt. Had they taken the truck? Of course they'd taken the truck. That was the whole point of the ambush. But who had driven it? He knew the answer before he even finished the thought.

". . . and I was like, 'Whoa, Nelly! Who is that at the bottom of the hill? But Oliver was all, 'Don't stop! It's a trap!'"

Cue irritating belly laughs.

Oliver rose slowly to his feet. Everything ached. His hips especially. A sore spot deep in his back. Must have slept on a rock. He patted his pockets. His knife was gone. Same with the .22 in his ankle holster. What was the name of the guy who hit him? Bobby? Brady? Something like that. He'd find him just as soon as he figured out what was going on.

He looked around. He saw the skeletons of cars circled around the camp, the low glow of multiple campfires. Men and women were speaking in low murmurs, and every now and then a child giggled or called out for mother. The smell of meat cooking made his stomach rumble. He headed toward the sound of Dennis' voice.

"There he is!" Dennis called when he stepped into the ring. "Good old Ollie! He doesn't like it when I call him that, but I call him it anyway. Sleep well, Ollie? Everything alright? You okay?"

Oliver ignored him. He looked at the people sitting around the fire instead, trying to figure out who was in charge. Dennis filled in the silence with laughter.

"Ha ha ha ha ha! That's good old Ollie for you! He doesn't like to talk much."

Oliver didn't see the woman with the dark skin. Nor did he see the man who hit him. But he did see the bait, the woman who stood half naked at the bottom of the hill. Dennis sat right next to her. Her beauty disarmed him. She smiled and he felt his face redden.

"Oh, I think Ollie's in love!" Dennis said, laughing.

The woman patted his shoulder and he quieted.

Oliver was shocked. He'd never seen anybody quiet that asshole down before. The woman had power. She was in charge.

"Would you like something to eat, Oliver?" she asked.

Without waiting for an answer, she picked up a paper plate filled with roasted vegetables and what looked like chicken. From the truck. His truck. He knew he wasn't supposed to touch it. Smith would have exiled him for it. Or even worse, added him to the patient list. But she wasn't here, was she? And he was starving, wasn't he? He took the plate.

"No fork?"

She smiled.

"The good silver's back at the house." She gestured to an empty lawn chair. "Have a seat."

He raised the plate in thanks and lowered himself into the chair.

"You're right, Dennis," the woman said. "He doesn't like to talk, does he?"

"Oh, you haven't seen half of it yet. This one time, he didn't say a word to me the entire ride, including drop off and load in. That's up and back, eight hours, plus two more for drop off and—"

Oliver tuned him out. He put a hunk of meat in his mouth and ate. Before he knew it, he was halfway through his food, so he slowed down. He sat back, chewing. The woman was watching him.

"My, you're hungry."

He nodded.

"Thank you."

"Oh-ho, he speaks!" Dennis said.

Oliver put a green pepper into his mouth.

"Your name is Oliver?" she asked.

He didn't say anything. He wanted the attention off him again, so he took another bite.

"Yeah, his name is Oliver," Dennis said. "I call him Ollie, though. He doesn't like it when I call him that."

The woman gave him a polite smile, and Oliver continued to nibble, quietly scanning the group. Nobody was outright holding. No pistols in holsters, knives in sheaths, not even a piece of rebar or a bat. They had to have something. Nobody wandered around without some form of protection. The woman watched him, her eyes following his, so he dropped them to his meal. He was going to have to do something he hated. He was going to have to speak to Dennis.

"Dennis, aren't you from around here?" he asked.

It almost backfired. Dennis, so unaccustomed to any sort of attention from him, let his mouth drop open and stared at him. Oliver cursed himself. He should have been nicer before, even if it was just a little bit, something to make their interaction a little bit smoother. But then Dennis held the look a little too long, opened his face a little too wide, and he realized that the idiot was just exaggerating. Then, right when everybody was just the right amount of uncomfortable, he burst out laughing.

"Hahahahahaha! I mean, whoa! Yeah! That's what I'm talking about!"

It worked. The woman was so startled by the outburst that she turned her attention away from Oliver. Dennis, tactful as usual, continued to blab away.

"Here we are, two months into knowing each other, and I never thought he was actually paying attention. Yeah, man. Yeah, dude. I'm from Pennsylvania, but I'm not from around here. I grew up in Harrisburg, man. That's like, two hours from here. Right on the Susquehanna. Man, we used to take road trips up to Sunbury, you know, when they inflated the damn in the summer? You wouldn't think such a small town would be the most popular boating spot on in the state, but it was."

And he was off, commanding everyone's attention just by running his mouth. The tenacity of societal politeness baffled Oliver. He didn't have much of it to begin with; as far as he was concerned, small talk was inane, even in situations that called for it. He thought that maybe the impetus for survival would have wiped it out entirely, but Dennis' continued existence disproved that. How could someone so blithely unaware of his surroundings make it this far? Could it be that his uncanny ability to get people to like him was actually an evolved survival skill? How on earth could that have happened? Tigers and bears don't care about personality. They just want to eat.

Hundreds of thousands of more intelligent, talented people were wiped out by the Catastrophes. Surgeons, athletes, professors, scientists, teachers, inventors, artists, musicians, yet Dennis continued to take breath. It was beyond all rational explanation. And his captors, the people who should have been beating him to a pulp, were just sitting there, politely listening to him babble about knee-boarding.

However he felt about it, the chatter took attention away, and he was free to scrutinize everyone around him. There were at least a dozen others sitting around the fire, and none of them were talking. But they shared looks. Worried looks. And they were barely eating. All of that food, the vegetables so fresh they still smelled like soil, the succulent chicken, and all they could do was peck and nibble. They were scared. Or waiting. He let his gaze wander beyond the circle. It was difficult to see much of anything in the dark. Mostly it was just shadows, the yellow dots of other campfires. He turned around in his chair, scanned the road behind him. The full moon outlined the cars and trees, black on navy blue.

There.

On top of his rig. A flash of light reflected by the moon. He squinted into the night, striving to see what might be . . . yes. There it was. A single form lying on the trailer, facing in. Sniper. The flash of light was from the scope. This was all a setup. But for what?

Dennis was saying, ". . . it's just like back at the hospital, man. Nurse Smith, I think she likes me alright. She's kind of a hardass, but at least she doesn't put me on the patient list."

"Shut the fuck up, Dennis."

The circle grew even tenser, but Dennis kept talking.

"I mean, times are tough, but I'd rather be hungry than suffer the way those poor guys are, let me tell you."

"Shut your fucking mouth, Dennis, or I'll break your fucking teeth."

"Jeez, Ollie. You don't say a word for months and this is the way you talk to me?"

Fuck it.

Oliver threw his plate on the ground and stood up.

"Where's Brady?"

"Calm down, Ollie."

"Shut up." He pointed at the woman. "There's a man here named Brady or Bobby. Gave me this fucking knot on my head. It's time for him to pay for it."

The woman didn't flinch. In fact, she didn't seem upset or even remotely surprised.

"Why don't you finish your meal, Oliver?" she said.

He looked around the circle, trying to catch someone's eye.

"Any of you know who did this? Where is he? Where's Brady?"

Nobody said anything. They kept their gazes firmly on their plates.

Oliver spun around, shouting out into the rest of the camp. "Brady! Brady you numb cunt! Come and get your ass kicked!"

"It's Brody."

To his left. A man with a black eye and split lip.

"Jamal," someone hissed.

Jamal ignored it.

"His name's Brody," he said.

"Where is he?"

Jamal looked away.

"I dunno."

"Where?"

"Out."

"Goddammit."

The woman finally spoke.

"I sent him out on patrol, Oliver," she said.

He summoned all of his anger. If he was going to get out of here alive, she needed to be afraid.

"Who the fuck are you?" he demanded. "What the fuck is all this?"

"My name is Isa. Nothing's going on. You're our guest here."

"Why'd you set that trap? Why'd you steal my rig?"

A few armed men stepped out of the shadows. And the woman, the one who tried to get Brody not to hit him, joined them. Dennis leaped up from his chair.

"Jeez, Ollie! Now look what you did! These people were nice to us. They could of just killed us."

"You dumb fuck," Oliver said, and threw a punch at him. It was a great big haymaker, and he put everything he had behind it, but Dennis ducked it easily and popped back, hands up.

"C'mon, Ollie. You don't wanna do this."

Fuck. How did such a dickhead like Dennis know how to fight? Oh right. The ARMY. So he wasn't lying about that. Maybe that's where he got all his confidence from. Oliver rapidly recalculated. He thought knocking Dennis out would cause enough chaos to allow him to duck out into the dark. From there he faced a couple of days of roughing it before he got back to the hospital, but it'd be worth it. Telling Smith what happened would be tough, but he could blame it all on Dennis, even make it look like the idiot had a hand in the whole thing. He could lead her back here. He'd like to watch her loose some of her creatures on these people, especially Brody. Seeing Dennis cut down would be a nice bonus. Hell, she might even let him start making the runs by himself if he pled his case right. Whatever happened, he'd still have a place at the hospital.

Now he might not be able to get away so easily. He decided to take a chance. He zoomed in on the woman from the truck, the one who had wanted to interrogate him, and her eyes wavered. Weak link. He advanced toward her, ignoring the cries for him to stop, hoping to get close enough for her to push the barrel of her gun into his chest. That's all he needed.

"Where is he?" he bellowed.

The woman retreated as quickly as he came. Had he made the wrong choice? No time to reflect. He doubled down.

"Where is he, goddammit!"

Someone fired a shot. He felt it thwack in the dirt near his feet. More people yelling at him, flying by in his peripheral vision. He heard the chunk of weapons being loaded. He backed the woman against the frame of a car. Why didn't she blink? Why didn't she cower? No time to pause. No time to worry. It was now or never. He felt the barrel push into his chest.

"Where is Brody? Tell me, goddammit."

She didn't flinch.

"Tell me!"

There it was. He saw it. Just like before. The doubt. The momentary flicker of attention. He reached up for the gun, meaning to rip it from her hands.

Then her finger clamped down on the trigger.

~

Shawn listened quietly as they told him everything. At first Topher thought his silence was politeness, but the more he spoke, the less Shawn said, and the less Shawn said, the more anxious he became, and he talked too much and too fast until he came to the part when Zorn beat the doctor to a pulp and Shawn, clearly disengaged, leaned to one side and farted.

Topher stopped, disgusted.

"Don't you care at all about what's happening?" he asked.

Shawn sipped his orange juice, nibbled on his roll.

"What did you expect?"

"I guess not this?"

"They were all bald, every last one of them," Zorn said. "Just like me, just like you. That's what's happening to us. That's what we're here for."

"I know."

"You know?"

"Yeah, of course."

"But . . . what . . . for how long?"

Shawn took a spoonful of mashed potatoes.

"I dunno. Probably figured it out about a year ago."

Zorn felt the anger start to boil up inside.

"You knew and you didn't tell us?"

"I did. I told him."

Topher balked.

"No, you didn't. You never told me they were turning us into bloodthirsty monsters."

"'Don't take the meds. Don't eat the food.' First day, when I jumped you. Remember?"

"Yeah, I do. But if you know about this, why are you still here?"

Shawn held up four fingers.

"Four times," he said. "Okay? It happened four more times."

"What did?"

"Same thing as what happened at school. Tore me up. Each time a little piece of me gone. I met good people. Good men with guns. Women who weren't afraid to fight. After the first two, I thought, 'It's okay. I'll find others.' The third time: 'I don't think I can do this again.' Then, that last one. Those maniacs in the red robes. They swarmed us. 'We love you! We love you!' Have you ever seen a man eaten alive? Have you ever seen a *child* eaten alive?"

Topher shook his head, ashamed, but Zorn remained still. He had. In his dreams. Yes, they were just dreams, but they were so real that he was sure they had actually happened. They went still as Gertrude's nurse led him to his seat and gave him his spoon. When he didn't move, she helped him scoop some potatoes into his mouth. After that, the motion was automatic. Topher watched, sad and disgusted.

"Well, we're getting out," he said.

Shawn giggled.

"Yeah. I tried that, once. Actually did it. Got about two miles away. Took one look around and turned right back and went to bed. Breakfast in the morning, lunch at noon, and back to bed. Nobody tries to rape me or eat me or cut off my head. Fuuuck that bullshit." He watched as Gertrude shoveled spoonful after spoonful into his mouth. "See? He doesn't mind, either. Plus, the power cuts out at midnight. They got plenty of staff food to eat in the kitchen. I got a whole stash in the ceiling in my bathroom."

Topher gaped.

Shawn continued.

"As far as I'm concerned, I'll stay here until the end of my life, and I plan on living a long time, my friends. Ask me how long I've been here."

"How long have you been here?"

"Longer than anybody else. I can game the system. Trust me, you're better off sticking around."

Gertrude dropped his spoon and it clattered to the floor. His arm kept moving, up, down, up, down. A rivulet of drool spilled down his chin. Topher and Zorn watched, horrified. Shawn shrugged.

That night, two hours after taking his meds, Nurse Smith and Tre burst into Topher's room while he was doing sit-ups.

"Well get a load of this," Tre said, marching over to him.

"No, wait!" Topher cried, but Tre grabbed him by his robe and yanked him off the ground.

Topher tried to summon the anger again, but it simply wasn't there. He'd been palming his meds, eating the staff food. He wasn't some super-creature with a deep well of strength and an endless capacity for violence. He was only a man. A man weakened by indolence and fear. Tre punched him in the face until he went limp.

The operating room had been modified to fit all of them. Three metal chairs were bolted into the ground, all facing the door: Shawn on the left, Zorn in the middle, Topher on the right. They were strapped to the chairs as if prepared for execution, each hooked up to an IV. Bags of green liquid hung from stands. Nurse Smith stood in front of them, holding a clipboard and a pen.

"Good morning."

Shawn spat at her.

"Fuck you! I told you everything."

"No, you didn't, Mr. King. How did you put it yesterday? 'I can game the system'."

"How did you hear that?"

"For someone who has been here longer than anybody else, Mr. King, you're certainly ignorant of the way things work."

"They broke more rules than me. I tried to help you."

"They did break the rules, Mr. King, you are correct. And they will be punished. Just like you."

Shawn struggled in vain against the straps, grunting and growling in frustration, and Nurse Smith turned her attention to Topher and Zorn.

"And you two," she said. "I've seen men like you before. Proud. Obstinate. Devious. I broke them all, just like I will break you."

"Please, Nurse Smith," Topher said. "I don't know why I'm here. I was just getting some exercise."

Nurse Smith held up her hand for him to stop.

"Don't embarrass yourself. Mr. King has already told me everything. Didn't you, Mr. King?"

"You told me I would be rewarded. You promised!"

"Mr. King, what do you think this is?"

Tre entered the room and whispered in her ear.

"Shawn, you leech," Topher hissed.

"Screw you," Shawn said. "Do you know what I could have been? They were going to let me in, be one of them, I know it. I know it."

Tre finished whispering, and Nurse Smith said, "Are they near?"

"Close. You want me to go, you know, get everything ready?"

"No. Not yet. I think we have enough time. Besides, you'll want to watch this." A creepy half-smile crossed her lips. She turned her attention back to her captives. "Now, gentlemen. It seems your behavior has forced me to speed up the timeline on my little experiment. Normally I would just raise your doses, maybe pull out a few fingernails. But one of our doctors came up with a new method, something that would be of great use to us. It's not been tested, of course. But that's what you three are for."

Without another word, she strolled over to Shawn's IV stand and pushed a button.

"What are you doing?" he cried. "No! Stop!"

The bag drained quickly, pumping the green fluid directly into his arm. He started to scream. The transformation began in seconds. All of the fat drained from his body, leaving spindly, ropy muscle. His fingers sprouted claws, and fangs shot out of his mouth. The scream cut off and he went into convulsions. His skin turned a sickly green and his eyes yellowed. The bag emptied out, he jerked some more then went limp. Nurse Smith ran a finger over his skin, smiled and pressed on his neck, searching for a pulse.

"Remarkable."

"Is he alive?" Tre asked.

She nodded and kneeled in front of the monster, peeled open its eyes and shined a flashlight on them.

"They dilated."

The thing that used to be Shawn woke suddenly, thrashing its body at her, and she leaped back into Tre's arms, then spun and planted a passionate kiss on his lips.

"Oh, Tre. Do you know what this means?" Something rumbled in the distance, a sound like thunder. "What was that?"

Another rumble rocked the building, followed by a massive crash. Dust sifted from the ceiling.

"It's them," Tre said.

"You said there was enough time!"

"What can I say? They're here."

He turned to go and Nurse Smith said, "I'm coming with you."

"No. You stay here. It might not be safe."

She hardened.

"You forget your place. I'm coming."

He looked over her shoulder at Topher and Zorn.

"What about them?"

"We'll deal with them later."

Then they left, letting the door close behind them.

The monster in the chair, the thing that used to be Shawn, a man, a teacher, a lost soul, thrashed and screeched and yanked against its restraints. The tendons in its neck contracted, ropy and thick, and its yellow eyes bulged. It began to slam its head against the metal rest, breathing through its nose, again and again. The strap loosened. It pushed and pushed and the leather pressed into its head so hard as to draw blood. The metal creaked. A bolt snapped, and then the strap broke off.

Topher turned to Zorn.

"Now would be a good time to channel your inner rage."

"I know!"

Another explosion, more dust. Topher heard the unmistakable pop of gunfire, men's shouts, more rumbling.

"Hurry up, Zorn."

"I'm concentrating."

The monster popped out of its right restraint and let out a triumphant roar. It ripped the strap off its chest.

"Oh my god, we're done for."

Zorn jammed his eyes shut, desperately trying to think of something, anything, that would spurt the rage. Mistreated kittens. Children dropping ice cream. Rainy Sundays. Wait, no, he liked that one. Yoko Ono? Dishonest politicians? Lazy highway workers? Nothing. Nothing seemed to work. If only someone could kick him in the balls.

Topher, in a sudden burst of inspiration, said, "Zorn, do you remember that show you used to love?"

"Not now, Topher."

"Do you remember the name of the show?"

"Delmont and Bunny? Of course."

The monster yanked on its one remaining leg, simultaneously swiping at him, its claws inches from his face. A small flicker of anger formed in his chest. *If that thing touches me, I'll press my thumbs into its eyes until they burst.*

"Delmont was a ladyboy," Topher said.

The flicker grew to a flame. Zorn flexed his arms, straining against the leather. The metal arms groaned.

"And Bunny was a pedophile!"

With a scream that came from the depths of his soul, Zorn broke both arm straps. The beast pulled free and leaped for him. He caught it in midair and threw it at the door right as Tre burst in wielding a butcher's knife. The monster struck him in the chest, and for a moment all Topher could see was claws and blood. Tre plunged the knife into its back and it let up a feral yowl, arms scrabbling to find the handle. Tre tried to scramble away, but the beast sunk its claws into his shoulder, opened its mouth wide, and bit into his neck. He screamed. Blood spurted out of the wound. The beast shook its head like a mad dog, and his flailing arms weakened and weakened and finally went limp.

Machine gun fire rattled out in the corridor, and the monster bounded out of the room, the butcher knife still planted in its back.

Later, after the piracy and adventure, the looting and danger, the death and war, when the world had calmed and begun to heal and the whole affair with Liam Chris had finally been rectified, Topher would describe his escape from the hospital to his grandchildren, Little Isa and Kenneth (eight and five, respectively), who more or less understood what he was talking about. Most of the family regarded him with awe, or fear, or that maddening brand of mixed condescension and respect to which only old people were subjected, but the children loved him, reveled in his long beard and what remained of the curly white locks.

Topher found comfort and legitimacy in his grandchildren's attention, even if it were a bit difficult to keep it. In fact, Kenneth, once he was old enough to stop pulling on his beard, was very interested in tales of the old days.

"But grandpa," he asked. "Was it really your men come to rescue you?"

"Of course!" Topher shifted the boy's weight on his knee. "Dear Lord, Kenneth. Either your rear end has gotten bonier or my thigh has lost even more muscle."

Little Isa, who was sitting on the sofa opposite him, traced circles on the cushion with her finger.

"But how did you know?" she asked.

"Honestly, I didn't. I hoped. We'd been so cooped up and drugged and Lord knows what else for so many weeks that I had no idea what was going on in the outside world."

"We went to the beach last summer," Kenneth informed him.

"I know. Did you find any three-eyed fish like I said you would?"

"No. But daddy got really sick and threw up all over the place."

"That's because your father's an alcoholic."

"Daddy said it was bad shrimp."

"He's always been a little thick. Now where was I?"

"You were talking about Uncle Zorn in the hospital," Little Isa said. "And about the monster with the butcher knife, and Delmont and Bunny."

"Ah yes. Well, I heard the gunfire and the explosions, and I naturally assumed it was my men coming to free me. Little did I know that, at least initially, it was the sounds of the enemy defending themselves against their own zombie breakout!"

Kenneth tugged on Topher's beard.

"Are the zombies all dead?"

"Oh dear, no." Then, seeing the boy's obvious terror, he added, "We destroyed many of them that day. The one's in the hospital, at least. But the zombies are never going away, my dear boy. That's why we live up here in the mountains."

Kenneth squirmed as he took this in. Then his innocent mind wrapped itself around this knowledge, and he said, "Because they can't climb?"

"Among other things."

"Is that why we live on a house on a stick?"

Topher guffawed.

"You, my boy, have quite the way with figurative language."

"What's figurine language?"

"Its language that talks about tiny glass models of fairies and elves."

"Grandpa, did Uncle Zorn save you?"

"I wouldn't go that far. I mean it was me who heard the . . ."

"Tanks?" Zorn asked.

"No. Tank. Singular. It's our people, Zorn. They came through for us! The Ton is here!"

He opened the door a crack and looked out into the hall.

"Coast is clear."

They tiptoed out of their torture chamber, making sure to drag Tre's body into the hall, a tempting morsel for any beast that might try to follow them. The wing in which they found themselves was unfamiliar, but the sound of the battle gave them a beacon to follow. They turned at random, heading ever towards it, hearts pounding down empty corridor upon empty corridor, until they finally turned a corner and skidded to a halt behind a group of the monsters busily munching on a body. Shawn, or thing that used to be him, was there, the butcher's knife still sticking out of its back.

"Just back away," Topher whispered out the corner of his mouth.

They edged back around and leaned up against the wall, terrified.

"There's nowhere else to go," Zorn said.

He was right. Unless they wanted to backtrack and try to find another way to their people, the only choice they had was to go through the monsters.

Topher edged closer to the corner.

"I'm going to check."

"What? No!"

"Maybe they've gone on."

Then he stuck his head around and came face to face the thing that used to be Shawn. It leaped back and Topher immediately turned, kicked Zorn in the balls, ran around behind him and booted him out into the middle of the intersection.

Topher saw the rage overtake his friend like a switch had been flipped. One second he was Zorn, the gentle giant, the next he was this mindless killing machine. The beast leaped at him, fangs bared, claws out, and Zorn caught it by the wrists and twisted. Bones cracked. It screamed. He threw it to the ground and the knife pushed the rest of the way through its body, exiting from its shoulder. Then he stomped on its neck, crushing its windpipe. The other monsters swarmed him as he turned around.

Topher couldn't do anything more than watch. He had no weapons, nothing he could use to help. Zorn's arms flailed, blood flew. Then the wall exploded, and concrete and rebar shot through the air, crushing the beasts on the top of the pile, impaling a few others. A semi burst into the hall, and Topher threw himself out of the way as it plowed through to the other side, slamming to a stop against the wall. Concrete dented the hood, broke the windshield, and the ceiling buckled and fell, exposing sparking wires like entrails.

Topher, covered in ceiling tiles and concrete, coughed as he pushed himself up and stared around him. His skin was coated white, his robe torn. Little cuts dotted his face and arms. He patted his body, stunned. All there. Good Lord. All there. He looked around for Zorn, but only saw a mound of blood slicked debris.

"Zorn!" he yelled.

He stumbled over and started to clear the broken ceiling tiles and copper pipe and cables. When he came across the first headless torso, he stopped. This was pointless. It was over. There was no way his friend survived. The sinking reality of it formed in his chest and belly. If he weren't so dehydrated, he would have cried. But he just stood there, empty.

The passenger side door of the semi-opened, and out stepped Saanvi.

"Mayor!"

She ran over to Topher as Isa emerged from the other side. She took one look at the situation—the wreckage and the bodies, the blank expression on Topher's face—and said, "Saanvi, don't!" but it was too late. Saanvi threw herself forward and embraced Topher, who was forced to stand there and take it, arms pinned to his sides. He wanted to feel something, but he couldn't. Amazement, maybe?

No. Just numbness. It did register as remarkable. Saanvi rarely emoted anything other than irritation and confusion. She'd never hugged him before. What had wrought his change?

"Mayor," she said. "I'm so glad to see you. We thought you were dead. We thought we'd lost you forever, but then Isa showed up," she let him go and pointed at her. "She told us what happened. She organized the whole thing."

Isa picked her way toward them, making sure to stay out of arm's reach. A bruise had formed on her forehead, and her face was grimed and sooty.

"I thought you were dead," Topher said.

Isa shook her head.

He nodded at the hole in the wall.

"How did you know?"

She turned and looked at it.

"You got lucky."

Yep. That was the way this worked.

"Where's Zorn?" Saanvi asked. "Is he here? Did he?"

Topher didn't respond at first, but finally, to stop her from asking any more questions, he shook his head.

He gestured at the pile, the body parts.

"Oh," she said, and let her head hang. She spotted something in the debris. "What's that?"

Oh dear lord, Topher thought. *Will she ever shut up!* Finally the rage he'd been trying to summon formed in his chest and spread to his limbs. He was about to scream, about to slam Saanvi's face repeatedly, turn it into a bloody pulp, but the thing she'd noticed in the debris caught his attention, too. He knelt down to get a better look.

It was a hand, a regular human hand, and it was slowly waving at them.

Topher jogged down the hall, steering around piles of ceiling tiles and chunks of concrete, looking for Gertrude's door.

"Gertrude? Or Kenneth? Whichever you remember?"

Machine gunfire echoed in the distance. The Ton was doing its work. He wondered how many creatures they had had to kill, how many of his own men had been cut down. Surely the hospital staff, all those horrible people who helped run the whole enterprise, the kitchen workers, the janitors, the doctors, had fled the building by this point. Perhaps some would join his group.

"Gertrude!"

Down the hallway, a door cracked open and a figure shuffled out, tall, bald, an expression of pure, unadulterated nothingness on its face. Gertrude. He was coated in white dust, just like everybody else, and he didn't look particularly well, but he was alive. Topher breathed a sigh of relief.

"Gertrude, thank God you're okay. I was beginning to—"

Nurse Smith came out behind him, pressing a syringe filled with green liquid to his neck. Her uniform was splotched brown and black. Her hair tumbled out of her hat, which, for the first time, sat askew on her head.

"Ah," she said. "How nice to see you."

"You're not dead."

"No. Not dead. Far from it, in fact."

"Nice syringe."

"Thank you."

He took a step forward and she pressed it a little deeper into Gertrude's neck, breaking the skin.

"I'll do it," she said. She started to back down the hall, peeking over Gertrude's shoulder.

Topher put up his hands.

"There's nowhere to go. My people are here. This whole thing, whatever it was, it's over."

The building shook, and she ducked, glancing at the ceiling.

"You people are animals."

She stumbled on some fallen ceiling tiles. More gunfire, another explosion.

"We can help," Topher said.

She scoffed.

"Why would you help me?"

"Because. It's what you're supposed to do."

Something changed in her face. She gave him a look he'd never seen before. He couldn't read it. Was it pity? No. Sadness? No. All he knew was that she softened. Just a little bit. Then the old coldness crept back in.

"Are you implying that I'm guilty of something?"

"No, of course not."

"That I'm evil?"

Topher didn't respond. She continued to retreat, guiding Gertrude as she picked her way back.

"The only thing you're supposed to do anymore is survive."

"You don't have to hurt him. Just let him go, okay? I won't follow."

A sneer formed on her lips.

"Do you think I'm really that stupid?"

"No."

"Don't patronize me."

"Okay."

"What did you do to Tre?"

"I didn't do anything."

"I said don't patronize me!"

"He's dead."

"You killed him."

"No, Shawn did."

She stumbled again, throwing out her arms for balance, and just like that, Gertrude spun and grabbed her by the throat and picked her up off the ground. She plunged the syringe toward him but he knocked her arm away and it hit the floor and cracked open and the green liquid oozed out. Then he squatted down, drawing her face right up to his, peering into her bulging eyes as her face turned pink, then red, then maroon. He turned it to the left, to the right. What was he looking for? Fear? Hate? Surprise? Remorse? Whatever it was, he didn't seem satisfied. He threw himself up and out of the squat, launching her away, and she flew through the air, hit the far wall, and crashed to the ground. She lay there, sprawled and motionless, like a broken doll.

Gertrude remained in position, a Greek statue, flexed and rigid. Topher hurried over.

"Gertrude?"

Gertrude didn't move. Didn't acknowledge him. Topher reached out and put his hand on his friend's arm. It lowered, slowly.

"Come on, Gertrude. Come with me."

Gertrude let himself be escorted away. They went to the closest intersection where Topher put him up against the corner. He brushed off his pajamas and robe. Patted him on the shoulder. Then he looked back at Nurse Smith.

"Stay here, Gertrude. I'll be right back."

He didn't know why, but he couldn't leave her there. After everything she'd done, after all the havoc she wreaked, he felt the need to forgive her. People were desperate. Some, like Rasheed, nailed women to poles. Some, like Nurse Smith, founded creepy hospitals and turned human beings into weird, green monsters. Even he had done some pretty horrible things, though not quite as horrible as that. Which was why he found himself standing over her, waiting for her to come around.

The sounds of battle had moved on, leaving a horrible silence in its wake. Nurse Smith coughed and opened her eyes, but she didn't move. She just lay there, stunned, alone, defeated. Topher extended his hand.

"Come with us."

She looked at it for a second, and for a second he thought she might take it. Then she reached up and slapped it away.

"Rot in hell. We had it perfect here and you ruined it."

Topher didn't know what to do. Part of him wanted to feel sorry for her, but another part was repelled by what he saw. If she were a child, maybe it could have been cause for alarm. Now it was just sad and pathetic.

"Have it your way," he said.

He turned to leave and ran right into Gertrude. He just stood there, staring at Nurse Smith with that blank expression of his. Topher touched his shoulder.

"Come on," he said.

But Gertrude wouldn't move. Just kept staring at her. Topher pulled on his robe and he resisted, like a dog pulling against a leash.

"Gertrude, let's go," Topher said. "Come on."

Gertrude's mouth worked, and for a second Topher thought he was going to say something, but no words came out. Then he tugged one last time and the spell was broken. Gertrude turned and allowed himself to be led away.

Back in the hallway near the truck, Saanvi and Isa had propped Zorn up against one of the tires. Blood coated his robe. Isa was helping him drink from her canteen. He swallowed a little, coughed it up. It cleaned a swath down his chin and neck. He looked up and saw Gertrude.

"Gertrude. Thank goodness," he said. Then, to Topher, "Did you find her?"

Topher thought for a moment. He looked at Gertrude, a cataleptic monolith. He looked around at the destruction, at the semi, at Isa and Saanvi.

"Yes."

"Well?"

"Well, what?"

"Did you kill her?" Topher didn't answer. "Tell me you killed her. Tell me you made her pay for what she did."

Topher opened his mouth like he was going to say something, but stopped and closed it.

"Topher!"

"Fine. I killed her. I made her pay for what she did."

Zorn relaxed.

"Did she suffer?"

Topher thought for a second.

"Immeasurably."

Before they left, they burned all the bodies.

James Noll

LIAM CHRIS

The days were warm. This he knew. He had a heart and a brain. This he knew. He knew how to eat and how to wash. He knew how to walk and how to take care of his waste. He knew that he'd come a long way because, well, because he was no longer lost in the fog, standing outside himself, watching others do those things for him. He also knew the anger, the rage, the bloodlust that bubbled up inside, bloodlust that, were he not so blank and numb, he would have a difficult time suppressing.

They traveled endlessly. He watched the trees as he rode along, first west, then south, then east. He liked to listen to the sounds of the horses, the clop of their hooves on the asphalt, their snorts and whinnies. He liked the feel of the sun on his face. One time they left him out for too long and it burned his skin, and he even liked that. The wind blew and he was cool. The night came and he slept. When there was food, he ate. When there was water, he drank. At some point, he realized that the carriage he was riding in belonged to the man with the curly black hair, the one who was always dressed in the white suit. White. He knew that color. More colors came to him in time.

Sometimes he woke up screaming, a strobe-light of blood and teeth and pale faces still in his head. Nobody came to calm him, bring him a glass of water, tell him it was okay. Why would they? Too many other people also woke up screaming. When he couldn't scream anymore he would sit in the dark, blinking, trying to remember who he was and where he was and why he was, but he could never figure it out. Then he'd lie down and cry himself to sleep and wonder why he was crying.

Sometimes snippets of the past returned to him. He was at a zoo being attacked by a gibbon. He was standing in front of a burning house, sirens peeling in the distance. He was in the payload of a bouncing pickup truck, his hands bound by zip ties. He was in a dark tunnel beneath a river, a mountain of jelly with eyes and rows of teeth blocking his way. Sometimes he saw other terrors: malformed wolves, walking dead, children with silver eyes holding dangerously sharp pencils. Sometimes the man with the curly black hair was there. Sometimes he wasn't. Who was he? How was he in his dreams?

Topher tried not to look at Gertrude too much. It was too disheartening. He had hoped his friend would recover as rapidly as Zorn, but it didn't happen. All he did was sit and stare, sit and stare. Not that Topher was able to do anything more than recover from the trauma himself. In fact, when he thought about it, the only real difference between the two of them was that he was aware of himself.

He knew he should be out there, giving orders, making plans, but for now he let Isa do it. He needed some time, some time to think. His body was healed, he was sure of it, despite the poison Nurse Smith had pumped into him and the toxic food they shoved down his throat. It took some adjustment, going from the sedentary lifestyle he experienced at the hospital to the constant hiking and weary wandering of the post-apocalyptic nomad. The sun was brighter and hotter than he remembered, and while he used to expose himself to it for hours at a time (without his hat on!), now he could barely tolerate the heat. It only took a few minutes before he'd sweated through his suit jacket, and his temples started to throb with the beginnings of a migraine, and he had to flee to the bench seat of his SUV.

If his body was barely healing, his mind felt little better. Anxiety hounded him, a relentless treadmill of worry and doubt. He tried to sleep, but the nightmares invaded, images of what he'd seen and done at the hospital. Monsters and teeth, buckets of blood. During his waking hours, he would suddenly panic for no reason, often curling up on the floor of the SUV, waiting for Nurse Smith to barge in and do something to him. But he was getting better. Little by little.

Isa made it easy.

People still flocked to her, adored her. At night, after they set up camp, ringing the vehicles and posting sentinels, they gathered around her at the fire. She listened to their problems, played with the children. She did not discriminate against any gender or age. It was sexual and asexual. The men seemed the most immediately affected by her, and Topher noted the growing number of pregnant women. But they never seemed to lust for her specifically, and she neither encouraged nor discouraged their affections. The women, however jealous they were at first, often became her most ardent followers. They listened to her every word, sought out her advice. Isa herself took no lover, but Topher did notice that Saanvi was almost constantly in her company. Out of everyone, she seemed to have utterly transformed the most. He liked what he saw. No longer was she the uncertain, shy, wallflower he once knew. In her place there blossomed a confident, poised, beautiful young woman.

And it was all because of Isa.

One day, as Isa guided them farther and farther east, he and Zorn retreated to the SUV for a nap. Topher fell asleep immediately, but once Zorn saw Gertrude, his mind started to race with worry, and he couldn't even think about resting. He watched his friends sleep for a while, then, discouraged, looked out the window. That was no better. He kept on seeing something that bothered him. It was carved into an old, rotting billboard advertising a gentleman's club, spray painted on the highway. After thirty minutes, he said, "six."

Topher roused himself with a deep breath and stretched.

"Huh?"

"Six. I've seen six of them."

"Six of what?"

"Six groups of those symbols. The ones from before. They come in threes. Look, there's another."

Topher looked out the window, and sure enough, there were three huge, ornate ankhs spray painted on the side of an overturned conversion van, arranged feet to feet, like a triangle.

"The symbol of Isis," he said.

At the sound of the goddess's name, Gertrude's lips twitched.

Zorn said, "Did you see that?"

"See what?" Topher asked, following his gaze. "Did he drool again? Fascinating."

"He smiled. Just then, when you mentioned Isis, he smiled."

"Even more amazing. About as amazing as your spiky head."

Zorn ran his hand over his scalp. Ever since Topher told him he looked like a porcupine fetus, he'd grown very sensitive about it.

"It was more like a twitch in the corner of his mouth," he said. "Just the slightest movement but movement all the same."

Topher eyed Gertrude. He was as much of a monolith as ever. He sighed and turned away. The rhythmic clop of horse's hooves filled the air, and every now and then a breeze filtered into the cabin, bringing with it the smell lilac and honeysuckle. Spring was here. Could the Earth be on the mend? Maybe they should find a place where they could farm? Or would a mountainous area be better, easier to defend, someplace near a river? Would there be fish? Deer? Would the water run clean and clear? He looked at Gertrude again.

C'mon. Twitch.

Twitch, you sonofabitch. Raise an eyebrow. Wiggle your nose. Anything but drool, anything but drool.

A line of drool ran down Gertrude's chin.

Dammit!

"It's nothing," Topher said.

"But maybe this means he's coming back?"

"You're projecting."

Zorn sat back and crossed his arms.

"I have to believe he's getting better."

"He was there a lot longer than we were."

"I know."

"We still don't know what those drugs were. They could have permanently brain damaged him. Maybe we don't want him to come back. Maybe he's a psychopath now."

Zorn didn't say anything.

"How are you feeling?" Topher asked. "Better?"

"I guess. I don't know what the measurement is for feeling better."

"Well, when's the last time you went into a murderous rage and ripped off someone's arm?"

"I see your point."

"Plus, your hair is growing back."

"If you compare me to a porcupine again, I'll rip off something more valuable than your arm."

"You mean my cock? Dear Lord, Zorn. Don't rip off my cock. I need that to piss. And fuck."

Zorn smiled. He didn't want to, but he couldn't help it.

Topher, heartened, said, "There's the Zorn I know."

"It wasn't funny."

"No, but this is."

And before Zorn could stop him, Topher removed his shoe and slapped Gertrude's head.

Zorn said, "Topher, stop." Topher did it again. "That's not funny."

"I'm not trying to be funny."

He hit him again.

"Stop."

"Make me."

He hit him again, and then it was there, the anger, the violence, the energy. It shot up and filled Zorn's soul.

"I said stop!"

"I said make me!"

He hit him again.

"Bastard!" Zorn cried, and lunged across the seat, wrapped his hands around Topher's neck, and pressed his thumbs into his windpipe.

On top of the car, sitting in the carriage seat they'd bolted into the metal, Saanvi frowned. The car was rocking, but she didn't remember Topher entertaining any of his usual favorites. In fact, none of the women had visited him since his return. Even stranger was the fact that he hadn't complained. If he suddenly reverted and started up the practice again, would Isa put a stop to it? Isa was firm and strong, there was no doubt about that, but she also encouraged the people to love one another in as physical a way as possible, and the people, reveling in her attention, complied. Saanvi herself had been at the center of that attention, and as she recalled Isa's voice and Isa's touch and Isa's smell, she realized that she was caressing her own neck.

Inside the van, Zorn strangled Topher with one hand and slapped around on the floor for the fallen shoe with the other. He found it, picked it up, and raised it over his head. He was going to smack him in the face with his own shoe. He was going to smack him in the face with his own shoe and choke him to death. It would be so satisfying, the irony, the justice. He felt like Goliath and Sampson and Hercules all rolled into one. Topher's face turned red, then purple. His eyes bugged out and he gargled and gasped, his hands slapping weakly, and Zorn gathered his strength for the blow, one of many to come, feeling his muscles contract, feeling the power surge through the tissue, but right when he was about to bring the shoe down, right as he was ready to strike, something caught his wrist. He craned his head around to look and gasped.

It was Gertrude.

He was still staring out the window, still drooling, but his arm was as rigid as stone. Zorn's grip on Topher's neck loosened, and Topher shoved him off, coughing and hacking.

"See!" Zorn cried. "He's back!"

Topher sputtered some more, took in deep, whooping gasps of air. When he was able to breathe without feeling like he was going to vomit, he said, "Zorn. You're an idiot."

"What? You saw that. He stopped me from hitting you with your own shoe. And killing you."

Topher swatted his head as hard as he could, which was to say not very hard at all.

"You mean like when he stopped Tre from killing Shawn? Remember when that happened? A few months ago?"

He fell into another fit of coughing.

Zorn sought for something in Gertrude's eyes, anything, a sign of comprehension, of understanding. He wanted his old friend back, his sensitive old friend who worried about other people, who cared about small animals, who cried at silly television dramas, but Gertrude didn't blink, twitch, or fidget; he didn't do anything but sit there, arm sticking out like a metal beam, Topher's shoe still gripped in his hand. Topher snatched it away and shoved his foot back in it.

"You do something that again and I'll be the one cutting off your cock," he said.

He yanked on the door handle and lurched out of the SUV. Isa was there, walking with everybody else, and all of the anger he was feeling toward Zorn transferred to her.

"Isa!" he yelled.

She shaded her eyes to see who was calling her.

Right at that moment, another man, short and pear-shaped, called out to her, too. Topher might not have been offended had she recognized him first. But she didn't. She turned to the other voice, the other man.

"Dennis!" she said, waving him over. "Come here. I want you to meet someone."

Dennis waddled her way, his head bobbing like a buoy. Sweat beads rolled down his face.

"How you doing, little lady!" he said, laughing. He reached out and put his arm around her waist when he finally reached her. "Whew! It's a hot one! But I guess every day's a hot one, huh? Hahahahaha!"

Topher slowed down. He couldn't decide how he felt about the man. That he was happy there was no doubt, but he was too loud, more off-putting than anything else. Especially that laugh. He assumed he meant it to be personable, but—

"Oh, Topher," Isa said. "It's so good to see you out. This is Dennis."

Dennis extended his meaty hand.

"Glad to meetcha. You know, it was touch and go there for a bit. Your people put up a helluva great fight, but if it wasn't for my intel on the layout, they would've been toast."

"Intel?"

"Dennis worked for that horrible woman," Isa explained. "Nurse Smith."

Topher extracted his hand.

"Yeah," Dennis said. "Transport and security. Mostly transport, but my military background gave me some expertise in security. I think that's why she gave me the transport job. I was in the ARMY. Hundred and first. Hooah!"

"Oh."

Dennis hitched up his pants.

"See, the complex wasn't exactly the easiest place to defend. Lotta ins, lotta outs. No real perimeter. More like a maze of buildings, you know. Plenty of high ground on top of each one, but she was too short-staffed to man the positions. Classic Khartoum. Classic Crimea. What a snafu. Situation Normal: All Fucked Up! Hahahaha!"

Topher tried to smile, but it came off more like a grimace.

An uncomfortable silence settled over them as they walked on. It was, as Dennis pointed out, hot. The sun gained strength as the afternoon wore on, burning off the clouds. The whitewashed landscape spread out before them. Topher grew tired again. The confrontation with Zorn had made him angry, and when he burst out of the SUV, he fully intended to rip Isa a new one. Why? He didn't know. He just wanted to. But this Dennis person confused him. Isa favored the man or at least knew his uses, but he was a moron, and Topher found his anger replaced by revulsion.

Isa said, "Isn't this a lovely day?"

Dennis laughed.

"Oh yeah. It's a beaut! You know, I'm awful glad I fell in with you people. A little weird, the way we got all hooked up. Too bad about old Ollie, you know? I mean, he wasn't the friendliest guy around, but me and him went back, you know? Well, not too far back. We just met and all, but I could tell he liked me. And he was a badass, too! Went through a lot. But I guess all of us did. Had twins. Girls. A wife. Lost 'em all. Didn't expect that little black-haired sweetheart to —"

"Dennis, would you mind if Topher and I had a word together?"

"No, of course not. Don't mind me. I mean, I know I talk a lot, so you just tell me if I need to leave, cause—"

"Could you please leave?"

It even shocked Topher. In any other situation, with any other person, such behavior would have been considered terrible manners.

But Isa had a way of saying something like that and getting away with it. Dennis looked like he was about to say something, but then she just smiled at him and it was suddenly okay. Not that a person like Dennis would have thought anything otherwise.

"Oh! Okay! I might have thought you were rude just then, yo! Hahahahaha! A little harsh. Hahahaha! I mean, you called me over. But, yeah, I get it, man. It's okay. It's all good. You got some catching up to do. I mean, if I met some people I knew before, you know, I'd need some time to catch up, too, but I don't know anybody from before, anymore. I guess the only person that close to counts is old Ollie, but that black haired girl—"

"Thank you, Dennis."

"Oh! Hahahahaha! No problem! I'm just gonna walk over here for a while. Met a guy said he was in the Air Force."

He dropped away, and Topher waited until his voice faded into the clopping of the horses and the general din of the caravan before he spoke again.

"Really?"

"We were desperate, Topher. And he had the information we needed. I'd rather have been able to turn his friend."

"'Old Ollie'?"

She smiled.

"It didn't work out."

"Did Saanvi kill him?"

A weight gathered in her features.

"Yes. He forced it. He didn't . . . he underestimated her."

"People always do."

He slowed his pace, and Isa put her hand on his shoulder.

"Are you okay?"

He shook it off.

"I want an update. Where are we?"

"Topher, are you upset?"

He caught himself. He didn't like to see that look in her eye. Like he'd betrayed her. Now his anger totally left him. Yes he was mad, but it shouldn't be directed at her, should it? Of course not. This was Isa. Everybody loved her. He loved her.

"No, no. Of course not. But, have you seen the symbols? The Egyptian ones?"

"It's nothing to worry about."

Topher was about to tell her about the ones he'd seen in Northern Virginia, the ones that said, "When she comes, run," but decided to let it drop. He looked around at the unfamiliar highway. The asphalt was cracked and potholed, more tan than black, and there three narrow lanes on each side separated by a Jersey wall. It was perhaps the bleakest stretch of highway he'd ever seen. There were, of course, vehicles abandoned all over the place, blocking the way, clogging the exits whenever they passed. It slowed them down, having to steer between them. Sometimes they had to stop altogether and use the horses to drag some onto the shoulder in order to clear a path.

"Where are you taking us?" he asked.

She threaded her arm through his, and he felt a little zing.

"Remember when you told Zorn you wanted to see the ocean one last time?"

"How did you know that?"

"A girl has her ways. But you did say it, right?"

"Well, yes. But—"

"That's where we're heading. This is the Jersey Turnpike. We're about thirty miles from 195. We're going to Point Pleasant."

Topher didn't know how to feel. The idea of seeing the ocean did appeal to him, just so long as there weren't any beach cults waiting to tear out their eyes and feed them to whatever ocean gods they'd decided to worship. But he wasn't comfortable at all with the route. The walled median, the woods on either side, made it too easy to be attacked. The back roads would have been a better option. They were less jammed up as a rule, and more often than not they led through deserted towns and strip malls, all of which contained supplies they could scavenge. Another cluster of ankhs, these painted in dripping red on a traffic sign, came into view. Isa leaned into him, put her mouth to his ear, her lips nearly grazing the skin.

"Look. Your bogeyman symbols."

She laughed, not in a mean way, but Topher didn't like the sound of it. Was she teasing him? Maybe. Maybe not. It felt wrong, though, and for the first time since they met, he was a little turned off. It must have shown on his face because she stopped in her tracks. Rather than try to make up for it, she slipped her arm out of his and dropped back without a word, seeking out different company. He watched as she found Dennis, and Dennis made some stupid comment and she laughed and tossed her head back, looking in his direction as if to taunt him.

That night they took shelter in the James Fenimore Cooper rest area. Topher decided to inspect the food van and was shocked at how low it had gotten. Who's job was this? Saanvi's. After a few minutes of stomping around looking for her, he spotted her tent near the edge of woods. He didn't even bother to announce himself, just unzipped the flap and ducked in, saying, "Saanvi, goddamit—"

Someone squealed, he saw flashes of skin, pillows flew, and he said, "Oh, sorry, sorry" and turned to leave but Saanvi said (from beneath her blanket) "it's okay."

He turned around, stooping, eyes averted. Then he heard Isa say, "You can look at us, Topher. We have nothing to be ashamed of."

"If it's okay with you, I'll just stay the way I am."

"Look at me."

"No, thank you."

"Just do it."

He did, and she was sitting up on Saanvi's pallet, hair mussed, cheeks flushed. Saanvi remained under the covers, eyes and nose peeking out.

"What did you want to talk to us about?" Isa asked.

"Well, you, nothing. I mean, I don't mind that you're here, but I just came to, not to interrupt. I didn't mean to, that is."

"Topher. Are you embarrassed?" She shifted, and it was hard for him to maintain eye contact. "Or something else?"

"Isa," Saanvi scolded. "Sorry, sir. Mayor, sir."

"No, it's okay. I, uh." He took a deep breath and tried to center himself. "Saanvi, I just visited the food truck. Did you know we were ridiculously low on everything?"

"Relax, Topher," Isa said. "Everything will work itself out."

"Work itself out? Are you kidding? Do you know how long it took us to build up what we had? How much work that took? That was supposed to last us through the winter. There's less than a month's worth of food left."

Isa laughed.

"What's the point?"

"What's the point? Living. Surviving."

"Yes, but like this? You can't scavenge for the rest of your life. Pretty soon there will be nothing left. And then where will you be?"

"I know that, but I'm not ready to give up. Not yet."

He stopped trying to explain, shocked at what had just come out of his mouth. Was this true? He searched his feelings. Yes. Despite everything he'd been through, the death and disease, the crazy people at the hospital, he really wasn't ready to give up. He really did want to find a new place to call home, where he and everybody else could put down roots, build a life, start civilization anew. Isa covered herself.

She stood up and leaned over and put her hand on his cheek. It was cool and dry. Her eyes were soft and loving.

"It will all be okay soon. I promise."

Topher searched out Zorn and found him setting up their tent next to the SUV.

"You're going to start guarding the food truck."

"What? Me? Why?"

"Isa's just letting everybody walk off with whatever they want. You've got to put a stop to it. We'll be completely dry in a week if this keeps up."

"Isa? Are you sure?"

Topher looked around, making sure there was nobody within earshot.

"Something's wrong."

"What is it?"

"I don't know. I can't put my finger on it. I spoke to her earlier, and something just seemed off."

"Didn't Saanvi post guards?"

"Yes, but they're taking bribes."

"How? Nobody has anything to bribe anybody with."

"Sex, Zorn. They're bribing the guards with sex."

Zorn surveyed the ragged faces of The Ton as they made camp for the night. They were a dirty bunch, with greasy hair and torn clothing. The women were scarred and exhausted; the men sported patchy beards and missing teeth.

"Really? Them?"

"Cock is cock. Pussy is pussy."

So Zorn took up guard duty.

Three hours later, with the sun long set, a woman and a girl approached him, smiling. The woman was at least thirty, but the girl couldn't have been older than nineteen.

"Ladies," he said.

"Hi, I'm Amy," the woman said. She nodded at the girl, who was twisting her hair in her fingers. "This is Katie. You're new, huh?"

Zorn tried to maintain his composure.

"I am."

Katie said, "What happened to Bruce?"

Zorn tried not to look at her.

"He was reassigned."

The women shared a glance.

"Poor Brucie," Katie said. "We really liked him, didn't we?"

"Oh yeah," Amy said. "He was so strong." She patted Zorn's chest. "Not as strong as you, though." Her hand wandered down to his waist, then lower. "Not as big as you at all."

Zorn gulped. Topher was right.

Maybe he could have put a stop to it, maybe he could have taken a deep breath and just said "no," but he didn't want to. He couldn't remember the last time he had sex. He once heard a heroin addict describe what it was like to kick the habit. Other than the sweating and pain and horrible abdominal cramps, she said she experienced a surge in all of her senses. Dope numbed everything. Once it was out of her system, all she wanted to do was taste things, smell things, feel things, but most of all she wanted to fuck. Brushing her nipples when she put on her shirt in the morning gave her an orgasm. Leaning against the corner of a counter sent her bucking. Whatever drugs they'd pumped him full of at the hospital must have had the same effect, because all of the sudden he felt himself twitch and grow hard.

Katie ran her hands over her breasts. Amy unbuttoned her blouse. His breathing grew rapid and rough.

"Please," he whispered.

Amy leaned in, her lips almost touching his, and traced the line of newly sprouted hair from his navel to his pants.

"You're Zorn, aren't you?"

The girl sidled up behind him. He felt her hand on his belly.

"Y-yes."

Amy kissed him, letting her tongue flit in and out of his mouth. Katie rubbed his chest, stood on her tiptoes and nibbled at his ear.

"I love your name," she whispered.

"We heard about what you did at the hospital," Amy said. "You were so brave."

"I-I was?"

"Oh yeah. Isa told us all about it. Me and Katie here just wanted to reward you."

She kissed his chin, his neck. Katie unbuttoned his pants.

"Don't you want us to show you?"

They traveled another ten miles the next day before it started to rain. It came down hard and fast, and they pushed through the best they could, but deluge didn't relent. Then the road flooded and they were forced to stop. That night Zorn swore he wouldn't do it again, but Amy and Katie came back, this time with blankets and a pillow. He learned a few things. One thing that he learned was that Katie liked to gasp Amy's name when she came. Another thing he learned was that there was nothing the two weren't prepared to do, no position too kinky, no act too depraved. They were insatiable, often continuing after he was finished. Later, as they lay on the floor of the nearly empty food truck, sweating, Zorn worried aloud about birth control and babies.

"Don't you worry about that," Katie said. "Now, do you have any more canned peaches left?"

"Of course, my dear. Of course."

Three days later, the road finally cleared up enough for them to move on. At first it was easy going, but after the third mile, Topher started to worry. They passed an exit choked with fallen trees. The next one was filled up with cars. The next one had been cut off by a deep gorge. Five or so miles farther, right next to the Woodrow Wilson Service Area, they were forced to stop by a line of cars blocking both sides of the highway. It was obviously a trap, but everybody was exhausted, and Topher had the feeling that if ordered them to clear the way, there would be a minor revolt. It rained again, albeit briefly, bringing a cool breeze. Steam lifted off the asphalt.

Isa seemed eager to push on.

"Why are we stopping? We're really close."

"What's the rush?" Topher asked.

She touched his arm.

"I just want you to get to the sea, that's all."

Topher considered it. He pulled out a map.

"We're only a few miles from 195, but it's at least another forty miles to the shore from there."

"Oh."

"Everybody looks done for the day, Isa. We should take the rest of the day off and set up here."

"Well, there's a rest station."

Topher looked at the line of cars, looked at the rest station.

How convenient.

At least he didn't see any ankhs or messages urging them to flee for their lives. The woods behind the station looked dangerous, he thought. If there was an attack, it would come from there.

That afternoon while on duty, Zorn decided that if he was going to continue to guard the food truck, he was going to have to try to look as tough as possible. All of the sex he'd been having made him feel warm and relaxed, and he thought that maybe the other men would try to take advantage of him. His softness, that is. To get food, not . . . well, maybe some of them would actually want to take advantage of him that way. Just because the end of the world happened didn't mean all of the homosexuals were oh for God's sake, focus! He leaned back against the door of the truck, but that just made him look tired. Should he cross his arms? Put one foot up? Maybe he'd look tougher if he strapped his gun over his shoulder, you know, like, "oh hey, look at that, I have a semi-automatic rifle on my back." Or should he cradle it in his arms like, "yeah, I got a semi-automatic rifle, what are you gonna do about it?"

He decided on the former.

He flicked dirt off his shirt. If he had hair, he would have run his hands through it. His nose started to itch, so he gave it a good farmer's blow. Good Lord, that made it worse. He swung around to the side view mirror and tilted his head back, trying to see up his nostrils. Then he heard footsteps approach from the parking lot and quickly threw himself back, sucking in a great breath of air when the handle dug into his spine.

Jamal appeared around the corner, followed by Gertrude, and he let the air out of his lungs with a pained whoof.

"You okay, man?" Jamal asked.

Zorn massaged his back, wincing.

"Yes, yes, of course."

"Okay, well, look. I was thinking about taking Gertrude out for a walk in the woods."

"Oh? That sounds like a fantastic idea. Have you run it by Topher?"

"Nah. He's over there jawing with Isa. Looks pretty intense."

"Oh."

"Look, I won't be long. It'll be good for him, you know. Fresh air. Sun." Jamal glanced up at the sky. "Looks like there's some peeking through."

"You're sure he'll be okay?"

"I had a sister. Miracle. She was like Gertrude. We had a creek behind our house and I used to take her for walks down there. She loved it. It was the only time I ever saw her be a part of the world."

Zorn finished rubbing his back and glanced at Gertrude, who was as statuesque and opaque as ever.

"I don't think you'll get that much out of him."

"Can't hurt to try."

He stood there, waiting.

"What do you want?" Zorn asked. "Permission?"

"I guess. He's your friend."

"Okay, well, go ahead."

"You'll tell Topher?"

"I didn't say that."

Jamal thought about it, weighing his options.

"I guess it's easier to beg forgiveness," he said.

He led Gertrude back behind the rest area, picking through the trees and scrub brush, making sure the branches didn't whip him in the face. The leaves were wet from the rain, and their shoes and pants were soon soaked. Gertrude lumbered along, arms hanging loose by his sides. He splashed through the puddles, seeming to marvel at the sights and sounds. They reached a little clearing where the sun peaked out from behind some clouds, and he turned his face to it, letting it warm his skin. Jamal thought he saw a hint of a smile creep up on his lips. He let him stand there for a few minutes, then said, "C'mon," and they pressed through the woods a little farther.

A little country road cut through the wilderness, and Jamal stopped there to pick some ticks off Gertrude's neck before continuing on. They passed some fields filled with corn rotting on the stalks, and then came upon a little stream. Jamal guided Gertrude over to a big rock in the middle of the creek and sat him down, then took off his own shoes and cooled his feet in the water.

"Nothing like cold water on your feet after a long hike, I tell you what." He looked at Gertrude, who sat on the rock, blank. "Yep. Nothing like cold water on your feet."

He leaned over and cupped a handful into his mouth. It had a tang to it, a clean zing, like real water. Ha. "Real" water. He cupped another mouthful. The taste pleased him just as much as the fact that it didn't sting his lip. He never thought the split would heal, but after they rescued Topher, Isa paid him a visit. Sewed it right up.

"Are you going to kill him?" she asked when she was done.

Jamal looked away. He knew she meant Brody. She was right to ask, of course.

"Jamal?"

"Yeah."

"'Yeah,' as in 'Yeah I'm going to kill him'?"

"If I wanted to kill Brody, don't you think I could have done it back there? At the hospital?"

"So you thought about it."

"Yeah."

"Yeah." She put her hand on his cheek. "We can't have any more of that, okay?"

"I know."

"I want your word."

He finally looked her in the eyes.

"Brody's a fool. A scared, angry fool. That's nothing to kill a man for."

He watched Gertrude sunning on the rock.

Poor bastard. Topher said that crazy nurse had done something to him back at that hospital in Philly, tried to turn him into a monster or a zombie. He shook his head. Even before the end of the world, people did crazy things, but for some reason, now that everything was over, it was like the craziest of the crazy had free reign to do whatever they liked. Good thing they had Topher. Good thing they had Isa. He looked at Gertrude again. He hadn't moved. What was going through that guy's head?

Leaf.

That was the word for it.

Leaf.

He splashed across the wet stuff to where the leaf was and reached out and brushed its surface. Tiny hairs, smooth skin shot through with veins.

Green.

Leaf.

It was a green leaf.

He thought about saying the word, thought about forming the letters with his lips and tongue. How do people make the "l" sound? He knew how to think it, but it was difficult to make his mouth comply. His first try made him look like an infant eating peanut butter; his second was no better. But on the third, he said, "Loof!"

No. Not quite right. Try again.

"Leouf!"

Again.

"Leeef!"

Close.

"Leaf!"

There it was.

"Leaf," he said. "This is a leaf."

The ease with which the rest of the words came back to him was startling. He looked around and named everything he could see. Rock. Bird. Wind. Sun. Hand. Cloud. Finger. Foot. Fly. Spider. Web. Then the bad thoughts crept in. Blood. Tear. Rip. Eat. Break. Gut. No! He focused, tried to stop the anger, the visions, the nightmares. He pushed it down, subdued it, built a dam to hold it back and, miraculously, it worked. For the moment. He hoped it wouldn't burst.

Calm now, he splashed back across the wet stuff (water?) and sat on the rock, beaming. The world had meaning again. He loved the sound of the creek (it was a creek!), the water rushing at his feet, the bed fat with the recent rain. He loved the feel of the sun twinkling through the trees. He loved the sight of squirrels scrambling from limb to limb. It must be spring, which would explain the naked woman ripping the throat out of the man to his left.

"Dear Lord!" he cried, and fell off the rock.

She was beautiful, her body full and ripe and round. Her mouth was dripping with blood, which spattered her chest and stomach. The man's hand dropped from her breast, and she looked at Gertrude and said, "We love you."

Maybe this was his mind. Maybe this was one of his dreams. He shut his eyes counted to three, reopened them. Nope. There she was. Mouth still covered in blood. So much of it rushing out of the neck of the poor man at her feet.

Suddenly he realized that he didn't know where he was or how to get to safety. How in the world had he come to be out in the middle of the woods with a cannibalistic nudist? He remembered the hospital and the food and gradually losing his hair. He remembered all that came before, the death and the bombs. And he remembered his life before that, all the way back to his days with Topher and Zorn.

Topher and Zorn. They were here, weren't they? They'd found him, right? He couldn't be sure of anything, but judging by how weird his life with them had been and how weird the current situation was, they had to be somewhere nearby. In fact, now that he thought about it, he was as sure of their proximity as he was sure that he had been a good boy, that he loved to read books, that his mother and teachers adored him, that . . . ha ha! He remembered! He remembered!

His face fell.

Oh God.

He remembered.

He searched the water, frightened, unsure. He needed to escape. He needed a weapon. His eyes were drawn to something strapped to the dead man's back, something long and cylindrical, and dangerous. The naked woman held out her arms to him and took a graceful step forward.

"We love you," she said again.

Her feet cut through the water with musical strides, lips glistening, full and slightly parted, red with blood, that poor man's blood, from his throat, which she had torn out with her own teeth, but my goodness those lips, they were so plump and firm. So luscious. And her breasts, also full and also luscious, and wobbling, and perfect. His eyes wandered down.

"We love you," she said.

She was suddenly only a few feet away. He could easily reach out and touch her. Perhaps she would let him kiss her? Of course the blood was an issue and he'd never kissed a girl before and . . . goodness, this was just like that horrid football game he'd seen once in high school with all of the sex and violence, only as far as he could recall the cheerleaders had remained clothed and had not ripped out the other team's throats with their teeth, although that might have made the game more interesting.

She grabbed his wrist. He wasn't even aware that she'd reached for him. He yanked it free and stumbled onto the bank. She frowned, curious. How could he? Why would he want to? She rubbed one of her breasts.

"We love you," she said, stepping out of the water and onto the grass.

More words came rushing back.

"Stay away," he said.

"We love you."

"Who is we?"

She pointed at the woods behind him. He turned. A dozen men and women dressed in crimson robes emerged from the trees. They spread out in a semicircle and surrounded him.

"We love you," they chanted.

He was trapped.

But instead of panic, something else welled up within him. The anger from before, from his nightmares, from the drugs. He concentrated on the reservoir, letting it build and build.

Zorn shuffled around, bored out of his mind. He glanced at the group sitting in the parking lot, glanced away, glanced back. Most of them were young men and women, some mere teenagers, though there were plenty of older people there, too. Isa seemed to be preaching to them, though it was unlike any church service he'd ever attended. She didn't seem to be judging them or telling them what to think, for starters. Also, nobody was sitting in uncomfortable, wooden pews. Some were lounging on their sides or leaning back on both arms. Heads rested in laps, fingers ran through hair. He couldn't hear what she was saying, but it must have been very encouraging because all of the sudden everybody started to make out. Girls with girls, boys with boys, girls with boys, in twos and threes and fours, Isa beaming down at them the whole time. Then Saanvi approached her from behind and wrapped her arms around her shoulders. Isa accepted them, leaned back and whispered something into her ear. Saanvi nodded and smiled, then kissed her full on the mouth.

"Sweet mama-jama," Zorn said.

A different group stood near the entrance of the service station, frowning and muttering. They were mostly older, middle-aged or heading towards it, their children running and playing in the parking lot, and they were all armed in one way or another. Those who didn't have guns hefted clubs or makeshift maces. Brody exited the station and spoke to some of the frowners. One pointed to the orgy in the middle of the parking lot. Brody took one look and stalked toward it. He barked something, a name perhaps, and a few of the couples stopped kissing and shot panicked glances at him. Saanvi moved away from Isa, her hand trailing to the gun on her hip, but Isa motioned for her to stop. She did, reluctantly, but kept a hard eye on the approaching man, who ignored them both. He headed right for two women who had not stopped kissing. My god! That was Amy and Katie. He yanked Amy up by her hair and smacked her across the face. Katie leaped on his back and he flipped her over. She landed hard on her side and lay still. Amy snapped something at him and he slapped her again. She screamed and raked her nails down his cheek.

And then Isa was there, standing between them. The man backed off.

"How goes the watch?"

Zorn jumped and spun. It was Topher. He hadn't noticed the altercation yet.

"Er, uh, good."

Topher opened the back of the truck and jumped up into the back.

"Christ, Zorn! This is worse than when Bruce was in charge."

Zorn turned his attention back to the fight. At first Brody gestured and jawed, spit flying out of his mouth. More than once he jabbed the gun at Isa, not intending to shoot, but out of anger. Saanvi circled around him, hand on her hip. Isa spoke only a few times, but with each word he seemed to calm down, until he saw Saanvi out of the corner of his eye and immediately turned and trained his gun on her, arm slightly bent. Isa scooted around him and put herself between them, talking to him, reasoning. He didn't say anything, but Isa kept talking.

Then she pointed at Zorn.

Topher jumped back out.

"Where's Gertrude?"

"Jamal took him for a walk."

"A walk? Where?"

"I don't know. The woods."

"The woods?"

Zorn peered around his friend. Amy pulled Katie off the ground. They both approached Brody, pleading, but he wouldn't take his eyes off Zorn. Topher finally noticed what was going on and said, "Have you been fucking Katie?"

Zorn tore his eyes from the fight.

"What?"

"Have you been fucking Katie?"

"How do you know who she is?"

Topher rolled his eyes.

"Please, Zorn. Everybody knows who Katie is."

Brody finally seemed like he'd had enough. He pointed the gun at Zorn, said something to Isa, and Isa nodded. Without another word, he strode away, heading straight for Zorn. His eyes were dead and black.

"Hey!"

"I see you've met Brody," Topher said. "Katie's father."

"Father!"

"He was sleeping with Amy. At least before we were kidnapped."

"Look at me, you fuck!" Brody yelled. "You been fucking my daughter? My girlfriend?"

Zorn waved, a feeble smile on his lips. Topher slapped him on the shoulder.

"Zorn, you dog!"

"Heh heh."

Brody puffed like a steam engine.

"Maybe you could summon your anger?" Topher said. "You know, like when you tried to kill me?"

Momentary hope spread through Zorn's chest, but it was quickly dashed. The sex, blow job after blow job, orgasm after orgasm, drained him of it. And Amy. The way she moved. How on earth could he get angry now? Brody was about fifty yards away. He raised his gun. Zorn raised his and closed his eyes, preparing himself. He wondered if he'd hear the report before the bullet entered his brain. Was this really the way it would end?

"I don't want to die," he said, and then machine gunfire rattled in the morning air and he cried out, but nothing hit him.

He opened his eyes. Brody had stopped and turned around, scanning the trees. Another burst fired, and this time everybody could tell it came from the woods.

Toddlers began to cry. Women scurried, calling for their children. Amy and Katie ran for the shelter of the rest stop building. Isa called out to her group, patting the air with her hands. Rather than running, they stayed put, listening to her.

"Didn't you say Jamal took Gertrude out there?" Topher asked.

Zorn nodded.

"Good Lord, Zorn."

He dashed away.

Brody, who, moments before was intent on killing Zorn, sprinted back to the station, crying out for his girlfriend and daughter. Topher caught up to him and grabbed his shoulder, yanking him to a stop. Brody took a swing and Topher ducked, then popped up and punched him in the face. Brody dropped to the ground, his gun skittering across the pavement. His men all ran up, uncertain as to what to do. They formed a semicircle around the pair. Topher ignored them. He snatched the gun off the ground, then extended his hand. Brody took it and pulled himself off the ground. Topher slapped the weapon into his hand and pointed north, and soon Brody and his men ran off in that direction, disappearing into the line of trees.

Gertrude had been in many fights before. He'd grappled with incubi, throttled werewolves, taken on massive squid monsters. Once he'd been assaulted by a gibbon at the National Zoo, and while it was not technically a fight, he did manage to give it a rather curt shake before it sank its teeth into his flesh.

He had not, however, ever fought a female human being, let alone one that was naked and beautiful. Indeed, he'd only seen a few nude women in his lifetime, usually by accident, like the time Topher found a box of lurid magazines buried in the woods behind their houses. ("Look at this!" he'd cried, shoving the centerfold into Gertrude's face. Gertrude promptly burst into tears. It took an entire week of watching *Brady Bunch* reruns to recover.) That he was chaste at middle age was not much of an issue for him. He'd never felt any real sexual desire outside of the incident at the football game with the hot dog and the cheerleaders. So as he fought off the naked woman with the pointy nipples and blood dripping down her chin, it was with a feeling of partial disgust for what she'd done, partial deference for her nudity, and (admittedly) partial titillation. The latter, however, disappeared entirely the moment she punctured his shoulder with her teeth.

"Good Lord!" he cried, and pulled her head back by her hair.

"We love you!" she said, and punched him in the eye.

He shoved her backward as hard as he could, sending her sprawling into the water. She stayed there a moment, a quizzical look on her face, then rose, languid and poised. She looked over his shoulder at the group that had gathered on the bank behind.

"Tear him to pieces," she said, and calmly turned and walked away.

The others removed their robes, letting them drop to the ground in twelve red puddles. Gertrude leaned over and rested his hands on his knees, pretending to be winded as they inched forward. The man who had escorted him to the woods (Jamal?) lay face down in the stream behind the circle, his boots anchored in the sand. His gun was still strapped to his back. That's what it was called, right? Yes. Gun. No, it was a semi-automatic. Perhaps they'd been out there hunting? No. People didn't hunt with semi-automatics. He surveyed his attackers. All he had to do was break the weakest link. There. She was tall and slim, waif-like, with bony limbs.

"We love you," they chanted, and then the noose cinched close.

The waters of his anger rose. He charged his target and barreled right over her. She clung to his legs for a moment, jaws snapping, and almost succeeded in tripping him up, but he found his strength and balance and he wrenched his leg free, raised his knee to his chest, and stomped on her face, crushing her nose. He stomped again, and again and again until her skull was nothing more than pulp.

One of the men grabbed his shoulder, and the waters boiled to the lip of the dam. Gertrude seized his fingers and bent them backward, snapping them in half. The man crumbled to his knees. Gertrude worked the fingers back and forth, back and forth, then kicked him in the face. Three more threw themselves on him, and he fell under their weight. He covered his head as they pounded away, letting the rage build, letting the sensors spike into the red. The concrete cracked.

"We love you!" they cried.

And that was it. It reminded him too much of the hospital, of Nurse Smith's repeated assurances that "this was best for him," and that she "only wanted to make him better."

The dam exploded.

He threw his attackers off and leaped to his feet, pure adrenaline rushing through his veins. One man stepped forward and he grabbed him by the throat, crushed his windpipe, tossed him aside. Another leaped for him and he caught him in midair, slammed him to the ground. A third jumped him from behind, put him in a headlock. Gertrude stomped on his bare foot, elbowed him in the teeth, and broke his wrist. The remaining seven paused, stunned, giving him the break he needed. He scrambled for Jamal's gun, tried to yank it free, but the strap caught something and stuck.

"We love you!" they said.

Gertrude turned and half-sat, anchoring the stock in the sandy bank. He clicked the safety off and pulled the trigger, sending a burst of bullets at them. He missed at first, but then two were hit right in the chest, another in the stomach. Another burst, and another one went down, her knee shattered. The air cleared. Silence fell. The last three cowered on the ground, awaiting their doom. He pulled the trigger again, but the gun jammed, and they looked up.

"She will get you," one said.

Gertrude bared his teeth.

They stood up now, unafraid.

As one they said, "When she comes, run."

And they turned and fled.

Gertrude dropped the gun into the creek with a disgusted grunt. There was a buck knife in a leather sheath on Jamal's belt.

That would do.

That would do just fine.

Topher dashed for the woods, followed close behind by Zorn. Everyone else had taken refuge in the service station, and Topher didn't blame them. Isa was a part of it. He knew it in his bones. That scene in the parking lot worried him. People were acting strangely. Zorn caught up to him a few hundred yards into the woods.

"You should have stayed back there," Topher said.

"If Gertrude's in trouble, I want to help."

"Fine."

They followed the same path as Jamal and Gertrude, crossed the same back road, saw the same rotting cornfield. They stopped when they came across the dead bodies in the creek. Topher toed one.

"Cut to ribbons."

Zorn let the water roll over his boots, staring at the only clothed body. He dragged it onto the bank, turned it over.

"Jamal."

He stared back at them, sightless, an expression of pain frozen on his face.

"His throat's been torn out."

Topher kicked at one of the corpses.

"This one has blood smeared all over her mouth."

Zorn looked around. So much blood. So much carnage. He recognized the rage. He recognized the art. He'd felt it himself at one point. He squatted over some muddy footprints in the bank, followed them to the tree line.

"I didn't know you could track," Topher said.

"I can't." Zorn pointed at the mud, the clear footprints in the grass. "It's kind of hard to miss."

They found the next dead body a few hundred yards into the woods. It was naked, lying face down in a little clearing.

Topher jammed his hands under its torso to flip it, but Zorn said, "Stop!"

Topher did.

"What if it's been booby-trapped?"

Topher thought for a second, then said, "Too late now." He flipped it over anyway, and Zorn screamed and held up his hands to block the blast, but nothing happened. He unclenched his eyes.

"Her throat's been slit," he said.

"Which means Gertrude's alive and functional." Topher examined the wound. It went so deep that her head had been nearly cut off. "Very functional."

They continued more cautiously, wary of an ambush. Their footsteps chunked and thudded through the dry leaves, sending an occasional bird or critter skittering through the trees. They passed two more bodies, one decapitated, the other gutted and pinned to the tree with the largest buck knife Zorn had ever seen.

"She looks pleased."

Topher examined the knife.

"This was Jamal's."

By the time they broke into the next clearing, they were sweaty and exhausted. A man stood at the edge of a cliff, his back to them. Bald, gigantic. Gertrude.

They approached him cautiously, peeking into the little valley below. A perfect idyllic image. Overgrown fields, a couple of farmhouses, barns, old dirt roads wending away into the distance. Topher wondered if Gertrude would recognize anybody, if he'd finally come back to himself. Or would he see everything as a threat, something to maim and gut?

He took a chance.

"Gertrude?"

Gertrude spun. His face was nearly black with blood, his chest and legs slick with it, his eyes white and wide and terrible. Zorn fell back into a crouch, ready to defend himself, but Topher said, "Wait."

Gertrude's studied them, deciding. No robes. These were safe. He beckoned them forward and they came, and when they reached the edge, he pointed down. Suddenly they weren't so worried about him anymore.

Gertrude took up the rear. He stopped at the woman pinned to the tree and wrenched the knife out and the body slumped to the ground. He gripped the knife in his hand, held it in front of him as he walked, his white eyes prowling the woods, alert, paranoid. They stopped at the creek to retrieve Jamal's semi-automatic. A few of the corpses were already stirring, so Gertrude shoved the knife in each brain. Zorn scooped up one of the robes and investigated the tags

"Huh."

"What?"

He turned it inside out and showed it to him. The tag read "Property of Tom's River Hilton Express."

The service station looked deserted when they finally made it back. Not a soul in sight. Had he not seen the horses and the food truck, Topher might have thought that Isa had run off. Just as he was thinking this, she came out of the front doors of the station, Saanvi close behind.

"What's happening?" she asked.

Topher told her about the massacre at the creek, how Gertrude had been attacked by a dozen naked psychopaths. He told her about the mob in the valley.

"They were lined up in a pattern. That ankh we've been seeing, all of them roiling and running through it. It looked like a tremendous waste of time and energy. There were at least two hundred of them."

"No," Zorn said. "Five hundred."

Isa took the robe from Zorn and slapped the dirt and mud and dead grass off it.

"A thousand," she said.

"I don't think—"

"A thousand. It's always a thousand."

Topher watched as she folded the robe.

"Exactly one thousand. How could you possibly know this?"

He could tell she meant it to be shocking, but couldn't figure out why. They were just another mob of idiots. Sure there were a lot of them, but they didn't even look dangerous. The red costumes were a little unnerving he supposed, but he hardly equated terry cloth with death hordes. If anything, they made him wonder where they were able to get the dye.

Isa said, "Remember on the barrier just outside Philly?"

"Philly?"

"I asked her how she got caught," Zorn said. "And she was telling us about the people she was with before, right?"

Isa held the robe against her chest.

"This is them."

"You were one of them?" Topher said.

She nodded.

"She's a monster."

"Who is?"

"She doesn't have a name. She just is."

Topher snorted. Isa tilted her head.

"You know, you're very similar to her, Topher."

"I don't surround myself with bloodthirsty cannibals."

"No. But there's something about you two. You attract people. They listen to you. They want to impress you."

Zorn said, "I'm sorry, are you talking about Topher?"

"When she first found me, it was just her and a few others," Isa said. "She was so charismatic, so beautiful. She promised to keep us safe, just like you did. She promised us that we were meant for greater things, just like you did. My husband was smitten from the start. I should have seen that. But my son, he was only thirteen. I had to protect him, and she offered her help. She fed us that night. The first meat we'd had in months."

She shook her head.

"Within a week, there were a hundred of us. Then three hundred. Everybody was loved, constantly. So much love."

"I think I see where this is going," Topher said. "Please don't tell me you let your son join in."

"The children stayed elsewhere. But me and the others, we did. Every night. It was intoxicating, sharing everything that way. It was weird if you didn't, like you were denying the group something vital. It went on for weeks, and it felt so natural, so what she asked us to do next felt more like an outpouring of the love.

"We hunted all day long together, one great mass. First she wouldn't let us wear anything, but it didn't work as well as we thought. We were just a mass of flesh. Naked freaks. People laughed at us, fought back harder when they realized what was going on. It was my idea to wear the robes. It was so simple. A uniform. We were intimidating, a wave of red sweeping down from out of nowhere. They didn't laugh anymore. They didn't fight. They ran. But they never ran fast enough."

"Can't we just sneak away?" Zorn said. "I mean, they're down in that valley and we're on the interstate."

Isa said, "You don't understand. There's no way out of this."

"No way out of what?" Topher asked. "They're morons in robes."

For the first time since they'd rescued her, Isa seemed to lose her cool.

"Didn't you listen to a thing I just said? They'll kill us. They'll kill all of us."

"Isa, calm down. They didn't see us. Gertrude killed any of the ones that might have raised an alarm."

"No. He didn't kill them all. You said there were only twelve bodies."

"So?"

"That was a scouting squad. She sends her best and strongest to find other groups, other people, to test the area, to decide whether or not to assimilate."

"And Gertrude killed a dozen of them. A dozen of her 'best and brightest'."

"And there are always thirteen."

"Oh."

"She knows everything," Isa said. "She knows exactly where you are. She knows exactly how many of you there are. She knows how much food you have, how many guns you have, how much ammo."

"I can't see how that's possible."

"She knows."

"They're northeast of here, right? We'll just turn around, head south, break off to the west?"

Isa started shaking her head the moment he spoke.

"They've already blocked all the exits. You saw it. It's a trap."

Topher thought for a moment.

"So maybe you're right. Maybe this is a trap. The rest stop has a roof. If they come for us, we'll just pick them off and wait them out."

"We don't have enough, Topher, and she knows. She'll just keep throwing more and more of them at us until we're out of ammo. And then that's it."

"We have more weapons than guns. We have knives and shovels, bats."

"That won't do anything when they swarm you."

"It'll do enough."

A roar sounded up from the north, and Isa sent a panicked look at the sky,

"Oh god. They're coming. They're coming."

"Isa, it'll be okay."

"No, it won't. What do you think is going to happen?"

"A fight. A battle. I've seen a lot, you know. And I keep winning."

"Not this time. When they catch you—"

"They eat you," Zorn finished.

Topher looked at him, surprised.

"How do you know?"

"Shawn told us, remember? Back at the hospital? He said something about this. About the red robes. 'Have you ever seen a man eaten alive?'."

Topher paused, shocked, suddenly remembering.

"That's what happened to Jamal," Zorn said. "Topher, what are we going to do?"

"I don't know. Let me think."

"We can't just do nothing."

"Let me think!"

Another roar from the north, closer this time, followed by the distant pop of handguns. Gertrude's head snapped toward the gunfire and he sprinted off, knife flashing in the sun.

"Gertrude!" Zorn called after him, but he disappeared into the brush.

"There's no time," Isa said. "She's here."

She was wrong.

The gunfire they heard was from Brody and his friends. They came limping out of the woods, their faces streaked with blood, their clothes shredded. Only three of them. Gertrude was with them, his knife and arms and torso covered in fresh gore.

"Where are the rest?" Topher asked.

Brody shook his head.

"Didn't make it."

"There were at least ten of you."

"They had more."

"How far out are they?"

"Half mile. They caught us in the woods. They were just there all of the sudden. Hundreds of them. Circled around us. Just kept coming. We emptied everything we had." He gestured at Gertrude. "He got us out. I've never seen anything like it. They couldn't stop him, no matter how many swarmed. He cut them to pieces." He took a deep breath and composed himself. "If he hadn't showed up, we would have died. All of us."

Topher ordered the children, the weak, and the old, to the roof of the rest stop, saddling them with as much food as they could carry and whatever guns and ammunition he could spare. The rest pulled the vehicles around in front to form two semi-circles around the entrance. He hid the horses inside. Isa watched.

"Why not use them?" she asked. "You need all the help you can get."

"The horses? We've tried the cavalry approach. We work better this way."

"No. The children."

Topher gaped at her.

"I'm not putting children down here."

"They're going to die anyway. They're going to see what happens to you, to their parents. They're going to know what's coming for them. It's cruel."

"I'm not putting children down here!"

She shrugged and wandered off.

Topher gave Zorn a look.

"See what I mean?"

"Yes. She's . . . that's not okay."

They took position behind the SUV. The rest of the men spread out along the innermost ring. Some had guns, some had spears, some just had knives. They stared grimly at the horizon. Isa sat on one of the benches in front of the rest station, stunned, silent, staring off into space. Zorn watched her as he loaded a shotgun.

"Do you think she'll be okay?"

"Does it matter? According to her, we're all dead anyway."

The crimson robes drew nearer, their shouting clearer. Three words, over and over again.

"What are they saying?" Zorn asked.

"It sounds like they're saying 'We love you'."

"We love you?"

"I don't think it's meant to make you feel good."

The cry came up again. "We love you! We love you!"

Zorn blanched.

"It works."

The enemy formed on the highway, first as a line on the horizon spanning all three lanes, men and women in crimson robes. More filled in behind them, hundreds more, and even more flowed in from the woods on either side, all of them chanting the words over and over, "We love you! We love you!"

Isa hugged her middle and started to rock back and forth. The children on the roof wept. Topher thought the cars would slow the enemy down, and he laughed at the irony of them getting caught in their own trap. But when the mob encountered one they swarmed it and pushed it aside as if it were nothing more than a toy.

He rested his gun on the hood of his SUV, and his people, those who still had guns and ammunition, did the same. The red robes marched closer, a solid mass. Isa was right. The whole thing was terrifying. The chanting robbed him of the ability to think; the sea of red stole his courage. Another roar came up, this time from the south. He turned and saw another army of red thronging the highway. There was no escape. They poured into the rest stop parking lot.

He yelled, "Fire at will!" and the world exploded. Red robes dropped, holes formed in the ranks, but more filled the gap and the mob marched on.

"We love you! We love you!"

So this is it, Topher thought. *This is finally it.*

They crested the first ring. He squeezed his trigger until there were no more bullets left, until the sound of gunfire all around him was swallowed by their maniacal chants. He was just about to throw his gun at them when a high-pitched whine filled his head, like someone had smashed a cymbal right next to his ear. His peripheral vision went black, and he grabbed his head and sank to the ground, his back against the car frame.

"Get up!" Zorn cried, still firing. "Are you hit? Are they firing something?"

Topher only managed a groan.

"My head."

The whine dissipated and the blackness receded, leaving him with a massive headache. Was that a migraine? Christ, of all the times.

The cannibals leaped over the second ring, and then suddenly she was there, Isa, standing on top of a car in the middle of it all. She was tall and magnificent, her long hair flowing, all of the pain and worry drained from her face. She'd put on the robe, the one Zorn found in the woods. The enemy stopped, whispering amongst each other.

"It's her," Zorn could hear them say. "It's Isa. It's the goddess."

Nothing stirred. A slight breeze shook the leaves in the trees. A child wailed from the roof.

Isa opened her arms to her people.

"My children!" They stared at her, enraptured. "I love you!"

And the chant came up in reply, thousands of voices crying, "We love you! We love you!"

She looked out over her flock, eyes glinting.

"I am your mother. I have cared for you. I have fed you. You are mine."

"We love you! We love you!"

She waited for the last of the words to die out. Then she turned and searched Topher's people, her eyes finally settling on Saanvi.

"Come, Saanvi."

Saanvi did as she was told, took her place next to her. They held hands.

"We have crossed the paths of people who were unworthy. Men and women who raped women, who tortured children, who slaughtered and killed and maimed for pleasure. We have given them what they deserved."

Her children roared in approval.

As soon as Topher stood up, another high-pitched whine spiked through his temples, and he leaned heavily against the SUV. He saw shadows lurking in the woods, lupine and hairy. A pack. Hunting them. At a signal from one of the leaders, the shadows dropped to the ground.

Isa continued.

"But these are not such people. I have tested them. I have been among them. I know." Her children looked confused, trying to balance the attack with what their goddess told them. Some beamed, beatific, forgiving. A few mouthed their words.

Isa said, "When the false god took me, these people came to my aid. When I needed medicine, these people gave it to me. When the heretics corrupted the world with their spawn, these people fought them."

Amidst the roar of approval, the shadows in the woods moved again, dozens of them, loping together, their eyes glowing red.

My god, Topher thought. *Are those werepyres? Could it be?*

"These men are your brothers!" Isa cried. "Their women are your sisters! Their children are your children!" She flung back her robe, exposing her naked body, scarred and pocked with old wounds. "I am your mother! I am your goddess! And I say it is so!"

The whistling sound returned, only this time it came from above, like something had been fired at them. Isa heard it, too, and she frowned, searching the sky.

"What is that?" Zorn asked, and then the missile struck.

It blasted a hole in the front line of the northern mob. Chunks of dirt and flesh rained down all around them. Topher threw himself to the ground. Three more explosions struck the ring, sending Isa flying through the air. She landed in a heap. Saanvi screamed and leaped for her.

The things in the woods shot out into the open, scattering Isa's people. Zorn went down. Gertrude went down. Topher tucked himself into fetal position. He spotted Isa lying flat on her back, arms spread, head turned in his direction. There was a hole in her stomach. Saanvi kneeled at her side, weeping. Then a mortar shell exploded nearby and she was gone. Isa's green and blue eyes focused on him and she smiled. A little line of blood trickled out of the corner of her mouth.

"We love you," she said.

And then she was still.

They were soldiers, not wolves. Fully armed. Machine guns, hand grenades, BAR guns, mortars. The fur Topher thought he saw was camouflage. Sticks and branches. When the attack was over, the soldiers rounded up the survivors—Topher's people, the remaining members of the blood cult, the women and children on the roof—and marched them out to the interstate and shoved them to their knees in front of a pile of the dead they'd massed on the median. The soldiers sprayed pile with gas and set it on fire. A black plume wafted into the air, followed by the stench of burning hair. Topher let his chin rest on his chest. Saanvi was in that pile. Isa. Where were Zorn and Gertrude?

A lone soldier swaggered down the line.

"I'm Sergeant Jason Mills. You're under my protection. Do what I say and nobody else dies." He strolled along the line. Children cowered, sniveling. Men and women stared at the asphalt. "Which one of you is Topher?"

Nobody moved. He yanked a woman up by her hair.

"Topher?"

The children kneeling at the woman's feet began to wail.

"Please," she said.

He put a knife to her throat.

"I'm not going to ask again."

"I'm here," Topher said, but Mills didn't hear him. He pressed the knife down and the woman began to scream.

Topher yelled, "I'm here!"

Mills stopped. Another soldier jerked Topher to his feet.

Mills said, "You're Topher?"

"Let her go."

"I'll need to verify your identity first. You answer correctly, she's free."

"Okay."

Mills motioned, and two soldiers pulled two men out of the line. They were beaten and bloodied, their mouths gagged, their arms tied behind their backs.

"Who are these men?"

"Michael Zorn and Kenneth Hughes."

"Why were you sent to Raleigh's Prep?"

"For murder and arson."

"That's not good enough. You have one more chance. Who did you murder?"

Topher clenched his jaw. Could he say it? Could he admit to that heinous crime, the thing he hadn't thought about in years? He saw the confusion on the faces of the people who had followed him up and down the east coast. Some he'd known from The Ton. Some he'd picked up along the way. He knew what they were thinking: This? This is the man we've been following? A murderer? When a minute passed, Mills said something to his men. Knives were placed to necks. Oh well. Not much to lose now.

"My parents."

A gasp from the crowd.

"Two more questions," the soldier said. "Why did you flee The Ton?"

Topher grimaced. So they knew about that too, did they?

"That's a loaded question."

"Why did you flee The Ton?"

"There was a cholera outbreak. We couldn't burn the dead fast enough."

"You left those people to die."

"I escaped before I was killed."

"There were children there." Topher didn't respond. "Last question."

"You already asked five!"

"I said last question."

Topher took a deep breath. He had no leverage here.

"Fine."

"Who is Liam Chris?"

Liam Chris? Was this supposed to have some kind of meaning? Was he supposed to be scared?

"I don't know. How am I supposed to know who he is?"

Mills paused, considering his options. Finally, he let the woman go and she collapsed to the pavement.

"You will soon," he said.

The soldiers dragged them into the woods. Topher first, then Zorn, then Gertrude. Topher had a difficult time keeping up but wasn't in bad of shape as his friends. Gertrude had been so badly beaten that his left eye was swollen shut and kept tripping over things. Zorn grimaced as they shoved them forward, suffering from some unseen wound. Once he fell flat on his face for no reason at all and didn't get up, and the soldiers stood around him and kicked him in the back and legs. When he still didn't move, they rolled him over and splashed water from their canteens onto his face until he sputtered awake, then they hauled him off the ground and shoved him forward again.

They crossed a creek and scrambled up a hill, finally emerging onto the shoulder of a secondary road. Mills's walkie-talkie squelched three times. He pressed the red button and said, "Subjects apprehended." A minute later they heard the sound of a vehicle approaching. A black SUV appeared on the horizon. They all stepped back as it roared up to the shoulder and skidded to a halt. The back doors opened and the soldiers shoved them inside. They slammed the doors shut as it made a U-turn and sped away.

The driver said, "I'm Billy, and this is Stewart. Keep your mouths shut and everything'll be fine."

It took a minute for Topher's eyes to adjust to his new surroundings. The interior was plush and clean. Air conditioning blasted out of the swivel vents in the roof. "Ride Like the Wind" played low on the stereo. He struggled off the floor and took a seat in one of the captain's chairs in the middle row, ribs screaming with relief as he reclined. Then he stretched his legs, carefully rolling his ankle around in circles, cracking the joints with a satisfying series of pops.

His suit was filthy. The knees on his pants were grass stained and torn, the buttons on his vest hung loose or were lost, replaced by little bits of thread poking out of his shirt like little worms. One of his suit sleeves was partially torn at the shoulder. He shifted to get more comfortable and it ripped all the way off. He let it hang there.

"Do you have any water?" he asked.

"I told you to shut up," Billy said. He reached forward and turned up the volume on the radio. Christopher Cross at high volume was its own brand of torture.

Topher settled back and tried not to worry. He looked out the window at the landscape, pine trees and scrub brush. It seemed familiar.

"Your heads are well-shorn," he said. The well-shorn heads bobbed along to the music. "Do you use product?"

Stewart cracked his neck. Billy's bear-like hands engulfed the steering wheel like it was a child's toy.

"The road is remarkably clear of cars," Topher said.

Stewart looked over his shoulder.

"Mr. Chris scavenged them."

"Stewart," Billy hissed.

"An excellent decision," Topher said. "I did the same thing with the vehicles outside of—"

"The Ton, we know."

Topher frowned.

"Seems like everyone knows about The Ton."

"Mr. Chris was there."

"Were you?"

"No." Stewart turned halfway around, muscles creaking. His face was broad and flat and perfectly nondescript, and he was sweating despite the air conditioning blasting in his face. "But Mr. Chris told us all about it."

"Okay."

Billy fiddled with some controls under the radio.

"I've had enough of his mouth."

"Gas is ready," Stewart said. "Just get the glass up."

Billy slapped at the dash again.

"Damn thing's broken."

"Just push the button."

"I am. It won't go up."

Stewart fussed around under his seat.

Billy said, "Did you bring the masks?"

"Crap. They're in the back."

"In the back? What good will they do us there?"

"I didn't think we'd need to use them."

Billy took off his sunglasses. His eyes were set deep in his head, and they were bloodshot and irritated.

"Didn't think, huh? Lemme ask you this: What good is an emergency backup plan if you can't implement it?"

"We were in a hurry. You saw how excited Mr. Chris was."

"Jesus, you're a real piece of work."

They drove in silence for a few minutes. Finally, Billy said, "Well?"

"Well what?"

"Are you going to do anything about this?"

"Like what?"

Billy adopted the kind of tone one might use on a thick-headed child.

"I don't know, Stewart. Why don't you figure it out yourself."

Stewart stared at him, hurt and angry.

"I hate it when you get like this."

"I don't know what you're talking about."

"Every time we leave the mountain, you get irritable."

"Would you just take care of it?"

"Take care of it?" Stewart held up his hand. "You remember what I did to my hand, right?"

"Then use the other one."

Stewart unbuckled his seat belt.

"Mr. Chris said he didn't want them damaged."

"What do you think the gas was going to do?"

"Fine."

Stewart turned around and punched Topher in the temple, slamming his head into the glass.

"Ah, fuck!" he cried, flexing his fingers.

Billy laughed.

"Should have used the other one."

Topher held up his hands.

"Please," he said.

Stewart looked confused.

"Please what?" he said.

Then he punched him in the face until he was unconscious, and then he punched him a few times more.

The stingray swam in graceful circles, its barbed tail swinging lazily with each turn. Its wings lifted and fell and slow strokes, sometimes pausing to glide, sometimes flicking the tips. Another one drifted into view, and another, and soon there were dozens of them swimming around the pool. Divers in scuba gear appeared, seeming to be just another part of the marine traffic, immune to the sight of the massive flying vessels and the possibility of being impaled by one of their barbed tails.

Watching them calmed Topher down, which was good. There was a lot he needed to calm down about. He was cold and hungry and bored and tired of being held hostage. This time in an aquarium, no less. Of all the ridiculous circumstances in which he had ever found himself, this seemed to be the most absurd by far. Liam Chris, whoever he was, was going to feed him to stingrays.

He opened his mouth, testing his jaw. It clicked. His teeth felt loose in their sockets, and his left eye felt like it was about ten times larger than normal. He looked around. Gertrude lay face down on king-sized blowup mattress, and Zorn was passed out on a beach lounger. None of them had been restrained in any way.

"I'm going to stand up now," he called.

He waited for someone to come and brain him into submission. Nothing happened.

"Here I go."

He stood up.

Nothing continued to happen.

His legs felt a little shaky, as if he'd been on a bender, and his head pounded, but it was nothing too horrible. He strolled over to an empty glass case and peered at his reflection. Sure enough, his eye was swollen, and the bruise on his cheek was large and round and purple.

The rest of the aquarium seemed to be in fairly good shape. A multi-tiered system of escalators crisscrossed from floor to floor, an old advertisement for a 4-D IMAX movie about tsunamis hung from the ceiling, two men were suspended by a rope over an open shark tank, and various tropical birds fluttered in the rafters. On the top floor, he saw a colorful exhibit on the declining rainforest, over which perched a delightful doomsday clock that had at one time displayed the correlation between the rising population, the ever-lessening rainforest, and the end of the world.

"A problem no more," he said.

He went over to Zorn poked him in the ribs until he stirred. Zorn sat up, wincing, and saw the stingrays, the fish tanks, the men hanging from the ceiling.

"Are those?"

"Yep."

"Are we to be sacrificed?" Zorn asked. "Again?"

"It's a strong possibility."

"Where are we?"

Topher shrugged.

Zorn looked over Topher's shoulder and said, "There's something coming out of the pool."

Topher turned around, his stomach turning to ice. Can stingrays breathe out of water? No, of course not. It was just one of the divers. He sat on the edge of the pool and removed his mask and mouthpiece, revealing a cherubic face framed by curly, white whiskers.

"Topher Bill," he said.

He stood up and limped backward toward them, twisting so he could see where he was going, his hand outstretched, ready to grasp and shake. He flipped his flippers off a few feet before he reached them, turned all the way around, and grabbed Topher's hand.

"*The* Topher Bill. I can't believe it!"

He led Topher back to the chair and nearly shoved him down. Topher put a hand on his cracked ribs, wincing.

"So you're Liam Chris."

"And don't wear it out!" Topher managed a small smile. "Tell me, Mr. Bill. Do you notice anything interesting about our names?"

"Not particularly."

"No? I was certain a man of your intelligence would have gotten it right off the bat."

"Sorry."

Chris stifled a frown.

"It's a riddle. Please indulge me."

"I don't think I have any choice, do I?"

"Indeed not. Now, let me think. How does it go? Ah. Here it is: Your name is my name and my name is yours; you'll understand if you shorten/reverse."

"Shorten reverse?"

"Shorten," Chris said. "Then reverse."

Topher thought for a moment.

"Your name is Llib Rehpot?"

Liam Chris shook his head, earnestly confused, then he laughed.

"Clever! But that's not what I meant. The 'Liam' is short for 'William,' just like your last name is short for 'William'. And 'Chris' is short for 'Christopher,' just like your first name is short for 'Christopher'. Now reverse it. Liam Chris. See?"

He threw back his head and laughed. It echoed throughout the empty aquarium. Something splashed in the distance, followed by what sounded like somebody moaning.

"Mr. Bill, I must thank you for leading that horrible woman to us. She always managed to stay just far enough away from my borders, as if she knew I was gunning for her. She must have thought she stood a chance this time. Or maybe she just got sloppy. When Mr. Mills told me that he'd seen you and her, and in the same place? Well, you can imagine my glee."

"What's going on here? What is all this? The stingrays, the shark tank. I'm not a spy in some silly action movie. You're not going to string me up by my thumbs and torture me to death. If you mean to kill me, just get on with it."

"Mr. Bill, I assure you that I mean you no harm. Not immediately."

"No? How wonderful for you. Good luck. A few months ago I survived a near-direct hit from a bomb." He pointed at Zorn. "His bomb. Didn't die. Didn't get a scratch on me. But all his men were killed. Did you know I was experimented on by a psychotic nurse?"

"You don't say?"

"Zorn lost all of his hair, and they nearly turned Gertrude into a zombie. It's bad enough with all of the real zombies running around out there, but they had to go and try to make their own!"

"Indeed."

"And then Saanvi turned out to be a lesbian, and Isa thought she was a goddess and she was going to indoctrinate us into her cannibal cult before you showered her with missiles. I daresay, Mr. Chris, if you mean me some kind of harm in the future, you're in for a wild ride."

"Are you trying to say you're immortal?"

"Of course not. I just keep winning, that's all, in spite of everyone else's best efforts."

"I find that hard to believe."

Topher spread his hands.

"And yet here I am."

Chris frowned, incredulous. How dare this cretin, this fool, The Butcher of The Ton, behave this way?

"You call my slaughtering of your forces, my capturing of your women and children, 'winning'?"

"I'm not trying to be flip. It's just the truth."

Liam Chris finished toweling off. He walked over to a chair with his clothes draped over it. A baby blue suit, a white, ruffled shirt, a powder blue bow tie. He swept his long, gray hair back off his forehead, and it fell wet and heavy around his shoulders. Zorn finally spoke up.

"If you don't mean us harm," he said. "Why did your men beat us? Why did you kill all those people?"

Liam Chris dressed slowly, not speaking until he'd buttoned up his shirt and shrugged on his jacket.

"Ah. The magnificent Michael Zorn finally speaks."

"Great. You know my name, too."

"Oh yes. I know every associate of Topher Bill's. To answer your question. I apologize for the behavior of my men. They were confused as to my orders." He pulled on his pants, buttoned his shirt. It took a minute for him to tie the bow tie, but when he was done, he plunked a white fedora on his head, picked up a black cane with a silver handle carved in the shape of a lion's head, and slipped into his shoes. He looked like an advertisement for a fried chicken restaurant. With a grand, sweeping gesture, he said, "Would you and your friends like a tour of my facilities?"

They tried to wake Gertrude up but he wouldn't budge. Zorn put his fingers under his nose, and when he was certain that he was still breathing, they left him there on the air mattress. Liam Chris found it difficult to hide his disappointment, and he pouted as he led them past the stingray pool.

"I must say this is not the way I'd planned things. I have half a mind to rouse him myself." He shook his cane in the air.

"Trust me, you don't want to do that," Topher said.

"I'll do as I please." Chris seemed to weigh the warning earnestly. "But still, I'm sure you'll fill him in, yes?"

He gestured with his cane towards a flight of stairs leading up to a platform from which extended a flat, black belt on an incline, walled on either side by clear glass panels topped with black running rails.

"I don't normally run the escalators, but for such a dignitary like you, Mr. Bill, it's worth expending the energy. This way, please."

He ushered them up and onto the belt, and when they were all aboard he cried, "Start it up, Charles!"

There was a clunking sound, followed by an electric buzz, and the belt jolted to life. Soon they were gliding up and across the aquarium. Zorn pointed out the educational pictures of fish and crustaceans hanging from the rafters.

"Gertrude would have loved those," he said. "The old Gertrude, that is."

He looked back at the prone form of his friend.

"Don't fret about him, Mr. Zorn. He's perfectly safe. Unless, of course, he wanders into the piranha tank." Neither man laughed. "A joke of course."

Topher said, "Where are you taking us?"

Chris smiled a little smile, arched his eyebrows and said, "To the top."

The escalator ended on the third level. They climbed another set of stairs and passed more fish tanks, these stocked with salmon and rockfish, trout and flounder. Then he led them up to a final door.

"Gentlemen, may I introduce you to the future."

He held the door open for them, and they stepped into a glass-domed sunroom.

Topher marveled. Zorn gasped.

So much food. So many colors. Red and green peppers, orange carrots, yellow bananas. Birds flitted in tropical fronds. Were those berries? Grapes? Tomatoes? An apple tree stood in the corner, the ground beneath it strewn with fallen fruit. From another corner came the scent of combating spices: cinnamon, basil, clove, rosemary, fennel, and mustard. Water tinkled down a tiered wall laden with roots and vegetables. Liam Chris's cane clonked on the boards as he made his way up a path that led to a charming little bridge overlooking everything. He leaned on the wooden rail.

"Fancy some fruit?" He picked a strawberry from a patch growing from a wooden planter.

"No thank you," Topher said, still wary.

Chris shrugged and popped it into his mouth.

"Delicious," he said.

He swatted the apple tree with his cane, and several apples thudded to the ground. One rolled over to him and rested against his foot. He plucked it up and crunched into it, the juice flowing down his chin.

"Gentleman. Please."

Topher eyed the apples dubiously, but Zorn picked one up and took a bite. When he didn't immediately die, Topher kneeled down (damn that popping in his knees!), picked one up, dusted it off, and took a very small, very delicate, very petite nibble. The juice and meat were ambrosia. Before he knew it, he'd taken two bites, then four, and then the apple was nothing but seed, core, stem. Chris beamed down at them, clearly enjoying watching them eat.

"Do you know what kind of store was the most looted immediately after Washington was firebombed?"

Zorn said, "Gun stores?"

"You would think, but those were actually the last to go. The owners had guns, after all."

"Supermarkets?"

"A close third. No. Electronics stores. Best Buy, Target, Wal Mart, any place with an iPod and video games. Even though the power was out. Even though people were killing each other in the streets. Even though the oceans were swallowing entire coastlines and the heavens rained down fire. Electronics stores."

He chuckled to himself.

"Makes you think we deserved it. Everybody thought that the government would take care of them. Everybody thought that what happened was akin to a hurricane or a blizzard. Idiots. Do you know where I went when the looting began? What store I looted?"

"Chuck E Cheeze?"

"You're joking. I get it. But no, I went to Meadow's Farms. Relieved them of every last seed packet they had. Then I went to TSC and did the same thing. Then to Feed 'N Stuff. I had a plan. I took it all back to my neighbors, showed them what we could do, how we could create our own community. Nobody was interested. The family across the street from me boarded-up their house. I thought they were preparing, that they knew something I didn't, but then we began to smell them. After a month without power, most of the rest fled."

He chuckled again, staring right at Topher.

"I soldiered on for a year. When the marauders came, I hid with my seed bank in the basement and waited it out. They didn't even bother to check. They just wanted to kill people and take the women. The cults were worse, and your Isa, she was the worst of them all. I did what I was told when I heard she was coming. I ran. Headed south. That's when I was truly desperate. Here I had the seeds to starting life anew stuffed into my backpack, but nowhere to plant them and nobody to protect me. I could escape the gangs only so many times. I was traveling with a good group of people, men, women, children. Isa caught us just outside of Richmond. That was a dark time."

He paused then, remembering.

"I barely escaped, but my seeds were safe. I wandered. Rumors began to swirl. A city in the wilderness. Farms and power. Government. Protection. The rumors were followed by the name. The Ton. Short, I soon learned, for Topherton."

Zorn stared at Topher, amazed.

"You named it after yourself?"

Topher didn't respond. He sat down hard on one of the benches and buried his head in his hands.

Liam Chris continued, "You can imagine my excitement. A *real* city. In the midst of all of this terror. I had to see it, join it, become a part of it. I had millions of seeds! Millions of them! I set out immediately. The road was as dangerous as before. Brigands, zombies, wild animals threatened me everywhere I went. But none of that mattered. I had hope for the first time in months. The world was about to be set to rights."

Topher would have buried his head deeper in his hands if he'd been able. He felt the older man's gaze penetrate his skull.

"Did we shoot you or brain you?" he asked.

Liam Chris clapped his thigh.

"I won't bother showing you the wound."

Zorn shot Topher a dark look, and Topher straightened up.

"Don't get all self-righteous on me, Zorn. My city was in crisis. We were overcrowded. People were starving, medicine was scarce. It was getting harder and harder to deal with the dead, so I closed the border until we could get everything under control."

Liam Chris limped down the stairs.

"That's enough for now. If you don't mind, I would like to apologize for Billy and Stewart. This way, gentlemen."

Billy and Stewart were the men suspended by rope above the shark tank. Their hands and feet were bound, and their mouths gagged. Blood dripped from a gash sliced ragged across Billy's ankle. The water frothed and boiled below, and the sharks, unable to control their frenzy, turned on each other.

Chris said, "Aren't they magnificent? Haven't fed them in days."

"Billy and Stewart?" Topher asked.

Chris patted him on the shoulder.

"So clever you are. So clever."

Billy snuffled and shook and was suddenly awake. He kicked, shouting against his gag, stirring up the sharks even more.

"No need to waste your energy, Billy," Liam Chris said. Then, to Topher, "So hard to get good help these days, wouldn't you agree?"

"I don't think you and I agree on very much at all."

"You disapprove? How did you keep your people in line?"

Topher didn't answer.

Some birds flitted by, and Liam Chris smiled at them.

"They're such delicate creatures, aren't they? So fragile, so easily crushed." He put a hand to his mouth and yelled, "Are you ready, Charles?"

A disembodied voice cried out an affirmative from somewhere below.

"Please, Mr. Bill, know that I no longer hate you, no longer revile you, no longer desire to harm you myself in any way. In fact, I consider you somewhat of a genius. Flawed, of course. Arrogant. Beyond reproach. But had it not been for your mistakes at The Ton, I'd not be in the position I'm in now. So because of that, I am going to give you that which you never gave me. A choice."

An electric thunk sounded above, and the rope holding the two men began to lower them into the tank.

"You can agree to run something I call The Gauntlet."

Billy's feet broke the surface and his body began to shake as if he were being electrocuted. He shrieked against his gag.

"Or you can refuse."

A different man in a black suit drove them away from the aquarium. He did not speak. They drove for over an hour. He made turns seemingly at random, not settling on a specific course until the sun set. When it did, he found a side road and headed in one direction. The air grew cold, and Topher's ears popped a few times as they climbed into the mountains. Gertrude woke up and he and Zorn spoke quietly in the back. Then the driver stopped in the middle of nowhere and told them to get out.

"Follow that road to the end," he said, pointing at what looked like a dirt driveway. "If you go anywhere other than that road, you're dead."

"Where does it go?"

"Follow that road to the end."

He put the car in gear and roared away. They watched until the tail lights grew into pale dots, then they turned around to look at the road. Trees lined each side as far back as they could see, darker and darker. A broken gate blocked the way, and when Topher went over and pushed it open, it almost fell off its hinges.

"Do you think this is The Gauntlet?" Zorn asked.

Topher shook his head.

"I think The Gauntlet is much worse than this."

They limped along for a mile or so. Topher's eye was still closed, and his ribs still hurt, and Gertrude had to take frequent breaks. The trees on the right thinned out, revealing open fields, freshly reaped, with huge bales of hay hulking like sleeping giants. A stream appeared on the left. They passed a white poster nailed to an oak tree. Liam Chris' face stared out at them. "Work Is Culture!" was printed under it. More appeared as they walked, all of them bearing some sort of Orwellian propaganda:

"Safety Is Fear!"

"Service Is Redemption!"

"Community Is Conformity!"

Others depicted a gleaming city with electric rail cars zipping over glass bridges, populated by teaming masses marching to work, or shopping, or building skyscrapers.

"Run the Gauntlet!" they cried. "Salvation Awaits!"

Zorn studied the images in the moonlight.

"He named his city 'Salvation'?"

Topher studied a picture of a smiling nuclear family eating a turkey dinner. This one read "Family Is Absolution!".

"My guess is that it doesn't even exist. It's all just another sick game. That's what all of this is."

They walked on. They saw another field brimming with pumpkins. The air began to smell like manure, and then on the other side of the stream they saw the shadows of livestock. The mountains here, it seemed, had recovered.

Soon they heard drums and flutes, the sounds of people talking, and they came upon a settlement of trailers, rows and rows of them, and RVs and tent cities, too. Men and women gathered around large bonfires. Horseshoes clanged. A raucous cheer went up. The people looked clean and healthy. A woman noticed them and tapped the forearm of another, and the two disengaged and came over.

"Hi," she said. "I'm Missy and this is Kristine. You're new here."

They looked nervously at Gertrude, bald and shirtless, blood crusting his skin.

Kristine said, "Would you like something to eat?"

Without waiting for an answer, they led the trio over to the nearest fire. Men were sitting on upturned stumps and lawn chairs, balancing paper plates on their knees. The plates were filled with potato salad and fried chicken, watermelon and grapes. People drank from red, plastic cups. Kristine handed Topher a plate and a drink.

"You must be starving."

More plates appeared for Zorn and Gertrude. Topher sniffed his.

"Is this man-flesh?" he asked.

"Goodness no!"

"I've been duped before." He sipped from the cup and said, "Beer?"

"Salvation's finest."

Gertrude finished his and held his plate out.

"More, please," he said.

Kristine laughed as she took it from him.

"At least we have one healthy eater."

A few of the men gave up their chairs and the three relaxed in front of the fire. The beer flowed. Topher grew warm and buzzed. Kristine sat on his lap, and drummers appeared out of nowhere carrying djimbes and congas, talking drums and shakers. They pounded out syncopated rhythms. Girls swirled around the fire.

"This is pleasant," Zorn said.

Missy watched them eat, smiling. She gave orders to other women, who always nodded, silent and serious, before heading off somewhere, then returned with more alcohol and food. She beckoned to Kristine, who strolled away from Topher, swishing her hips. He did not look away. A gruff-looking man with a full beard and thick slabs for arms appeared and squeezed his shoulder.

"Hey, brother! This is great, isn't it?" Topher tried to shrug him off, but the man was too strong. "I'm Chuck."

Chuck chugged his beer.

"I tell you what. Just last week I was lost in NYC, running from packs of dogs, scrounging for food." Kristine swished by, catlike, and placed another beer in his hand. He downed it and crumpled the cup and threw it on the ground with an angry belch. "Now look at me. I'm living like a king!"

He wandered away, hailing the other men with a hearty "Hey Brother!"

The night was filled with laughing faces, and Topher, drinking beer after beer, had a hard time keeping up. Chuck returned and cried "Like a king!" The fire grew higher and higher. The dancing girls shucked their tops and shimmied and shook. Kristine was on his lap, and then they were kissing. Dennis appeared, pale and dazed. An angry biker sucker punched Gertrude, who fell sideways onto one of the stumps. Zorn broke a flaming log over the angry biker's head. The stars shined in the clear night sky, spinning, spinning overhead.

Topher awoke the next morning in a tangle of limbs and hair and breasts. His ribs ached. Kristine lay with her arm across his chest, and another girl he'd never seen before lay face down over his legs. Men and women sprawled all over the floor in various states of nudity, a complex arrangement seeing as the trailer they were in was narrow and already cluttered with women's underwear hanging from clotheslines. Bags filled with produce sat on the counter, and men's clothes piled up in corners.

"Get up," he said, pushing feebly at the woman on his legs.

She moaned.

Kristine sniffed and stirred.

"Stay in bed, baby." She threw her leg over him and kissed him full on the mouth. "Only a few more hours."

He shoved her aside and she squealed, then started hitting him.

"Fine, then! Get the fuck out!"

He struggled off the bed and waded through the river of naked people, a pillow strategically placed over his crotch. It took a moment to locate his clothes, his torn pants and jacket, his Panama hat, but when he finally gathered everything up in his arms, he slammed open the door and was nearly capsized by the brightness of the sun. He rubbed his eyes and blinked until he could see again.

The campsite sat nearly at the base of a tall mountain, about an hour's walk to the west. It was covered in trees, thick and green, and the sun sent the shadows of an occasional cloud against it, like a canvas. Nearer by ran the stream, peaceful and serene. The charred remains of the bonfire sent a little trail of smoke into the air, its skeleton logs grayscaled and coated with ash. Missy stood between the trailer and the bonfire, fully clothed, waiting for him.

"Hi there. Look who's up all bright eyed and bushy tailed." When he didn't answer she clucked her tongue. "Not in the mood to talk?"

Topher coughed and tasted tobacco. Had he really smoked the night before? He coughed again, and his cracked ribs screamed. He bent over and tried to clear his lungs carefully, but the more he tried not to cough, the more his throat tickled. He ended up hacking and moaning all at once. The last time he'd been this hungover, the world was still the world. Indoor plumbing, electricity, flat-screen televisions. When he was done he stood up and rested his hand on his ribs.

"I need water."

Missy crossed her arms.

"I'm not your mother. There's the stream right over there."

"I didn't mean it like that. I just . . . I'm really hungover."

"Better hurry. The race begins in an hour."

"Race?"

She smiled.

"Surely Liam explained things to you."

"We just got here last night," he said. He made his way down to the stream, clothes still gathered in his arms. "And I never said I'd run his stupid gauntlet."

He felt her watching him as he dunked his head into the cold, clear water. He drank deep, washed his arms and legs, cupped it under his legs and scrubbed.

"Enjoying the show?"

She walked away, and soon he heard her banging on the trailers.

"Kristine! Girls! Get 'em up and out!"

The doors swung open to the whines of the women.

"Oh, c'mon Missy. Just one more hour."

Missy continued undaunted.

"Get 'em up and out," she kept saying. She moved from door to door until all of the women had scurried away to some other part of the camp, leaving the men to blink, crippled with hangovers, in the early morning sun.

Chuck said, "I call bullshit on this! Where's that whore?"

Missy walked right up to him and smacked him across the face.

"You mind your manners," she said. "We're not whores. You're nothing to us."

He grabbed her by the neck, but before he could even begin to squeeze, she kneed him in the groin. When he keeled over, she brought an elbow down on his neck, sending him face down in the grass. She straddled him, wrenched his arm up behind his back and he cried out.

"Say you're sorry."

"Fuck you!"

She grabbed his forefinger and broke it with a snap. He cried out again.

"Say you're sorry."

He huffed into the ground, eyes clenched.

"Fuck you."

Another snap, another finger broken.

"Okay, okay! I'm sorry."

She left him there, snuffling in the dirt, and strode up the line of confused and frightened men. Dennis looked even paler in the light of the sun, and though he didn't show any physical signs of injuries, he seemed barely there.

Missy said, "The Gauntlet starts in less than an hour." She pointed west. "Starting line is at the bottom of the mountain. I suggest you gather up whatever you own and get going"

One of the men, another shirtless beard wearing a pair of torn cargo pants, started to laugh. His belly jiggled.

"Little girl, I'm not going anywhere."

"I strongly suggest you move."

"No."

"Your choice."

She turned and waved with both arms over her head, and then the man's chest exploded. He collapsed, eyes wide open, the contents of his insides splattered against the outside of the trailer. The report from the sniper rifle sounded a few seconds later.

Missy said, "Anybody else want to argue with me?"

Nobody said a word.

"Good." She looked up at the sun, shielding her eyes. "Now you've got less than fifty minutes."

They jogged along the dirt road, thirteen men in various states of dehydration. If one fell behind, a shot rang out and a bullet dusted at his heels. Soon all that could be heard was their panting and groans. Chuck fared the worst, and by the end of the first quarter mile, he'd been shot at two times. He was soon joined by two others, one for falling down, one for running to the side of the road and squatting, the victim of a disagreeable stomach. Topher slowed to a jog to keep pace with Zorn, who was trying to help Gertrude along.

"What's wrong with him?"

"I don't know. We're all dehydrated. Didn't he get into a fight last night? I think something's broke inside."

Gertrude's breaths were ragged and hoarse, and he ran with one hand pressed to his side. Topher took him up under his other arm and they slogged forward. At the half-mile mark, Dennis fell flat on his face and didn't move. They left him there, and a bullet thunked into his back and another one into his skull and he shook and lay still. Chuck shot a look over his shoulder.

"Oh god!"

"Still living like a king?" Topher asked him.

"Shut up."

The sun beat down.

Up ahead, shimmering in the noon heat, they saw something. It looked like a utility pole, only one without any lines. As they jogged near, they saw it wasn't as tall as they thought, that it was like a lifeguard stand, or a chair for a tennis referee, with a ladder on the side and an umbrella anchored atop to block the sun. Liam Chris sat there, dressed in his baby blue suit. He placed a bullhorn to his face.

"Come on, you lazy slugabeds! Salvation awaits!"

He raised a pistol into the air and fired three times.

The group struggled on, and when they were within one hundred yards they saw a second structure, a crow's nest on a raised platform just behind him, like a smaller version of the barricade in which Topher and Zorn and Isa rested on outside Philadelphia. Two armed soldiers stood on it.

Liam Chris pointed at his wrist as they stumbled to a halt.

"Tick tock, gentleman. Tick tock."

The men groaned. Sweat poured off their faces. A few fell to their knees and rolled onto their backs.

"We need water," Topher said.

Liam Chris laughed.

"Oh, my dear Mr. Bill, I have nothing for you, just like you had nothing for me. I do have the mountain." He gestured behind him. "I do have my men." He gestured at the soldiers. "And I do have The Gauntlet."

"Why run the race if you're going to kill us anyway?"

"You mistake me entirely. Think of this as an opportunity. An opportunity to rejoin civilization. If you win, you become a citizen."

"Bullshit," Topher muttered.

Chuck yelled, "Come on! Let's do this!"

"I've got a plan," Topher told Zorn, but Zorn was busy trying to hold Gertrude up. "Leap on the weaker ones from the start. The more we can take out when the gun goes off, the less competition."

"But Gertrude's one of the weakest."

Liam Chris held the gun in the air.

"Runners on your mark!"

"I didn't mean him, Zorn."

"Get set!"

"Then who were you talking about?"

The gun went off, and Chuck leaped upon the shortest one of the bunch, an old man whose ribs were poking out of his skin, pummeling him in the face with his good hand.

"Never mind," Topher said, and he lurched forward with the rest. After ten minutes, the mountain seemed no closer. Topher threw a look over his shoulder. Chuck was running behind the pack, grimacing. The old man lay face down in the dirt. One of the soldiers in the crow's nest aimed at his body and fired.

There were only eight left by the time they made it to the trees. One by one they spread out and disappeared into the canopy. Topher didn't see where Chuck went; he hoped to avoid him altogether. The air was cool but thin, and Gertrude seemed better and worse for it. His face wasn't as red as when they'd been jogging in the sun, and he was able to stand on his own, but a dark purple bruise had formed on his ribs, and it was still difficult for him to breathe.

They were bound to be attacked. This was The Gauntlet after all. Topher searched the ground something he could use as a weapon. He kicked aside some dead leaves and saw the top of a rock boiling out of the ground. It took a minute of digging with his fingers, but he was finally able to pull it out. He hefted it in his hand and showed it to Zorn. Zorn took it.

"Better than nothing," he said.

They hiked up the mountain, shuffling through the brush. Topher went from feeling sick and sweaty to miserable and shivering. Pinecones crunched, and the trees took on a dark, ominous quality that he found eerily familiar. Every now and then he saw a claw mark carved out of a pine tree. They were huge, with red rivulets dripping from them, as if the tree were bleeding. He stopped at the third one and called Zorn over.

"Should we follow these?"

Zorn inspected it, tracing his finger along the grooves, and as he did, Gertrude fell to his hands and knees.

"They're old. Maybe they'll lead us to water? Maybe there's a stream farther up?

Gertrude pulled something out of the dirt and held it up to them. A long metal cylinder. Zorn took it from him.

"It's a shell."

"From a gun?" Topher asked.

"No, from the ocean."

Topher spun around.

"What was that?"

"What was—"

"Shhh!"

Zorn crouched, alert, listening. The last time he was in the middle of a forest like this, he was attacked by werepyres.

They didn't see him coming. One second they were crouched, alert, the next, a massive form leaped out from behind an outcropping and tackled Gertrude. Chuck. The two rolled down the slope, slammed into the base of a tree and broke apart. Gertrude bared his teeth, but he was weak, and before he could even push himself off the ground, Chuck was on him, trying to wrap his hands around his neck. Topher and Zorn slid down toward them, Zorn holding his rock over his head. Gertrude managed to press him up, using every last ounce of strength, just managing to keep Chuck's thumbs from his throat. Then there was a hole in Chuck's chest and he fell over.

Topher only saw him fall off. He thought Gertrude had done it, and it wasn't until they skidded to a halt a few feet away that they saw the hole and the blood. Gertrude coughed and hacked and waved them away.

"Run," he gasped.

"What?"

Another bullet took a chunk out of the earth at his feet.

"Run!"

Topher yanked Gertrude away just before another bullet thunked into the ground where he'd been, and they ran up the mountain. They ducked and juked and zigzagged, and the gunfire chased them as they ran, higher and higher.

"They're toying with us," Topher said.

Up ahead they saw the gleaming light of day. Surely they hadn't reached the summit?

The gunfire stopped suddenly, and Topher took the lead, and yes, now that they grew closer he could see that the trees ended in a line, but how? They were not even a quarter of the way up. They ran for it anyway. What else could they do? Ten feet to the line. Five feet. Then they broke into the sun and skidded to a stop. Before them was a cliff facing a rocky valley. The mountain rose up to their left, white crags and sheets of solid granite. To the right they saw what looked like a lake shimmering in the distance, three rocks poking up in the middle of it. More forest lay beyond, and peeking out of the treetops was what looked like the top of a clock tower. Topher was struck dizzy. Could that be?

"What are you doing?" Zorn said. He threw a panicked look behind him. "They're almost here!"

Gertrude pointed at the valley below.

"Look."

They all peered over the edge.

Bodies.

Hundreds of them. Piled one atop the other as though they'd been bulldozed over. Or pushed. Or shot. Or forced to jump.

This was Liam Chris' version of population control. Maybe Salvation existed, maybe it didn't, but what did it matter? This was their fate, what he intended all along.

"This is it," Zorn said.

Topher shook his head.

"No. This isn't it. It can't be."

"Oh, right. You always win, don't you? Look around, Topher."

"You'll see. Something will happen."

"Yes. They're going to kill us."

The first of the soldiers emerged from the tree line. Sergeant Mills. Four more men followed him. Their faces were painted black and green, and they wore camouflage shirts and pants, their helmets festooned with leaves and branches. Topher, Zorn, and Gertrude turned to face them. The soldiers didn't raise their guns. They didn't need to. Mills said something to his friends and they laughed. Then he said, "Hi, Topher. I'd hoped I see you again."

"You'll forgive me, Mr. Mills, if the feeling isn't reciprocated."

"No. I don't mind that. But I do mind that you got Billy and Stewart killed."

"Not that I care, but that was your boss's decision."

"You know, Mr. Chris usually tells us to make these things quick. 'Don't torture them,' he says. 'Clean shots and over the cliff,' he says. But with you three, he gave us permission to enjoy ourselves." He withdrew his knife.

Then a voice cut through the air, hoarse and reedy, but loud.

"No," it said.

They all turned, and there stood an old man, seemingly out of nowhere. He was dressed very formally. A gray, three-piece suit with a red bow tie, a red pocket square, and shiny, black shoes. He leaned heavily on a cane. An old chill, one Topher hadn't felt since he was a boy, crept up his spine. Behind the old man ran a razor-wire fence concealed by branches and bushes, and on the other side was a grass-covered mound, tall and perfectly round, as if someone had constructed it, had poured the dirt there and shaped it that way.

"These young men are coming with me," the old man said.

"Who the fuck are you?" Mills said.

The old man didn't answer. He beckoned to Topher instead.

"Come along, boys. Come along."

Without a second thought, all three trotted away, away from the cliff and the horror that sat at the bottom, away from the mercenaries, first Topher, then Zorn, then Gertrude.

"Told you, Zorn," Topher said.

"Hey!" Mills cried.

Topher heard the metallic chunk of rounds being loaded. The old man smiled as they approached, then he turned and ducked into a square hole that had been cut out of the fence, a small square hole that was nearly unnoticeable in the chaos of brown leaf and green pine in the background. He headed toward the mound and slowly descended into the ground and then was gone, as if the earth swallowed him up.

The soldiers opened fire again.

Topher dove through the fence, ignoring the pain as a sharp edge cut into his side, and rolled into a hole at the mound's base. Zorn about to follow when four of the things from the hospital, the pale monsters, appeared on the top of the mound. He drew up, putting a protective arm around Gertrude. They'd followed them here, but how! Their red eyes settled on Zorn, brimming with malice, but then Gertrude stepped in front of him and they softened. He reached out for one, his hand shaking. He didn't know why he did it. He felt like he should touch it, connect somehow, and when his fingers brushed its forearm he felt a little zing rush through his body. Then a bullet struck it in the shoulder and it screeched and took a step backward, adjusting its focus on the soldiers.

The other monsters let out a terrible cry and leaped off the mound. Bullets flew, and men screamed, and Zorn tackled Gertrude and they fell into the hole.

James Noll

RALEIGH'S REDUX

It wasn't a hole but a trap door with a latch built into it. Zorn pushed it up, using a bolt anchored into one of the beams to hold it in place. The door was made out of wood, and he was sure that one of the soldiers would shoot into it, shredding him, or smash it open and jump inside, but all he heard were their shrieks as the monsters tore them to pieces. He and Gertrude cowered until the last of the squeals and grunts subsided, then he said, "Are you okay, Gertrude?"

Pause.

"Yes."

Yellow light filtered in through the cracks in the trap door, and they could only see a few feet in front of them, but Zorn was certain that this was their tunnel, the one they'd used to escape years before, the one that led to the secret room under their dorm. Two yellow flashlights had been left for them, leaning up against the dirt wall. Zorn swiped one up and turned it on. The beam was strong. He gave the second one to Gertrude and motioned for him to move forward.

They stooped as they walked, brushing the occasional cobweb from their eyes, slapping their necks at imaginary spiders. Roots dangled from the ceiling, rocks boiled up at their feet. The tunnel intersected with another, and a fluorescent yellow arrow directed them to the right. They followed it. Soon they heard crunching as they walked. Gertrude pointed his light downwards.

"Bones."

The dirt was littered with them. Human bones. Bleached white. Rib cages, thighs, feet. A clavicle. But there were animal bones mixed in, too, horribly disfigured, twisted or elephantine or both, elongated skulls with different sized eye sockets. They kicked what they could out of the way as they walked. Some crumbled to dust. Some rolled away and struck others with a hollow clonk. They came to an open door, beyond which stood a hallway aglow with warm, orange light. They passed through, followed the light to the right, and rounded the corner into the room.

Six tapestries along a wood-paneled wall. Antique furniture. A knight's armor on a stand. It was amazing. All still there. Unchanged.

Topher and the old man warmed themselves in front of a roaring fire, large mugs clasped in their hands. Two more mugs sat on the rustic trunk before them. Topher was dressed in a clean linen suit. A newly blocked Panama hat rested on the end table at his elbow.

"Ah, boys," the old man said. "You made it. Please, please come in. Sit! Sit!"

Zorn and Gertrude each took a seat and, at the old man's bidding, poured themselves a draught from the pitcher. Zorn eyed it suspiciously. He'd been drugged enough of late. But Gertrude held it up to his nose and sniffed. His eyes went wide and he smiled.

"Hard cider," he said.

He took a long, satisfying gulp.

The old man tapped his cane.

"Raleigh's best. We make all kinds of alcohol here. We got the idea after a bumper harvest of pumpkins one fall. Too many to eat, too many to trade, too many to turn into pies or carve into decorations. I balked at first, of course, but in the end it just didn't make any sense to let all of it rot."

Zorn waited for Gertrude to start vomiting blood, or for his eyes to shoot out of his skull, or for his stomach to erupt with locusts, but he only gulped it down, finishing with a smile, the first smile anybody had seen on his face since they found him.

"You have a foam mustache on your lip," Zorn said.

Gertrude licked it off and belched.

The fire crackled. The old man beamed at them. He held his cane between his legs, twisting it with shaking hands.

"I cannot tell you how pleased I am to see you. So many years, such horror and catastrophe, and yet you're here. I knew it. I knew it! You were the only ones, the only ones to ever escape, and kudos to you! But I knew you'd be back. You had to return. This is, after all, the only home you've ever had."

"I'm sorry, sir," Zorn said. "I mean, I'm grateful that you saved us, and for this wonderful cider, but I . . ." He looked at Topher for help, but Topher just smiled at him. "Who are you?"

The old man's pleased expression suddenly fell, and just as suddenly Zorn found himself back in school, sitting in the headmaster's office, facing down the glare of authority, wondering (just as before) what it was that he'd done wrong, and how much he would be blamed, and how horrible the punishment would be. When the old man spoke, his voice was flat, menacing, monotone.

"You don't recognize me?"

Topher covered his mouth with his hand. Was he laughing? Zorn's mouth went dry.

"Er—"

The old man's face shook, his lips pressed tight. *My God. The rotten coot's going to explode.* And the old man did explode. With laughter. Zorn and Gertrude, each gripping the arms of their chairs, ready to leap away should the old man attack, exchanged a confused look.

"Oh, dear, dear boy. I'm sorry, I'm sorry. It's just that I'm well aware of the way I used to be, and I've been here for so long all by myself. I don't get to interact with people very much."

He withdrew a handkerchief from his suit pocket and dabbed at his eyes.

"I do suppose I've changed. We all grow old. Just look at you three! The last time I saw you, you were nervous, pimply little fellows. But so strong. And so confident, so smart. Outsmarted me, that's for sure."

Realization dawned upon Zorn's face.

"Stoneman? Are you Mr. Stoneman?"

Stoneman nodded, and suddenly Zorn saw him. He was nearly completely bald, with only a few wispy strands of white hair covering a liver-spotted pate, and his eyebrows were in dire need of trimming, and his nose was round and bulbous, but the eyes were there. Piercing, bold, filled with light.

"I want you boys to sleep here for a while," Stoneman said. "Not too long, mind, but long enough to recover from your ordeal with that madman."

He stood up, leaning on his cane.

"I'll be back in a few hours. Then I'll show you something amazing."

He went to the door and gently closed it behind him.

Zorn said, "Topher, what's going on?"

"It's incredible, isn't it. But that really is Stoneman."

"What does he want?"

"I don't know, and I don't care. All he'll say is that he's been here all along. Waiting."

"For us?"

"Maybe." Topher settled back on the couch. "We'll talk later. Right now I'm exhausted."

To sleep without fear for the first time in years was a novel thing. Topher was wary. He wanted to set up a guard, but he was too exhausted to do it himself, and before he could make a decision he was out cold. The next thing he knew, Zorn was shaking his shoulder, Gertrude was already up, and Stoneman was tottering in the door.

"How long were we out?" Topher asked.

"I don't know," Zorn said. "At least four hours."

Stoneman rapped his cane on the stone floor.

"Come along. Come along," he said.

They let him take the lead, shuffling slowly through the secret walls of their old school. He paused at a spot and stepped on an iron handle sticking out of the floor. A wooden panel slid aside and the boys followed him into a wardrobe and then into a bare dorm room. Their old room. It had been gutted. They wandered around, wondering at the streaked walls, the dusty floors. Zorn was amazed at how small it was. Had all three of them really lived here?

Stoneman cleared his throat.

"We had to scavenge the furniture, of course. And most of the plumbing and fixtures. Follow me, please."

He led them to the cobblestoned courtyard. The overpasses, the open tunnels, the clock tower, all of it was untouched by time. A little dirty, in need of some repair, but intact, existent, whole. It seemed to Topher as if he'd stepped quite literally back into his childhood. Memories flooded. His face flushed, his eyes filled with tears. He ached for his youth, even his time spent here. Everything was so innocent in comparison to the terror of the past few years. He turned to his friends and saw the same desire reflected in their faces. Stoneman's golf cart was still parked off to one side, just like when they were kids.

"How is this possible?" Topher asked. "The rest of the world is in tatters. The tsunamis, the bombs, the riots. How did you keep this place whole?"

"And those creatures?" Zorn added. "The last time we were here, they'd overrun the campus. How did you survive?"

Stoneman nodded, smiling.

"All in good time, boys. All in good time." He pointed to the golf cart. "Climb in."

He piloted them across the campus, through the shortcut between Merton and Croix, out to the gravel access path. Gertrude thought, *here is where Topher lost his boot running from the wolves.* Stoneman turned right onto the shell path that led to the Athletic Fields. Zorn thought, *this is where Mr. Floyd let us go after we found that poor dead boy.* They stopped outside of what used to be the track. Topher thought, *this is where Gertrude threw up.* It was now a cornfield, with tall, healthy stalks.

One hundred and twenty yards long. Fifty-three and a third yards wide. Full of food.

Stoneman waved his cane all around him.

"We planted the other fields with berries and lettuce, tomatoes, broccoli, squash, zucchini, cucumbers. We have chickens, too. And cattle."

Topher said, "Mr. Stoneman, this is amazing."

"Yes, my lad. You probably didn't know it when you were here, but Lake Perish is stocked with fish. Bass. Carp. Catfish. And Chainwrought Creek has crawdads. Chainwrought Forest has ten lifetime's worth of game."

"And wolves," Zorn added.

Topher glanced at the sun as it slipped behind the trees. A shadowy hand stretched across the corn, and a howl, low and lonely, broke the peace of the afternoon. Stoneman put the cart in drive.

"I suppose it's time to get back, isn't it?"

It seemed to take forever to drive back to campus. Afternoon turned to evening. Another howl rang out as they reached the courtyard. Topher was tempted to get out and run. Stoneman seemed tense.

"The cart doesn't go as fast with so many people in it," he said.

They all breathed a sigh of relief when he pulled up to the administrative building, nearly leaping out of the cart as they followed him to the door. Stoneman glanced around, muttering, "Shouldn't have gone out so late. Shouldn't have let you sleep so long." He pulled a keychain laden with keys out of his pocket and it jangled in the air. More howls pierced the evening. His hand shook as he looked for the right one, so bad that when he did find it he couldn't fit it into the hole. The trio gathered together behind him, wishing for a gun, a knife, a thick tree branch, anything. The shadows lengthened, darkened. The old man's hands finally steadied, the key caught the hole, slipped in, and the lock tumbled. The door creaked open into a dark foyer, and all four pressed in. Gertrude slammed it behind him and turned the bolt.

Stoneman's apartment was small and cozy. He pointed at his fireplace.

"Be a good lad and start a fire," he told Topher.

Kindling and dry twigs sat in a basket to the left; split wood stacked against the wall to the right. Topher set to work, and in no time the apartment was aglow with the warm light of the fire. The old man lit a few candles, then retired to his bedroom, returning a while later dressed in a soft bathrobe, tottering as he carried a tray filled with fruit salad and vegetables.

"No matter how warm it is down-mountain, it's always cold up here. Even in the middle of the summer." He set the tray down on the coffee table in the middle of the room. "Please. Eat."

They helped themselves to the food, and when they were done, Stoneman produced mugs of clean, clear water, "fresh from the well." They sat back in their chairs, satisfied. Stoneman looked around at all three of them, a faint smile on his lips, head nodding, hoary eyebrows aloft. Topher sat up straight, ready to talk.

"Mr. Stoneman, you have to tell us how you did all of this. Who is the 'we' you keep talking about?"

"You're not going to like the answer."

"Does it matter?"

He pointed at the window.

"Them." He looked around at each of them, his steady eyes holding each of them. "They're not always animals, you know, but they do live out there now."

"How is that even possible?"

"After you escaped, we reached a tenuous truce. I promised not to hunt them down, and they promised not to feed on the students. They turned their interests elsewhere. When the Catastrophes struck, we came to rely on each other. Eventually, we were able to cultivate the fields. My idea. My knowledge. Their work. Their protection."

"That's it?"

"That's it." Stoneman thought a while. "Well, not entirely. Luck seemed to find its way here. That woman from the hospital came calling. They needed food. I gave it to them. In exchange, they provided me with the product of their research. First I fed the nasty things to my friends in Chainwrought, but then I realized I might be able to use them. Those that could be tamed and trained were spared. I used them for labor until that fellow set up shop in the aquarium. Then I had them patrol the fence. Meanwhile, the seasons changed, the fields grew prosperous, and I waited. And now you're here."

"And now we're here."

"I want you to kill them."

Topher spat out the water he'd just sipped.

"What?"

Stoneman nodded at the window.

"Them."

"But I thought . . . you just said . . ."

"Yes, but they've served their purpose. The fields are green. There are women down-mountain. There are books and knowledge here. And we have her." He turned in his chair and said, "You may come out now, my dear."

A female voice floated from his room.

"Are you sure?"

All three froze, especially Gertrude, who looked like he was about to cry. Stoneman tapped his cane impatiently.

"It's entirely safe, I assure you."

There was a short pause followed by tentative footsteps, and then Nurse Smith entered the room. Zorn stood up so fast that he nearly knocked over his chair.

"Now, now. Now, now," Stoneman said, struggling to his feet. "I understand there is some history here."

Topher stood up, too.

"History? She tried to kill us! Nearly turned Gertrude into one of those monsters!"

"Topher, please."

"Why shouldn't I strangle her right here, right now? Cut her pieces and feed her to your friends in the woods."

"Because I will not let you!"

The old man's voice cracked when he yelled, but his eyes glowed with the familiar fire of his youth. His anger quelled Topher's.

Stoneman calmed down. He said, "She told me, you know."

"Told you what?"

"How you let her go. How you spared her life. You even offered her protection."

Zorn looked at Topher, stricken.

"You said you killed her."

"Obviously, I lied."

"She's smart. She's controlled. She knows what she wants and how to get it," Stoneman said. "Don't get me wrong, you're a powerful force, Topher, but there is a reason The Ton did not survive. You're impetuous, just like when you were here. Sometimes you're blinded by your own ideas. Isn't that right, Mr. Zorn?"

Zorn didn't know what to say. He agreed, of course, but this was Nurse Smith they were talking about. Finally he said, "Yes."

Stoneman continued.

"Plus, she's tough. She's a survivor. She made it all the way here from Philadelphia by herself."

Topher sneered.

"Only because I let her go."

"A wise decision, no doubt. Because if you hadn't, I wouldn't have known you were still alive, and I wouldn't have known to look out for you."

Stoneman smiled as the realization dawned on all three of them. He finally felt it safe enough to sit down.

"Yes, I can see you understand now," he said. "She showed up a month ago. I don't know how she got in, but she did. 'They're in danger,' she said. I didn't know who she was talking about at first, and then she told me everything."

Topher looked Nurse Smith in the eyes.

"Is that true?"

She cleared her voice, choosing her words carefully.

"You spared my life. You didn't have to, but you did. I can't be obligated to anybody."

"Okay, very good. You've repaid my kindness. He might not want you to go, but you can do the right thing and leave on your own."

"She's not leaving," Stoneman said. "I will not let this place fail. You can make it work, but you need her to do it."

The three men bristled and glared.

"Sit down," Stoneman said. None of them moved. "I said sit!"

Topher took a deep breath and did as he was told, however reluctantly. Zorn followed suit, then Gertrude. Nurse Smith remained where she was, close to the door. The old man sighed.

"Boys, I'm dying. Not right now, but soon. I can feel it."

"Mr. Stoneman."

"No need to go on. I'm not there yet. I've lived a long time. I'm proud of what I've done. At one point, my life was dedicated to helping young men recover from the evils of the past. Give them the tools they need to rejoin the world. This is no different. You have what you need. Now it's your turn to carry it forward. Finish what I've started. Rebuild civilization here." He gestured at the window again. "It's a new world, my friends. And those things, those abominations, can't be a part of it. Set them on that fool in the valley, then finish what you started when you were younger. Of course, you'll have to deal with the cursines."

"You kept the cursines?"

Stoneman struggled to his feet, yawning.

"An unfortunate necessity. So. Do we have an agreement?"

"You want an answer now? Can't we talk about it?"

"Oh, I don't know. At my age, there's no knowing what might happen in the night."

"We just need a little more time."

The old man paused.

"Fine," he said. "You have the night to discuss it, but I think you know what you need to do, don't you?"

He tottered toward his bedroom, stopping next to Nurse Smith and fishing around for something in the pocket of his robe.

"It's in here somewhere. Ah." He produced a key and placed it in her palm. "You may have the room across the hall, my dear. You needn't worry about these three."

Nurse Smith ducked her head and whispered a contrite "Thank you." Then she left.

Stoneman opened his bedroom door.

"Goodnight, boys. Please don't harm her. She's misguided, certainly, but she will make a good ally."

With that, he retired to his bedroom and shut the door behind him with a gentle click.

The fire crackled in the fireplace. Topher strolled over to the window and pulled aside the curtain to have a look at the courtyard. Night had completely fallen. The windows of the dorms were dark, hollow eyes. His gaze wandered up at the white face of the clock tower, forever stuck at seven fifty-seven. Maybe one day they could figure out how to turn the power back on. Something moved below, and his eyes snapped down. Black smudges swarmed the cobblestones, dozens of them. They sprinted along the overpasses, teemed along the path to the Grotto. More spilled out of Chainwrought. Suddenly they stopped and, heeding some instinctual command, turned their snouts to the full moon to let up a howl.

Gertrude's head whipped towards the window, and Zorn's too, their faces slack with terror, their eyes wide. And that's when Topher knew what he had to do. A mantra began to form in his mind.

We will begin again.
We will begin again.
We will begin again.

Thank you for reading *Topher's Ton*! Read on for the first chapter of *The Rabbit, The Jaguar, & The Snake*, the first novel in the Bonesaw Series

James Noll

THE RABBIT

Hey, how's it going?

Lemme tell you the story about the time I saved the world.

Looking around right now at the burned out buildings and the churned up streets and the bodies in the gutters, I know what you're thinking: "This is how you save the world?" So I guess my answer is that I don't really know. And I don't really care. I kind of look at it as something that happened to me, like jury duty or a colonoscopy. But hey, that's jumping ahead now, ain't it? Let's start from the start. And there ain't no better place to start with than my Ma and Pop.

Pop came to America from the old world before the Model T, if you can believe it. Met my dear old Ma on the boat on the way over, and even though I knew it wasn't the truth, I like to think that the whole thing was a whirlwind romance. Love on the high seas. A jealous suitor. Fist fight in first class, a triumphant right hook followed by a wedding on the main deck, with the ship's captain and the clear blue skies and the icebergs floating by. In reality, pop was a penniless Jew from Minsk, and ma, she wasn't no better off. Their getting together was probably more like a scrum and a moan behind a crate in steerage, a pauper's union at the neighborhood temple, and nine months later, me.

I grew up in the slums of the Bottom with about five million other street rats. Living in a place called the Bottom was exactly like what you'd think it'd be like living in a place called "the Bottom." The one room tenements, the baking hot summers, the midnight bum-rolls, the cholera, the TB, the dysentery. Ah, the golden years. Ma toiled long hours as a seamstress in a heat box deathtrap, and Pop worked a whole bunch of miserable jobs. He was a fish monger, a ditch digger, a stone-cutter. He buried gas lines. Dug subway tunnels. I don't know how he did it, but eventually the old codger saved enough money to buy his own business. A newsstand. Established himself as a true entrepreneur.

Me, however, I was free as a bird. Lived like a king. I hung out the usual gang of gutter punks. Skinny Pete. Squinty. Slappy. The Mangler and the Jew. We got up to all kinds of hi-jinx, me and them. Alley smokes. Heel hacks. Knife fights. But then Ma died in a factory fire, and Pop didn't know how to put up with me. Granted, I was a bit out of control, and short of drowning me in the river, there wasn't nothing he could do to keep me in check. Plus, he'd just got that newsstand off the ground, and he couldn't have a liability running around, that liability being me, so his only option was that free school them papists run.

And by that I mean Catholic School.

And Catholic School was Catholic School.

I know what you're thinking. You're thinking, "ain't you a Jew? Them papists don't let no Jews in Catholic School."

Well, you're right, you're right. But pop, he wasn't no dummy. About three months before he signed me up, we started attending mass. Every Sunday morning, every Sunday night. Pop got himself in thick with the priests, told them that he wasn't no religious type, that it was too late for him but that he didn't want his only son to go to Hell. Next thing I knew, they're swinging that censer all over the place and tracing the sign of the cross on my forehead with water. And just like that, I was a mackerel snapper, with all the privileges and blessings and hope of heaven.

He packed me off to Our Lady of the Bleeding Hands and Slit Throat that very fall, and then my education began in earnest. And boy oh boy did it suck. Sure I got me a nifty uniform and three squares a day, and oh yeah, they taught me how to read, rite, and rhythmatic, but I also got myself a hefty backhand whenever I done anything to offend anybody, which, given my natural constitution, equated to a considerable amount of backhanding. I'd always thought I was pretty clever, a real yuk yuk guy, you know? I even got The Mangler to laugh on occasion. In my opinion, my mouth was the best part about me, but them priests didn't seem to share my sentiments. (Well, they did and they didn't, but more on that in a sec.) They hit me so much their knuckles'd swell up just looking at me. Unfortunately the kind of behavior in which I specialized also drew a different kind of attention, the kind ain't nobody want, and from there my story went from pitch black to pitch blacker.

Satan black.

Ninth bolgia of Hell stuff.

I don't feel like going into all the details cause there ain't no point in grossing nobody out. The only thing you need to know is this: all the things that happened to poor kids with no resources in Catholic School happened to me. Pretty unconceivable a century later; run of the mill back then.

I got my revenge, though, right? Not after they fucked me up permanent, and not until I was much older, old enough for everybody who hurt me to forget about who I was and what they done, but revenge was got. I won't go into the particulars. That story's been told already anyhow. Some jerk wrote it up in some dumb book he published. *A Stick in the Eye* or . . . what's that? Oh yeah. *A Knife in the* Back. Anyway, it's a good read. A real pot boiler. Seven short stories and a novel. You should check it out. Especially the one about me.

Go ahead.

I'll wait.

Okay, maybe we ain't got the time for that kind of thing right now. For those of you who don't want to, or who ain't got the time or the patience, or who can't read, think of it this way: That priest's head looked good up there on my wall, didn't it? Not as good as them two goombahs, dumbass Basilio and fat little Arko, but good enough for government work.

So look, enough with the exposition. Here's where the story really begins.

About a year after that, I was killing time at Pop's newsstand, selling the typical newsstand type stuff, like newspapers, and magazines, and chocolates, when The Widow Mrs. Feldman stuck her head out her window.

"Howzit," she said.

It was a slow day. The war'd been over for three years, and the twenties was roaring like a lion. After the morning rush, ain't nobody was interested in the good news, so I sat back and put my feet up on a stack of City Sentinels to read the science section.

"Fuck you, you old witch."

"Hey, language, language. Is that any way to talk to your elders?"

"No. But it's the way I talk to you."

She laughed that chuffy laugh of hers. Half phlegm, half soot: "Huh huh huh. Huh huh huh."

"Jesus," I said. "You inhale a smoke stack or something? You gonna be alright?"

"You're a funny one," she said. "Real wiseass. You get that from your pop or your ma?"

Ma'd been dead for centuries, but Pop, he kicked it only a few months before. Lasted pretty long, him. Ninety-five years. Not bad for a time when most people died at half that age. It's fantastic, actually, unless you consider how he died, because he died kind of shitty, if you ask me, with the cancer eating away at his lungs until there wasn't no lungs left. I was already irritated before she reminded me of all that, but now I was irritated considerable more. I took my feet off the papers and plonked them on the sidewalk.

"You need your attitude adjusted?"

She waved me off.

"You don't scare me. Mr. Feldman was the last one who tried and look at what happened to him. Plus," she nudged her chin at the old abandoned townhouse. "I know what you done over there. And I like it."

I gave the old place a glance. It was all blackened at the base from when them two idiots tried to burn it down, and the windows was still cracked and grinning at me, but it was still standing, proud and unbeaten. I returned my attention to the article I was reading.

"Oh yeah?"

"Yeah. You got style, kid. And I know you been thinking about expanding your services."

Now that one shocked me a little. How the fuck she did know about that? She wasn't wrong, but, well, after I finished "The Unholy Triumvirate," I ain't had no inclinations to carry on. I felt I'd done my duty, purged my demons. Lived along with the knowledge them fucks who did what they done to me and mine would never be able to do it to somebody else and theirs. Until recently.

I'd heard things about what was still going on at that school. Good old Ronnie Resnick told me about it, and let me tell you something, I was none too pleased. In fact, I was so unhappy that I was actually thinking about giving them a little taste of my scalpel and bonesaw, add a few more trophies to my wall. But that was as far as I got, just the thinking about it, and as far as I knew, thinking about a crime wasn't a crime. That wasn't the problem, though. The problem was that The Widow Mrs. Feldman knew about the crime I was only thinking about.

"You know fuck all about it," I said.

"About what?"

I stared at her over the top of my paper. She wouldn't look me in the eye. Looked everywhere but, mumbling and muttering to herself. Dead giveaway. Finally I said, "You know fuck all about fuck all."

"You're a laugh riot. A gaggle of giggles. I don't know fuck all? You just told me everything I needed to know."

"Ah you're a crazy bitch," I said.

But she wouldn't let it go. Kept laughing that hoarse laugh. I won't lie to you. It pissed me off.

"The fuck you laughing at?" I snapped. She laughed harder. A little ball of energy swirled up in my chest. I tried to keep reading, but it wasn't no use, so I folded the paper and slapped it down on the stand. "Can I help you with something?"

"No, but I can help you with something."

"Not interested."

"No really. Listen. You look in the mirror lately? You look good for a guy your age."

"Watch it, you old hag. I might be horny, but I ain't desperate."

"What are you? Thirty-three? Thirty-four? You don't look a day over twenty."

"Sorry, you're not my type."

"I heard that about you."

Sometimes a body just got to absorb the insult. That was one of them times.

She said, "I know you know what I'm talking about. I know you seen it, too. You're in your prime. You'll never look better. I'm just trying to help you out a little. Give you a boost." I pretended to read again. "Look. I'm on your side here. You wanna stop them fucks from doing what they do?"

Fine. Fuck it. She knew. How she knew what she knew, I don't know. But she knew. I put the paper down.

"Yeah," I said. "I do. I'm gonna kill every last one."

The Widow Mrs. Feldman nodded.

"That's what I thought. C'mere a second."

"Fuck that. I ain't going nowhere. You come here."

"Got a bad hip." Her cat jumped up on the sill next to her and arched its back against her shoulder. She pet it. "Hey there, Demon. You come out to say hello?" Demon meowed. The Widow Mrs. Feldman reached behind her and put a glass of something on her sill. "Demon made you something to drink."

I looked at it. It was tall and skinny and filled up with something green and goopy looking.

"I ain't drinking that."

"It's cool and fresh, and it's a hot day, no?"

"Yeah, but I ain't drinking that."

She seemed to take that in, studying me, reading me, but she finally shut up so I was able to get back to the news. Whoo boy, the world was in a ton of shit. The Great War really fucked things up good. Unemployment rising in Germany. Some asshole in Italy and his black shirts. The old lady started to hum a tune. I didn't notice it at first cause she sung it under her breath, but then it seeped into my head, into my bones. I'd heard me a lot of music in at that point in time. "I Ain't Got Nobody." "Ain't We Got Fun?" "I Ain't Nobody's Darling." Streets was positively filled with that new jungle bunny shit. But this was something different, eerie and earthy, like the trees and the rocks and the wind all got together to start a band. It was the most beautiful thing I ever heard, and I felt transported by it back to a time when there wasn't no bricks or buildings, no assholes or asphalt, just the sky and the ground and the oceans and the rivers, and the next thing I knew, I felt something rub my calf, and when I looked down I seen Demon winding his way around my ankles. I got dizzy. And out of the haze came The Widow Mrs. Feldman's voice.

"You sure you don't want that drink?" she said.

And you know what? I did get a thirsty right then. Parched, even.

Years passed, and it was around that time that I started noticing something different about me. My old friends, Slappy and the like, they got older. Fatter. Sicker. Slappy caught a case of the Nationalism, enlisted in the Army, and ended up a corpsesickle when he tried to fight the Bolsheviks in Siberia during the Russian Civil War. The Mangler was too smart to sign up for any government sham but dumb enough to get himself killed in a drunken pub brawl. I heard Squinty went blind, which anybody with half a brain could of predicted, and then I never seen him again. The Jew was the only one who made it out somewhat prosperous. Owned himself a pawn shop near the Industrial District. I seen him every now and then, always alone, muttering to himself, stooped over and worn, like the trials of life weighed on his shoulders so heavy that he couldn't take it no more.

But me?

I stayed the same. Like my body got to the ripe old age of twenty two and said, "Fuck it. I'm done." And that's when I knew. I knew what I was going to do. I was going to follow through on all them thoughts I'd been thinking.

Look, I got a lot of regrets in my life. Who don't? I regret not running away from them fucks at the Our Lady of the Bleeding Hands and Slit Throat before they got to me. I regret not taking on extra work somewhere so Ma didn't have to work in that heat box deathtrap. But one thing I don't regret is drinking the potion old Mrs. Feldman made me that afternoon. Changed my life, it did. Or at least I think it did. Who knows? All I know is that once I realized what was what, all them ideas that'd been swirling around in my head solidified, and the guy I was after wasn't the guy I was before, and everything I'd ever known, the fear, the pain, the helplessness, vanished, replaced forever with an anger that nearly consumed me.

So I expanded my services. And by that I mean killing any fucks what fucked with the well-being of a helpless kid. This took some creativity. You know, before you start in on the judging, you should remember who I was going after. I wasn't duping no co-eds into helping me carry my groceries up a flight of steps. I wasn't leaping out at grandma from alley corners. I went after the kiddie diddlers, the pedo-pokers. Remember what I told that priest?

"I wish I had someone like me around when I was a kid."

Well, I took that serious, and for a while, it worked out pretty well. I find you been diddling kiddies, I hunted you down and slit your throat. Worked out well for about five or six years, but unfortunately, no matter how skilled or careful or sneaky or creepy, there comes a time in every great killer's career when he ends up caught. Well, not every one, because has anybody ever heard of Jack the Ripper?

So, yeah, this was some time around '51? '52? I got wind of a local cop whose tastes ran unconscionable. First some kids started spreading rumors. Scumbag took Jerry Blumczech for a ride in his cruiser. Gave Arnold Gold an option in an alley. Then this new cop showed up, lo and behold, fresh out of nowhere, young guy, slicked-back hair, square jaw, and a bit swarthy in the palms if you know what I mean. I seen him talking with the kids on my street, and then he's walking them to school, buying them ice creams. Classic profile. I also noticed that little Robby Resnick—Ronnie Resnick's grandson— wouldn't go near the guy, avoided him at all costs, ran across the street when he offered him a chocolate, took the long way to school. Once I seen that . . . there ain't no words for it. I felt an anger I ain't never felt before, and not for me, but for that poor kid. I didn't save Ronnie Resnick's ass from a priest way back when just to have his grandson get his plowed by no cop.

If only I'd known.

Them kids was paid to spread them rumors.

Robby was paid to act like he was afraid of the jerk.

Blumczech never took no cop car pleasure cruise.

Gold remained just as pure as his name.

And I fell into it like the sucker I was.

One night, returning home drunk from a date with one of The Widow Mrs. Feldman's bottles, an opportunity presented itself. I seen that sonofabitch pedophile cop walking across the street a block in front of me, and the dark twirlies descended. I didn't normally snatch nobody on the spur of the moment, and I definitely didn't do it when I'd been drinking, but up until that point I'd enjoyed a string of successes and I let it go to my head. Isn't that always the case with people like me? They call it a cycle or something; we plan and we stalk and we kill and we drink to forget it, even if we're not supposed to be bothered by it, and then we plan and we stalk and we kill again, a little sloppier this time, and a lot sloppier the next time, and worse and worse and then you're spiraling out of control like an idiot. So yeah. Pedocop spotted. Dark twirlies descended. I don't remember what happened after that. One second I was walking behind the guy, the next I'm surrounded by a bunch of dicks screaming at me to hold up my hands, goddammit or they'll shoot.

"Alright, alright," I said, and did what I was told.

Unfortunately for me, my hands was covered with gore. So was my face. And my chest. And them cops is shining the lights in my eyes and I can't tell if it's real or fake, can't see nothing, really, except them lights, and suddenly I realized I was straddling somebody, and when I looked down I seen a busted open chest cavity between my legs.

"Oh shit," I said.

"Oh shit's right," someone said, and slugged me solid right in the temple.

What'd they do? What do you think they done? They dragged my ass to the station and worked me over with a rubber hose. Ripped out my adenoids. Showered me with the old lead sprinkler. They could have saved their breath. I had no intention of lying. I wanted them fuckers to know what I done. Maybe they'd see the light. Maybe they'd understand that I was actually trying to help them out. So that's why when the beatings stopped and my face had time to unswell, and they hauled me into a little room with a bright light overhead and a two-way mirror (you seen TV), and the one cop was breathing down my neck and the other acting all official and polite, and they asked me "Did you fucking do this shit?" I said, "Yeah, I fucking did that shit" and that was that.

I don't think the cops expected me to do that, kill their boy so soon. I think they thought they were going to do some serious investigating, whip up the media, maybe fabricate an event, something they could use during an election year. They certainly didn't think any of theirs was going to die, and if they did, they didn't think it'd be as unpleasant as the way I made it. The guilt must have been phenomenal. The one I killed was fresh out of the academy. Top of his class. Asshole tighter than a corncob. True blue, him, and his dumbass superiors set him up to be gutted like an animal.

I seen the realization dawn on them right then and there in the interrogation room. Their eyes went dead, and they broke out another round of rubber hoses and wooden clubs and brass knuckles and beat the ever-loving shit out of me, punched my half-swoll eyes 'til they was fully swoll, pummeled my bread-basket until it was mush.

When it was all done and I wasn't nothing more than a bloody pulp, they drug me down to the deepest, darkest, dankest part of the jailhouse, threw me in the moldiest cell, slammed the door, cut out the lights, and marched off, slapping each other on the back and giving each other hand jobs. Okay, maybe they wasn't giving each other hand jobs, but they was jerking each other off. I'd like to say I took it all professional, but I was scared out of my mind. I soiled myself silly. Them fuckers threw away the key. I was gonna die down there. I curled up on the thin mattress in the corner and cried myself to sleep.

The main think I had was "what happened?" Why didn't they parade me around in shackles? Publish my picture in the newspapers? Slap me in the chair and let me do the electric jiggle on live television? I'll tell you why. Because things didn't turn out the way they planned. Because I didn't do it the way they wanted me to. Because I didn't follow the rules, didn't fit into a box, and that makes normals itch, and no matter what anybody tells you, no matter how many times they say "live your dreams and be an original," they don't mean it true. Sure, live your dreams. Sure, be an original. But don't do nothing too dreamy or original or you'll freak us the fuck out and we'll throw you in the dungeon.

And that's all it was, them sticking me in that cell. Fear. Pure fear. I educated them on the limits of all that freedom they said they loved so much, and all the sudden they started to think maybe too much of it wasn't such a good idea, that were was people like me who took them serious, took them at their word, who didn't give a fuck. That scared the crap out of them more than anything else, because where there was one dumb enough or sloppy enough to get caught doing the kinds of things I done, there were probably a hundred more waiting in the wings, just itching to cut and slash and slaughter, and once they seen what the people in charge had in store for them, who do you think they'd be coming for?

Well that wouldn't do.

That wouldn't do at all.

Fortunately, there was another group of people that'd took notice of my talents. Powerful people. People like me. Violent, ageless. Better than that, they were from the Neighborhood. Not the neighborhood, the Neighborhood. There's a difference. What's the differ . . . ? Just give me a minute. You'll see.

One morning after breakfast (a rotten orange and moldy bread) I got a knock on my cell all polite like, like I had a choice not to answer.

"Yeah?" I croaked.

The voice on the other side sounded like the streets. Asphalt and brick. Dumpsters in alleys.

"That you?"

I worked my jaw and it clicked.

"Yeah it's me."

"Lemme in."

"What do you mean, lemme in'? I'm in here. You're out there."

"No. You're in there, and I'm out here."

"Six to one, and go fuck yourself." A pause. "Please."

Another pause. Then the guy said, "You gonna let me in or what?"

Seeing as I'd just spent the last few weeks getting my adenoids ripped out, I really didn't feel like screwing around, you know?

"Remember what I said before about 'go fuck yourself'?"

He laughed. Can you believe that shit? Laughed.

"That's a good one," he said. "Good to maintain a sense of humor. But you know what? You ain't got no manners."

"I got plenty manners. For example, I said, 'Go fuck yourself,' then I added 'please'."

The silence on the other side of the door hung thick in the air. A mausoleum at midnight.

He said, "Maybe I'll come back another time."

His footsteps clopped away down the hall.

"Hey, I can be good!" I cried. "You come in here and I'll give you a shot of my bologna, how about that!" I couldn't stop laughing. "Oh sure, I got some cheese to go with it, too. And a little grease for extra flavor!"

After that, nobody came to visit no more. They stopped everything, the beatings, the food, everything. The former was a relief, the latter, a problem. I got creative. You ever eat a spider? It's not as traumatic as people think. I mean, sure, you gotta, you know, actually eat a spider, but then the stomach acid burns it to bits and you're ready for more. I became quite the arachnid connoisseur. Never reached Renfield status, but after ten days, twelve days, thirty days—who the fuck knew—I decided that, yeah, there really wasn't going to be a trial, and, sure, there really wasn't going to be no electric chair, neither, but the cell? The cell was my sentence. Twelve feet by twelve feet of eternal punishment. Four water-stained walls, a gray, concrete slab, a metal bed bolted into the wall, and that slate iron door.

So I ate spiders.

And flies. And silverfish. And cockroaches. And ants. And anything else that showed up. Catching a rat was like Christmas dinner.

Years passed, I guess. I stopped keeping track. Toward the end there, though, I couldn't really tell what was what no more. I can't remember when I started seeing things, but I started seeing things. Entire cities demolished by a ball of fire. Houses swallowed by earthquakes. Children snatched from porches. At first, I knew it wasn't real, then I thought it might be real, then I wasn't sure no more, and at a certain point, it didn't matter. There it was, and I was seeing it, so it was real.

And then one day the guy came back.

I was standing on my bed trying to coax a roach into my cupped hand when the knock came at the door again. I eyeballed it. Thought for a second. Almost had the fucker. Just. One. More. Second.

Another knock came and I said, "Just a minute."

The third knock came harder, and my hand shifted and the roach scurried up and away into a crack in the mortar and I pounded the cinderblock with my fist, crying "Motherfucker!" I turned my anger at the door. "You sonofabitch! You just cost me my lunch!"

"Tsk tsk," the guy said. "I see we haven't learned our manners yet, have we?"

I stared at that friggin door a long, long time. Sometimes when things started talking to me, if I stared at them long enough without saying nothing, they went away. So I stood there kind of hunched, my hands held up like I was about to pounce, my stringy hair covering my eyes. What was left of my prison uniform hung in tatters off my shoulders, and I didn't have no hips left, so I had to make a belt out of a strip of one of the pant legs to keep them from falling off. Not that it mattered. When the guy didn't speak again, I relaxed.

Phew, I thought. *He wasn't rea*—

"Hello?" he called. "You still there?"

"Oh," I said. "It's you."

He snickered.

"Yeah. It's me. You want to let me in now?"

"We gonna have this conversation again?" I sat down on my metal bed.

"I guess we are. So what's it gonna be?"

"Let's see. How's it go again? You want me to let you in, but you're out there and I'm in here."

"Noooo . . ."

"Yeah, yeah, I know. I'm in here and you're out there. Still don't change nothing."

"I don't begrudge you your bitterness."

"Bitterness? Bitterness? You got any idea how long I been down here? Because I don't. You should get a look at me. I'm a ghost. A fucking wraith. And all for what? Getting rid of the scum who did what they done to them poor kids? I was helping them out! And they locked me away!"

There was a long pause after that, and ice started to form in my belly. Did I scare him off? Right when I was about to plead with whoever it was not to go, he said, "You mind I can ask you a question?"

Oh thank fuck.

"Go ahead."

"You ever wonder if there was other people out there like you?"

I thought for a minute.

"Like scraggly macs who's been thrown in a hole until the sun explodes?"

"I think you know what I mean."

I took a deep breath.

"Yeah," I said. "The thought did cross my mind from time to time."

"That's good. That's real good. So you wanna let me in or what?"

"I can't," I whispered.

"What's that?"

"I said I can't!"

"Oh yes you can. Yes you can. All you go to do is stand up and open the door."

"But it's locked! They locked me up! They threw me down here and melted the key!"

"So you won't do it?"

"The door. Is. LOCKED!"

"Is it? You ever try opening it?"

The fuck was he talking about? Of course I'd tried opening it. I hung on the handle until my fingers broke, kicked it until my toes bled. Or maybe not. Who knew. One second oozed into the next down there. I could cup my hands against the wall for hours, waiting for a beetle to crawl into it, or lick at the water trail until my jaw ached, and I wouldn't know if it was the next day or the next week.

"I dunno," I said. "Maybe I haven't."

"Well, why don't you give it a shot? If it opens, great. If it don't, well, I ain't like you'd be any more disappointed than you already is."

That was some hot logic right there. Couldn't even start to think of an argument against it, so I said, "Okay."

I stood up shaky and shuffled toward it, and the whole time I'm thinking, "It's a joke. The fucking fuck is fucking with me." I knew that when I grabbed it, I'd feel the metal in my fingers, the same icy handle that I'd been yanking on for years (or hadn't been), and once again I'd push on it, and once again it'd creak and whine, and once again it wouldn't open. And then that son of a bitch on the other side would laugh and laugh, and I'd scream until my voice gave out.

Well. No time like the present, right?

I put my hand on the handle.

I pushed down.

You can imagine my surprise when, with a rusty squeal, the frigging door swung in at me.

The Rabbit, The Jaguar, & The Snake is the first book in the Bonesaw series.

An epic tale of adventure and survival, *The Rabbit, The Jaguar, & The Snake* follows the story of Bonesaw, a hood from the early 20th Century, Wheeler, a city detective from 2021, and Coatl, the last remaining general of a primitive, jungle empire.

Bonesaw is kidnapped by the Brotherhood, a mysterious clan whose members never age and never get sick. They give him a choice: either compete in The Gauntlet (Golgotha, Hell, and The Battle Royale), or they'll kill him. Unfortunately, the contest is designed to produce maximum body count, and even if he can make it out alive, he might not like what they have in store for him afterward.

After surviving an attack from an otherworldly beast, Detective Katherine Wheeler investigates a string of murders with similar, horrifying details: each victim was killed by something that erupted from inside their bodies. As the corpses pile up, she realizes that an invasion is underway, one that could wipe out mankind.

Finally, Coatl faces his most dangerous foe yet: the monstrous tecuani. When they overrun the last stronghold in the empire, he realizes the world has one last hope for survival: Ka-Bata and his army. To reach him, Coatl must travel hundreds of miles through the jungle, a journey treacherous enough without the tecuani larva growing in his leg.

Separated by time and space, these three unlikely allies, The Rabbit, The Jaguar, and The Snake, must find a way to join forces. If they can, the human race has a chance to survive. If they can't, it is doomed.

Sign up for updates and new releases here:

www.jamesnoll.net

Thanks for reading!

A NOTE FROM TOPHER

Hey you slugabeds! Topher here. That roustabout Noll was too busy napping to write this, so he begged me to do it for him. Seeing as I am considered quite the talented wordsmith, a man of letters, if you will, I cannot blame him. Also, he has the tact and charm of a drunken car salesman.

Unfortunately, he actually makes a living from the books he writes, if what he does can even be called writing (I liken it more to the random appearance of letters on a page.) Nonetheless, he needs help from readers such as you. Please review *Topher's Ton* (my personal favorite, of course) so he can write more books, particularly anything that feature me.

ABOUT THE AUTHOR

James Noll has worked as a sandwich maker, a yogurt dispenser, a day care provider, a video store clerk, a day care provider (again), a summer camp counselor, a waiter, a prep. cook, a sandwich maker (again), a line cook, a security guard, a line cook (again), a waiter (again), a bartender, a librarian, and a teacher. Somewhere in there he played drums in punk rock bands, recorded several albums, and wrote dozens of short stories and a handful of novels.

He has published short fiction and poetry in *Whurk* (www.whurk.org) and the *Fredericksburg Literary Review* (www.fredericksburgwriters.com).

Experience his presence online at:
www.jamesnoll.net
www.facebook.com/knifeback